Freedom Run

Freedom Run

A Novel

Jim Riggs

Susan,

Enjoy the Run!

Jim Riggs

26 July 2018

ISBN: 1515152634
ISBN 13: 9781515152637

Recommendations for Freedom Run:

Some reviewers would say, Freedom Run is a real page-turner. I have read of real-life escapees who lived for decades and eventually were found out and forced to spend the rest of their lives in a fetid prison. I kept wishing these characters well. I like the way Riggs weaves the action through Federal and State Parks, describing the scenes and features with such good words that I can really see each place. It's neat to have attention drawn to parks that don't get much play in the press. I think he was reading his log books and studying his photos when he described all the scenic details.

Geraldine Fromm Schwarz, author of
PACKIN' CATS FOR THE ARRR-MEEE:
Fun on the Farm in the 'Forties

"The words of Freedom Run are teachingly creative and forgivingly wise."

Dean Schwarz author of The Boy and the Old Dam

Cover Photo by Jim Riggs

Acknowledgements

I'm deeply grateful to my friend, Barbara Schacker, who used her skills as an English teacher and many hours of her time to read <u>Freedom Run</u>, penciling in crucial suggestions that improved my writing and made this a better novel.

I appreciate my long-time college friends, Dean and Gerry Schwarz for pushing me to the finish line and giving me words of encouragement.

Thanks to Valerie Palmer whose proofreading skills were very helpful.

My wife, Darlene put up with hours of seclusion while I was writing and editing <u>Freedom Run</u>. Her gentle words of positive criticism made this process easier.

A decade ago I took a creative writing course from Des Moines Area Community College. My professor, Seeta Mangra, made the comment on one of my papers, "I'd really like to read a novel that you have written." Thanks for the inspiration, Ms. Mangra.

I

The Ranger

After five years in prison, five months in a halfway house seemed like a walk around the block. It also seemed like a 50 mile hike. The day I finished my third month, I remember thinking, *All you need to do is keep your head on straight for sixty-one days.*

My name is Paul Hartman. I was two months from completing my prison sentence. To arrive at my check-out day, I would have to handle a huge problem that would face me for almost every one of those sixty-one days. Our new guard, Roger Stewart, or The Ranger, as we called him behind his back was the definition of trouble for me. The man was trouble for each of the prisoners, but especially for me.

There were four prisoners in this marvelous new halfway house. Each of us had problems with The Ranger, but mine were the worst. The guy reminded me of my seventh grade English teacher. Both Mr. Don Bartlett, my English teacher, and Roger Stewart, our vindictive guard, loved finding a male victim -- a student or a prisoner -- to pick on, put down, and destroy. Both men of power chose me for their victim.

The Ranger was the worst excuse for a prison guard that any of us had encountered in our cumulative twenty-some years behind bars. Five nights a week for eight weeks, I had been holding my tongue, controlling my temper against a man who had absolute authority over me. He was evil personified. But, if I could tolerate The Ranger, stay out of trouble for sixty-one days, then I was out of the halfway house, into a new part of my life.

One night in late winter my relationship with The Ranger exploded. Our halfway house was down to four prisoners, Mary Swartz, Rod Dodge, Bob Johnson, and me. We cooked and ate our supper.

Our tasks included planning tasty, nutritious meals on a tight budget. Mary made sloppy joes, vegetable soup mixed with hamburger. Earlier, I had stirred up some strawberry Jell-O with bananas and pineapple. Rod and Bob set the table and cleaned up.

I liked working with Mary. When I knew nobody was look-ing, I touched her hand. She gave my fingers a little squeeze. I am nearly forty. Mary is not yet thirty. My mind pictured the two of us together someday. I wondered if there was a way for us to make it happen when we left prison. There would be worse people to spend the rest of my life with. Mary had grown up poor. She had drifted into dancing, prostitution, and fraud. Besides being a beautiful, sexy woman, I saw her as bright, in-quisitive, full of life. I could sense her determination to leave her past life behind and start over. In my life as a teacher I never imagined being romantically involved with a prostitute. Somehow, this was different. We were like two teenagers, making tentative contacts, gently testing feelings. Her touches excited me; I sensed a person who could make life interesting.

While Bob and Rod finished the dishes, I read my book. <u>Papillon</u> was about a guy who was imprisoned on Devil's Island, a French prison off the coast of South America. He eventually escaped in a home-made raft. The story had my attention, but when Bob suggested a game of cards I joined the group. We all played 500. Breaking out a deck, removing the twos and threes, adding a joker, we sat down for a game.

We were well into our first game when the guards changed. Roger Stewart came on duty. We all cringed a bit, sensing that there would be some kind of trouble. We all thought Roger (The Ranger) Stewart believed he was here on earth to save the world from us. I also suspected that our guard thought that Mary would love having sex with him.

When The Ranger saw us playing cards, he said, "Sorry guys. Time for all good prisoners to go to bed. Break up the game. Get to your rooms."

I asked, "Mr. Stewart, would you mind if we finished the game? The score is 420 to 380. It should be over in just a few minutes."

The Ranger moved toward me and placed his face and index finger in my face.

"Hartman, you think because you got a couple of college degrees you are something special. You think you can fast talk your way into doing anything you want. Well, you're wrong. One of the things you need to learn before we parole you out of here is that when someone in authority tells you to jump, you ask, 'How high, sir?' If you learn that, then you might succeed on the outside. I really doubt if you'll make the grade, Hartman. You are just too sleazy a crook to ever make it for long in the real world. Who would ever trust you after what you did?"

I didn't even answer the idiot. The man was sick. He had chosen his profession simply as a way to show his authority. He didn't really give a damn about people.

It was useless to argue. I gathered the cards, stuffed them back in their box, and headed for our bedroom. Rod, Bob, and I shared a room, while Mary had her own room. Rod and Bob followed me.

As we closed our door, we heard The Ranger start on Mary.

"Just a minute, Mary. You and me need to talk."

"I've done nothing wrong, Mr. Stewart. Let go of my wrist, please. We have nothing to talk about,"

"Yah. I reckon we do. Sit down on the couch."

We couldn't see it, but Mary pulled away and The Ranger jerked her arm. She landed on the couch with Roger dropping beside her.

He pointed towards our bedroom.

We heard, "Those three guys are going to have a rough time making it on the outside. On the other hand, you, Miss Mary, can make it anyplace. You can make it with any man you choose. Tonight, you choose me, Mary Swartz. You and I are going to spend the rest of the night together. When you're out of prison, you're gonna remember what a real man is like, sweetie."

In a clear voice that we all heard, Mary responded, "You know I'd be in serious trouble, if I said yes to that proposal, Mr. Stewart. You can just bolt my door and I'll be alright by myself."

"I wasn't really asking, Miss Mary. I been thinkin' about you all day. I think I'll just take what I want. It might be more fun if you was to be willing, but I'll be having a good time even if you ain't."

Roger moved his hand around her shoulders and pulled her closer.

We heard his voice. "You and me are going to have some fun, Mary. And you're going to earn real high marks on your performance reports."

The prison guard reached over and grabbed her breast.

"Take your hands off me," we heard Mary scream. "Being a guard gives you no right to touch me, you bastard."

Three prisoners stood at a closed door. We glanced at each other and I saw two nods that mimicked my own. We had heard every word of the exchange. I took a deep breath, turned the handle, felt the door opened quietly on well-oiled hinges.

II

Escape

We saw Mary and The Ranger sitting with their backs to us on the couch. The Ranger had one hand around Mary's neck and the other on a breast. I looked left and right, watching Bob and Rod moving beside me. The Ranger glanced to his left and saw Bob.

"In your room, Johnson. This has nothing to do with you."

The Ranger heard my footsteps from behind him. He turned just in time to meet my fist. It was a long blow, over the couch. My fist connected lightly with our guard's jaw. My swing was poorly timed with little power. The Ranger dived over the couch and tackled me. We both went down. The big guard hammered my mouth with his fist as he scrambled on top of me. He pulled his meaty hand back for a finishing blow. Mine was already back. Swinging up with all my power, my fist made contact with his mouth. Roger flopped flat on his back. His lips were suddenly grotesque, the size of his nose.

Struggling to my feet, I was a step behind Roger. His swing caught me in the gut, but I was moving away. His head came past me. I swung from my hip, stepping into the punch, the blow hit him flush on the nose. I heard a crunch and saw a mist of bright blood. Roger, The Ranger, went down like a bag of corn, his head crashing into the edge of an open door. I heard a sickening thud like a bat hitting a baseball or maybe a cantaloupe. Roger lay still. Blood was streaming from between his swollen lips and from his nose. The back of his head looked dented where his hairless skull had collided with the door. Our guard's face glowed in a ghost-like, bleached-out white. I dropped to the couch. As I glanced around the room, three faces were staring at me.

Mary said, "You okay, Paul?"

I touched my nose. Blood was filling my mouth. My head felt as if a herd of cattle had stampeded over me.

"No, but I think I'll live. How's The Ranger?"

Rod said, "Not moving. I think he's out."

Bob was worried. "What now? All four of us were about to be be freed. Two months and we'd have been out. Now this asshole spoiled it all. Why did he have to go after Mary? What will we do now? Maybe we should call 911."

Rod said, "And be presented with four tickets back to the State Pen at Fort Madison? That ain't a good idea. We need to get the fuck out of here."

Bob said, "The fight just involved Paul and The Ranger. Maybe we should call 911. The rest of us might be all right."

"All of us will be back in prison for our full terms, Bob," said Mary. "I'm sorry, but you're going to take the hit just like the rest of us, my friend."

My eyes turned toward our guard. "The Ranger's not moving," I said. "Maybe we should check him out."

Rod bent over The Ranger. He pulled him flat on the floor. The look on Rod's face was incredulous.

"I don't think he's breathing."

"Check his pulse."

Rod grabbed the Ranger's wrist. "I don't feel nothing."

"Let me try," said Bob.

Bob's hands gently slid along Roger Stewart's neck. Then he moved to his mouth.

"Nothing. No pulse. No breathing. The man is dead. You killed him, Paul."

Mary said, "Paul didn't kill him. They had a fight. Paul was protecting me. The bastard hit his head on the door. It was an accident. An accident."

"What do we do?" asked Bob. "Maybe we should turn ourselves in. We're innocent,"

Rod asked, "How'd that work for you eight years ago, Bob?"

The room was quiet as a tomb.

Then Bob said, "Not well."

Rod asked, "Wanna try it again?"

Bob looked at the floor.

Then he responded, "I'm with you."

I asked, "Any other thoughts? Escape? I'm leaving. Does anybody want to try to convince the cops that you're innocent?"

"Mary?"

"I think I'd better go. I don't trust the cops. Best case, they give us more time in jail. I don't want any more prison time."

She looked up at me with big brown eyes.

"I'm leaving," she said.

"Me too," said Rod.

I turned to Bob and put my hands on my friend's shoulders. "Bob, if you think you can beat this thing by staying here and testifying, we'll tie you up and make it look like the three of us are responsible. You stay and tell them the truth. They might just believe you."

It got real quiet.

Bob was looking down. He seemed to be doing some deep thinking.

"I can't believe this is happening to me," he moaned. "I did nothing wrong before being busted for drugs. I've served seven years. Before I'm paroled we're tangled up with this worthless bastard of a prison guard who's now dead. Nothing about this is my fault. Now I have the choice of fighting for my innocence again in court or serving life in prison for killing a prison guard or spending the rest of my life as a fugitive."

"Got a better idea?" I asked.

"What can happen?" Bob reasoned. "We turn ourselves in and either they believe us, letting us go in two months, sentence us to life in prison, or hang us for killing a prison guard."

"Wanna gamble with that," asked Rod.

"I haven't paid much attention to Iowa's death penalty law," I corrected, "but I think they repealed it before any of us were born. The death penalty isn't an option, folks. Besides, it was my fight. I'm out of here."

Bob looked me in the eyes. "Me too," he said. "I'm with you."

"Anybody else? Rod?"

"I'm out of here while we have a chance. Regardless of the circumstances, they'll say we killed The Ranger in cold blood. We won't be able to convince anyone that we tried to prevent this asshole from raping Mary. I'm leaving."

"Anybody need any clothes?" I asked.

"We should leave," said Bob.

"I'm thinking long term," I offered. "I'm going to need clean underwear."

We found plastic bags under the sink and collected most of our clothes. The bags weren't very full. None of us had much.

We gathered near the door.

"Wait a minute," I said. "Think about this. We've got some time. Nobody's going to check on us until morning, after we're supposed to be gone to work. What do we need?"

"Wheels," said Rod. "The Ranger probably has a set of car keys in his pocket and maybe some cash and credit cards. Can we travel far enough to be safe? I'd say our chances are mighty slim. What do you all think?"

"You're thinking about stealing The Ranger's car?" asked Bob.

"He won't be needing it," suggested Rod.

I reached into the dead man's pocket. My hand came out with a big ring of keys. My second hand filled with a plump wallet.

III

Leaving

We searched The Ranger's pockets, found three bucks in change and a Swiss Army Knife. His wallet had several credit cards, an ATM card, a debit card, and three hundred forty dollars in cash.

"Here's something that might be handy," I said.

"What's that?"

"A list of banks with security numbers. We might make a stop at an ATM."

"Prison didn't cure you of being an embezzler, did it, Paul?" kidded Mary.

I frowned. "We're desperate. The more money we have the longer we can stay free, Mary." I glanced up at her eyes. They were filled with humor.

"Just kidding, Paul. Don't be too serious."

"This is a serious time," said Bob.

I smiled. Then I asked, "What do all of you think about withdrawing some money tonight on these credit cards and bank cards?"

Rod said, "Just as well. Maybe we can use them to buy some things we need."

"And fill up our gas tank," said Bob.

"We better do it just once though," Rod said. "They'll be able to trace the credit cards to us if we use them tomorrow."

I opened the drawer of the desk and pulled out a pad of paper and a pen. I wrote the words:

This asshole of a guard tried to rape Mary Swartz. We tried to stop him and he died after he bumped his head in the struggle. We are getting the hell out of here. We'd rather stay, but who'd believe our side? We think Stewart was drunk. Check his blood for alcohol.

We turned down the lights inside the halfway house as they might be if people were in bed. We left Roger lying with the pool of blood around his head. I felt kind of sad and very guilty that the man was lying there dead because of a struggle with me. I knew he had been doing something evil, but I was still sad that Roger Stewart was dead. I said a little prayer asking God to forgive him and accept him in heaven, if there was such a place. I didn't think he deserved to die.

The four of us were piling into Roger Stewart's Toyota 4Runner SUV, when Mary declared, "Anybody need a beer? Here's a half a case of Bud on the passenger seat."

Rod said, "There's a half a case of empty cans on the floor of the back seat."

I thought for just a moment. Then I advised, "Don't touch those cans, guys. See if you can pick them up without leaving prints. Maybe you can stick a finger in the opening. Put them in this plastic bag the beer was in. We'll leave them beside Roger. If whoever finds him, thinks to check for fingerprints, maybe they'll believe our story that he was drunk and we aren't completely responsible for his death."

Bob tried the door to the halfway house. It was locked of course.

"The place has an automatic door," said Rod. "We knew that."

I handed him The Ranger's key ring.

"The Ranger should have a key. Try these."

We were standing near a street light. All of us were uncomfortable with our visibility.

Rod found the key on The Ranger's ring. I hated to go back into the halfway house and look at Roger Stewart's cooling corpse again, but I took a deep breath and carried the plastic bag of cans to The Ranger's body and laid them beside him.

I scrambled back in the SUV, turned the key, and drove north.

"Where you going, man."

"I'm thinking we should go south, where it's warmer."

"You're driving north."

"Let's find a convenience store in the wrong direction and max out his ATM cards."

"Maybe fill the gas tank too?" offered Bob.

"Good plans. You're devious men," accused Mary.

I drove north, full of fear. Fear of using stolen credit cards; fear of showing up on a video at an ATM machine, fear of driving several states away from Iowa without being stopped by the cops, fear of establishing some kind of new life; and fear of being caught escaping from Des Moines with three other escaped prisoners.

IV

Roger's House

Looking in the rear view mirror, I saw that Rod had popped the top of a Bud and was enjoying the bite of the beer. The rest of us decided we could wait a bit longer to let beer into our lives. I don't even like the stuff.

I had climbed behind the wheel and driven a couple of blocks before I pulled over to the curb.

"Look at that address from The Ranger's wallet, Rod. Let's go over to The Ranger's house, see what else he has that we need. Rod, you and Bob are close enough to his size, I'll bet you can wear his clothes. Why don't you keep his wallet, and his license too? Scowl a bit. You might be able to pass for him on a dark night."

"What about his family?" Bob asked. "We can't just bust in on his wife and kids, Paul."

I recalled The Ranger complaining about his wife. "One time I heard him say that he and his wife are separated. She has the kids except for one weekend a month. I'm betting his house is empty of people."

The address was for a house in West Des Moines. I pointed Roger's 4Runner for the suburbs.

We passed a K-Mart Store and I turned in.

"Now what, Paul? Don't you think we better be driving to Roger's house?" asked Mary.

I had an idea. "We may keep this Toyota for a while, guys. It might slow the cops down if we had some different plates."

I drove to the back of the parking lot, where the employees parked. I stopped next to a Chevy.

"Do we have a screw driver?" Bob asked.

They searched the back of the SUV to no avail.

Rod deduced, "Roger must not have been mechanical. No tools in here."

"Wait a minute," Bob said. "Here's the Swiss Army Knife I took out of his pocket. This thing has a screw driver on it."

Bob slipped out and removed the front plate from our Toyota and from the Chevy. He switched the plates and moved to the rear as the lights of a car swung down our aisle. Rob opened the back window as if to reach in with a package.

The car passed and drove closer to the store, probably looking for a parking spot with a shorter walk.

Bob bent behind the Chevy, removing the license plate, then quickly made the switch. We had gained us a few hours and some safer miles.

I suggested, "Before we leave town, we'll go see if Roger can help us some more."

It didn't take long to find Roger Stewart's little bungalow on Elm Street. Mary hit the button on the garage door opener. I drove right into his garage, and Mary shut the door behind us.

Sitting in the other stall of the two car garage was a red Ford Ranger pickup with an extended cab and four wheel drive. It seemed about ten years old.

As we looked at the bright colored pickup parked beside us, Rod said, "Looks like we might be able to travel in two pairs. What do you guys think? Should we split up?"

"I don't think I have much chance on my own," Bob said. "How do we escape and then establish new identities so the police can't find us? I was hoping you guys might help me."

Rod comforted him. "I talked to enough crooks in prison. I think I know how to procure some false ID's. One guy told me that you have to go to a cemetery and find some kid who was born about the time you was and died at a very young age. The kid probably never filed for social security, so you just send for a duplicate birth certificate. Then later you can apply for a social security card."

"It sounds like new identities are possible," agreed Mary. "I also think Rod is right. We'd just as well go in pairs. Should we split up now or travel out of town first?"

"I agree," I said. "We'll be better off in groups of two. Then we need to spend the night putting some miles between us and Des Moines."

My attention shifted to the red pickup. "It looks like *The Ranger* left us a Ranger. Who wants the Ranger? Does anybody have any preferences?"

Nobody said anything. I glanced at Mary. "Mary, how about you and me?"

She quickly nodded, "We could try it together."

Bob asked, "Rod, are you willing to partner up with me?"

"You bet," Rod smiled. "We can get along."

Then Rod turned to me. "How about if me and Bob take the Toyota? I don't like a straight transmission much. That pickup has a stick."

"I don't mind a bit," I offered. "I'll smile about The Ranger's Ranger every time I see the word Ranger on the truck. Now, let's see what else we can find in this house that he would want us to have now that he's passed away."

I looked at Rod. "How about you and Bob head upstairs. Either of you can probably wear Roger's clothes. If you find anything really big or really small, Mary and I might use them. We'll search this floor. You just pack a couple of bags."

V

Bonuses From the Ranger

Mary and I found a cooler in the garage and another in the basement. We filled them with food from his refrigerator and freezer. We threw in silverware, a can opener, and a handful of book matches with all kinds of motel and bar advertising on them. In the basement we found a sleeping bag, a couple of foam sleeping pads, three blankets, a 2-person tent, and a two burner Coleman camp stove. Mary grabbed an old skillet and a sauce pan. In a closet I found a spinning rod and a tackle box with a bunch of crappie jigs and a little fillet knife. There was a rechargeable electric drill in the garage that I put in the Ranger. I grabbed a beat-up tool box with a collection of sockets, pliers, and screw drivers. A hatchet fit behind the seat. I liked tools when a person had a job to do.

Rod and Bob showed up with two duffle bags and a suitcase full of clothes. Each of them had a couple of blankets thrown over his shoulder. Rod was carrying a Winchester pump shotgun and a big black automatic pistol in a holster.

"Look what we found under his bed." said Rod.

I didn't like the idea of guns. "If they catch us with guns, that will just compound our troubles, fellows. I'd vote to leave them here."

Mary nodded her agreement. "So far we really haven't done anything bad. *The Ranger's* death wasn't our fault. I don't feel guilty about taking his stuff, but I don't like the idea of guns. Besides, Rod, wasn't a friggin' gun the reason they sent you up to start with?"

Rod rubbed his jaw. "S'pose you're right, Mary."

He laid the guns on the carpet.

Bob thought we were funny. "The cops will think we're strange criminals. We raid The Ranger's house and steal food and clothes and leave a pile of guns on the living room carpet."

"Should give them a chuckle," I laughed.

"We found a couple of changes of clothes for Bob and I," Rod offered. "Paul, I think you can wear some of his underwear, maybe these shorts and sweat shirts. We also threw some t-shirts and sweats in a gym bag for you, Mary. It could do you until you buy something better. He didn't have no bras, but we did find a couple of pairs of fancy lace underwear hanging above his bed." Rod laughed as he dangled them on his finger and then threw the panties to Mary. She caught them and stuffed them in her pocket.

"Thanks for thinking of me, Rod."

He paused and then pointed at our food. "What are you two planning to do? Set up housekeeping?"

I answered, "We figured that if we could put distance between us and this town without stopping and spending money it would be better."

Rod and Bob glanced at each other. "We may not have too much problem with money for a while," Bob suggested. "Look at this." Bob flashed a stack of bills about an inch thick. He riffled through them. We could see they were mostly hundreds and a few twenties. He handed Mary a pile of cash. "Here's about half of it. $1700 in that stack, sweet lady."

"Our friend Roger had this in a safe under his computer desk. The key was sticking out the top. He must have been doing pretty well as a prison guard," Rod continued.

"Wow!" I exclaimed. "This could make the difference between our escaping cleanly and going back to prison. I'd guess Roger was hiding some cash from his ex-wife and kid. Nice guy, our friend Roger!"

Rod looked at our pile of camping equipment. "What the hell are you doing with the tent and the camp stove, Paul? You aren't planning to go camping. It's cold out there."

"I figure the longer we can hold out without spending what money we have, the more chance we'll have to establish new identities. If we use his credit cards after we leave Des Moines, we'll leave a trail, as easy to follow as a wounded deer through fresh snow. We can camp pretty cheap after we're down south someplace and then we won't have to spend much money. I've slept in a car before and I didn't like it at all. You guys might not be too bad off in the back of that 4-Runner."

I had some more thoughts. "We can keep his bank cards for an emergency, but we'd be better off not ever using them again after tonight. In fact I have another idea. Let's each use a credit card to fill up our gas tank in the opposite end of town to the direction we are going. Convenience stores sell everything these days. Stock up on whatever you think you'll need. When the cops check those credit card receipts, that could throw them off for a while and encourage them to look in the opposite direction."

I reached into my pocket and handed Bob The Ranger's ATM card. I wrote the code on a piece of paper. "Here. Take this ATM card and see how much money an ATM machine will give you. I've got a card from another bank. Mary and I will get some cash with it. It's going to take money for us to escape and get a clean start."

We loaded our vehicles and said our good-byes.

I said to Rod and Bob, "Give us a couple minutes start with the Ranger. We don't want a neighbor to see us both leave at the same time. It would be kind of hard for our friend, Roger, to do that. We'll probably never see each other again unless they arrest us and we meet in Fort Madison. We are all damn good people. Figure this thing out and make a new life for yourselves. I hope I never see you again, my friends. You can do it and you deserve it. Good luck, gentlemen."

We shook hands. Mary gave hugs to Bob and Rod. She and I climbed into the Ranger.

VI

Extra Cash

Mary pushed the button that opened the garage door. As we backed out of the drive, she closed The Ranger's garage door behind us. We found a main street and drove west. As we passed a bank, I stopped at the side of the street. I was wearing an Iowa Cubs hat that I had found at The Ranger's house. I pulled the hat low over my eyes and hunched the collar of my jacket.

"Let me see that ATM card."

Mary looked at the card under the street light. "It's not an ATM card. It's a debit card. Does that matter?"

"I think the difference is that we can use the debit card in a store for a purchase. Probably with a pin number. I don't remember what the limit might be. Maybe we can withdraw more money."

Mary frowned, "Isn't the limit still $500?"

"Typically, but it depends on what the maximum is for the account. Let's find out."

I reached out the window and tried the numbers. I told the machine I wanted to know the balance.

It spit out a piece of paper. The account balance was $1,623.29.

The screen asked if I wanted to make another transaction. I told it to give me $500 and it spit the money right out. I tried again and the machine gave me a rather rude message denying my request. I tried the $100 and the machine gave me five twenties. I did it twice more before it told me I had reached the limit.

I asked Mary, "What's the time?"

She squinted to see the clock on the dash. "11:50"

"Let's go get a cup of coffee."

"Are you crazy, Paul. We want to get out of town."

"Ten minutes. Let's see what happens in ten minutes. Let's see what happens at midnight."

There was a McDonald's just around the corner.

Mary suggested, "Why don't we just get a large coffee and share. We can save a buck."

We drove through the drive-up. It was a new day when we drove away.

Back at the bank, It was twelve-fifteen. I tried the debit card again. I gave it the pin number from the Ranger's wallet. Soon we had another $800.

I told Mary, "I feel like a thief."

"You are a thief, Paul Hartman. That's why you were in the Iowa State Penitentiary."

Rod and Bob waited impatiently in the garage for about ten minutes. Bob walked around, looking on shelves for anything that might be useful for them. His eyes coveted the bicycle hanging from a hook on the ceiling.

"I loved biking. I wish there was room for it in the SUV."

Bob saw a set of wrenches, pliers, a hammer, and some screwdrivers on a rack. He threw them in a cardboard box and set it in the back of the 4Runner.

"Tools are good," he told Rod.

"Anything else we need here?" said Rod. "It's time to hit the road."

Rod backed the Toyota out of the garage and Bob hit the button on the opener. They watched the door go down on the Ranger.

Rod drove to I-35 North. Near the intersection was a Quick Trip. He pulled up to the pumps.

"You fill the tank and I'll buy some supplies," Bob suggested. "Maybe you should stay out of the store. The clerk might think you are a hold-up man."

"That ain't funny, man," Rod muttered. "I didn't rob every store in Des Moines. Besides those clerks don't stay on too long. The ones I robbed are probably working for new businesses by now."

"I remember these automatic pay machines," Bob commented. "They were just getting popular before I went to prison."

Rod ran the credit card along the slot. Then he turned it over and tried again. The third time the pump was ready to run.

In the store Bob took a little red basket and walked the aisles. He gathered supplies, food, and grabbed a case of bottled water.

The clerk totaled the groceries.

"This it?"

"Yep."

"The total's $199.43."

Bob handed her The Ranger's credit card.

"Slide the card right there." She pointed at the machine in front of Bob.

This machine is something new, he thought.

This time it only took two tries for him to slide the card the right way.

The clerk pointed at the machine again. "Punch the green button that says the price is right."

Bob did it.

"Sign your name in the box, please."

Bob found the place on the screen and signed the credit card slip, *Roger Stewart,* just as if he wrote that name every day. He looked at the signature on the little screen and frowned. *I can't read it.* He nearly panicked when she asked for identification. He fished out The Ranger's driver's license and showed it to the clerk. He gave her a dirty look. She seemed satisfied. He took his receipt and picked out slots in the wallet for the license and the credit card. He was shaking visibly by the time he stowed the bags in the back of the 4Runner and climbed into the passenger seat.

"Problems?" Rod asked.

"She made me slide the credit card and sign my name in some fool machine. I was scared shitless when she wanted ID. I had The Ranger's wallet and his driver's license. I didn't know we looked that much alike. I was scowling like a pit bull, when she looked at the picture and glanced up at me. Thought I'd faint, I was so relieved when she handed me the Master Card and the license. She made me awful nervous, Rod. I'm glad we aren't using his credit card again."

Rod was ready to move. "Where to, man? I think we should go to St. Louis. Find us a way."

"Interstate or backroads?"

"What do you think? Interstate would be easier driving."

Bob pointed at the Atlas. "If cops want to block us, it's easier for them on Interstate Highways."

"Ok. Find us a two lane."

Bob smiled. Head south on I-35. Then I'll take you through some pretty country."

"It's night, man."

"It'll still be pretty, Rodney. We're going to Hannibal, Missouri, my friend. Have you ever read Mark Twain?"

VII

Detour to Mary's Mom

Mary and I were in The Ranger's Ranger searching for a black-top road headed south out of Des Moines. The gas tank on the Ranger was on empty. We stopped at a convenience store where we filled the tank and stocked up on groceries, including over-the-counter medications and anything we thought might be nice to have in the next few weeks. We split up while I was looking at Maglites. As I dropped a heavy three-cell flashlight into my basket, she showed up with both hands full of make-up.

"This make-up isn't the greatest, but it will work. Anyway, The Ranger's buying. Thanks, Roger."

Our total came to $307.25.

Back in the Ranger, I glanced over at Mary. She seemed to be engrossed in thought.

"What's going on, Mary. You're awfully quiet."

"I was just thinking," she answered. "We aren't going to be back in Des Moines for a long time, right?"

"Maybe never, if things work out alright for us. Is that a problem?"

"Would it screw us up if we were to stop and see my mom for just a few minutes, Paul? I want to give her a hug and maybe grab a few things I might need. It would only take a few minutes."

"It's a risk," I cautioned. "Time is a definite factor. We ought to be out of Des Moines by now. They could discover The Ranger's body any time. Where will they start looking for us? Your mom's place?"

I was concerned about Mary's mom as well. "It's best for us and for your mom if she doesn't know anything about our escaping. Especially, that she doesn't know where we are headed."

Mary was quiet.

Then she said quietly, "I've got a box at home with some jewelry and some cash. It's not a lot, but it could help us until we get established somewhere, Paul."

I hesitated only a moment. "Maybe we can take a risk. It would be good if you could say goodbye to your mother, Mary. Where does she live?"

"She has a little house in Saylorville Township. It's just north of the interstate."

We parked on a tree-lined street in a quiet neighborhood. I could hear the sound of the trucks on I-80 and I-35 a half-mile south of us.

"Will you wait here, please, Paul?" Mary asked. "I'd like to handle this by myself."

I nodded and she walked to the door. The dog barked at Mary's knock.

She whispered to herself, *Shut up, Winston. You fool mutt. It's just me.*

The porch light came on and the door opened a crack. Winston growled deep in his throat and then wagged all over when his memory clicked in and he recognized Mary. He got a huge hug as he slathered Mary with his sloppy tongue.

"Mary! What the hell are you doing here? Did you break out of jail? What the hell is going on?"

"Quiet, Mom. Just open the door and let me in. I'll explain."

Mary slipped into the living room, greeted the excited dog, and hugged her mother. "I have to pick up some of my things, Mom. I'll explain what's going on while I pack a bag."

She grabbed an old suitcase, filling it with clothes and a pair of running shoes. On the floor of the closet, she found a lock box. With the key from the bottom of her jewelry box, she opened it, smiling to see that her cache was still there.

As she worked, she explained to her mom about the attempted rape and the guys that had helped her.

"I can't go back there. There is no way that they wouldn't give us all life in prison for the death of the guard -- even if he deserved it and even if it was an accident. We are leaving. I'll probably never see you again, Mom. Maybe I can find a way to get in touch, but if I do I'll run a big risk of spending the rest of my life in prison. The guy I'm traveling with is a good man.

He and I will be great together, Mom. I love you. Don't even look out the door."

Teary-eyed, Mrs. Swartz grabbed on to Mary's arm. "Wait, Mary. I have an idea. It will take me five minutes. She hurried to her bedroom, opening a bottom drawer of her dresser. In a cardboard shoe box, she found an old pink wallet and an official looking sheet of paper.

Back in the living room, she handed them to Mary. "I don't know why I kept these, Mary. When Michelle was killed in the car wreck, she was eighteen. She looked so much like you. Here's her driver's license and her birth certificate and her Social Security Card. They may help you start a new identity. I don't know how that stuff works, but who knows? It might be useful to you."

"Thanks, Mom. Great idea. It might just work. At least if I get a job, I can give them some ID. I love you, Mom. Forever!"

They hugged again and Mary jogged for the pickup.

Mary climbed into the Ranger and slid over towards me. I started the engine, drove to NW 14th Street, and turned south.

"Turn on the dome light," Mary requested. "Mom got me a new ID."

"What are you talking about?"

She held up a driver's license.

"My sister, Michelle, died in a car accident a year ago. Mom found her driver's license, birth certificate, and social security card. From now on you can call me Michelle Swartz. My sister lives again."

I glanced at the photo. "It looks like you, Mary."

"Michelle. Call me Michelle from now on, Paul."

"Michelle it is. Remind me. Mary's a habit."

"It'll take us a while."

Michelle and I drove out of Des Moines on 14th Street which was Highway 69. It soon joined Highway 65 which we thought might be a safer route to Missouri than I-35.

Surveying snow-filled ditches, we quickly decided that south was our best direction of travel. Michelle and I talked about a plan of action. We agreed that we should go south until the weather was warmer. We would obey the speed limits rigorously and make sure we came to a full stop at every stop sign. We'd avoided yellow lights like poison ivy. Driving at 55 mph down state highways, we didn't have to worry much about yellow lines and tickets for illegal passing. We just didn't want to be stopped by a cop for anything. Michelle's driver's license could help us. We agreed that she should do a lot of the driving. If something happened she could flash her license. The resemblance between her and her sister's photo on the license should be plenty close.

We passed through most of Missouri on US 65. It was just before dawn when we reached Sedalia. Stopping on a back street, I listened for barking dogs. The night was as silent as the Christmas carol. Using The Ranger's electric screw driver, I removed the license plates from a maroon Ford Ranger pickup and handed them to Michelle. The pickup wasn't exactly red, but it might be close enough for a non-discerning cop. Inside the unlocked pickup I found the registration certificate in the glove compartment. After driving to the next town we stopped on a quiet side street and switched the new Missouri plates to our Ranger.

By the time the sun was coloring the sky with tinges of pink and blue and gray, we were approaching Arkansas. The weather wasn't a lot warmer than it had been the night before, but the radio said the high in Joplin would be 55 degrees. Des Moines was predicted to reach 38 degrees with a couple of inches of snow later on. We were on our way to better weather.

Michelle said, "Paul, I'm really tired."

"Me too. Maybe we should find a place to stop and nap for an hour."

"Find it soon. I'm very sleepy. I can hardly keep my eyes open."

"This might be a truck stop up ahead."

"I could sleep anywhere, Paul."

We turned into a Pilot Truck Stop. I filled the gas tank, shoving the old Ranger plates deep in the trash. Michelle used the restroom and then we parked in the back. We locked the doors. Michelle leaned against me. In minutes we were both asleep.

An hour later a county sheriff's car cruised past. I opened an eye, catching a glimpse of a deputy scouting out our license. I held my breath for about two minutes until he left the truck stop and turned back on the highway.

VIII

To Run Or To Hide

It was nine o'clock and the sun was shining when we stopped at McDonald's. We bought a couple of Sausage McMuffin's with egg and two cups of coffee.

Sitting at a tiny table on high stools, I said, "I can't believe how good fast-food tastes after three years of eating prison cooking."

Michelle nodded in agreement. She flashed a pretty smile. but her eyes were drooping. "Paul, I'm awful tired. I think we should find a place to spend the night."

"Or maybe to spend the day. Let me drive for a while. I'll see what I can find."

Feeling refreshed after our break, I got behind the wheel. Mary was sleeping as we turned west on I-44. Two hours later, I drove into Fayetteville, Arkansas.

Down the street was a brick building with an American flag flying in front. The sign said, *Ozark National Forest, US*

Forest Service, Fayetteville Regional Office. I turned into the driveway and parked.

"Take a nap, Mary. I love camping in National Forest Service campgrounds. I'll ask for some maps."

"Michelle," said the sleepy voice. "Michelle. Remember, Paul, I'm Michelle now. My sister's name is on my driver's license. Say, 'Goodnight, Michelle.'"

"Goodnight, Michelle. Sleep tight."

Inside the office was a dark-haired young lady in a green uniform. My mind immediately thought *Cop.* My stomach did a flip at the sight of her uniform. A second later, I relaxed, telling myself, *She's just a forest ranger, not a cop or a prison guard.*

"Can I help you, sir?" she smiled.

I smiled back. She seemed to be the age of one of my high school students.

"Sure," I answered. "We're on our way to a week on Bull Shoals Lake over by Mountain Home. Thought we might need a stopping place on the way home. Do you have a map showing camping areas in the National Forest?"

The ranger had a name badge on her shirt that said, "Martha Dye." Martha handed me a brochure. "Take one of these," she offered. "It shows the roads and campgrounds and some of the short trails in the forest."

I opened the booklet and glanced at the map of the forest and then over Martha Dye's head at a television set that was tuned to the morning news. The volume was low, but I saw the headlines, "FOUR PRISONERS MURDER GUARD. ESCAPE IOWA HALFWAY HOUSE." The TV flashed a picture of me, then of Mary Swartz, Rod Dodge, and Bob Johnson. As the picture switched from me, Martha's eyes followed mine to the TV. She glimpsed the photos of Mary, Rod, and Bob.

When the TV news switched to another story she looked at me and said, "That's awful about those prisoners killing a guard and escaping. Kind of scary. Strange though. I was listening to the radio on the way to work. Strange. All of them were about to be released from the halfway house. Then they killed a guard and escaped. Why would they do that?"

I agreed with her. "I heard that too. Made no sense to me. If I was about to be released from prison, I sure wouldn't kill a guard and run away. Seems silly."

"Anyway, keep your eyes open."

"I saw their pictures," I said. "If I see the escapees, I'll go the other way."

"They'll catch 'em," said Ms. Martha Dye. "There's too much news and there are too many law enforcement people looking for them. They won't be free for long."

I said, "Be alert."

"They won't be here. This is the last place a gang of escaped prisoners would show up."

I looked around and bought a National Audubon Society bird book and a pair of binoculars. I thought, *Maybe we can look like birders. Nobody would look suspiciously at a couple out birding.*

Michelle was sound asleep. She didn't even stir when I got in the pickup and headed it down the road. Then she leaned to my side and rested her head on my lap. That felt really good. When we drove into the Lake Wedington Campground, I hated to disturb her rest.

She was waking up as I was stopping to get a self-registration envelope from a rack.

"Have you ever been camping, Michelle?"

"Camping was never my style," Michelle reflected. "I always liked *things*. Diamonds and pearls and nice clothes always sounded better to me. This place is awful pretty though. I like it. The forest is gorgeous. Are we going to spend the night here?"

"We need to talk," I suggested. "Let's sit at a picnic table and make a decision."

I picked up a self-registration envelope and drove around the campground.

Pulling into a gravel parking spot at a lovely wooded campsite, I shut off the engine.

"Let's sit at the picnic table."

"What's wrong, Paul? Something's wrong. What happening?"

I sat on the table with my feet on the wooden bench. I rested my head in my hands and my elbows on my knees. I wanted to think.

"Paul?"

"I'm scared, Mary."

"Michelle."

"I'm scared, Michelle."

"What happened?"

I told her about seeing the pictures of the escaped prisoners on TV. "That girl is going to see a news broadcast again.

Maybe this afternoon. Maybe tonight. She'll probably say, 'I saw that guy this morning. He was in my office this morning. I had a fucking murderer in my office this morning. He might have killed me.' We're in trouble, Mary."

"Michelle."

"We're in trouble, Michelle."

"Maybe she won't remember you?"

I had no doubt that Martha Dye would remember. Tonight's news would include possible sightings of the escaped Iowa prisoners in Fayetteville, Arkansas. Their search was narrowing.

"OK. What are our options?" I asked. "What choices do we have?"

"We could get back in the Ranger and run. We could drive west, south, or east."

"We could set up camp right here." I said. "Hope the Ranger lady thought we were just traveling through."

"We could give ourselves up."

"That isn't happening. When I have a 5% chance to have a free life, I'm not going to give it up for a 100% chance at life in prison."

Michelle said, "We're together on that one, Paul."

"I'm leaning toward spending a day or two here," I suggested. "We have stolen plates on the Ranger that might or might not be in the law enforcement computer system. The red Ranger is a red flag that will show up in front of every cop we drive past. I almost think we should ditch it. Drive it off a boat ramp at night."

"Maybe we need to buy another car first," Michelle suggested. "How much money do we have?"

"Check your purse. We got $1700 from The Ranger, $1400 from his debit card, and you picked up some money from your house. Maybe $3100?"

Michelle took out her purse, started adding.

"I've got $3600 here, Paul."

"Maybe we should buy a $1500 car."

"Seems silly trading an almost new Ranger for clunker."

"It's just money," I laughed. " And freedom."

"So," Michelle agreed. "We camp here for a couple of nights. Then we drive into town and buy a new vehicle in my name. Later that night we drive the Ranger down a boat ramp into a lake."

"Good plan, woman," I agreed. "I was thinking exactly the same thing."

IX

Camping In the National Forest

We located a level campsite that was relatively secluded. The late winter weather was still quite cool and the park was mostly empty. We decided to skip the tent and sleep in the back of the Ranger, under the topper. I spread our guard's foam sleeping mats and laid a blanket on top. Both of us were bushed. A nap seemed like a good plan for the early afternoon. The sun was warm. We were afraid, but we were still free. I wasn't sure how well we would sleep.

I said, "We only have one sleeping bag, Michelle. Sorry."

"It's all right, Paul," she chuckled. "I'll use the bag. You can have the blankets."

"Or we can share," I responded.

We shared. Michelle and I stayed really warm spooned together in the sleeping bag. We slept like children with no worries.

It was late in the afternoon when I awoke. We were lying face-to-face and Michelle's hands were under my sweatshirt, massaging my back. Her lips were inches from mine so I bent my head and kissed her.

My mind flashed to my first serious kiss. I was a college freshman and she was a high school girl with way more experience than me. Now I was an adult and Michelle was a former prostitute with way more experience than me. The kiss with Michelle felt exponentially better than that first one with the high school girl. Michelle's tongue traced my lips and then twined with mine.

My hand moved to Michelle's bra. I unhooked it as if I was a man of quantitative experience, which I was not. I matched her gentle back massage on her bare back. Her strong ribs and spine were covered with muscles that made smooth paths for my hands to explore. I rolled her gently toward her back, my hand moving under her bra, attempting to cover her left breast. Not much chance of that. I had never touched a woman with such bodacious breasts and such a slender waist.

Then we were both naked. Michelle reached into her make-up bag and handed me a box of condoms.

"Where did you get these?"

"They came with the make-up from the convenience store. Thank The Ranger. It was his money."

That could have destroyed the mood. But it didn't. A half hour later, we were both asleep again.

In another hour I sat up and dug a Pepsi out of the cooler. A couple of big brown eyes were looking at me.

"Want to take a walk?" I asked

"Sure."

She took my hand as we walked along a dirt path. I was thrilled to feel her hand in mine. We found an overlook above a pretty lake. The sun was low in the sky. We sat on a rock outcropping, leaning together, feeling the warmth of the spring sun on the rocks. The air was mellow. Michelle and I shared the can of pop. I had forgotten that there were days like this. We watched clouds turn pink and purple and peachy and blue. God was presenting a spectacular show just for the two of us -- to let us know his power and how good life could be.

"Isn't it lovely?" murmured Michelle. "I don't remember ever seeing anything like this before."

She squeezed my hand.

I squeezed back.

We stayed on the warm rock until the light was almost gone. After sunset, the sky rewarded us with deep grays, dramatic pinks. The glorious colors reflecting in the lake, doubled our pleasure from the sunset.

We walked back to the campsite as a damp coolness begin to descend upon us with the night. Gathering dry sticks and branches from the dark forest, I built a fire. Soon we were roasting hot dogs and marshmallows and warming our toes.

Later, we snuggled together in the back of the pickup under our sleeping bag.

At dawn I awoke early. I sat up in our bed under the topper. I thought, *Here we are with every law enforcement officer in five states looking for us while we are living a life as relaxed citizens on a quiet vacation. Today or tomorrow, we need to make a change and put more miles between us and Iowa. I guess we'll enjoy this while we can.*

I zipped Michelle into our sleeping bag and slipped out to build a fire. I mixed up pancake batter with an egg and milk in a plastic bag. Firing up the propane stove, I put on a pan of water. When it boiled, I dropped in a handful of coffee. After a couple of minutes, I added a bit of cold water to settle the grounds, and filled two cups with steaming coffee.

As I set a cup near Michelle, she smiled and said, "That smells super. I could get used to having you around."

We sipped hot coffee as the sun rose high enough to begin to warm our cozy little nest in the back of the pickup truck. Soon, we were sitting at the picnic table, enjoying hot pancakes, smothered in butter and syrup. Freedom was alright.

The warm spring sun and the budding forest made us feel really alive for the first time in years. Michelle (I was beginning to like her new name) and I walked the rocky, forested trails of this Ozark woodland. The rugged yellow rock of the Ozarks was everywhere. Dogwoods and the redbuds were blooming, the forest blazing with white and pink flowers.

"I love the smell, Paul. I never smelled anything so fresh. My eyes and my nose are feasting just like my stomach did on your pancakes this morning."

We sat on another rocky outcropping above the pretty little blue-water lake. Michelle reached into the pocket of her jeans, pulled out a pair of scissors, and handed them to me.

"What do you want me to do with these?"

"Cut my hair," she demanded. "Give me a real short haircut."

"I can't cut hair."

"You mean you never have cut hair."

"Right," I agreed.

Michelle gently squeezed my hand around the scissors.

"And you want me to cut your hair," I said. "Now."

"You got that right. I want it short."

"Short."

"Real short," she demanded.

"I can't."

"Do it. Make it all about two inches long. Cut it, Paul."

I started cutting. Michelle handed me a comb. Pull it out with this first. Then cut along the comb. You can do this, Paul. I can't go to a beautician. They watch the news. I'll get it trimmed a thousand miles down the road. Cut it, Paul."

Twenty minutes later there was a pile of blond hair on the rock.

"I don't think they'll match you with the picture of Mary Swartz. You're still beautiful, but you're beautiful with a bad haircut."

"My goal."

"Glad you're happy. I've got a question."

"Yes?"

"Can we buy some hair dye and change your color to black? Or dark brown?"

"We can do that."

"Let's go to town and find a drug store."

"No need," said Michelle.

"What do you mean?"

Michelle reached into her knapsack.

"Here," she said as she handed me a box.

"What's this?"

"Read it."

"Natural Instincts? This is hair dye."

"Yep."

"You already bought it?"

"Planning ahead," Michelle bragged. "You didn't see all the shit I threw in that basket of stuff The Ranger bought for us."

I said, "Condoms. Hair dye. What other surprises did you pick up at that convenience store, Michelle?"

"I'll let you know. Anyway, it's time for you to dye my hair a dark brown."

"Who do you think I am, your personal hairdresser?"

"Is this an affront to your manhood?"

"No. I'll dye your hair. I can love you with black hair as well as blonde."

"Paul."

"Yes."

"Look up."

"What?"

"Those birds. Way up high. What are they?"

"You are a bird watcher," I answered, "aren't you?"

"I was watching while you were cutting."

"They're Turkey Vultures."

Turkey Vultures sailed on a gentle breeze in the blue skies above us. The huge black birds drifted in the air currents with hardly a move of their wings. Their wing feathers were spread to the maximum, forming open V's between them. Were the buzzards searching for food? Were they smelling the breezes, hoping to find a scent of some dead, rotting animal?

"I read about Turkey Vultures when I was in prison," I reflected. "They can smell carrion from two miles away. I also read that they can eat a rotten carcass containing enough salmonella to kill every person in a large town and never get the least bit sick. They are amazing birds. Our environment is much better with them hanging around; cleaning up dead things."

"Look over on that point," Michelle pointed. "There must be ten of them roosting in that dead tree. They don't seem to be feeding. I guess the big birds don't eat all of the time."

I sat on the rock with my arm around Michelle. This was such a pleasant place. This woman was a delightful companion. I whispered in her ear. "I think I love you, Michelle."

She turned to my ear and said softly. "I'm sure I love you, Paul."

She raised her head and I kissed her. Life in the Iowa State Penitentiary moved behind me, like ancient history. People were looking for us -- people with radios; a huge network of police and sheriffs and highway patrol officers and FBI agents. We didn't have time to fall in love. Michelle and I had lives to plan. We had to find ways to stay free. We had to find a place to live safely without looking over our shoulders for danger.

"Michelle. Will you live with me the rest of your life? Will you live with me as my wife?" I asked.

"My, aren't you the poetic one, Paul."

"I'm sorry, ... I didn't mean to say it that way, Michelle. I just ..."

She interrupted me with a finger on my lips. "Hush now. You just said a real nice thing."

For a few minutes the only sound was the chirping of the birds in the forest. Then she touched my cheek and said, "I wrote a poem while we were in the halfway house, Paul. I memorized it. Do you want to hear it?"

"Sure. Of course."

She looked into my eyes.

"I'll be your wife, for all your life. I'll love you true, never make you blue.

I'll have your babies, all the way to Hades. Together, we'll both stand tall.

Forever, I'll love you, Paul."

...

...

"I could reverse that, Michelle. I pledge that I'll love you, ... forever!" I answered.

X

Unlicensed Fisherman

Walking back to the campsite, we held each other. My right arm was around Michelle's waist and her left arm around my waist. We tried to match steps as if we were in a three legged race at a Sunday school picnic. By the time we neared our campsite, we were pretty good. I liked the feel of Michelle's hip and thigh against mine.

Near a dry creek, we heard a rustle in the leaves. I spotted the box turtle crawling down the ravine. It was the size of my hat. The tan-colored, high arched shell was like a beige plastic checker board wrapped over a cantaloupe and attached to the body of a reptile. The color was a perfect match for the dry oak leaves lying in the gully, brownish-green with yellow blotches.

I bent down, lifting the pretty creature for a closer look. Its legs and head disappeared within the shell as the front flap on the bottom shell levered closed. The animal was about as safe as a slow-moving reptile could be.

"What is it, Paul?"

"It's a turtle."

"I knew that, smarty. What kind?"

I thought for a moment.

A wave slid across my brain.

"An Eastern Box Turtle. See the way the front of its shell hinges. Most turtles don't do that."

"Pretty neat. I love it, Paul. Can we keep it? I never had a pet turtle."

"You want it to die? It will die if we keep it. Out here in the woods, it will find another boy or girl turtle and raise babies. It will be much happier. Their biggest hazards are people who take them home for pets and death on the highway, as they cross slowly in front of cars. I can't resist the temptation to stop along the road and carry a crossing turtle along its way to its destination side of the highway."

"You're right. I think we should let it go."

I set the turtle on the ground. We watched, as a minute later, it extended its head and feet, took a look around, and continued on its way down the dry creek bed.

Back at our campsite Michelle searched through our sacks of food and cooking supplies. She found a bag of potatoes.

"Do you like fried potatoes, Paul? My daddy used to fix fried fish and Canada fries. Why don't you go down and catch a mess of fish and I'll wash these potatoes and put them on the camp stove to fry?" she asked.

I found the spinning rod we had taken from The Ranger's garage. Tying on a tiny jig with a rubber body like a little grub and walking down the trail to the lake, I was filled with the eternal optimism of a fisherman on his way to water.

The bay was secluded, a perfect place for a guy who was wanted for murdering a prison guard. I spotted an open pool among the trees and cast the little jig. Hitting the water with a tiny splash, it sank slowly. Before it hit bottom the line took a turn to the right. I twitched the rod and hooked a nice sunfish. In minutes the pretty yellow-bellied fish was flopping on the shore.

In twenty minutes, I had four chunky sunnies swimming in my bucket. Using the fillet knife from the Ranger's tackle box, I soon had eight thick, white fillets of succulent sunfish waiting for the skillet.

As I walked into camp, Michelle asked, "How'd you do, Paul?"

The smile on my face gave me away.

I buried the carcasses of the sunfish back in the woods. I washed the fillets in a pan of fresh water and soon had them sizzling in hot canola oil in our skillet. Before long, our plates were full of fried potatoes and golden fish.

"This tastes great, Michelle," I commented. "I love these circles of crisp brown potatoes. You are a terrific cook. Now I've got another reason to keep you as my wife."

"I'm afraid I am susceptible to flattery, Paul Hartman. Thank you."

I lay down on the bench of the picnic table, listening to the sounds of the forest. Birds sang, squirrels chattered, a gentle breeze moved the branches of the spring forest.

Michelle said, "Paul. Are you awake?"

"Sure."

"I was just thinking. We nearly made a big mistake."

"What's that?"

"What if a conservation officer had wandered up and asked you for your fishing license?"

"We'd have been on our way back to Des Moines. Dumb, wasn't it?"

"Yup."

"Guess I'd better pack the fishing tackle away."

"At least until you get a fishing license."

"Can't do that until I get a driver's license."

We washed the dishes and pans and began to organize food and cooking supplies in some cardboard boxes we had picked out of a dumpster behind a strip mall.

I dug through the camping gear and pulled out the tent. The directions were sewn into a seam. I started to read about how to put it up and fell asleep again in the warm sun. Michelle found me there and curled up beside me. The afternoon nap felt really good. We woke up feeling groggy, so we went searching for the camp shower room. Soon we were back with the new knowledge that the campground had no shower. We heated a big pan of water and used a wash cloth and soap to transform ourselves into people who felt clean and fresh. Together, we followed the directions and set up the little tent.

I said, "We have to figure out a cover story about our past that is vague enough so that people can't say, 'Oh, you're from Springfield, Illinois. Do you know my cousin? He's from Springfield.' We need to find a place to live and work where we don't tell people much of anything about us."

Michelle asked, "Won't we have to give background information when we apply for jobs? How do we get a past when we don't have one?"

"I haven't figured that out yet," I answered. "Let's keep sharing ideas. You, at least, have an identity. Your sister's Social Security records and her job records are yours now. Her driver's license is your identification card. You could probably even get a job as long as the personnel people don't check back with folks in Iowa."

"Let them check. My sister didn't work anywhere except at McDonald's. Nobody Michelle worked with will still be there. She will have left a bit of money in my social security fund. Who will remember her? I think I'm good with her ID. What are we going to do about you?"

"I just don't know."

XI

Loss of a Ranger

We packed most of our gear into cardboard boxes and covered them with a plastic tarp. The Ranger was pretty much empty as we drove into Fayetteville.

We stopped in a grocery store for a loaf of bread. As we walked out of the store, Michelle elbowed me. "Keep walking, Paul. Don't stop at the truck. Don't even look at it."

Out of the corner of my eye, I saw the police car parked beside the Ranger and the cop standing behind it, writing down the number of our stolen Missouri license plate. Michelle was right. We had to disassociate ourselves with this town. We were finished with the Ranger.

We walked down the block and did a zigzag course away from the grocery store.

Michelle suggested, "Let's hike back to the campground."

She started to walk ahead of me in that direction.

"Wait!" I commanded. "We may still be alright, Michelle. Let's be calm and formulate a plan. I saw a library up town. Let's go up and do some reading."

"Are you nuts, Paul? We've got to leave this town. They are about to track down our truck. We have to run!"

"No. We have to walk calmly. Let's go to the library. I have a couple of ideas. Trust me, Michelle?"

"Of course, I trust you. You are just a swindler and a murderer." She laughed. "Let's go to the library and talk about your ideas."

We walked the back streets until we located the small-town library.

I searched for a local newspaper, while sending Michelle for a road atlas and some travel books on Texas. While she looked for places we might like to be, I searched the want ads for "Cars for Sale."

Michelle was contemplating pictures of Big Bend National Park, when I found the ad for the pickup.

"Look, Michelle. Here's a 1995 Chevy S-10. Four cylinder, 172,000 miles and they're asking $1900. I think we have about thirty-five hundred dollars, right?"

Michelle looked up at me. "We have that much, Paul."

"Good. Let's go buy a car."

"Can we take a minute to look at the map first? I found a place in West Texas called Big Bend National Park. It looks to me like the kind of a place we want. It's close to the Mexican Border. It's wild, wild country. Some of these little towns are so far from anywhere that I don't think anybody could ever find us. Can we get us a map and see how to get there?"

We did.

"Big Bend looks great. Almost all of our camping stuff is back at the campground. We still might be able to find a way out of this situation. Let's go look at this S-10."

Michelle called Jack Wiggins. He told her the S-10 was in great shape, with new brakes and new tires. He said that he changed the oil regularly and it ran like a top. Jack also told Michelle that the little pickup got 28 miles per gallon out on the highway, 30 with a good tailwind. He gave us direction to find his place. We told him we were close by and would just walk over.

As we were walking out the door of the library, I told Michelle to go out and sit on a bench in front of the building.

"I've got an idea. Be back in ten minutes."

Seven minutes later I took her hand and said, "Come on."

"Where the hell you been, Paul? What's going on?"

"I asked the librarian where I could find some information about Southeastern Alabama. Told her I wanted to visit the Gulf Coast. If she remembers me, maybe she'll tell the cops."

"You are a devious man, Paul Hartman. A devious man."

Ten minutes later we were having a test drive. Jack was right. The truck ran like a well-tuned watch. It had a cheap aluminum topper with a few dents and scratches that made it look experienced.

Back in Jack Wiggins' driveway, I told him, "I'll give you thirteen hundred cash, right now," I offered.

Jack said, "Let me talk to my wife."

He came back in five minutes. "$1500 and its yours. Sally thinks we can get $1700 for it if we wait. I thought $1500 was a fair price. Anyway, that's our low price. That includes the topper and I'll throw in a bed board and a set of drawers that fits between the wheel wells and a mattress for camping. It fills the back of the truck. You'd be getting a heck of a deal."

Mary and I walked to the end of the driveway and had a talk.

"Can we afford that much, Mary?"

"Michelle. My name is Michelle, Paul." She pointed her index finger in my face. "You be careful. You could screw us up if you aren't careful," Michelle whispered.

"Sorry."

"About the money. I think we can afford it. If we buy the pickup and license it in my sister's name, we can stop worrying about them finding us with The Ranger's truck. This whole deal may be a blessing in disguise. Besides, it looks pretty good for as old as it is. It has a CD player. And I love that sexy blue color."

We walked back to where Jack was waiting. "$1500 and you throw in two CD's."

"Deal. I'll sign the registration and y'all can take it down to the courthouse and get your license. I'm supposed to keep the plates. Y'all have insurance? You're supposed to have insurance to drive it."

"No problem," I lied. "My Dodge Ram blew a piston and it was going to cost more to fix it than it was worth. We needed a vehicle that runs. This will be good for us."

Jack gave us a Candice Glover CD and a Mozart: Oboe & Bassoon Concerto.

"Candice Glover is a black woman who won American Idol a couple of years ago. Mozart is nice listening. I think y'all will like them."

Car insurance was a problem we hadn't thought about. We had no address. Michelle might have a credit history. I think that was something insurance companies checked.

We drove back to the library where I waited outside while Michelle found a listing in the newspaper of *For Rents*. She copied down the address of an apartment for rent.

I was a little worried about the plates. The lady in the auto department had to see Michelle's driver's license. Then she wanted to see evidence of insurance. We went looking and found a AAA Insurance office a few blocks from the court house and bought a cheap liability policy. By the time we were done with the license and the sales tax it cost us $127 that we hadn't wanted to spent . We gave her the address of the apartment for rent in Fayetteville. We could send a correction once we were settled in Texas.

It was after dark when we got back to camp. We threw our gear in the back of the S-10 and hit the road. We didn't want to be around if someone sniffed out our stolen license plates and traced them to the campground. I didn't think that would happen. Still, we didn't need to take any unnecessary chances.

In two hours we were in Tulsa where we found a Walmart, parked in the midst of a bunch of campers and motor homes, settling down in the back of our little blue S-10.

"I think it's funny, Paul."

"What?"

"These folks spent what? A hundred thousand dollars for one of these giant motor homes? Then they spent their nights in Walmart parking lots."

"I agree. I can't understand people. It would have been a lot more fun for them if they had found a park like the one we were in last night. I wish we were in a place like that tonight. We could be walking around in the national forest disguised as birders."

"At least we are saving money," Michelle reasoned. "That's probably why these folks are here too."

"They spent all their money on huge RV's."

While we were in the library, Michelle had made notes of highways through Oklahoma to Texas. We checked the Oklahoma route. It looked like a straight shot west to the Panhandle. Lots of little towns; plenty of miles between them.

XII

A Restless Night

Rod Dodge and Bob Johnson also heading south toward Missouri; Rod at the wheel and Bob navigating.

Glancing at the speed zone sign and then at the speedometer, Bob said, "Forty-five, Rod. We're coming into a town."

"Thanks, man." Rod responded. "I guess I'm in a hurry to get out of Iowa. I doubt the Missouri cops will be as serious about us as the ones in Iowa."

"Don't mean to bug you," Bob answered, "but I'd hate for a traffic ticket to send us back to prison."

"No problem, man. I'll drive. You make sure I obey the laws."

The two ex-cons rode ten miles in silence. Then thoughts of The Ranger filled Bob's mind.

"I keep thinking about that guard. I'm really sick about him, Rod. He looked so white, like every drop of blood flowed out of that little cut in his head. I can't believe he died. Paul hit him solid, but I didn't think he hit his head hard enough to kill the asshole."

"He's dead, man. Forget it. He's dead and there ain't nothing we can do about it. We need to escape Iowa. We need to find a place to hide in St. Louis. The Ranger don't matter any more. He's history, man."

"You're right. I'm glad we're in this together."

"Two heads are better than one," Rod assured his friend. "You're doing a great job of finding us back roads to travel. I don't think we need to worry too much about the highway patrol in these little towns we've been going through. Runnells, Dallas, Melcher, Bussey, Lovilla, Albia, Moravia. Where the hell are you finding these lonesome little towns?"

"Actually, I used to be a bicycle rider. For about ten years, I spent a week each summer riding on RAGBRAI, that bike ride across Iowa. I rode my bike through almost every town in the state. When you ride a bike through one of these little burgs, you learn a lot about a town. Rural Iowa is filled with really friendly folks. People who lived in these little towns came out and made us bikers feel like welcome visitors. At each host town, where the riders stopped for the night, somebody in our group always knew a local person who would put up a bunch of us. They'd give us a free shower and either a bed or a bit of soft carpet to spread some blankets on."

"I hear it's a drunken blast. Sometimes, I wished I'd been a biker and in good shape. Be fun spending a week drinking beer and watching biker girls in bikinis."

"That was a part of it, but there's a lot more," observed Bob. "It's a unique feeling to be one of 10,000 riders dipping their wheels in the Missouri River, being a part of a moving party traveling like a tidal wave across Iowa. Gave me a lot of satisfaction dipping my wheels in the Mississippi, knowing I was one of those who was tough enough to have peddled almost 500 miles."

"You must have gotten pretty close to those guys you peddled with."

"We ended up being good friends. My chief biking partner was my brother, Stan. He's a terrific brother as well as an exceptionally talented acoustic guitar player. Stan plays in lots of bars around the state. Really, around the world. You might have heard him."

"Don't think so. My kind of guitar music is country-western."

"Anyway," continued Bob, "we drank a few beers along the way, but neither of us got blasted like some of the crazy people you'd see in the beer tents. We were always too tired to party at night. It's pretty strenuous. Biking a hundred miles a day, you can eat all kinds of great food and still lose weight. You should try it, man."

"Ain't there cops who bike? My luck, I'd run into a biker cop and he'd say, 'Ain't you Rod Dodge, the guy who killed the prison guard. You're under arrest, dude.' I don't think I'm ever coming back to Iowa, unless it's in handcuffs."

"What's next?" Rod asked, "What metropolis are we going to slip through in the dead of night on our way to someplace warm and quiet to hide out until things cool down a bit?"

"The state line is coming up directly. I'll find Missouri in The Ranger's atlas and chart a course to the south."

Bob studied the map under the dome light.

"How about finding a place near a motel or shopping center or McDonald's or something?" asked Bob. "Just park and sleep in the back for a couple hours. Then we can be down to St. Louis around mid-day. I'm anxious to find some new ID. What do you think?"

"I was wondering about gravel roads," Rod offered. "If we could take back roads to St. Louis, maybe we wouldn't have to worry about the Missouri Highway Patrol. Ought to be able to find us a cheap motel in St. Louis by early afternoon."

"St. Louis and a motel bed sound pretty good to me," Bob agreed. "I'm bushed. This has been a crazy day."

"According to guys in the slammer," Rod observed, "There are places there where a guy can buy a legitimate driver's license, birth certificate, social security card, even a credit card if you want to do something really crooked."

"I'm not much into doing things that would hurt somebody else," Bob responded. "I never thought much about identity theft. All I want is to do is metamorphize myself from Bob Johnson, escaped prisoner running from the cops to Joe Blow, working citizen from Hobunk Center, Missouri. Then I can settle down, live my life, stay out of trouble."

Rod glanced at the clock on the dash. "Three-fifteen. I'm ready to find a place for a catnap. How far is Hannibal?"

"Maybe an hour. I remember a pleasant riverfront park there. Might be a good place to stop."

"Just find us someplace where no cops'll be shining flash-lights in our eyes to hassle us. I'll sleep."

Fifty-five minutes later, they were parked on a quiet side street in Hannibal, Missouri.

Sunup found Rod and Bob rolled in blankets in the back of the Toyota. The two escaped prisoners had fallen immediately into a deep sleep. Rod slept soundly until daylight surrounded them.

Bob tossed and turned, searching for a comfortable posi-tion.. Each time he closed his eyes, it was like someone was hitting the PLAY button for his dream video. Roger Stewart's white face filled the screen. The dead guard was lying on the floor of the halfway house, surrounded by a pool of blood. A prison guard in uniform threw open the door and burst into the room. Bob ran. The guard ran after him, yelling, "Murderer! Stop murderer!" The jailer drew his automatic pis-tol and began firing. He must have been shooting .22 shorts, because the crack of the gun was no louder than a cap gun. Bob heard the bullets whining over his head. He ducked and swerved.

Then he was in the rural Iowa countryside near the south-ern Iowa town of Dallas. He and Rod had stopped to pee. The guard came running up the road. Again the uniformed prison guard yelled, "Murderer! Stop, murderer!" This time, the guard had the bloodless, stark white face of The Ranger. Bullets cracked and sailed over his head. This time he and Rod jumped in the Toyota and drove away. As Bob began to relax, he heard the whine of the bullets. One of them hit the rear window of the SUV. It left a dimple, a small hole in the glass.

Then they were standing in a park in the old river town of Hannibal. Bob could see signs directing tourists to Samuel Clemens' boyhood home. In his dream he saw a river boat moving up the Mississippi River pushing six barges north toward Iowa. Then, there was the guard again. Again, the man had Roger Stewart's white face. "Murderer! You killed me! Stop murderer!" he yelled. Bob ran and ran and ran. He heard the pop of the pistol and saw the muzzle-flash of the little automatic. The guard was a terrible shot. He kept missing. Bob ran harder. He was out of breath, but he continued to run and pump his arms. He felt a hand on his shoulder. He swung his fist and connected, a glancing blow to a solid face.

"Cut it out, Bob," yelled Rod Dodge. "It's me. Wake up. You're ok. I'm going to be pissed if you gave me a shiner."

Bob was awake, sitting up in the back of the Toyota. Down the street, he could see the Mighty Mississippi rolling along. Heavy gray mist floated above the river. The fog was thick enough to hide the Illinois side. The scene was much more beautiful than the one in his dream.

"Is it time to go?"

Rod said, "It's quarter to seven. We'd just as well be on our way. Let's blow this town before some local cop comes by asking us what we are doing here."

They drove up the steep hill to a Casey's gasoline station. Digging into their cash they filled the tank. In the restroom, Bob brushed his teeth.

"I feel better," Bob said. "Sorry about the dream. Some damn prison guard in uniform was chasing me. Then it was Roger, The Ranger. His face was spooky white as if the blood was all drained out of his body. Every time we stopped he started chasing me and shooting his little .22 automatic pistol at me. The guy was a terrible shot. The bullets kept sailing over my head. Sure glad it was a dream."

They bought large coffees and a dozen day-old donuts at Casey's General Store.

As they walked back to the car, Bob glanced at the rear license plate.

"Rod, we've got a problem. Look at the rear plate."

Rod said, "What's wrong with it?"

"Our plate. It's shining like a light from a fishing boat on a dark night. The plate's shiny clean and the rest of the truck is dirty as a pig sty. We need to find a gravel road and throw some dirt on these license plates"

XIII

Missouri Plates

South of Hannibal, Rod and Bob turned west on a gravel road.

"Look for a spot with no buildings in sight," suggested Bob.

After a couple of miles, Rod pulled to the side of the narrow gravel road.

"How's this?" asked Rod. "We're at the bottom of a ravine. We shouldn't see nobody."

Bob had picked up a Pepsi bottle from the trash at Casey's and filled it with water.

"Pour it on the plate," said Rod. "I'll throw handfuls of dirt and gravel on it."

A minute later, Bob directed, "Throw some more on it. Throw it all over the back of the SUV so it will look even. Then we'll give the front bumper the same treatment."

The two escaped prisoners stood back and admired their artistry.

"Nice job, Bob," complimented Rod. "If some County Mounty had seen our clean plates, he'd have stopped us for a talk while he called in our number. We'd have been dead meat. Now you can hardly see the numbers."

Bob gazed at the back of the truck. "Maybe we should ditch the Iowa plates and steal us some Missouri licenses."

"Good thought, man," agreed Rod, "Where do you suppose we'll be in two days? They must be looking for us by now. They couldn't know for sure which direction we headed. If they're smart they'll figure we either went someplace warm or someplace where we got relatives or friends."

"You thinking Florida?" asked Bob.

"I'm thinking Missouri. St. Louis."

"Ok," Bob agreed. "Then we oughta have Missouri licenses on our car. Even better, Missouri licenses off a Toyota 4Runner."

"Makes sense to me, man."

"First we get Missouri plates," said Bob. "Then we see if we can find a 4Runner. The Missouri cops are going to be looking for a 4Runner with Iowa plates. The sooner we're driving a 4Runner with Missouri plates, the better chance we stay free."

Rod laughed, "You shoulda been thinking of that last night when it was dark."

"Couldn't. The Ranger was chasing me down the road shooting at me all night long."

"Ha!" Rod chuckled. "Anyway, where we gonna get Missouri plates in the daytime?"

Bob said, "We're going back to prison if we go back to Hannibal and try to steal plates now. Any cop will be checking 4runners from Iowa so we're dead if we even pass a cop."

"Seems to me," Rod said, "we find a farmhouse with no-body home and a car in the yard."

Bob suggested, "If there's a car in the yard, then there's probably somebody home. We'll have to stop at a farmhouse that has a car and just knock on the door. If somebody answers we'll ask them for directions to someplace we're not going."

"Like how to get to Lake of the Ozarks by the scenic route along the back roads."

"And where have we come from?" Bob asked.

"Lemme see the atlas."

They spent a couple of minutes looking at the Missouri map."

"We left Canton, Missouri this morning," Bob explained. "We have to meet our wives at Lake of the Ozarks for dinner tonight."

"Why ain't we wearing wedding rings?" Rod asked.

"Good question," Bob answered. "I got high blood pressure. Makes my hands swell."

"And I broke my finger," said Rod. "Almost had to cut the ring off."

"Where we staying tonight?" asked Bob.

"Tan-Tar-A Resort."

"Is that in Lake of the Ozarks?"

"Sure is. Betty Lou and I stayed there on our honeymoon."

The two convicts found a narrow blacktop road going south. Rod pulled into the driveway of a run-down farm with a Honda Pilot parked in front of the garage. Bob knocked on the door. A pretty young woman dressed in tight jeans and a

NE Missouri State sweat shirt answered. Two toddlers hung on her legs. She told Bob to find Highway H and go south.

Five miles south, they stopped at a farm with a dirty, maroon GMC pickup parked in the yard. Again Bob knocked. A tall, slender farmer in bib overalls came to the door.

Bob thought, *This guy is three days away from his razor. He must be a decade older than me.*

"How are you doing today, sir. We were exploring the back roads of Missouri and we kind of lost our sense of direction, what with the cloudy day and all. We're supposed to meet our wives for dinner tonight at Tan-Tar-A Resort in the Lake of the Ozarks. We'd like to see some real Missouri countryside and thought we'd take some back roads. My brother and I were arguing about which way to go so we decided to stop and ask for some local advise."

The farmer's bib overalls were strapped over a long-sleeved, blue work shirt that was frayed around the edges. His skin was bronzed from much time outside.

"Well, come on in," the guy offered. "I'm about to have coffee. The missus baked some fresh apple pie. Join me and we'll find you a route. I'm Howard Fleshner."

Howard held out his hand. Bob shook it, felt the firm grip of a man who worked for his living. Bob said, "Bob Barnes."

Rod walked up behind Bob. He shook hands with Howard Fleshner and said, "Rod. Rod Barnes. Pleased to meet you, Mr. Fleshner."

"Howard. Ain't nobody calls me Mr. Fleshner."

"Ok, Howard," said Rod. "We sure didn't plan on pie and coffee,. This is just great."

"If we eat it while it's fresh," said Howard with a wink, "maybe Margaret will bake me another when she gets home."

"Good plan."

"I see you boys are from Iowa."

"We are," said Bob.

"Where at?"

"Cedar Rapids."

"Your license says Polk County."

"My brother, Rod's, car. He lives in Des Moines."

"Gotta cousin from Parkersburg. That's Butler County. Dick Fleshner?"

"Don't know much about Parkersburg."

"Got hit by a terrible tornado a couple years ago."

"I remember," replied Bob. "It was awful." *I couldn't go help. They had me locked up in the Iowa State Penitentiary.*

"It was terrible. Luckily it missed my cousin's house. I went up and helped clean up for a couple of days. The town was back on its feet real fast."

"People must have had good insurance," said Bob.

"Hard working folks," explained Howard. "Iowan's are people who turn out and help when trouble hits."

"There were lots of volunteers," complimented Bob.

"Lemme clear the table off and get a map."

Howard poured three cups of stout-looking black coffee. He cut three generous pieces of apple pie with a crunchy crust, dishing up the pie for his guests. He folded an Official Missouri

Highway map to the area that included Hannibal and Lake-of-the-Ozarks. He spread the map between the coffee cups and pie plates. With a hot pink highlighter, Howard marked a route via Highway H to Highway 19 to Highway 94 to US 54 to Lake of the Ozarks.

"You can take Nineteen all the way to Ninety-four. It runs up the north side of the Missouri River. It'll give you some right fine views. Fellow can just imagine Lewis and Clark running up that river a couple hundred years ago.

"Ninety-four'll take you to US 54 which'll take y'all right down to Lake of the Ozarks. No problem. Pretty scenery."

Rod said, "This looks easy. Terrific."

Bob said, "It's so kind of you, Howard. We don't need to be in Tan-Tar-A until late afternoon. It'll be wonderful to see some of the Missouri River Valley."

Howard Fleshner insisted they take the Missouri Map with them with their route to Lake of the Ozarks highlighted. It took ten minutes to say goodbye. Finally, they were on the road south.

Rod began to giggle. "Can you believe we stopped to steal his license plates and that farmer treated us to pie and coffee."

Bob was tickled as well. "What do the kids say? LOL?"

"What's that mean?"

"I think it's Laugh Out Loud."

"Or is it Lots of Love?" asked Rod.

"Right now, it's Laugh Out Loud. Nobody'd believe this if we told them."

Rod took his time driving down the narrow blacktop road. It was a little rough and he and Bob were in no hurry.

Bob said, "This map is better than the atlas at finding back roads that will take us to St. Louis. Lucky break."

"And great pie. I ain't had nothing that good that for ten years."

They drove another five miles before pulling into a farmstead with an old beat-up F150 Ford pickup sitting up on jacks in front of a shed beside a barn. The grass was unmowed around the truck.

Bob knocked on the door.

Nothing.

He knocked louder.

Nothing.

One more time.

He hollered, "ANYBODY HOME?"

Rod said, "Nobody home, man."

Bob grabbed a screwdriver and loosened the screws holding the pickup's plates. He handed the plates to Rod, inserting the screws back in the old Ford.

"Put the Missouri plates in our car. I'd hate to have someone come home while we're stealing their licenses."

Rod laid the Missouri plates on the floor of the back seat. They continued south on the narrow blacktop road. After about ten miles, Rod pulled over near a small stream.

"Is this a good spot to switch licenses, Bob?"

"No traffic. Let's do it."

"Hustle."

In three minutes the plates were switched. Bob laid the Iowa plates on the floor beneath his feet. Soon they would be buried deep in a garbage can at a convenience store. Now the Toyota was from Missouri.

XIV

Fake Papers - St. Louis

Three hours later Rod and Bob were sitting in a bar in Saint Louis. Bob was at a table in the back. Rod was at the bar, sipping a beer, having a conversation with the bartender, a tall brunette whose name was Jenny. Rod guessed her to be thirty. She was six foot tall and must have weighed a hundred eighty pounds. The woman had an infectious smile and loved to listen. Rod wanted her to talk.

"Must be fun to work near a college," offered Rod. "These kids must keep your life lively."

"Absolutely!" said Jenny. "They make my days interesting."

"They're away from home," offered Rod, "away from parents, away from churches. I'll bet they begin to rebel. Now they can go to a bar and get drunk and act crazy."

"That happens mostly late at night," said Jenny. "I get the basketball players. They drink too much, cause trouble. Usually that's after midnight in the wee hours of the morning, when athletes should be home in bed."

"These kids come to college when they're eighteen," Rod commented. "Do they show up in your bar. Try to convince you to serve them beer?"

"They do, but we're pretty tough about checking ID's. Anybody who looks under twenty-five is asked for an ID."

"What then? What if they can't produce one?" asked Rod. "You call the cops?"

"No, we just send the kid on his or her way," explained the bartender. "Tell them to come back when they're twenty-one. Their group typically goes on and the whole crowd tries another establishment."

Rod asked, "Do they use false ID's?"

"Probably," said Jenny. "If they do, the cards are pretty well done."

"Must be pretty tough to get one made these days. The state uses holograms and all sorts of shit to foil counterfeiting."

"Some of these geeks who major in technology figure it out."

"Do you ever catch the guys who forge the ID's?"

"It isn't my job.," Jenny said defensively. "Don't know. Don't care. Let the cops handle it."

Rod asked, "Do the kids ever talk about who makes the fake ID's?"

"NO. Why are you asking me so many questions about this? What are you after, mister? Excuse me. I've got glasses to wash."

Rod finished his beer, took a glance at Bob who seemed to be pretty friendly with a couple of college coeds. He turned to the door and left the bar.

Meanwhile, Bob had bought a beer. He had taken it to a table in the back of the bar. He sat back, relaxed. *I'll let Rod handle this one. I'm not much for beer, but it's nice just sitting here.*

Two young college coeds came into the bar. They stopped at the bar to pick up a couple of beers and took them to a table next to Bob. They plopped a couple of textbooks and notebooks on their table and sat down.

One of them took a big sip of her beer. Bob heard her complain, "Sarah, I think we're wasting our time. I'm never going to understand trigonometry."

"Patricia," encouraged Sarah. "We have to try. Get your book open and let's start over at the beginning of the chapter. See if we can figure it out."

"Ok. But I think it's a waste of time."

As books and notebooks opened, Bob stood, picked up his beer, took three steps, and sat at an empty chair at the table between the two pretty college girls.

"Excuse me, girls. I have a daughter who must be about your age. I was eavesdropping and heard your frustrations about trigonometry. About the time you were born, I took trigonometry. Actually, I took it in high school, at Iowa State, and at UNI. I think I know the subject pretty well. If you don't mind me butting in, I'd be glad to give a shot at seeing if all three of us can understand it tonight."

Sarah gave him a cautious glance. "I don't know. We don't know you, mister." She looked at Patricia. "What do you think?"

Patricia smiled, "He's a big guy, but he looks harmless. What do we have to lose?"

"Certainly not your virginity," answered Sarah. "Let's see if this guy can teach us trigonometry. You have a name, mister?"

"Donald. Donald Jenks. I live in Kirksville. My daughter goes to Truman State."

"Well, Mr. Jenks. Where do you want to start?"

"You tell me. Can we start at the beginning of this unit, so I know what approach your teacher uses?"

Patricia opened her book to the first page of the chapter. "Here it is, 'Unit Circles.'"

"I remember unit circles. Give me a minute."

Bob read the first few pages.

"Do you have some paper?"

Sarah tore a sheet from her notebook. "Here."

Bob took the pencil out of Patricia's hand and drew a nearly perfect circle on the notebook paper, then a coordinate axis centered on the center of the circle.

"Ok. Here's a unit circle. Do you know what that is?"

"Sure," said Patricia. "It's a circle with a radius of one whose center is at the origin."

"I thought you girls didn't understand this."

Patricia smiled.

"Now, I'm going to draw a tangent to the circle through the point (1,0). Do you know what a function is?"

Both girls nodded.

"That's algebra," said Sarah. "I got an A in algebra."

"Good." said Bob. "Then you should get an A in trigonometry."

Twenty minutes later Sarah and Patricia gave each other high fives.

"I can do this shit," said Sarah. "It makes sense."

"I hate to say this," agreed Patricia. "This is almost fun. Why don't you come and teach our trigonometry class, Mr. Jenks?"

"What do we owe you," offered Sarah.

"The answers to a couple of questions."

"What?"

"I've been wondering. How old are you?"

"What do you think?" asked Patricia.

"I think you are my daughter's age. About eighteen."

Sarah said, "You missed that, Donald. We're both twenty-one."

"No way."

Both young women reached into their purses and slid driver's licenses across the table.

Bob read birth-dates and calculated ages. "You're both twenty-one? These have to be fake."

"You don't expect us to admit that do you?" asked Sarah.

"OK. I've got a situation. My daughter is eighteen. She goes to school at Truman. At home, we all drink a beer or a glass of wine occasionally. At school, she has to drink Diet Coke. You don't suppose I could get her an ID that was as good as yours?"

Sarah looked at Patricia. Patricia nodded.

"We're going to give you a phone number and a name. Call this number and ask for George. Tell him what you want and that Patricia and Sarah sent you. Please don't screw him over, Donald. This guy does great work. The kids at St. Louis University would not like to lose him."

"Thank you. You're pretty classy young women. If you ever need another father let me know. Jackie would love to have a couple of sisters."

"Thanks for your help, Donald Jenks. You saved us.

"Somebody once told me that evidence of a good student is that she works hard. You two are good students."

Patricia and Sarah gathered their books and headed for the door. They left the bar with a wave to Bob.

Bob waited two minutes and then he headed for the 4Runner.

"Where the hell you been, dude? I thought maybe you was going to make it with them college girls. I struck out. Couldn't come up with a clue as to where we'd find new ID's. Sorry, man."

"Not a problem. Here's a phone number for George. He's the guy who did the impressive looking ID's for Sarah and Patricia. Let's go find him."

"You rascal, you. Are you serious?"

"I think it's a good chance," promised Bob. "Let's find a phone."

Rod called the number and talked to George. They drove to the address he gave to Rod.

Bob knocked. The door opened. A slender young man in a long-sleeved flannel shirt and jeans, looked out, glancing up and down the street.

"Come on in. Call me George."

"I'm Rodney. This is my brother, Robert. We understand that you are really good at producing official papers. We don't like our old names any more. We'd like to be new people."

"I might be able to help you out. Let me get some information."

"What do you need?" asked Rod.

"I want to know your ages. Also tell me your birth year."

"I'm 26," said Rod. "Born in 1989."

"And I'm 43, contributed Bob. "I was born in 1971."

George said, "I'm going to study obituaries from around the country. I'll find a couple of dead guys about your ages. I'll find a birth date and the county court house, say in Terra Haute, Indiana. I'll call them and say something like, 'Hi, I used to live in Indiana, but I've been living in India for the last ten years working as a Christian missionary. Any chance I could get a copy of my birth certificate?'

"If this scheme works, I'll get the birth certificate to you. You can call a motor vehicle office and apply for a driver's license. Once you have one good piece of identification, the driver's license and social security cards should be easy for you."

"How long will this take?" asked Bob.

"To get a birth certificate? Maybe three days. Maybe a month."

"I hope sooner rather than later," said Rod.

"You should be able to go to a local court house with your birth certificate and the driver's license should take you an hour. With the driver's license and the birth certificate, you can apply for a social security card. No big deal."

Bob asked, "How much?"

George said, "You can pay me two hundred bucks a piece and I'll get you birth certificates. Guaranteed. Or you can do it yourself for free."

Rod paid George $400 in cash.

XV

East St. Louis

Rod Barnes drove the Toyota past Busch Stadium and the giant arch, over the Mississippi River into East St. Louis, Illinois. Bob led him off the highway into a depressed neighborhood. They found a run-down motel on an old highway winding through the inner city. The sign said, "$25 – SINGLES."

"What do you think about this place, Rod?"

"I can't imagine any place much cheaper," he responded.

"My wife always wanted the Holiday Inn," Bob recalled. "Paul was right in suggesting that we live as cheap as we can. Let's check it out."

Rod paid cash for two nights for one person. He registered in the name, Sam Adams and gave them a license plate number of **842 PEI** instead of the number on their stolen Missouri plates of **824 PIE**. The clerk was engrossed in a TV movie and approaching asleep. He didn't seem to care about the name and the license number. The motel guy wouldn't know there were two of them. Rod walked back to the Toyota, drove toward the back of the crumbling asphalt lot, and parked in front of Unit 12.

They carried the suitcase and duffle bags into the room. Bob sat on the bed. It sank about a foot.

"Nice bed. Maybe we should have paid an extra ten bucks and got a room with two twin beds. This shitty excuse for a bed's gonna funnel our bodies right to the middle."

"I don't know about you," announced Rod, "but I ain't the kind of a guy to sleep with another man."

"I ain't that kind of a guy either," Bob assured his friend. "But, I have enough confidence in my manliness, that I can sleep in the same bed with you and know that nothing improper will happen. Whatever, it will be better than last night in the back of the SUV. You can sleep on the floor if you're worried about touching my body."

"I want a woman, not you, pal," observed Rod.

"You've got that right, Rodney," agreed Bob. "I'll guarantee, I will sleep better than I did last night in Hannibal. What do you think about going out for a first-rate meal? Then we can come back here for a good night's sleep. Tomorrow, we go looking for an apartment to rent. We need to figure out the answers to a lot of questions. Can we find jobs and make some money? Do we stay around here. Should we go someplace farther away from Des Moines? We need to find a way of settling into a real life. Do you think those birth certificates George is producing will do the job for us?"

"You are full of terrific questions, man," responded Rod. "Let's sleep on them. Tomorrow, we'll do some serious planning. Anyway, figure a week before our papers is ready. We ain't gonna rent an apartment 'til we have names to write on the forms, dude."

"For the moment, I could use supper," said Bob.

"I'm ready for some chow," reflected Rod. "I picked up some coupons in the office. There are some restaurants around here that offer buy one, get one free meals. We can stretch our budget a while with them."

"Terrific," Bob agreed. "I'll be glad to move into an apartment where we can cook some of our own meals. I like to cook. I know I can fix meals a lot cheaper than we can buy them in a cafe."

The two escaped cons and murder suspects drove their stolen truck, with stolen Missouri plates onto the streets of East St. Louis, Illinois. The neighborhood looked as if it had been left behind. Trash was collecting on broken walkways. Paper was blowing about in the breeze. Damaged buildings lined the streets. Shabbily dressed little kids were playing ball in the street. Reluctantly, the kids moved aside for the SUV. Little black and brown faces glared at the occupants of the SUV as Bob and Rod passed.

Bob said, "Listen. I hear rap music and barking dogs."

"And kids yelling."

"Half the lots are empty. Most of the windows are broken. Plenty of little black kids on the street. We seem to be the wrong color for this neighborhood, man."

They smelled the smoke and the barbecue before they saw the sign.

"Smell that, man?"

"We must be close." Rod pointed ahead. "There's the BBQ place. We're here. Let's try it. What have we got to lose?"

"Our lives maybe."

"Hey man," chuckled Rod, "There's cars parked beside the restaurant. Must be safe?"

"Do they have hubcaps?" asked Bob.

"You're a pussy, man."

"Probably."

"How many of these dudes is wanted for murder?" Rod asked. "We're more dangerous than most anyone in East St. Louis."

"Funny. I don't feel dangerous."

After supper Bob rubbed his stomach. "The BBQ place was funky, but I think that might have been the best barbecued ribs I've ever eaten, Rodney."

"I agree. We can come back here, partner."

"How long do you want to live?"

"Ha, ha. Tomorrow we explore St. Louis. This freedom shit ain't bad, Robert. It ain't bad at all."

XVI

Random Plans

Bob studied his receding hairline in the bathroom mirror as he pulled the Bic razor over his round face. *I'm getting old*, he thought.

My daughter, Jackie, graduated from high school last year. I missed her wedding in October. Then she told me in her last letter that she was pregnant. I had all those plans; to be released from prison, get a job, and hold my grandson on my knee. Now I may never see the kid. I may never be able to see my little girl again.

The mirror showed a stream of tears running down each side of his nose. As he turned to face Rod, he saw a questioning look in his friend's face. "What's going on, man?"

"I love that girl so much. My daughter, I mean. How can two kids be so different? I fathered a son who seems to care only for himself. I guess I love him too, but wouldn't it have been easy for him to have stepped up to help me when he could have kept me out of prison? Maybe, he could have found himself a new direction at the same time."

Bob turned and stared back at his face in the mirror. "I can understand my wife not sticking by me. It must have been tough on her. When she sent me a letter, telling me she was leaving, I felt deserted and angry at first. Later, I told her to go ahead. She had a life to live. It didn't make any sense for her to spend half of it hanging around, waiting for me to be out of prison.   I just thank God I have a daughter who still cares enough for her old man to keep loving me. I feel bad about not being there for her."

Bob looked toward Rod. "Is there some way she and I can keep in touch? Could I do something with this internet stuff? Can they trace e-mail messages?"

Rod said, "I'm not sure, but I think one of them computer geeks can probably tell what you had for lunch before you sent a message. I'd be real careful about sending an e-mail to your daughter, man."

"What about a web site, Rod? Could she post pictures on a web site? They couldn't catch me if I pulled up that site and looked at the pictures, could they?"

"Maybe we need to go into Best Buy and talk to one of those computer guys. We could ask him, *If we had a web site, could we tell who accessed it?* You know how devious I was when I was robbing convenience stores. We just have to make people think we are trying to find out who hits our own web page. I'm pretty sure you could look on her web page and nobody would know it was you."

"What about Facebook?"

"Lot's of young folks are using Facebook, but I don't think you can stay anonymous on Facebook, Bob."

"It would be great if she put pictures on a web page and I could see them. I need to work on that. There must be a way I can communicate with her. I just have to figure it out."

"That might work, man. I think it'd be a one-way deal. You could read her stuff. It sounds real dangerous to go the other way though. If the cops ever found out about it, I'll bet they'd be knocking on our door quicker than ants could find a picnic."

Bob said, "We don't have a computer or internet access or anything right now. I guess the first thing we need to do is to settle down some place. Then we can sign up for a computer class or buy a book on computers."

"I seen an ad in Sunday's paper for computers," offered Rod. "You can buy one for five hundred bucks. I don't know how much memory a cheap machine would have. I heard somebody say memory's real cheap. Buy plenty. He said you always want more later if you don't have it."

"First, we need to find a place to settle down," reasoned Bob. "Then we need jobs. Are you still figuring on sticking together, Rod? There are advantages and also disadvantages of living together for a while. We can cut our expenses quite a bit if we share an apartment."

"You're right. Only one set of dishes and pans, one toaster, and one set of furniture. Heat and air conditioning won't be any more for two than for one. On the other hand, I wouldn't want people to think we was gay."

"That might not be so bad, Rod. We both know by now that we like women, but maybe if people thought we were gay then they wouldn't have ideas about us being ex-cons. I say let 'em think what they want."

Rod nestled his chin in his hand. "You could be right, man. You see any other problems with us living together?"

"The only problem I see," Bob answered, "is if one of us screws up, does something stupid and gets caught, then the cops would have a pretty good chance of nabbing the other guy."

"Well, we'll just have to be smart," smiled Rod. "I think we should find a medium-sized town and settle down for a few months. Buy us a cheap car; dump the Toyota where nobody will notice it for a while."

"I was thinking about that, too," offered Bob. "If we find a town in Missouri or Arkansas to settle in, then we should take the Toyota over to someplace in Illinois like Peoria or Springfield. When the cops find it they'll think we are going in that direction."

"Great idea, dude," agreed Rod. "We could park it some place like a hospital lot. There are people parked in a place like that for days. It would take a hell of long time before anybody discovered The Ranger's 4Runner. But first, we need those identification papers and we have to figure out where we go from here. What are your thoughts? Which direction do you want to go? A few years ago, when the cops showed up at my door, I was all set to go to Texas. I'm afraid to suggest it again. Could be bad luck."

"Do you want someplace warm?" asked Bob. "I'm kind of tired of Iowa in the winter. Summer's coming. I was thinking about Florida. It would be great in the winter and spring and fall. Could we handle the heat in the summer?"

"It can't be any worse than Iowa in the winter," Rod answered. "Another place I went to once with my grandparents is Hot Springs, Arkansas. They took me to an Intergenerational Elderhostel for a week. I went to classes in the science center, hunted for crystals, and hiked in the mountains. Did some snorkeling in a big, clear mountain lake. I wouldn't mind if we bought us a boat and went back and caught some bass and crappies."

"I could go for Arkansas," said Bob. "Summer in Florida sounds pretty humid and I don't really like the idea of hurricanes, but I still may head for Florida when we get this identity thing settled."

"I guess we'll just see what happens, man."

"First, let's add up our money and make a budget," reasoned Bob. "Then pick up our new birth certificates so we can work on driver's licenses and social security cards. I think our future is beginning to look bright."

"We got plans, dude. Makes it better."

"What do you think about doing some touristy things while we are in this area, Rod? We have lots of spare time."

"You bet. I'd be bored just sitting around."

"Like you were never bored for seven years, sitting around in prison?"

"You know what I meant, Robert. I'm ready to get out and see things and do things. Do you realize that we could go watch the Cardinals play a ball game?"

"Or we could rent a canoe and float one of Southeast Missouri's wild rivers. Did you ever paddle a canoe?"

"I can't even swim, man. I don't think I'd feel real comfortable in a canoe."

"We'd wear life jackets. You would absolutely love it. We are free, Rod. We can do anything we want to do."

"I'm all for this fun stuff, dude, but we have some chores to do. I'd hate to have The Ranger's car get us in trouble. We really need to lose the Toyota, ... soon."

"I keep telling myself not to be in too much of a hurry," said Bob. "First we need permanent ID's. Then we buy another cheap car. After that, we ditch the Toyota at some hospital or all night truck stop in Illinois. Finally, we set up new lives in some place like Hot Springs."

"You're right, man. We just have to keep reminding each other to be patient. I've never seen a major league baseball game. Let's do it."

XVII

Overnight in Tulsa

Sometime during the night, Walmart turned out some of the street lights. I hung a sweatshirt over the side window of the topper to keep the light out of my eyes. Night slipped quietly away. The dim light of dawn surrounded our parking lot campground. I was sleeping soundly, when Michelle awoke, her eyes greeting the dawn.

Day broke quietly in the parking lot. The night had been untroubled. Early in the evening Michelle had nervously watched the police car's hourly trip through our campground. Gradually we realized that they were just checking to make sure no bad people (like us) were there who might bother peaceful RV'ers. We had worried a bit about them running our plates and checking our ID. Slowly it registered to our brains that we were in a legal vehicle with legal plates, that Michelle had a legal ID. If they decided to check us out, we were probably alright. It was pretty unlikely that any cop would find anything suspicious about us.

Michelle was starting to dress when I opened my eyes. My timing was good. I lay there admiring the beauty of her body, reminding myself how I loved the gentle lines of her face. Knowing this stunning woman loved me as much as I loved her gave me a powerful feeling. I smiled as I complimented myself on my good fortune. My life was changing. Good luck was surrounding me.

I thought, *The Fickle Finger of Fate is moving in Paul Hartman's direction. Or perhaps I should be calling myself Paul Swartz. Michelle has an ID. Being her husband might take some suspicion away from me if I used the name Swartz. Maybe we should buy some cheap wedding rings.*

"You're awake, Paul. Why didn't you say something?"

"I was busy," I responded. "I was admiring the pretty face and the magnificent body of the woman I love."

"You are simply full of the Blarney. Are you an Irishman or something?"

Michelle reached out, gently caressing my neck. The soft touch of her hand sending chills up my spine.

"I'm probably mostly an Englishman," I replied. "I think maybe one of my grandfathers had some Scottish blood running in his veins."

"Well, whatever it is that runs in your blood, I like the combination," she smiled.

In the back of her S-10 pickup in the Walmart parking lot in Tulsa, Oklahoma, Michelle kissed me good morning.

Is this heaven or what?

Then she destroyed my mood with, "I don't like this parking lot stuff, Paul. Are you ready to hit the road?"

"Sure," I agreed.

I had slept in my clothes. We made the bed, stowed our gear, and headed west. The back of the S-10 was perfect for camping. The long drawers under our sleeping platform held our tent, cooking gear, and some food. The plywood platform over the wheel wells and the thick foam pad made our bed much more comfortable than our smaller pads had been. We could snuggle under our blanket and sleeping bag and stay pretty warm until just before dawn.

I asked Michelle, "Do we have a scrap of paper? I want to make a list of stuff we need." I wrote down sleeping bag and blankets. If we stopped at a garage sale, we might be able to buy some things to keep us just a bit warmer at night.

Michelle glanced at my list and teased, "Good idea. I have you, but I was still just a little chilly by morning."

"Your butt was like a giant ice cube."

"Number one: who told you you could touch my butt. Number two: My butt is not giant sized. You may have just lost some touching privileges, mister."

As she drove west I worked on my list. We weren't in too much of a hurry. Oklahoma was not a state adjacent to Iowa. We could afford to drive slowly, taking our time. The Ranger's Ranger was gone. Now we were birders from Arkansas driving a blue, Chevy S-10 pickup.

XVIII

Lazy Time in the Great Salt Plains

Michelle and I drove up Highway 11 going north out of Tulsa. At Pawhuska, we picked up Highway 60, following it west through the thriving Oklahoma town of Ponca City. After we crossed Interstate 35, we continued west on Highway 64 past the little town of Jet, the gateway to Great Salt Plains. Much of the flat prairie was covered with green fields of grain. We wondered if it was winter wheat that had been planted in the fall. Now in early spring the grass was several inches tall and a bright green. In bare, red-dirt fields, the south wind pushed whirling dust devils carrying away the rich, light Oklahoma soil. Scattered trees seemed to have a definite bow toward the north.

Near Jet were a lake, a state park, and a national wildlife refuge all bearing the name Great Salt Plains. Great Salt Plains Lake was a marshy salt flat on the Salt Fork of the Arkansas River. At a roadside kiosk, we learned that native Americans had gathered salt from these flats before the dam formed the shallow lake. We wondered why the river was salty. What would make a fresh-water stream run with salt water?

At a picnic table along the shore of the lake, Michelle made cheese sandwiches while I sliced a couple of apples onto a paper plate. The spring sun on the shore of this lake warmed our bodies as it warmed this land. Out on the lake large white birds were swimming. I walked back to the pickup for our binoculars.

"What are the white birds, Paul?"

"No clue. Here's the bird book. I'll take a look through the binoculars."

"What do you see? They look awful big for ducks. Maybe they're snow geese or swans. They are a long way away."

"You have to see these birds, Michelle. They are huge. Notice the big yellow bill? They're Pelicans. Take a look through the binoculars. I'll see if I can find them in the book."

Michelle focused on the Pelicans. "Wow! They are beautiful, Paul. Look at the size of that yellow beak. It's like a snow shovel."

I said, "I remember reading where Lewis and Clark shot a Pelican on the Missouri River when they were going west two hundred years ago. They filled the bill with five gallons of water."

In our bird book, I found a Brown Pelican and the American White Pelican. "Here it is. They've gotta be American White Pelicans. Aren't they marvelous birds?"

Michelle gazed at the sky behind me. "Look up, Paul. A huge black and white kite."

The Pelican, gliding slowly toward the lake was almost over our heads. Its wings were locked in a slow, graceful glide toward a landing just beyond us. It did look like a huge white kite with black tips. We watched in awe as it extended big, flat, orange, webbed feet and came to rest gently and gracefully on the salty lake, like a water skier settling into the water after letting go of his tow rope.

"Wow!" exclaimed Michelle. " Isn't that a thrilling sight? I've never seen anything like it."

"Isn't it easy to look like birders?" I asked. "Both of us look like country bumpkins in a big city -- looking up in awe at giant sky-scrapers."

I wrote the date and the place in our bird book beside the picture of the American White Pelican.

"This is a nice place, Paul. Maybe we should check out the campground. I'd rather sleep here in our tent than in a Walmart parking lot."

"I was thinking the same thing. Let's go find Sandy Beach Campground. Maybe we can camp where we can see the lake."

We took a while to remember how the little backpack tent went together. When we finished, we were proud to see the graceful lines of green nylon in front of our sleek blue S-10.

I commented, "*The Ranger* had a nice choice of tents."

"Please don't mention him, Paul. I want to forget that part of my life. I want to put it behind me and start over fresh and new. OK?"

"I'm sorry. You're right. This is a new life for us. Starting today we are free and clear of the past. We should talk about developing a new *past* that we can talk about as if it is real."

We spent the rest of the afternoon walking trails and sitting in the warm spring sun. A found a rocky beach covered with rich brown crystals; one of the signs told us that they were selenite crystals.

"It says here that they were formed by the salt in the lake," explained Michelle.

"Does it tell you why the lake is salty?"

"Apparently, the rivers that feed it run through an old ocean bed. Can you believe that this used to be an ocean?"

"It looks a little like an ocean beach," I observed. "And the water is certainly salty. Did you taste it?"

Michelle put a finger in the water and then in her mouth. "Salty!"

A sign told us about the birds of Great Salt Plains Lake.

"Look here, Paul. It said the pelicans feed on salt brine flies."

"Those are mighty big birds to survive on a diet of brine flies," I commented. "They must eat fish too."

"Everybody needs a balanced diet."

We crawled into our sun-warmed tent and took a two hour nap.

It was starting to cool just a bit when I woke up and saw Michelle's big brown eyes staring at the sky.

I put my hand on her cheek.

"Whatcha thinking?"

"Nothing. Maybe about how lucky I am. I like this life with you so much better than the life I had before I went to prison. I'm so lucky to be with you, Paul. You're a good man. I was thinking about those big white pelicans eating those little brine shrimp. How graceful they were when they landed. Selenite crystals. How beautiful they are. How nice it is to be in a warm tent with you."

"And how lucky we are to have hamburger we can cook for supper?"

"Yeah. That too," she smiled. "You hungry?"

"I reckon I am."

"How about hamburgers and fried potatoes?"

"And a can of peas," I added. "We need a balanced diet."

"Good plan," agreed Michelle. "Let's do it."

She pulled me down and kissed me like she might be hungry for something else.

We devoured a good meal, cleaned up dishes, took off on another walk. Michelle identified some beautiful ducks with long necks and long pointed tails as Pintails.

Some little birds with orange breasts sent us back to the bird book. With binoculars Michelle saw the blue sides and backs. Bluebirds. Our list was growing.

I awoke before dawn, wondering what time it was, trying to find enough of our covers to stay warm. Michelle was snuggled close to me trying to absorb some of my body heat. We needed another sleeping bag.

Gradually, I heard an escalating sound. Birds were coming awake. I heard a call that sounded like, 'bob white, *bob white*.' I could see why they called that quail a Bobwhite. Its call sounded exactly like its name. Out on the lake I began to hear the quacking and calling of thousands of ducks and geese that had landed at dusk. How wonderful to awaken to a wild world on the shore of Great Salt Plains Lake. I wished I was warm. The tent felt like the inside of a refrigerator. We were sleeping on a couple of short, quilted, foam rubber mattress pads covered with a light cotton blanket. I had rolled over regularly to ease the pain in my hips. Then, we lost the blankets and had a short struggle to see who who had bare skin exposed to the cold air. We were covered by two blankets and a sleeping bag, spread out over the two of us. Michelle was shivering beside me. Finally, I sat up and zipped the bag.

"What are you doing, Paul. I'm cold. Don't take the sleeping bag away from me."

"Just relax, sweetheart."

I wrapped her in a blanket and helped her slide into the bag. Then, I spread the last blanket over the top of her.

"That's nice. You are a good man. I don't care what anybody says. Goodnight, Paul."

"Goodnight, Michelle."

I was shivering now. I crawled into my jeans, pulled sweat pants over the top, found a t-shirt, a long-sleeved flannel shirt, a sweat shirt, a Polartec jacket, and a stocking cap. I crawled from the tent and wished for a winter coat. The grass was white with frost. Some puddles were solid ice.

I built a fire. Soon I was warming my hands on a little blaze. I remembered a story I had heard as a child about an Indian who described fires.

"White man buildum big fire -- sittum far away. Injun buildum little fire -- sittum up close."

My fire was one I could sit up close to.

The story has always stuck in my mind as the proper way to build a campfire. I put on a pot of coffee on our camp stove and mixed up pancakes. By the time the spring sun touched the tent and brought a sleepy Michelle to the door, the coffee and a couple of cakes were ready.

"You are such a sweet man. I was freezing my butt and you tucked me in. Now you've built a warm fire and made me coffee and pancakes. I love you, Paul."

"That goes double for me, Michelle. I like making you happy. You make me feel like the luckiest man in the world just to be around you every day."

I sat on the ground near Michelle, drank my coffee, contemplating how lucky I was.

Then Michelle said, "Paul. I'm scared."

"Scared?"

"Yes. This is so good. Everything is going too well. I'm scared that we'll get caught. All of this will end. We'll be back in prison in Iowa. This will be over and we'll never see each other again. I don't want this to end, Paul."

Neither of us guessed that our next change of luck would come from a surprising direction; an air-breathing Arthropod with eight legs and fangs.

XIX

Brown Recluse Spider

After breakfast Michelle crawled back in the tent to stuff the sleeping bag and fold bedding.

I was cleaning up from breakfast when Michelle's scream pierced the quiet morning.

"What's wrong?"

"Ouch! Damn it!"

"Are you all right?"

"Something bit me!"

"We have a rattlesnake in our tent?"

"I'm serious, Paul. It wasn't a snake. A bug bit me on the shoulder. It hurts like hell! I don't know what it was, but it was a sharp, burning bite."

I crawled into the tent and began searching.

"There are scorpions in this country, Michelle. I've read about them crawling into the boot of a cowboy camped on the desert and stinging the foot that comes into the boot in the morning."

Michelle was kneeling by the door. "Look!" she exclaimed. "There he is! A big spider. Back in the corner."

I saw him. It was a big spider, half an inch long, grayish-brown, kind of leggy.

"I know him," I assured her. "We had these critters when I lived in Carbondale. I read more about them while I was in prison. I think this one is a Gray Recluse Spider. Maybe a Brown Recluse. Look closely. Does it have a violin on its back?"

"Paul, my shoulder hurts. All you do is look at the pretty little spider and wonder what kind it is. Worrying a little more about me and a little less about the stupid bug that bit me might be something you can involve yourself with."

"If it's the Brown Recluse, you could develop serious problems, sweetheart. Some people have a severe reaction to the bite. I read that the enzymes in the bite can produce toxins that break down cell membranes. Sometimes the surrounding tissue dies and scar tissues form. It can lead to skin grafts to repair the damage."

"Am I going to die? I don't want to die of a spider bite, Paul! Do we have to find a doctor? What do we do now?"

I looked closely at the spider. Sure enough, there was the violin-shaped mark on its head. This was the Fiddle Spider or the Brown Recluse.

"First, I'm sure this is the Recluse. It's fairly common in the south. Second, the bite sometimes causes really bad reactions. More often, people who are bitten have a natural immunity to the neurotoxins and the bite is not bad. When I lived in southern Illinois, we had them in our house sometimes. They like really dark places. I've been bitten more than once. My bites developed into little pimple-like things that disappeared in a few days without a trace. We need to watch it, but probably that's what will happen to you."

"You've been bitten?"

"Sure. We often found them in our bathtub. They can't climb out of the smooth surface of the tub."

Michelle said, "You scared me, Paul. You told me all of those terrible things first. Then you said it was probably no problem. Sometimes you're mean. I'm thinking about not loving you any more. And I am leaving this tent. You can take care of the blankets and the sleeping bag. Make sure you shake them out. Kill all the bugs or we're staying in a motel tonight."

"Listen to me first, Michelle. Seriously, these bites can be really bad. I've seen them fester into a huge hole in the skin that takes months to heal and requires skin grafts. The best thing to do would be to go to a doctor and get an antibiotic."

"We have no insurance, Paul."

"It's a gamble. The odds are in our favor. Ninety percent of the time you get a little pimple and it goes away."

"That means ten percent of the time my skin falls away and the poison eats away at my flesh."

"Yup."

"What shall we do?"

"Two choices," offered Paul. "We can get some ice on it. Pray that it heals without a problem. Or we can find a doctor in one of these small Oklahoma towns."

"So what shall we do, Paul?"

"If it was anyone else, I'd do the ice, head on our way, hope that good odds take care of you. It's you. I don't want anything to happen to you, Michelle. We don't want a big hole of raw tissue in your shoulder. I think you should see a doctor."

"We have no insurance and not much money."

"Let's get packed and find a doctor."

We still had a bit of ice in our cooler. I wrapped some in a towel and had Michelle hold it against her shoulder. In the trash can, I found a used plastic cup with a lid. I trapped the spider inside the cup, slid the lid over the opening, and sealed it. Then I packed our tent and bedding, throwing the breakfast dishes in the back of the pickup without washing them. We drove toward Alva, Oklahoma to look for a doctor.

"Paul?"

"Yes?"

"Is there danger of being arrested here?"

"You have an ID. The doctor won't be able to tell that you're not Michelle. We don't have insurance."

"Will it take more money than we have?"

"We should be ok. A couple hundred max? Maybe I can bargain. They won't have to deal with the insurance company."

"Maybe you should stay outside," Michelle suggested. "That way the doctor will see a single woman, not a couple who might be escaped prisoners from Iowa."

"Good plan," I agreed. "You're from California driving to South Carolina to join your mom. Maybe you can negotiate the price. You can afford to pay $50. Any more, you won't make it to your mom."

"I'll try."

In Alva we found a medical clinic. The sign on the window said, *Dr. Pamela King MD, Family Medicine.* Michelle dropped me off a block away. I went for a walk around a residential neighborhood. She drove to Dr. King's office.

The receptionist smiled and greeted Michelle, "May I help y'all?"

"I was bitten by a Brown Recluse Spider," Michelle explained. "He's in here." She held up the plastic cup. "I have no insurance, but the devastating consequences are so scary that my mom says I need an antibiotic. Can Dr. King give me some pills?"

"I think she'll want to see you first."

"I'm not sure I have enough money."

"I'm sorry for you, ma'am."

"So I guess I have to just risk getting a bunch of my flesh eaten away?"

"Perhaps we could work out a payment plan."

"Fine. If I had hope of finding a job. How much will it cost?"

"An office appointment is $130."

"How much would you get if I had insurance?"

"I don't have those numbers, ma'am. I'll put you on the list and when you see Dr. King, you can talk to her about payment. Perhaps you can work something out. It will be about half-an-hour."

"Thank you, nurse."

"I'm not a nurse, but you're welcome."

Thirty-two minutes later a nurse came to the door at the back of the office. "Michelle?"

"Right here." Michelle stood up.

"This way."

The nurse weighed Michelle, took her to an examination room, sat her down, and took her vitals.

Eleven minutes later, she jumped as a knock on the door startled her. A pretty, busty, dark-haired woman came into the room. An aura of confidence surrounded her.

"Michelle?"

"Yes."

"A spider bit you?"

"Yes."

"When?"

"This morning. I was camping. In a tent."

"And you think it was a Brown Recluse?"

"Yes."

"Are you sure?"

"Here it is. In this cup." She held out the cup to Dr. King."

"Smart." She looked at the spider and then carefully took off the lid and looked again."

"It's a Brown Recluse alright. There's the perfect little violin on his back and head. Where did he bite you?"

"In the tent."

She smiled. "I mean where on your body did he bite you?"

Michelle smiled, "I'm sorry. You wanted to know that he bit me on the shoulder. Right here." She rolled up her sleeve.

Dr. King said, "Looks slightly swollen. A little eruption."

She rubbed her chin. "Usually these things are no worse than a bee sting, Michelle. But, a small percentage of the time the poison begins to eat away at the flesh and it could leave an ugly cavern in your shoulder. I'll give you a prescription for an antibiotic and we'll make sure you're not in that group that reacts badly to the spider bite."

"I have a problem, Dr. King. I don't have any money. Well, I'm traveling across the country. I'm moving from California to live with my mom in South Carolina. I have just enough money to pay for my gas and eat a couple of meals a day. Could I give you, like fifty dollars and maybe you can give me some free samples of antibiotic? I'm sorry. I'm embarrassed to have to do this, but I have no insurance and almost no cash."

Dr. King looked at Michelle for about twenty seconds. Then she took a big breath and said, "Ok. I'll make the bill for forty-six dollars and you can go to the pharmacy and use the four dollars to buy this antibiotic. It's a generic and only costs four dollars. Be sure to follow the directions and take them all. One a day for ten days."

"Oh, thank you, Dr. King," Michelle smiled. "I really appreciate your seeing me. You don't know how much that helps."

"You're welcome, Michelle. Good luck to you."

An hour later, I was driving south from Alva on Highway 281. Thirty miles down the road we saw a sign for Little Sahara State

Park. I made a quick right turn through drifting sand into the parking lot. At a picnic table, Michelle and I made peanut butter, mayonnaise, and lettuce sandwiches and shared a Pepsi. Then we stretched out in the back of the S-10 and tried for a nap as we listened to the roar of Jeeps and ATV's cruising the dunes. I kept nagging Michelle to keep ice on her shoulder. Finally, we climbed to the top of one of the sand hills where we lay and watched the vehicles drive up and down the steep dunes for an hour.

We slid back down the steep, sandy slope, then spent an hour in the Nature Center learning about local birds and animals. Exhibits explained the shifting sand that covered 1600 acres above the Cimarron River with dramatic dunes.

It was nearly dusk, when I turned our little blue truck south toward Texas. I was feeling fresh, so I drove as Michelle slept with her head on my shoulder.

Midnight found me struggling to stay awake. At San Angelo State Park in Texas, we self-registered for a campsite, sleeping in the back of the S-10 for about seven hours. We took early morning showers. Then, we were driving south, putting more miles between us and Iowa. By noon, we were nearing the Texas border town of Del Rio.

Michelle's immunity and bargain medical treatment for the spider's poison seemed to be working. The bite had swollen just a little and looked like a bee sting. She was working on her ten day's supply of antibiotic.

XX

Drug Raid

Bob Johnson awoke to the wail of sirens. He sat up in the sagging bed, threw his feet on the tattered carpet, and felt icy cold sweat cover his body.

How did they know we are here? he thought.

Then he sensed that the sirens must be coming for someone else. There was no way that the police or anyone else knew that he and Rod were at the Sweet Dreams Motel in East Saint Louis, Illinois. *The sirens were for someone else.*

He glanced over his shoulder at Rod. His friend was lying on his side facing the opposite wall as far away as a man could lie on the narrow double bed. His knees were drawn up so that his body was in a fetal position. The noise of the sirens was gathering volume, but Rod was deep in predawn slumber.

Bob slipped his pants over his underwear and threw yesterday's long-sleeved t-shirt over his head. Suddenly, yellow, blue, and red lights made pretty patterns on the wall as the flashing lights from police cruisers showed through the holes in the heavy old drapes. The sirens sounded as if they were in the room. Then they stopped, the silence brought Rod to a sitting position.

"Those were sirens, Bob! And they're right outside our door. Let's get the fuck out of here."

Bob was buckling his belt and slipping into his shoes. He pulled the curtain back an inch, glimpsing three police cruisers parked at odd angles in the lot behind their Toyota.

"There are at least three cops behind our truck and they have shotguns. Put your pants on, man. I think we can kiss our days of freedom goodbye."

Rod pulled on his pants and slipped into his tennis shoes.

"Fuck! Fuck! Fuck! We were on our way to a new life. It's all over. We ain't bad guys. We don't deserve to go back to prison."

Bob took another peak out the curtain.

"Wait just a minute, partner. Those guns are pointed toward the motel room next door to us. We may not be dead yet. Don't give up hope."

"I think we should turn ourselves in so they don't shoot us," said Rod.

"On the other hand," Bob continued, "if the cops and robbers suddenly start shooting, we could be dead in one big hurry. I think we should hide on the floor of the bathroom and pray that one of those stray bullets doesn't hit us."

Rod grabbed his shirt and dove into the tiny bathroom, finding a safe spot in the cheap fiberglass bathtub.

"That tub ain't going to stop no bullet, man."

"You just stay down low and keep your fuckin head down. I'm as low as I can possibly be in here and I ain't moving."

They stopped talking. For about five minutes the silence was complete. Then the phone rang in the motel room next door. They could hear muffled voices, but no words.

"Bob, I think you should take another peek outside to see what's happening. Nobody is shooting. Maybe it's safe to leave this place."

The light knock on the door made both criminals jump about a foot.

The whispered voice said, "Open up. Police."

In the bathroom, Bob whispered to Rod, "Oh God, we're done. They ran our license plate. We're going back to prison, Rod."

Rod said, "You're right man. There ain't no way out of here. Open the fucking door."

He got up out of the tub, holding out his hand to his friend. They walked toward the door together as Rod buttoned his shirt.

"We're coming," Bob said. "Don't shoot."

Bob slipped the dead bolt, opening the door to the biggest cop he had ever seen. The guy was about six foot eight inches and must have weighed more than two hundred sixty pounds. He was holding a big black automatic pistol to his side.

"Sorry to bother y'all. We've got us a situation in the room next door. There are a couple of drug dealers with guns over there and we want you out. Now."

"Yes, sir," said Rod and Bob in chorus.

"Is that your 4Runner? If it is, move it. You can come back later for whatever is in your room. Go!"

Rod got behind the wheel and the police covered the window next door as the two escapees moved their stolen SUV onto Highway 3, turning south through the western Illinois forest and farm country.

"Anything you needed in that motel room, Rod."

"Not me. I don't ever want to see that room again, man."

"Do we need to worry about fingerprints?" asked Bob. "I think I left some back there."

"Well, maybe we should find a productive way to spend the day," suggested Rod. "Then slip back to the old Sweet Dreams Motel, do a little clean-up project. I don't want to spend tonight there, but I still have the key. We can go in and wipe the place down. Give the cops plenty of time to do their job and catch those druggies. Then we'll go back and make sure they're gone. I learned how to clean real good in prison. I'll bet we can make every one of our finger prints disappear from that motel room."

Bob put his hand on his chin like *The Thinker* and pondered. He reached into the back seat and got The Ranger's road Atlas.

In a moment he said, "There's a decent-sized town, Waterloo, just down the road about twenty miles. Maybe we rent a Super 8. Then, I think it's time to solve another problem."

"Yeah?"

"The Ranger's 4Runner."

XXI

Clean-Up At Sweet Dreams Motel

For $62, Bob rented a motel room in the Super 8 in Waterloo, Illinois, while Rod took a walk around the block. Later, Rod was sprawling on one of the beds as Bob sat in an easy chair.

Bob suggested, "If some cop gets real interested in our Toyota, we'll just slip away and let him have it. By now Missouri and Illinois cops are sure to have the description of the 4Runner."

"For sure."

"We have to figure our pictures are out there," said Bob.

"With the cops or with the press?"

"Both," answered Bob.

Rod argued, "On the positive side, remember, we've got stolen Missouri license plates on the truck. And they have the descriptions of **four** people so the cops might not immediately link us up with the Four-Runner."

"I don't know," answered Bob. "They've surely been to The Ranger's house. They must know by now that we've stolen two vehicles from Roger Stewart. They're surely looking for two of us with the 4Runner and two with the Ranger. I've got a real bad feeling about that truck. When the East St. Louis cops did that drug bust this morning, they surely got a good look at our car and probably at us. It won't be long until they put two and two together and it comes out us. Seems to me we have two big problems, man. Well, a lot more than two, but we've got two big problems we have to solve very soon. First the car. I love it, but we can't afford to keep it. Second, a place to live. If the cops figure out that the Toyota at the motel was ours, they'll be after us like flies on a jam sandwich. We need a safe place to stay until our papers are ready. And we need to get rid of that 4Runner."

Rod said, "We got a third problem, man."

"What's that?"

"Them cops at the Sweet Dreams Motel. If they put two and two together, and if somebody read his reports, and if they run a plate on our 4Runner and find it bogus, then they could be waiting for us when we go back."

"Shall we run?"

"We're already running, man."

"You know what I mean. Should we get on some back roads and drive south?"

"What do you think?"

It was a minute before Bob answered.

"I think we should go park a few blocks from the Sweet Dreams, walk close by, and check it out. If the cops aren't around we go in with a bottle of 409 cleaner and a roll of paper towels. Clean it up. Eliminate our finger prints and clear the hell out."

"Let's go do it, dude."

They bought cleaner and paper towels, drove to within a couple of blocks of the motel, parking on a side street.

"I'll walk ahead a block," said Bob. "If I see anything of the cops, I'll turn around and walk back toward you. You run like hell back to the car. I won't run. If they're still there, they'll be looking for a car, not an old white guy. If I don't see any cops, I'll check around the room. If it's all clear, I'll wave to you. We'll do a fast clean-up and be on our way. Then, we'll figure out how to get rid of the Toyota. It's making me damn nervous, Rod."

"Me too. I have an idea for later."

"What?"

"Later. Let's clean up the room first."

The clean-up went without a hitch. No cops. When Bob and Rod finished, no prints. By mid-afternoon they were back at the Super 8. The 4Runner was parked a couple of blocks away on a quiet side street. Rod and Bob lounged on their beds and talked.

"Here's the deal," Rod said. "I knew a guy from prison, who was there for buying stolen cars and cutting them up for used parts. Maybe this truck might get us some money if we could find us a chop shop."

'Is the guy still in the pen or is he outside?" asked Bob.

"I'm pretty sure he went out a couple of years ago. Guess where he lived."

"St. Louis."

"He lived in St. Louis of all places. I think his name was Danny."

"And his last name?"

"It's on the tip of my tongue, man. It'll come. Just give me a minute."

For three minutes, the motel room was silent.

Then, "Evans! Danny Evans. Let's get a phone book and find him."

There were thirteen Dan, Daniel, or Danny Evanses in the St. Louis phone book.

"What do we do now?" Rod asked. "How are we going to find out which one is my friend, Danny Evans?"

"Easy. You call. Say, 'I used to have a friend named Danny Evans when we both lived in Fort Madison, in southeast Iowa. You wouldn't be my old buddy would you?'"

"That's going to take a lot of calling."

"All you have to make is thirteen calls and you have him. Pick up that damn phone and get to dialing, my friend. We'll get *The Ranger's* Toyota off our hands and turn it into some extra cash at the same time."

XXII

Chop Shop

Thirteen phone calls didn't quite do the job. Rod found six people at home. One woman said she had no idea if Dan Evans had ever lived in Iowa. "I've only known him for four months. Shall I have him call you?"

"That wouldn't be a good idea. I'll call back. When's a good time to reach him?"

"He's usually home by six or a little after. If you don't contact him then, try about nine. We may go out for dinner tonight."

"That's great, ma'am. Thanks."

By six o'clock Rod had struck out on all but two of the Dan Evans'. The last two still didn't answer so he tried the new girlfriend again.

She answered. "Yeah, he's here. Just keep it quick, please. He's just getting out of the shower. Then we're going out for pizza."

After a moment, a deep voice came on the phone. "This is Danny. What do you want? Sharon says you knew me in Iowa. I'm not sure I want to talk to anyone I knew in Iowa. Who are you?"

Rod recognized his voice right away. "Hi, Danny. This is Rod. We roomed together for a while. I thought we was pretty good friends. I was passing through St. Louis and I thought we might renew our acquaintance."

Danny's voice became really soft. "Rod. I remember you. You were always a regular guy, but I don't really want anything to do with my old friends from Iowa. I have a good business going and I just don't want my past to screw it up. Understand?"

"You bet. I understand that, my friend. I liked you too, man. We always watched each other's back. I'd like to buy you a meal, visit a bit about old times and new times, maybe offer you a chance to make a few, almost honest bucks."

"Almost honest bucks sounds bad, Rod. I really like it on the outside. I have a girl. I have a business. I have a nice truck. It's honest money. Almost honest money probably won't do it, friend."

"Ok. I understand. At least let me take you out for a meal. How about supper tonight? Me and my buddy ain't got no plans. Your girl friend said you were going out for pizza. How about we meet you at the pizza place and we buy? Then I'll stay out of your hair. We both just left the system and it would be good to talk to a real woman for a change. OK?"

"Let me ask Sharon. I'll be right back."

A minute later, Danny was back on the phone. "Sharon would love to meet you. She said you sounded real nice on the phone. Where are you? We'll find a pizza place someplace between you and me."

Twenty minutes later the four of them were sitting in a big booth. They could see the St. Louis Arch from the restaurant. Rod and Bob thought it was a really classy place.

The four of them seemed to hit it off really well. It turned out that Sharon had served time in an Arkansas prison on a series of charges ranging from shop-lifting to drugs to breaking and entering with an old boy friend. She was working as a waitress and was up for a job as a manager at a really nice restaurant in the west part of St. Louis.

Bob and Rod were both impressed with Sharon's plunging neckline and her lovely monarch butterfly tattoo. Both men had trouble concentrating on her pretty face.

Two large pizzas were nearly gone when Rod said, "Danny, we was going to request a favor, but I really don't want to ask you to do something that might cause you problems with the law again. You guys are doing so well."

"What were you going to ask, dude? Least I can do is listen. I remember when that big black dude was pissed at me. He would have knifed me bad. You stepped in and karate chopped him in the back of the neck. He never figured out what hit him. Never bothered me after that. Every time he looked at me, he rubbed his neck and then looked behind him. I owe you one. The least I can do is listen to you."

"Well, here's the situation," Rod explained. "Bob and me aren't really out on parole. We were in a halfway house in Des Moines when this fucked up guard tried to rape a woman prisoner. Another guy stepped in, trying to protect her. We kind of walked into the fight. The guard fell. Hit his head real hard. The dude stopped breathing. The bastard was dead, man. We decided we didn't have a chance if we stayed and faced the music, so we took his car keys and left him. Drove to his house, stole a bunch of stuff the guy couldn't use no more. Then we left the state. Now we have his Toyota 4Runner. It has to be hotter than that first slice of pizza that just burned my mouth. We were going to leave it in a parking lot somewhere, when I thought of you. Bob and me thought you might be able to make some good bucks and we might be able to help our cause a bit if you just parted it out."

Rod paused for a breath. Then he continued, "After we heard your story, we sure don't want to do nothing to cause you trouble. You are free and clear, man. Bob and me'd both feel like shit if we made a deal and anything happened to you because of it. So we'll just be on our way and say I'm real glad to hear of your success. You're a real great guy, Danny. I'm glad we had a chance to see you."

The booth became silent.

"Rod, why don't you wait just a minute?" suggested Danny. "I want to talk to Sharon a moment out in the parking lot."

Five minutes later, the four of them huddled near the 4Runner. Danny said, "Here's the deal, man. I have a buddy who has a body shop in an old barn out in the country on Highway 65 down toward Lake of the Ozarks. The guy does a few rebuilders. It should be no problem for him to find a wrecked Toyota to rebuild. He might have a vehicle that he would trade for your truck and all of us could make a few extra bucks out of the deal. Your hot Toyota 4Runner could just disappear. It's the kind of a deal where there are no victims, Rod."

Danny moved closer to Rod and lowered his voice.

"If you're still offering, I can call him right now. He has a 2002 Ford Escort. It's a fair mileage car, pretty dependable. We could trade cars with him tonight."

Rod said, "That'd be perfect, man."

In the final deal, Rod and Bob received two thousand dollars cash plus the Escort. It had a new baby blue paint job and ran like a top. The deal made everybody happy.

XXIII

Del Rio, Texas

Del Rio, Texas has a nice ring to it. Michelle and I were beginning to feel safer now that we had a big state between us and
Iowa police. As we parked in front of the National Park Service
Office along the highway, the tones of the Val Verde County
Courthouse Clock chimed noon. We picked up flyers and
maps from state and federal parks near town. This time, the
uniform of the woman officer didn't make my blood pressure
rise more than a few points. Being free people was beginning
to feel more natural. Michelle and I visited with her about bird
watching in the Del Rio area. She gave us a map of promising
birding locations.

"Have you ever seen a Green Jay?" she asked.

"A Green Jay? I'd love to see one," I assured her. "We hoped
we might add the bird to our list. They are a very pretty bird
and I've heard they are fairly common along the Rio Grande.
Can you tell us where we might find them?"

The ranger smiled. Her badge told me her name was
Nancy. "You can find Green Jays almost anywhere around Del

Rio. They spend a lot of time in the open forests and the scrub oaks along the river. They also show up pretty regularly at our feeders."

"So where would you recommend that we go to see them, Nancy?"

She thought for about ten seconds, then suggested, "Take Highway 277 south until you reach a spur to the right. Take the 277 spur for a block and turn south on Pecan Street. It will curve right, just past the Val Verde Winery. All of that scrub oak by the river is great habitat for Green Jays and also for migratory warblers. You won't be sorry. The jays are beautiful birds and the warblers are a bonus. You can find them any time of day, but sometimes when they are migrating, they just seem to fall out of the sky in the morning. They fly all night on the spring breezes from way down south in Mexico. When dawn comes, they just drop from the sky like colored snowflakes. You can never tell what kinds or what colors you might see."

She gave us way more information about birds than I wanted. Her greatest gift was her enthusiasm. It was catching. As we left, Michelle asked me, "What do you think? Shall we get up early and find us some warblers, Paul? I'd love to see those birds fall out of the sky. Warblers are pretty small, aren't they? I'm glad you bought binoculars. This could be fun. I've never been bird watching before."

I explained, "According to the bird book, a Green Jay is about 11 inches long. A Blue Jay is also 11 inches long. Warblers are tiny, about five to six inches. They winter in Mexico and Central America and then breed in Alaska and across northern Canada. That's a big trip twice a year for a tiny bird. No wonder they call these old folks that are running around down here *Snow Birds.* They act just like the warblers. They head south when the weather gets cold and pick up a southern breeze and go back home when the snow is gone in Iowa."

We drove to the scrub oak forest south of town and found a trail. We took the binoculars and the bird book and walked a couple of miles. The country was pretty wild. For a while I thought we were lost. Then we found Green Jays. They were gorgeous birds, with blue heads and black bibs and masks. Their backs were green and their breasts yellow. Michelle and I agreed they were the prettiest birds we'd ever seen.

Michelle conjectured, "I wonder if God gives little children who die a color-by-number set and has them paint each section of the body of the Green Jays a different color."

On the way back to the pickup, we passed a marsh. There were some big white marsh birds wading. I didn't know what they were. We found ourselves whispering to each other so we wouldn't disturb the birds.

"They look like Great Blue Herons who ran into a bottle of bleach," I joked.

Michelle looked up Great Blue Herons in the book. She found a Great White Heron that lives in Florida and a Great Egret that winters along the Texas-Mexico border. Our bird was about three feet tall and had black feet and legs, just like the Great Egret.

"I think it has to be the Great Egret, she decided. "Look at the big yellow beak."

We were getting good at this birding stuff. I wrote the date and "Del Rio, TX" in the margin of the bird book next to the picture of the Great Egret.

"I always thought you weren't supposed to write in books, Paul."

"This book is ours, Michelle. We bought and paid for it. In school they didn't like us to write in the books because somebody else was going to use the book the next year."

"Still doesn't seem quite right. It must be an ethic that's ingrained in my brain."

"I took an algebra class once from Mr. Jack Spain. He gave me my book and told us to look through it to make sure we wouldn't get charged for somebody else's ink marks. Inside the back cover, the person who had the book last had written, 'FUCK SPAIN!' Mr. Spain wasn't too happy when I showed him that and told him I hadn't written it. He told me he had seen the remark in the spring when he had checked in books. He had separated it, but somehow it had gotten into his book pile again over the summer."

Michelle said, "That kid was pretty disrespectful. How do you suppose Mr. Spain felt?"

"I know how he felt. He was pissed off. He told me he had the list of who had that book the year before. No one had checked it out, but one kid hadn't handed in the book that he was supposed to have. I had the impression that Mr. Spain had a talk with the kid and that he not only had to pay a premium cost for the book he'd lost, but that he'd had to listen to a lecture on how much books cost and how bad it is to destroy a book for whoever got it the next year."

"Did you like him?" asked Michelle.

"Mr. Spain was a great guy. He and I became good friends. Later in the year, we had a conversation about it after class one day. He said he had found the book as he was giving a final exam for another class. He had just read a really nice note from one of his advanced algebra students who was also on his track team. The note told Mr. Spain what a wonderful teacher he was and what a great influence he had been for the kid. He had credited Mr. Spain with teaching him math and track and also how to live his life. Mr. Spain put the note in his drawer to save and then started checking in books. The first book said, *FUCK SPAIN!* under the back cover. He said, he figured God was trying to tell him, *Don't get to feeling too smug, Jack. You may have done a good job with one of your students, but there's still a lot of work left for you to do.*"

Michelle chuckled, "That's a funny story, Paul. Mr. Spain must have been a great teacher."

"He was incredible. He's one of the reasons I decided to go into education. Now I've screwed up my life so that I can never teach again. I'll have to find a new career direction. When I went to prison, I got a letter from Mr. Spain. He said he was disappointed that I'd made a mistake. Told me he had confidence that I'd find a way to make something better happen in my life. Said he knew I was a good man. I doubt if he's too proud of me today."

"Both of us will be needing new careers, Paul. Except I was really ready to find a new life. I didn't like myself too well for the things I was doing to other people before I got caught and sent away. I feel like I've started moving up a new path already. I owe you a lot, Paul. You've treated me more like a person than anybody I ever knew. No wonder I fell in love with you. Besides, you being so sexy."

"Not nearly as sexy as you, woman. Let's get back to town, buy some groceries, find a place to camp."

Before I could get back in the pickup, Michelle gave me a hug. All I could think of was setting up the tent and crawling into a sleeping bag with her.

As we drove away, Michelle said, "Can we come back here at dawn? I want to see those warblers fall out of the sky."

"Let's do it," I said.

At a super market we bought a copy of the Del Rio News Herald from a rack out in front. We were glad to see there weren't any articles about escaped murderers from Iowa on the front page. We checked the want ads and the grocery advertisements. We needed jobs and food.

It didn't take long to fill our grocery order. Our list was short. We topped it off with some Texas grapefruit and a hunk of ice for the cooler. We had our meals covered for several days.

This time there were no police cars parked behind the S-10. The police didn't worry us as much right now. The pickup was ours and Michelle's I. D. was fairly solid. I worried a little that they might trace an auto transfer from Fayetteville, but there was nothing we could do about that. If it didn't work, they'd show up on our doorstep.

XXIV

Lake Amistad

West of Del Rio, a blacktopped road took us to Amistad National Recreation Area. We followed the signs to the campground sitting on a hill above Lake Amistad. Camping was cheap at eight dollars a night, with concrete slabs for motor homes, pickup campers, and trailers. The thermometer on the Del Rio National Bank sign had registered 78 degrees. The air felt mellow.

Michelle said, "The paper says Des Moines had a high yesterday of 31 degrees."

"And the low here?"

"Sixty-two."

"Where would you rather be?"

"If we were in Des Moines," she reasoned, "we'd be in jail. We wouldn't have to worry about the weather."

"Shall we sleep in our tent again?"

"I'm willing. This is a good place to be, Paul. Look at all those campers. Does this place even allow tents?" Michelle asked. "All I see are motor homes and solid-sided campers."

"That's because everybody else is afraid of the bears, Michelle."

She frowned and then snuggled up to me, "You'll protect me? Right, Paul?"

I returned her hug. "There are no bears within 500 miles of here, but protecting you sounds like fun. See the flat places that are cleared out behind the concrete slabs. I think those are for tents."

"I want a camping spot under a shade tree," Michelle demanded. "We need shade."

"Which tree would you like to camp under, Michelle?"

She studied the park in a circle around us. There wasn't a tree in sight.

We did find an empty camp site on the hill. It had a tent pad that was nearly flat. Flat seemed like a good idea if we were sleeping in a tent. This was rough, barren country. Sharp spiny plants covered the ground.

"Maybe we can buy a book to tell what all of these plants are," suggested Michelle. "I think I saw some plant and cactus books at the ranger station in Del Rio. These plants surely have names. I think it would fun to learn them."

"How's our budget?" I asked. "Do we have money for plant books?"

"Probably not."

"What's your priority?"

"What I really need is a shower," confessed Michelle. "Where's the shower room, Paul?"

"I don't think this campground has a shower, Michelle. That's probably one of the reasons it's so cheap. It does have a nice rest room with a pit toilet. It looks really clean."

"Paul. We have to have a shower. We even had showers in prison," she begged.

"We'll find a way to wash. Maybe we can have a sponge bath tonight. Tomorrow we'll look for a shower. Sometimes truck stops have showers, don't they?"

"I don't like the idea. You promised to protect me from the bears. I would think you could find me a shower."

"After dinner we can heat a pan of water and I'll take a wash cloth and give you a sponge bath and you can do the same for me. How does that sound?"

"Not as good as a shower, but maybe it'll be fun. We will find a shower tomorrow, right Paul? Promise?"

"I promise to do my best to find us a place to shower."

We worked together to set up the little green tent and make our bed. Then I fixed grilled-cheese sandwiches while Michelle heated up some canned tomato soup and stirred up a batch of instant chocolate pudding.

After supper I washed the dishes. Michelle dried and put them away in the drawer in the back of the pickup. Then we followed a trail to Lake Amistad and skipped rocks into the calm water.

Warm, golden, evening sunshine bathed our campsite as we returned from our hike. We were happy for our tent and mattress pads.

As we cuddled together beneath our sleeping bag, Michelle whispered in my ear, "Paul?"

"Yes?"

"Have we run far enough?"

"What?"

"Can we find a place to live? Like in a house?"

XXV

Making Plans In Del Rio

In the morning we spread the Del Rio News-Herald on our picnic table and began searching for jobs and apartments. Del Rio might be a town for us to settle in for awhile. Having a street address, might be a step toward getting me a birth certificate, a social security card, and a driver's license.

"This extended vacation has been fun," Michelle observed. "I'd want to continue it forever. How long do you think our money will last?"

"Not long enough," I reasoned. "Can we live on a thousand a month? Our pickup cost us basically, $1700 including license and insurance. So we have about $1600 left. We have to eat and pay rent and have money for food and gasoline. I agree with you. We should find a place to live. Then we can sit down and add it all up."

Michelle said, "We'll have to get real jobs, Paul. But I think we can live pretty cheap and still enjoy ourselves. If we don't buy too many things, we can keep mobile, be ready to travel light if we need to. … I can't believe I just said that. Me, who spent my whole life living for the *things* I could own. What am I saying, Paul?"

"That there is a new you? That your experience in prison has reformed you?"

"Something has changed me. I'll have to think about this some more."

I glanced at the front page of The Herald. The headlines read, "*Investigation into Superintendent's expense records continues.*"

"Look at this, Michelle." I pointed at the article. "Now I feel right at home in Del Rio. Do they steal from schools in every town?"

"Things are the same everywhere," agreed Michelle. "I'll bet they have prostitutes in their city jail sometimes. Aren't you glad our old lives are behind us? The only things they want us for now are escape from prison and murder of a prison guard. And I don't think either of us feels too guilty about what we did back in Des Moines."

One section of the want ads was labeled, "Apartments."

Most of the apartments were renting for closer to $1000 than $500. Then we found an ad for an unfurnished two bed-room apartment for $400.

"We could afford that for a while," Michelle said.

I wrote down the address.

"Look at this ad, Paul."

Free Stuff: Very Playful Black Lab, Female. 6 months old. 273- 3960

"Can we have a dog, Paul? Do you like dogs?"

"Those are two different questions. I love dogs. *Can we have a dog?* A dog would really complicate our lives. Notice, the ad says *Very Playful*. Do you know what that means?"

"What?"

"She is out of control."

"She likes to chase tennis balls."

"She jumps on everybody."

"She plays tug-of-war."

"She's a pain in the butt."

"We should go see her and see if we like each other," Michelle argued. "I think a dog would be wonderful. If we were sleeping in our tent, she could keep me warm at night and protect me from the bears. My man doesn't seem to be willing to protect me from bears."

"Ha. Ha. You don't know how hard I'd fight to protect you from a bear."

"I would probably lose you both," Michelle said with a frown. "You and the dog would both die fighting for me."

"If we had a dog, you would have to divide your love for me in half," I proclaimed.

"That's not the way love works, Paul. Actually, I'd love you so much more if we had a dog. Can we go look at her?"

"Michelle, I'd do anything for you and you know it. Write down the phone numbers of the lab and the apartment. We'll find a phone and check on them. Maybe someone already took the free dog."

"I'll cry."

"If we get the dog," I argued, "we'll have to add another twenty dollars a month to our budget. Can we afford it?"

"I'll get a job in a restaurant waiting tables. I don't know about you, Paul. How are you going to get a job with no driver's license and no social security card? You may have to stay home with the dog and be a stay-at-home dad." She gave me a shy smile.

We studied the employment ads. The jobs required references and special training which we couldn't produce or didn't have.

Michelle said, "Look at this, Paul. The City of Del Rio is looking for a part time driver to transport the elderly and deliver meals to homebound old people. You could do that. It says you need a high school diploma and must pass a CDL. That's a driver's license with an endorsement for passengers. If we could get you a driver's license and a social security card, you'd be perfect for that job." Same shy smile.

"You know, Michelle, I've been thinking about this problem. Can the Iowa officials check out my social security record? Or is it private? I think those records might be private. If I used my real social security number, I don't think the cops could access those records. Also, I graduated from Carbondale High School in southern Illinois. If I obtain a copy of my diploma and showed an employer, the Iowa people might never know, would they?"

"I don't know about that, Paul. I'd guess the cops can get any records they want. If you had money coming into your social security account from Del Rio, Texas, I think the Des

Moines Police would find out and be on our doorstep quicker than sweat bees find your pop. And what about your driver's license? You would have to get that special Commercial Driver's License. Will they check your past record? Will that lead them back to Iowa?"

"I've been thinking about that, too," I reasoned. "Suppose, I have just returned from ten years in India. I don't have an old license, so I'm getting a brand new one. I'd obviously have to pass a driving and a written test. What do you think? Would that story fly? I know my real social security number. If that can't lead the Iowa people to us, it might be alright."

"Even if the police can't acquire Social Security records, you can bet that as soon as you apply for a driver's license, the Iowa BCI will be on our doorstep.

"Also, if you decide to use the lie about coming from India, you'd better work on your tan. You look real white right now. Doesn't India have a lot of sunshine? I think we should be awful careful about this new identity shit, Paul. We shouldn't be in too much of a hurry. I'm still thinking you should use a name from a tombstone. Then we could get married and you could take my name. Paul Swartz. That has a nice ring to it. We could be a real modern couple. Why should the woman always be the one to change her name?"

She continued. "Mr. and Mrs. Michelle Swartz. I love it."

I surprised her. "I like the idea. Marry me, Michelle. I'll take your name."

"I wonder if you shouldn't use Paul Swartz anyway. Let's check out a flea market and see if we can buy some cheap rings. Fake diamonds. Fake gold. Just enough so we look married."

"Let's do it."

That night was great. I think both of us were loving sleeping in the tent. I woke up in the middle of that night to go outside and pee. The sky was clear. The stars were bright. I crawled back in the tent and kissed Michelle awake.

"Come out and look at this, I whispered. Tonight, I'd like to offer you the sky."

She crawled sleepily out of the tent and looked up.

"Wow! That is wonderful, Paul. I have never seen anything like it. Are we smack in the middle of the Milky Way? Is that what they call that mass of stars? And look at the lake. It is so calm. Every one of those billion stars in the sky is reflected in that lake. This is incredible, Paul. Thanks for waking me." She kissed me, then turned and leaned back against me. I put my arms around her and held her close. A few minutes later, we sat on the picnic table watching the stars for a half an hour. It was another half an hour before we finally fell asleep. I was glad I woke her.

At ten after nine, warm sunshine brought me out of our tent. I dug in the drawer in the back of the pickup for a couple of towels. Michelle crawled out of the tent a moment later.

"Are we ready to go search for a dog and an apartment?"

"Or an apartment and a dog."

"Get your priorities straight, Paul."

"We're on our way. I might have a surprise. Hop in."

"What?"

"It wouldn't be a surprise if I told you, sweetie. Come on."

"Ok. I've got to get some makeup on if we're going to see other people."

"No. Skip the makeup for now."

"Paul! What's going on?"

"Surprise. Trust me?"

"Sure. You better not embarrass me."

"I'd never do that, Michelle."

I'd caught a glimpse of an ad in the paper for a campground. I drove toward town and back onto Highway 90. I turned into the drive for the Holiday Trav-L-Park.

"What's this," asked Michelle, as I parked in front of the shower house.

"You wanted a shower. Pretend you are staying here with your big Winnebago motor home and are taking your morning shower. Take your towel, soap, shampoo, hairbrush, makeup, and act like you live here for the winter. I'll meet you back here in half an hour."

"We can't do this, Paul. Somebody will arrest us and send us back to Iowa."

"It'll be ok. Nobody asks people in the shower if they are camped here. Just act like you come and shower every day. You'll be fine and you'll be clean. Enjoy."

"Ok, Paul. I love you for getting me a shower."

She kissed me and whispered in my ear. "In case they send us back to two separate prisons, remember I'll love you forever."

"Forever."

XXVI

Del Rio - An Apartment and a Dog

The Val Verde County Library had a concrete bench under a shade tree.   Michelle and I filled a plastic bottle in the water cooler in the library.   Then we sat on the concrete bench and drank the water.   We used the phone in the lobby to call Tillie Teasdale, the woman who advertised the apartment for rent. She invited us to come and see it right away.

The apartment was pretty basic second floor accommodations; kitchen, living room, and a single small bedroom.   From the front door vestibule we climbed a long, straight stairway to the second floor.   An old refrigerator, a beat-up gas stove, and space for a small table and chairs filled most of the kitchen. Everything about the apartment was old, but it had a clean, scrubbed look about it.   Mrs. Teasdale also had an old, yet clean and well-scrubbed look about her.   Her face had deep wrinkle lines as if she had spent a lot of time smiling as a younger person.   She had the kind of face that made me think she had been a beautiful woman in her youth.   She was tall and still slender.

Age was giving her hips and her stomach a little more flesh than she had probably carried as a young woman, but she obviously took good care of herself.

When we told her we had no furniture, Tillie said she had an old double bed with an iron frame. State law wouldn't let her rent the apartment with the bed, but we could use it. She even had a set of sheets we could use. They were thread bare, but we didn't care. The price was right. We gave her $400 for the first month and a $400 deposit that she would return if there was no damage other than normal wear and tear when we moved out.

She also gave us phone numbers for the power company and the phone company. Those costs would be extras she said. We would have to handle them ourselves.

Mrs. Teasdale asked us to call her Tillie. She wanted to know where we came from. We told her "Arkansas."

"Why, my cousin, Harriet, is from Arkansas. She lives in Little Rock. That is close to where our former president is from. Actually, he was from Hope originally. I declare, I believe Harriet was one of the few women in Little Rock that Bill Clinton wasn't able to seduce. You ain't from Little Rock are you, honey?"

"No, we're both from Eureka Springs," said Michelle. "It's up in the mountains up in the northwest part of the state. I really liked Bill Clinton. I wish I had met him. I thought he was cute. If he'd have put the make on me, I'd probably been in bed with him. Oh, sorry Paul. Y'all know you're the only man for me any more."

Tillie said, "Well, if he'd have seen you, he'd have sure fallen in love with you. I think you are as cute as a bug and with your figure any man I know would go bonkers over you. I guess you know what a lucky man you are, Paul, to be married to Michelle. You better watch her close. Some of these Texas cowboys will try to steal her right away from you."

I gave Tillie $800. The thought crossed my mind, *Does it draw suspicion to us if we pay all our bills with cash? Would we look more normal if we paid by check? Maybe we should put some money in the bank and start a checking account.*

When I drove up in front of the Del Rio National Bank, Michelle asked, "What are we doing here?"

I explained my thoughts about checks.

"What if we have to leave town in a hurry, Paul? It's not like we have a lot of money to spare."

"My thought is that a checking account might lower our risk. People who pay cash for everything are often drug dealers."

"Let's not keep a lot of money in there then. I think most of our cash should be distributed between you and me fairly evenly."

We opened a checking account with $800 cash. Michelle put the account in her sister's name and social security number.

We had seen a couple of garage sale signs on the way through town. One had a small chest of drawers that would hold all of our clothes just fine. Michelle found a couple of blouses that were almost new and very cute for a dollar each. At another sale we found an easy chair and an old beat up rocker that just filled the back of the S-10. The chair was worn and ragged on the edges, but it would be better than sitting on the floor. Our best bargains were a couple of backpacks for a dollar each and a set of nested aluminum pans for camping for two dollars. We were beginning to like camping.

At a third garage sale, we bought a radio/tape player. The lady plugged it in so we could assess the radio. She also gave us a cassette tape to try. It worked like new and had good airy sound for a cheap radio. Michelle and I decided we could live without TV, but it would be nice to be able to listen to the AM-FM radio. Almost all of the stations in South Texas were in Spanish, but both of us enjoyed Mexican music. I had a year of Spanish in high school. Michelle knew none. Learning Spanish was something we should do if we were going to live in this part of the country very long. We talked about checking out a guide book and a Spanish instruction tape at the library.

That sale also had an old broken table and a couple of loose-jointed wooden kitchen chairs. The woman who was selling them told us that if we bought the chairs for $3 each she would throw in the broken table. I thought about offering her less, but she probably needed the money more than we did. I gave her eight bucks for the table, chairs, and the radio. I took the table apart and fitted it all into the pickup.

"Are you ready to head home, Michelle?" I asked.

"Paul, I'm thinking we should call about the dog," Michelle said. She looked at me with those big brown eyes of hers and what could I say?

Back at the library, Michelle sat on the bench under the shade of the oak tree while I called about the free Lab.

Then I turned to Michelle. "We're in luck, Michelle. They still have it. Somebody had come to look at her, but for some reason they hadn't taken her with them. The people said something about not being sure and they would get back to them. The owners want to meet us before they gave the dog to us."

We drove out to a little house on the south edge of Del Rio. The streets in this part of town had no curbs or gutters. Houses were small. Most had a well-cared-for look about them. As we parked, a big black Lab ran to greet us. She jumped up on Michelle and began to lick her face. Michelle reached her arms around the big dog and gave her a hug.

The dog came over to me and started to jump up on me. I said, "SIT!" She sat. Then she looked at me as if waiting to be given a reward. I was impressed. When I patted her head and rubbed her ears, she seemed pleased and gave my hand a good licking.

A woman came to the door. "Hi. I'm Gladys. You must be the people who called about Sally. I see you've already met."

"Good afternoon," I greeted her. "I'm Paul and this is Michelle. Sally is a beautiful dog, Gladys. I think she and my wife like each other."

"Sally likes everyone," bragged Gladys. "That's one reason we have to get rid of her. She's just too friendly. She greets everyone who comes to our door or who walks by on the street.

People don't like taking a licking every time they come to our door."

It didn't take Gladys long to decide that we were deserving master and mistress for her dog. She disappeared into the house and came back with a couple of dog dishes, a leash, a rope to tie her up, and a half a sack of dog food.

"I needed to meet you before I gave Sally to you," Gladys explained. "I wanted to make sure she was moving into a really good home; that I wasn't giving her to some murderers or something. I think you folks will be real nice to Sally and take good care of her. I'm a pretty good judge of character. Those other folks who came yesterday weren't a good fit. I can tell you will love her and she will be a good dog for y'all."

Gladys walked us toward the pickup.

"It looks like you got yourself a load of furniture."

We explained that we were moving into an unfurnished apartment and that we were trying to find furniture at garage sales.

"Need a couch?" Gladys offered. "We've got a pretty good old couch in the basement. I've been wanting to get rid of it. We was going to get the city to haul it to the dump when they have the spring cleanup next month. It's still good if you want it. You'd have to carry it up the stairs. My husband, Ralph, and I can't handle it."

We checked out the couch. It was a lot better than nothing. We carried it upstairs and told Gladys we'd come back to pick it up after we unloaded.

"Thanks for your trust, Gladys," I said. "We like the dog a lot. We will take good care of her."

I opened the door of the pickup and pointed. Sally looked at Gladys, who nodded and said, "OK." One leap and the dog was sitting proudly behind the steering wheel.

Sally (we had to have a new name) sat on the seat of the pickup with her head out the window crowding Michelle over to my side. I didn't mind. At least the big dog wasn't coming between us.

Michelle rubbed Sally's chest. "Look here, Paul. The only white mark on her body is this blaze on her chest. It looks like a letter or something."

I glanced at the white mark. "It looks like a bird to me. We could call her 'Bird.' What other dog has her name printed on her chest?"

Michelle wasn't too happy about the name, Bird. "Sounds kind of dumb to me, Paul. But, maybe you're right. It would be unique. It's a whole lot better than Sally."

"What do you think girl. Do you like the name, Bird?" The dog wagged her tail. Anything was fine with her. She was easy to get along with.

"I'm not sure I like Bird either. Try something different," I suggested.

Michelle paused, then said, "Mandi."

She gazed into the dog's big brown eyes. Then she declared, "Mandi. . . . Yup. I think we should call her Mandi."

I agreed. "Looks like Mandi's her name."

"I like it," I said. "Mandi sounds great to me."

"Mandi!" she said to the dog.

The Lab lifted the front corners of her floppy ears, tilted her head, and almost nodded at Michelle. Our dog's name was Mandi.

Back at the campground, we packed up our tent. Mandi roamed through the brush around our campsite, sniffing every tuft of grass, checking for interesting smells.

On the way to our new apartment, we stopped again at one of the garage sales. I bought a pair of jeans, a pair of dress slacks, two t-shirts, and a sweat shirt. We found a couple of books for a quarter each and a woven rug for 50 cents. Mandi would need a place to sleep. I hoped she wasn't a *sleep-in-the-bed* dog.

We drove back to Second Street and our new home. The pickup was full of stuff. We were happy to unload our new furniture into our apartment and pack our clothes into our chest of drawers. The drawers were sticky and it needed a coat of varnish. We didn't care. We were happy to have things of our own. It had been a long time for both of us.

We made one more trip to pick up Gladys' couch. The subject of our sticky drawers came up in our conversation.

"I've used a bar of soap," suggested Gladys. "Rubbing it on the bottom of the drawer where it rides on the slide will sometimes keep it from sticking and let it slide in and out more easily."

Back at the apartment we tried the soap trick. It worked great.

I flopped on the couch and Mandi jumped up beside me. Now we had all of the comforts of home. Really, it probably wasn't as nice as prison, but it was ours and Michelle and I were both thrilled at having our own place.

Now we needed to find some jobs.

XXVII

A Waitress and a House Husband

After a week in Del Rio, Michelle and I were learning to like the life style we were living. Almost every day we were getting up early, going somewhere new, and doing something special. On many days, we explored birding spots near Del Rio that the forest ranger had told us about. On the weekend, we cruised garage sales, buying things we needed for our apartment. In the evenings we did a lot of reading and were often in bed by the time the sun went down -- although I think we got out of town and saw more sunsets than either of us had ever seen before.

One day, I looked at the map and found a state park that was unique and close. I spread the map on our kitchen table.

"Look at this, Michelle. Out west of town. Here. There's place called Seminole Canyon State Park. It's a state historical park that has pictographs that are 4000 years old."

"Pictographs?"

"I always confused pictographs and petroglyphs. I learned many things in the prison library. Pictographs. You paint pictures. So pictographs are painted on rock walls. Petroglyphs. Petroglyphs are scratched into rock walls. The brochure says that Seminole Canyon has pictographs. The pictographs are marvelous primitive pictures that are painted on the rock by ancient Indians more than 5000 years ago. For three bucks a piece we can tour the place. Sounds kind of interesting to me. What do you think?"

"Sure, I've never seen a pictograph," responded Michelle. "Is that like the graffiti that kids paint on the bridge over Saylorville Lake?"

"I guess those would be pictographs. Sure."

Michelle paused, then changed the subject. "Paul, I'm getting worried about cash. You and I are spending a lot of money and we have nothing coming in. Do you suppose I should look for a job? There is a truck stop on the way out of town. I could stop and ask if they need help."

"I feel guilty about us using your money, Michelle. If you get a job, I'll feel even more guilty."

"Paul, I want to be working. I used to *love* working as a waitress. I really want to go back to work. You can't get a job until we work out what to do about legal papers. You and I shouldn't be arguing about this. I know you'd be working if you could."

It was quiet for a minute. I hung my head and closed my eyes.

Finally, I looked at Michelle and said, "Ok. You go to work. I'll keep trying to figure out what I can do for our finances."

"Thanks for understanding, Paul." She threw her arms around me. Her hug, with her long slender body wrapped into mine felt perfect.

"What are you going to tell a restaurant manager?" I asked.

"I'll just tell him or her that I haven't worked for a while. I've been home keeping house and when I did work, it was at some restaurants back in Arkansas and I can't remember their names."

"That might work. Give it a try if you want to, Michelle. We'd be better off having some money coming in. We sure aren't balancing our budget right now. We don't need a lot, but we won't have a chance if we don't bring in some wages."

I dropped Michelle off at the truck stop and waited while she looked for the manager. I decided that I needed to take some steps that would let me go after a job. I had the never-ending task of figuring a way to acquire a social security number and a driver's license.

I was reading a Louis L'Amore novel, nodding my head, half asleep, when Michelle slid into the pickup beside me.

"Do you want to know what I found out in the restaurant?"

I said, "You bet. Did you get a job?"

"She wants me to go to work right now, Paul. They just had a waitress quit this morning and they've been going crazy all day. I can work as many hours as I want. I'll get $3 an hour plus tips. She said 'With your figure, sugar, you'll do real well on tips from the truckers.'"

"Wait a minute. I don't know if I like that too much, Michelle. I'm a pretty jealous guy. All those men ogling you might be more than I can handle."

Michelle took my hands and looked into my eyes with her big brown eyes. "Paul, I love you for ever and ever. I will never look at another man the way I am looking at you right now. You are the only one for me forever. You can trust me, Paul."

"I know I can trust you, Michelle, but you are so darned beautiful, I know every man who sees you is going to be drooling over you. It's ok. I'll be alright."

"Anyway, if it's cool with you, I'm going to work. Another gal is coming in at 5:00 tonight. I can work eight hours today. You take care of Mandi and work at organizing our apartment. Maybe you can find out about getting a Texas driver's license. What do you think?"

"Go to work, woman. Let's get some fresh money in our checking account."

I kissed her. "Don't forget me. Remember, I love you like a bald eagle loves fresh fish."

Seminole Canyon would wait until Michelle and I could go together. I could find enough to do to keep busy and productive.

I stopped at the hardware store and bought some wood glue and some waterproof varnish. At home, I started in on the table. It didn't take long to put it back together. It wasn't quite *like new,* but it was pretty good. I should have stripped and refinished the wood, but it wasn't like we needed fancy. We needed a table. I used a piece of rope to tie around it and a stick to twist the rope really tight so it held together while the glue set. Some glue in the joints on the chairs made them feel a lot more solid. I felt good to be making us something useful out of junky stuff.

Then Mandi began getting anxious to be outside. She started prancing the floor. I decided it was time to let the glue set. I drove east on Highway 90 to Calderon Elementary School and found a nature trail behind it. The flyer the park ranger gave us said there were upland desert birds there. I hung my binoculars around my neck and slid the bird book in my jacket pocket.

I let the dog run around the trail for a while, then called her back and attached her leash. She wasn't too happy about that. I worked at making her heel. She caught on fast. Mandi wanted to please me. She did whatever she could to make me happy. Our Lab was a grand dog.

Birding is a tough activity to do with a dog, but we walked the nature trail and I spotted some neat birds. The first was a kind of a dove. We have Morning Doves back in Iowa and in Southern Illinois, but this one had scalloped feathers on its breast. They were layered like shingles. When it flew, its wings had reddish or chestnut colored patches on the ends. Its tail was long and spread out to show white edges. The bird book said those were all characteristics of an Inca Dove. I was fond of this dove. It was as if the bird had come from ancient Mexican tombs.

Mandi got pretty excited about the other bird I was able to identify. The bird leaped across the trail and ducked through a grassy opening in the cactus and mesquite like a streaker at a football game. It was there. Then it was gone. Later, we saw another that stayed awhile. It was feeding in the grass. I recognized it right away, thanks to my misspent childhood, watching Saturday morning cartoons on TV. This was my first real-life look at a Roadrunner. The bird must have been almost two feet long and was streaked brown and white. Through the binoculars, I got a look at the red spot behind the eye. While I was watching, the Roadrunner caught a little snake. It looked so proud running around with that snake in its mouth. I was thrilled to have seen the bird. It was easy to understand why the Roadrunner became such a hit on kid's TV programs. Bird watching was fun.

I sat on a bench, watching a brilliant sunset spread over the desert. The vibrant reds and deep grays were stunning. I was in awe. I wished Michelle was there with me. A strange feeling of loneliness came over me. Then a different feeling replaced the loneliness. Celebration. I realized that every time I saw a sunset or a sunrise, I commemorated my freedom. Mandi roamed for a few more minutes, then the dog and I turned back to pick up Michelle.

Her smile was as lovely as the sunset. I could tell right away, she was excited about her day.

"I earned seventy bucks in tips plus my wages," she announced. "I had such a good time. The people I work with are wonderful. The manager is wonderful and the customers were wonderful and generous with their tips and with positive comments about my service. This was a fun day."

She pulled me over and kissed me. "And I'm happy to see you and Mandi."

I didn't even mention being lonely. Why poke a pin in her balloon? Mandi was happy to see her too. Her tail rotated in a circle and her body shook. The woman and the dog were in love with each other.

"What did you two do today?" Michelle asked. "Anything fun?"

"I organized some things in our apartment. You'll have to see for yourself. Mandi and I went for a walk in a nature preserve over by the high school. She ran around the desert for a while. I worked on teaching her to heel and we did some bird watching. The Roadrunner was the neatest thing. Remember the Roadrunner cartoons on TV? Mandi and I saw two of them in real life. They are crazy looking birds. It was great! I'll take you back there soon, so you can see for yourself. We also saw a little Inca Dove. It was like our Mourning Doves except smaller with a kind of scaly breast and chestnut bars on its wing. It was pretty neat too."

"I'm jealous. That sounds exciting."

"Then we saw the most beautiful sunset I have ever seen. The red was the brightest red in the world. You could probably see it from the truck stop. Isn't it great to be free people? I am so happy we have each other to share joys with."

Two escaped prisoners and suspected murderers walked up the steps to their apartment hand in hand, celebrating life and liberty -- for one more day.

XXVIII

Birdwatchers from Des Moines

The next morning we were up early. I dropped Michelle off at the truck stop at daybreak and drove toward Mexico on Highway 239. I followed the signs to Laguna de Plata, a 70 acre plot of grassland and marsh that was set aside by the city of Del Rio just for birds. I parked, using the binoculars, I checked open spots in the marsh for waterfowl. Mandi sat beside me. She was pretty patient for a big pup.

Birds were wading on the sandy beach below me. I focused the binoculars and saw a sandpiper type of bird with a white breast and black spots. I looked in the book and found a dozen shorebirds that looked similar to the bird in my binoculars. I guessed that it was a Greater Yellowlegs. This little bird didn't have a spotted breast and looked to be half the size of the Greater Yellowlegs' 14 inches. I was pondering all of this when a car drove up. An old couple got out and walked over to me. They didn't look like any cops I'd ever seen.

"What are you finding?" the gray-haired man asked.

"I thought it might be a flock of sandpipers or Greater Yellowlegs. Then I figured they are too small to be Greater Yellowlegs and there seem to be a hundred different kinds of sandpipers. Want to take a look?"

I handed my binoculars toward the kindly looking gentleman. He politely refused and said, "Mine are focused for my eyes and I'm partial to them."

Then to his wife in the car, "Hand me my binoculars, hon. There's some shorebirds down below. I want to check them out."

In an instant the guy had me pegged as an amateur birder. And I had him pegged as an expert. Before he looked through the binoculars, he said, "If you look in your book, you'll find maps beside the birds, they'll tell you if the bird is found in this part of the country. That will narrow your list of sandpipers down to just two or three."

He focused his binoculars on the birds. "See the spots on the belly. It seems to me that makes them Spotted Sandpipers. Come and take a look, Harriet. See what you think these birds are."

Harriet also had a pair of binoculars hanging around her neck. She quickly focused and said, "You're sure right, Charles. Those are Spotted Sandpipers alright. See the yellow legs and the yellow bill with the darker tip, like it was dirtied in the mud."

I took another look at the Spotted Sandpiper and then reached out my hand to Charles and then to Harriet. She had a firm handshake. "Thanks for the information, Charles. My name is Paul. I'm pretty much a beginner about this birding business, as you probably guessed. I'm thrilled at seeing these birds and learning their names and watching them do interesting things. Yesterday, I saw a Roadrunner catch a snake. It darted around back and forth through an open area and looked proud as a Peacock. Things like that are thrilling to me."

Charles said, "A Roadrunner with a snake would be thrilling to anyone, Paul. Seeing interaction between wild critters really makes birding a special hobby. Everybody has to start someplace. Once you begin to see things like your Roadrunner and the snake, the bait's been cast and you are hooked.

"Where are you from, Paul? I see the Arkansas license plate on your Chevy. We have retired friends around Bella Vista. They built a house down there a lot cheaper than we can build the same house in Iowa."

I glanced at the license on their Saturn. The Iowa plate said *Polk County* in smaller letters. A chill shot up my spine. *Had these people seen my picture in the Des Moines Register?*

"We lived in Eureka Springs for a while," I answered. "That's not far away from Bella Vista. All of those retired Iowans come over to the tourist shops in Eureka Springs. I'm really from southern Illinois mostly. You're from Polk County. Is that Des Moines?"

"Sure is," Charles answered. "We bought us a trailer house in Del Rio. We come down here to keep warm during the winter. It snowed about eight inches in Des Moines yesterday, and tomorrow is the first day of spring. It won't last long, but we're sure glad to be down south this time of year."

I asked, "What's happening in Des Moines these days?"

Charles said, "Not much. We get on the internet and read the news articles from the Des Moines Register pretty regularly. I guess the big news last week was the escape of a bunch of prisoners from a halfway house. The paper said they killed a guard and stole his car. Then they went to his house and stole his pickup and a bunch of other stuff."

"Didn't make any sense to me though," Harriet commented.

"What do you mean?" I asked.

Charles went on, "Those four convicts were about to be released from prison on parole. Why would they escape from prison and kill a guard? Also the paper said the guard had a real high alcohol content in his blood. They found him with a cut on his head and a bruise on his jaw. Now it seems to me that the guard either just slipped and fell and had the bad luck to hit his head or he got in a fight with the prisoners and got hit and then fell and hit his head."

"I see what you mean," I said. "If prisoners had a fight with a drunken guard and he bumped his head and died, I think they'd run."

"What was those prisoners suppose to do," Charles continued, "wait around and get caught with a dead guard? They'd figured nobody would believe their story so they'd just skedaddle out of there as fast as they could go."

"What do you think, Paul?"

"It sounds like a strange deal to me, Charles. I don't know much about it, but I think I agree with you. Why would people try to escape from prison when they were about to be paroled? It doesn't make sense to me either."

Harriet had been using her binoculars. "Excuse me, Charles. Is that a Turkey Vulture up there?"

Charles and I moved our binoculars toward the soaring bird.

"I don't think so," he declared. "There are both Turkey Vultures and Black Vultures in this part of the country. That's a Black Vulture. See, the line of its wings goes straight across. A Turkey Vulture's wings form kind of like a shallow V. Also, the tips of the wings is lighter. In a Turkey Vulture, the wings look two-toned from below and the tail is long, extending well beyond the feet. The Black Vulture's feet extend to the tip of the tail and sometimes even beyond."

"Charles, you are a walking bird book," I commented. "How do you know all of this?"

He said, "I've been studying birds for a few years, Paul."

His curiosity was getting the best of him. "You on vacation, Paul? What brings you down to this west Texas country?"

I paused just a few seconds. "Well, actually, I'm kind of between jobs. I've spent about four years in India working for a guy who was trying to start an independent electric company. He kind of ran out of money and here I am in Texas trying to start over again."

Harriet thought just a moment. Then she said, "Are you a handy guy, Paul. I mean can you fix stuff? Us old folks in the trailer park are always needing things repaired. These people aren't rich, but if there was someone around who knew how to fix things, I think he could make a pretty good living. Right now we have a toilet that overflows about once a week. We'd like to put in a new toilet, but the plumber wants a hundred dollars even to come out and look at it. Meantime, we scrub the bathroom floor every week."

"I can put in a new toilet, Harriet. Would you like me to have a look at it?"

She said, "I'd just like you to buy a new one at the lumber yard and install it for a reasonable price. Let's see what kind of work you do."

I agreed to go with them to choose a new toilet and then install it. Luckily the job went like clockwork and by mid-afternoon, Harriet and Charles had a working toilet with a new wax ring in their bathroom. In my pocket I had their check for $100 made out to Paul Swartz. I also had three small jobs to do for their friends the next day. Luckily, I had a set of The Ranger's open-end wrenches and a putty knife in my truck so I didn't have to buy any new tools.

On the way home, I stopped at the pay phone in front of the library and called the Val Verde County Court House. I told the lady I was born in Little Rock, Arkansas and wanted to know how to acquire a new birth certificate since I lost mine and wanted to get a passport.

"Y'all need to keep your birth certificate, passport, driver's license, and social security card in a really safe place, honey. Treat them like they was gold. Now you just get on the Arkansas Department of Health Website. Look for the Vital Records Section. You'll probably have to fill out a form and send them a copy of your photo ID.

"And if I don't have a computer?"

"Then you go down to the Val Verde County Library over on Spring Street. They have computers there for you to use."

You're very helpful, honey, I thought. *Now if you could tell me how to get a photo ID, I could be a new person.*

"Thank you, ma'am."

"You sure are welcome. Good luck now."

I'd need a lot of luck. A new birth certificate with a new name might be tough to come by.

I needed a driver's license to get a birth certificate and I needed a birth certificate to get a driver's license. Establishing a new identity was not as easy as it was purported to be.

I found the phone number for Social Security and called them. I asked who could access my social security records. The guy said the only people who could obtain the records were me or some other social agency like someone from the food stamp division.

If I could locate a copy of my birth certificate and my passport, maybe it would make sense to use my real name and get my driver's license in the name of Paul Hartman. I'd feel safer with a new identity, but my old one might just work. Michelle and I would have to sit down and talk about it. Soon.

When Mandi and I stopped at the truck stop to pick up Michelle, she asked me to come in and eat with her. One of the perks of her job was some free meals. I guess they figured the waitress would know more about the menu if she had eaten some of the features. She introduced me to her boss and our waitress as her husband, "Paul." We had prime rib and a steak. It was pretty good food for a truck stop.

I gave Michelle my $100 check and told her my story of the Iowa birdwatchers and the new toilet. She had earned wages and tips of more than $100 again. Our bank account was growing. We had already made almost enough to pay for another month's rent. I shared my excitement about other fix up jobs at the mobile home park.

When Michelle left the cafe, she was carrying a sack of beef bones. Mandi would eat well tonight.

At home I turned on the radio to an FM station that was playing some classical music and sat on the couch with my book. Michelle sat beside me as I told her about my conversation about the Iowa prison escape with the birdwatchers from Iowa.

She reached for the check.

"Paul, for a smart guy, you were awful dumb today."

"What do you mean?"

"Look at this check."

"Yes?"

"Paul Swartz? The escaped prisoners included Paul Hartman and Mary Swartz. You told those Des Moines people to write the check to Paul Swartz. Do you think that was dumb?"

"Stupid as hell. Should we leave town?"

"I don't know. I was just beginning to like this town, Paul. I like living in a house. I like having a dog. I don't want to start running again already."

Tears were streaming down her face. I put my arms around her and held her close.

Ten minutes later, she dried her tears and looked up at me. "What are we going to do, Paul?"

"It seems we have two choices. We can pack up and hit the road."

"I don't want to leave."

"Or," I continued, "we can pray that Harriet and Charles don't know the names of the escaped prisoners and don't put Paul Hartman and Mary Swartz together and get Paul Swartz."

"They've got the name in their check book."

"Risk it or run?"

"Let's go out to the lake and watch the sunset."

Michelle was tired. It had been a long day for her. Now, thanks to me, we had a major problem to resolve.

We drove out to the lake and watched the day end. The sky was not as dramatic as the day before, but it was still pretty and the reflection in Lake Amistad doubled our pleasure. Mandi was the happiest member of our family as she crunched down on the steak bones.

XXIX

A New Life in Waterloo

The baby-blue Ford Escort matched the color of the morning sky. The car was parked in front of room number 8 at the Super 8 Motel in Waterloo, Illinois. Rod and Bob felt safer knowing The Ranger's 4Runner was in a shed in rural Missouri, probably chopped into many pieces by now. Danny had assured them that any part with a VIN number was melted down to a glob of steel.

Rod liked the way the little Ford ran. It was a tight fit for Bob's hefty frame. Both men were pleased to know that the Escort wouldn't be a magnet for the cops.

Bob was making a list of things they needed to do. First was finding a cheap place to live. $62 a day for a cheap motel room would eat up what little money they had very quickly.

"Maybe we should just drive around town and look for a for a house or an apartment for rent," Rod suggested. "These big apartment complexes require long term contracts. They want to know where we work, our salaries, our legal history, all that shit. If we find a private individual, they might not have this formal application. We need a place where we can just pay a month's rent plus a deposit and move in. We really can't sign a six month contract. We ain't going to be here that long."

They drove the streets of Waterloo. At the Waterloo Chamber of Commerce office they got a map and some suggestions from the clerk about an old neighborhood that might have some cheap apartments. After another hour of driving the streets of the Western Illinois town, they had a list of three apartments and a small house for rent. They had the phone numbers and addresses listed on a note pad from Super 8.

"I think we may be premature, man," said Bob. "We have no ID. Not even a name to give a landlord. I think about all we can do now is find us a cheaper motel."

Rod argued, "Getting two grand for the 4Runner is gonna help us to keep us going a while longer."

"I think we should find another flea bag motel," suggested Bob. "If we find something for $25, we'd save $36 a night."

"I don't know, man. I like these beds. Maybe we should sleep on it tonight."

XXX

Real Identities

Bob and Rod awoke early, even though the two queen-sized beds at the Super 8 were the most comfortable beds either of them had slept on for years. They planned to drive to St. Louis and call George to check on their new identification papers.

After passing the Gateway Arch, they drove the streets looking for a pay phone.

"There ain't so many pay phones as there used to be when we went to the can," observed Rod.

They found a pay phone in the lobby of a library. Rod dialed George's phone number.

"This is George."

"Hi, George. This is Rodney Barnes. You were doing some work for me and my buddy. I wondered how you was coming."

"You guys are all set," responded George. "I got lucky; found just what you wanted. Come by this morning if you like. I'll set you up."

Rod was excited. "That's good news, dude. We can be there in a half an hour or so if that's alright with you."

"Terrific."

The line went dead.

"Let's go get our new ID's," smiled Rod. "We can start a new life. This is kinda like a religious experience, like being born again. I hope I get a cool name."

At 8:57 the two escaped convicts were standing on George's front porch. Rod pushed the doorbell. A minute later he rang again.

"I heard the bell," said Bob.

At 9:00 George opened the door and looked up and down the street. Then he greeted Rod and Bob.

"Morning, guys. Come on in."

The men entered the apartment.

George motioned toward a low couch. "Sit down, gentlemen."

George sat in an office chair. Rod and Bob dropped into the couch.

George reached into a desk drawer and pulled out a big black automatic pistol.

Rod and Bob opened their eyes wide.

"Don't know you fellows too well. This is just to make sure nothing crazy happens, guys. I'll show you what I found. A guy named Joseph Jorgensen was killed in an auto accident about ten years ago, when he was twenty. Could be you, Rodney. You told me you were 30 years old, right?"

"Exactly. When was my birthday?"

"Your birth certificate says you were born on April 1. That makes you a joke, an April Fool's Day joke on your parents. By the way, your parents are both dead. Both of them had heart problems, as did Joseph Jorgensen, even at his young age. If I were you, I'd be real careful to watch my weight and avoid smoking. Keep those heart attack risks down, bro."

"Very funny."

"And, here's a birth certificate for Jonathan Wilson. The guy was forty when he died of cancer in Cleveland. He was born in Perryville, Missouri. It's just down the Mississippi River from St. Louis. His parents are still alive. They live in St. Clairsville, Ohio. If I were you, I'd stay away from eastern Ohio, Robert.

"In order to get real driver's licenses for Joseph Jorgensen and Jonathan Wilson you'll have to study the book and take the test."

"It's been a while since I took the driver's test," said Rod. "I'll have to study."

"I was sixteen when I took the test," said Bob. "That was twenty-seven years ago. Scares me just to think about it."

"I have a good business going here, guys," George explained. "If you can help keep the cops away, I can help a lot of people get going straight again. We protect each other. I know nothing about you and you know nothing about me. Make sense?"

"Gotcha," assured Rod. "Nobody will ever find out about you from us."

Rod and Bob shook hands with George. In the Ford, they shared high fives.

"Let's blow this place, dude," said Rod. "We have some celebrating to do."

XXXI

Celebration

Rod and Bob headed their Ford Escort back over the Mississippi River toward their Super 8 Motel in Waterloo. Beside them on their seats rested two clean white business envelopes. Each contained an official birth certificate with a raised stamp that came from a County Courthouse. Rod's was in the name Joseph Jorgensen. Bob's had the new name, Jonathan Wilson.

Bob slapped his envelope between his palms. His smile filled his face. He said, "This makes me feel like a bird, man, a bird in the open sky. I'm on my way to living free again, Rod."

"Joe, my name is Joe. Joseph Jorgensen. Don't ever call me Rod again. The only time I'll ever be Rod again is if some cop writes me a ticket and I ain't got a new driver's license yet. I'm Joe Jorgensen. You're Jon Wilson. Or do you like Jonathan?"

"I think I'd prefer to go with Jonathan. Jonathan Wilson is a good name. I'm Jonathan Wilson and I'm forty-two years old. I think we should celebrate," Bob suggested.

"Shall we stop at a bar and have a beer?"

"Actually, for some strange reason, I never learned to like beer that much," Bob admitted. "I'd have a glass of wine though. Why don't we drive to Waterloo first and find a bar close to our motel? Somehow, drinking and driving seems like a bad idea."

Jonathan and Joe walked to a sports bar a block from the Super 8. The Falcon was parked in the back of the motel parking lot. Both men felt as high as soaring hawks as they walked into Bo Beck's Bar and Grill. They pulled up a couple of stools and sat at the bar.

On the stool next to Joe sat a washed out blonde with a pretty face and a body that was carrying about twenty pounds more than ideal for her five foot four inch frame. Jonathan guessed that the woman was close to legal drinking age and that the bartender would card her before he served her a drink. The two escaped cons couldn't help but notice the young woman's low neckline.

Her blouse left more of her copious breasts outside than inside. As she sat on the stool beside him, Joe quickly moved his attention away from their celebration. He had never seen breasts so luscious. He felt like a largemouth bass who had sighted a big juicy night crawler. Joe Jorgensen was ready for a woman and he thought this woman might be looking for a man.

Jonathan leaned in front of his friend.

"Excuse me, ma'am. We were thinking about the burgers here. Are they any good?"

"They are just great, honey. That's one reason I drove over the River. The burgers and the music are fantastic. You'll love them."

"Can I buy you a drink and a burger?" Joe offered. "We are celebrating and you sure are welcome to join us."

"Sounds real great," Angie responded. "I'll have a Bud Light, please."

She looked at Joe and glanced at Jonathan. "What are you boys celebrating?"

Joe was stumped. *I can't tell Angie that we are celebrating the acquiring of new birth certificates. What else might we be celebrating? A job? A divorce?*

Jonathan interrupted the pause, saving his friend. "We're celebrating Joe's getting fired from the worst job in the world by the worst boss anyone ever had. All the bitch could do was criticize. She was the sorriest excuse for a boss that anyone in the world ever had. The woman was just plain shitty. Sorry about the language, ma'am."

"I've heard those words before, Jonathan. If you'll stop calling me ma'am, I'll forgive you some bad words. My friends call me Angie. My teachers called me Angela. You're Joe." She leaned toward Joe to offer her hand. He nearly fell off the bar stool as her cleavage opened for his eyes to see.

Joe finally managed to reach out his hand and shake the smooth four fingers that Angie offered to him.

She shook his hand and pulled Joe toward her out-thrusting lips, kissing him as if they were old friends. Their lips stayed together just a little longer and a lot firmer than lips should that were meeting for the first time. Then she reached around Joe, took Jonathan's hand, pressing her breasts into Joe's side.

"Hi. I'm Angie."

"Pleased to meet you, Angie. I'm Jonathan. We're glad to have you join our little celebration."

Angie pulled Jonathan to her and gave him an imperceptibly shorter kiss on the lips. Jonathan felt just a little of her tongue caress his lips before she pulled away.

Joe was hoping that the kiss between his friend and this woman with her breasts in his side would last as long as possible. As she moved back to sit up straight he wanted to order drinks, but somehow his tongue would not say the words.

Again Jonathan saved him. He told the bartender, "I'll have a glass of red wine and a glass of water. My friends want Bud Lights. And I hear you have great burgers. How about three of those?"

"Fries?"

Jonathan glanced at his friends and saw two gentle nods. "Sure."

The bartender took a long look at Angie and said, "Sorry, young lady, I have to ask you for your ID."

He took a glance at her driver's license and returned it with a little smile. "You didn't make it by much, did you."

Joe thought, *She's young, but at least she's of age. That's good.*

An hour later three burgers and Jonathan's wine were gone, four beers had disappeared; the trio had shifted to a round table, and

Jonathan was tired. He excused himself. "Pardon me, but I need to go to bed. I have some things to accomplish tomorrow. You two enjoy yourselves."

"Goodnight, Jonathan," said Angie. "It was so nice meeting you." She got up off her chair, wrapping herself around Jonathan with a full body hug, following it with a kiss whose quality rivaled anything he remembered from his ex-wife.

I wonder if it's time to fight my friend to see who takes this woman home.

"Goodnight, Angie. Goodnight, Joe. You and Angie have a good time. I'll see you later, Joe."

"Sleep well, man. Later."

Sometime in the middle of the night, Jonathan heard the door open and quiet steps move to the other bed. A bit of muffled laughter told him that he and Joe were not alone. Rolling over to face the wall, he tried to go back to sleep.

In the morning Jonathan awoke early. He glanced at the other bed. He wasn't surprised that it was full. After climbing into yesterday's clothes, Jonathan went for a walk around the neighborhood before coming back to the motel for the free buffet breakfast.

He sat at a table, watching a bit of the morning news, wondering, *Where am I going from here?*

XXXII

Separate Ways

Jonathan Wilson was troubled. He poured a cup of coffee, added skim milk, and popped a wrapped pastry with a strawberry center into the microwave for fifteen seconds. He carried it all outside the motel, sitting in a chair near the pool, pondering his situation.

I like Rod's company. Or I guess I mean, I like Joe Jorgensen's company. I like the support I feel from the young guy. Adding another person to our lives makes our capture more likely. Angie could be just a harmless diversion. Or she could send Joe and me back to prison.

A feeling of danger settled around Jonathan like an early fog on a cool August morning. His partner's enjoyment of alcohol worried Jonathan. *Joe was obviously a little drunk when he came in last night.*

Jonathan sat with his hands linked on his stomach and his feet propped on a chair pondering his situation. *What if the police had arrested Joe for being drunk and disorderly? It happened all the time. Back at the University of Iowa, football players were arrested regularly for being drunk and acting stupid. Iowa's multi-million dollar football coach couldn't seem to find tough, mean football players who would stay home and twiddle their thumbs at night. The kids liked to party in Iowa City bars. By 2 AM, they often had too much to drink, then they did dumb things that got the attention of the police. Joe Jorgensen and I will soon be back in prison if Joe can't control the alcohol.*

Jonathan understood his friend's attraction to Angie. She was a delightful woman who was looking for a man when she found him and Joe. He thought, *I was as much attracted to Angie as Joe was. If my friend had not gotten together with her, she and I might be upstairs in our motel room right now.*

The sun peeking over the top of the motel roof splashed bright light into Jonathan's face. It seemed to fill him with a new thought like the gathering spring storm.

The time to split with your partner might be near, Mr. Jonathan Wilson. You're nearly broke. You have about eight hundred dollars left from the cash you took from The Ranger. It won't last long if you take off on your own. Joe has the two thousand that Danny gave us for the 4Runner. That brings me up to eighteen hundred. The Ford Focus is half mine. It might be worth twenty-five hundred. If I took off on my own with the car, I'd owe Joe half of that. That leaves me less than six hundred dollars. If he kept the car and paid me, I'd have about three thousand. I'd have to buy a cheap car and live on what I had left until I found a job.

Jonathan sat by the motel pool, drinking coffee, reading USA Today, but mostly pondering his new situation. He was realizing that Jonathan Wilson and Joe Jorgensen's days together were numbered. It was time to think hard about where he wanted to go. It was time to think about setting up a new life on his own.

$1800 won't last long. I couldn't rent an apartment or even a room from an old lady and still have money to eat. Someday, I'll need clothes that aren't leftovers from The Ranger. If I travel, I'll need gas money. I can't hit the road hitching rides. The first cop who saw me would be checking me out. Maybe I'm stuck with Joe until I get a job and begin to accumulate some money in the bank. Or, ... I wonder if Joe would come up with the cash for another car? That would be a step toward giving both of us independence. It's time to split.

Jonathan strolled back to the buffet to refill his cup. Angie was gathering coffee, a banana, and a bowl of Rice Krispies. She caught his eye, walked toward him, set her food on a table, giving Jonathan a hug and a kiss.

"Good morning, Jonathan. It's nice to see you. I'm late for work. It was a nice night with you and Joe. You are real swell guys."

"Where do you work, Angie?"

"I'm a helper in Loving Your Kid Day Care. I love working with kids. I'm taking night classes at the community college. Some day I want to be a teacher."

"Good for you," complimented Jonathan. "Teachers are the most important people in our country."

"I ain't got time to talk," Angie said as she finished her cereal. "I need to be at work in fifteen minutes and it's a ten minute drive if the traffic is good. Thanks again for a nice evening. I'd like to spend some more time with you and get to know you better, Jonathan."

"Maybe it'll happen. You have a great day, Angie. Enjoy those kids."

"Bye for now."

XXXIII

Hit the Road Jon

Jonathan filled his cup with coffee, poured another for his friend, and carried them to their room. As he was reaching for the handle, the door opened.

"Room Service," he muttered.

Joe, took a cup of coffee and smiled. "Hey, thanks, man. Maybe you should stay around. You might be worth your keep."

Jonathan had a morning paper tucked under his arm. He handed it to Joe and whispered, "I didn't find any stories about escaped prisoners from Iowa. I guess that means they haven't caught us yet and maybe they haven't caught Paul and Mary either."

"At least not yesterday."

Joe glanced at the headlines and then turned to the sports page. "The Cardinals are in first place. A half a game ahead of the Cubs. Maybe we should slip over to Busch Stadium for a game."

"Can we afford it? How are our finances? I sat at the pool for an hour trying to figure out how we're doing. I'm worried about how long our money will last."

Joe looked him in the eyes and pointed his right index finger in Jonathan's face. He said, "Look, man. I ain't gonna live my life worried about money. I have a birth certificate and a woman. This is a big town. I'll find me a job. Things are going good."

"Do you want to go down and eat some breakfast?" Jonathan asked. "It's not great, but it's food and it's a meal we don't have to buy. Then we can talk about where we go from here. Now that we have names maybe we ought to go rent that house we looked at."

"We need to talk about that, man. I got an offer this morning. This Angie chick likes the sex with me. She asked me this morning if I want to move in with her. She says she has a house in St. Louis and would like a roommate."

"What did you tell her?"

"I told her I'd talk to my friend, Bob, about it."

"You called me Bob? That was pretty stupid, man."

"It slipped, but it's alright."

"What did she say to that?"

"I was still a little drunk. I couldn't even remember your new name. She said she thought your name was Jonathan. I told her that your middle name was Robert. So I sometimes called you Bob, especially when I want to piss you off. She told me you was a real nice guy, that I should be nice to you."

Jonathan snapped, "We cannot have you getting drunk, man. You do or say something dumb, then both of us go back to the slammer."

"It ain't going to happen again, dude. It's been a long time since I laid one on. I won't do it again. I promise."

"I was thinking about this situation this morning," Jonathan explained. "Can we afford to buy another cheap rebuilder from your friend in St. Louis? I was thinking it might be time for me to head out on my own. If this thing with Angie works for you, then if I had a car, I could head west and look for a job. I always wanted to see the mountains and living in a place like Colorado or New Mexico might be alright. What do you think? I appreciate you getting us new identities and all. Now I wonder if we might both be safer on our own."

For a couple of minutes, the room was silent. Joe stood with his hands in the front pockets of his jeans, gazing at the pattern on the carpet. Jonathan had his hands in his back pockets as he watched his friend.

Then Joe said, "I still got a bit of a hangover from last night, Jonathan. You're right about the booze. I can't afford to drink more than one beer. Let's go get some more coffee and some toast. Sit out by the pool and talk this over. I'd love to move in with Angie. She's great in bed and I like her a lot. We seemed to hit it off real good. I think I'd sure enjoy going to bed with her every night a lot more than I've enjoyed you. No offense, but you understand. Alright?"

Over coffee, the men agreed that the time to split was close. Jonathan was about to bring up the car situation when Joe said, "I think you're right, man. We need to buy another car. I don't think either of us needs anything real new. As long as a car runs good and handles alright, I can live with it for awhile. Is that ok with you?"

"I think that's exactly the way we should go," Jonathan agreed. "Let's figure out what we have to do. I don't want to stick around here forever. I'd really like to be a little farther from Des Moines; someplace where Iowa events don't make the newspapers."

Jonathan went to the front desk for a pad of paper and a pen. They started on some lists of things to do.

1. Send for Social Security cards.
2. Buy a car license.
3. Work on driver's licenses. Maybe from two different states.
4. Buy a cheap car from Danny.
5. Rent a place for Jonathan. Maybe a single room. Maybe in another state.

Jonathan said, "Maybe what we need to do is go to the library and use their computer. I earned my license in driver's ed class when I was sixteen. What kinds of identification do we need now? Is a birth certificate enough?"

"You're right man. I mean about the library. Let's go and use their computer. If we Google *driver's license in Illinois*, we should have some answers."

The warmth of spring was in the air as the two men walked to the Waterloo Public Library. The librarian was very helpful in showing them how to use the Internet.

An Illinois driver's license had four requirements:

A. Written signature on a document such as a cancelled check, Social Security card, or passport. "We need them Social Security cards," said Joe.
B. Date of birth: From a birth certificate, or a passport. "Bingo. We can do birth certificates," said Jonathan.
C. "We don't have a Bingo. We need four in a row for Bingo. We got B."
D. Social Security Number: From a Social Security card. "We have to write for Social Security cards, Joe."
E. Residency: Utility bill, lease agreement, voter registration card, vehicle registration card. "Looks like we need to have a place to live and be there long enough to get bills in the mail."

Joe said, "We only have one in four and then we will probably need to take a written and a driving test. Looks like a snap to me."

"This could take time, Joe. You'll have a place to live if you move in with Angie. I'll need to find a room, maybe in Illinois. Then I'll need to apply for a Social Security card. That should give me a lot of time to study for the written test."

"I'm thinking you're right," agreed Joe. 'It might be a good idea if we were licensed in different states. No red flags that way."

"I don't want to drive us apart, but if you're hooked up with Angie, you'd have a place to live. You can share expenses. You might even register your car with her for a while. You could receive mail there, maybe even put a phone in your name. That would give you a utility bill as a record of residence."

Joe went back for more coffee and toast. Jonathan smiled and thought, *It's time for Jonathan Wilson and Joseph Jorgensen to part company.*

XXXIV

An Old Friend

The weeks in Del Rio were pleasant times for Michelle and me. She worked as many hours as she wanted at the truck stop. Snowbirds were calling me for fix-up jobs that were keeping me in spending money. I was developing a word-of-mouth reputation as a guy who could repair broken stuff around the house. I purchased a prepaid cell phone so that old folks in the trailer court would have a number to call.

My new friends, Harriet and Charles, were computer people. Harriet had a program she used to print business cards for me. I posted a note on the bulletin board at their mobile home park telling people that I was available for small jobs. The carpentry required tools. I acquired a used circular saw at a garage sale; so dull that the only way it could cut a piece of two by four pine was by burning its way through. I bought a new saw blade and the saw cut straight and true. I also found a used sleeping bag. It was in good shape and very warm. We stopped at Big

Bubbles Coin Operated Laundry and ran the bag through their largest washing machine.

Our lives were developing some order. Early one morning we sat across from each other at our little kitchen table drinking coffee and eating toast.

"Michelle, you like your job at the truck stop and I'm enjoying doing carpentry work for these old people, but I know, both of us would be happier if I had a real job. I have an idea."

"What do you have in mind?"

"Yesterday, I spent twenty bucks for a phone card. I want to call my mother and see if she can find my birth certificate, passport, and my old driver's license and send them to me. What do you think, Michelle. Would it be worth the risk?"

Michelle thought about the idea for a moment, then said, "I'm a little worried that the FBI might put a trace on your mom's phone, Paul. They probably want us pretty bad. I'd worry about your mom sending anything to us. We might lose everything we've worked hard to get."

"I worry about the same thing," I agreed. "After I bought the card, I went to the library and started to call Mom's number in Carbondale. Before I dialed the last digit, I hung up. I was scared. I asked myself the same question. How much do they want us? How badly do they want our butts back in prison? Would they put a phone tap of some kind on my mother's phone? I'm not going to take that chance."

"Calling your mother would have been really dumb, Paul. Really dumb."

"As I was dialing, a picture of you flashed in my mind. I didn't want to do anything to threaten your freedom, Michelle."

She moved her face close to mine. "You're way too smart to even think about doing something like that, Paul."

I looked down, hiding from her eyes. "I guess I'm getting kind of desperate. I can't think of any way to come up with legal papers. Driver's license, social security card, birth certificate, passport. It seems to take two of those to get the third. Before September 11, 2001, this could have worked. Now, they're keeping the terrorists from getting false ID's and they've made it really hard for us honest American citizens."

"Who happen to be murderers and escaped prisoners."

"Ouch!"

"So what are you going to do, Paul?" Michelle asked. "She's your mom. She's probably worried. You should probably let her know you're ok."

"I killed a prison guard, Michelle. Cops don't like guys who kill one of their own. I woke up in the middle of the night with another idea. I've got an old high school buddy in Carbondale named George Dunkelberg. We fished and hunted and played basketball and football together."

"What are you getting at, Paul? What does George have to do with this?"

"George and I are best friends, Michelle. I'd do anything for George Dunkelberg and I think he'd do anything for me. I want to call him and ask him to call Mom; invite her over to his house for coffee; then I can call George back while she's there.

If they have a tap on her phone, a call from George to Mom isn't going to raise any red flags."

"You're sure you can trust George? I don't like the idea of anyone knowing where we are right now, Paul. I wouldn't even tell my Mom."

"Nobody will know where we are. I don't intend to tell him or Mom that we're in Del Rio, even though I'd trust George with my life. I guess I am willing to try using him so I can talk to Mom."

"It sounds like a plan with just a small amount of risk, Paul. Do it."

I dropped Michelle off at work at eleven. At the library, I used my phone card to dial George's number. After six rings, his answering machine answered. Leaving a message didn't seem to be a good idea.

I drove to the trailer court and built some storage shelves for an old couple. I liked building shelves. As I was finishing the second coat of paint, Mrs. Miller mentioned that she and her husband, Ken, were from Iowa. I hoped she didn't notice me swallowing hard and ending our conversation quickly.

I was glad to finish and collect a check for $190 for labor and materials. I had them make it out to Paul Swartz. Ken and Karla Miller seemed pleased with their shelves.

On the way back to the apartment, I stopped at the library and used the pay phone to try George's number again. This time he answered on the first ring.

"This is George."

I said, "Hi George. This is Paul."

George paused. "Paul? Paul Hartman? I can't believe I'm hearing your voice. Where the hell are you, buddy?"

"You don't want to know that, partner. You probably heard some things about me."

"I've read all the papers," George declared. "They say you killed a guard and escaped from a halfway house in Des Moines. I know better, Paul. That's bullshit. You wouldn't kill nobody. You want to tell me what happened?"

I paused this time. ... "Sure. One of our guards was on my case. He sent us guys to our rooms, then he tried to rape a female inmate from the other side of the house. I came up behind the guard and pulled him off. We had a scuffle. I smacked him a good lick on his jaw. When he went down, his head hit the corner of a door. We tried to revive him, but the guy was dead. He had it coming, but I guess I did kill a prison guard. Anyway, all four of us escaped. We learned later that he had drunk a half a case of beer before he came on duty. We left the empty beer cans beside his body."

"That's quite a story, Paul. You were almost ready to be released and this happened. Tough luck."

"Tough luck for four of us. We were all short-timers and now we're all running from the law. It's really hard finding a new identity so that I can work and have a life."

"What can I do to help you? You know I'll do anything I can."

"I'd like to talk to Mom and let her know I'm alright. I'm guessing they probably have her phone tapped. I had a wild idea. What if you invite Mom to your place for coffee, say ... Saturday at 10:00 a.m. I'll call your house at 10:05. Please don't say anything to her about why you're really calling. You never know who may be listening at her phone or even in her house, George. Ok? Would you feel comfortable doing that? Is there any way this could lead to you being in trouble?"

George didn't hesitate. "She'll be here. All I'm doing is having her over for coffee. Can't be in much trouble for that."

"You're a real friend, George. I'm trying to establish a new life for myself. I feel like one of those guys in a witness protection program -- except it's not the bad guys who want to find me, it's the cops. You be careful, buddy. I don't want to create any problems for you."

"Don't worry about me, Paul. I don't think what I'm doing can cause me any trouble. You take care of yourself."

"I will. Not a word about this to anybody, George -- not even your wife."

"That'll be tough, but I'll do it."

"Thanks, George. Good to hear your voice."

"Goodbye, my friend."

I hung up the phone and wiped the dampness from my eyes.

A few minutes later, when I picked up Michelle, she took a look at me and asked, "What's wrong? Are you crying?"

"I just talked to George. How can a guy be blessed with such a friend? He's going to call Mom and have her over to his place for coffee tomorrow at ten in the morning. I'll call him shortly after ten and talk to her. He said, 'I know you didn't kill anybody, Paul.' I told him what really happened. I knew he would trust me. I'm so lucky to have a friend like George."

Michelle said, "Well, you're a pretty good guy, Paul. George and I both figured that out. And I haven't known you nearly as long as he has.

XXXV

A Talk With Mom

My birding friends, Harriet and Charles, suggested we might enjoy visiting Big Bend National Park in West Texas.

"It is a wonderful place with tons of great birding," reflected Harriet. "You'll love it."

Michelle and I had been heading for Big Bend, when we found Del Rio. After Harriet's suggestion, we decided to spend a long week-end camping at Big Bend. I also wanted to call George and talk to Mom from someplace besides our new home town, in case there was some way someone could trace our call.

Since Big Bend didn't allow dogs on the trails, Tillie Teasdale offered to take care of Mandi while we were gone. Tillie and Mandi hit it off well. We dropped Mandi off downstairs at Tillie's apartment late Friday afternoon after Michelle finished work. We would miss the big dog, but we would have a lot more freedom in Big Bend without her.

It was late, about eleven thirty, when Michelle drove into Marathon, Texas. A brown sign told us to turn south toward Big Bend National Park.

"We should probably fill up our gas tank," I suggested. "It'll to be cheaper here than in the park."

She pulled into the gasoline station, put her head on the steering wheel, and fell asleep. I filled the tank, checked the oil, and washed the windows. Michelle stole a cat-nap. When I climbed back into the passenger seat, I kissed Michelle on the neck.

"You drive," she mumbled. "I'm asleep."

"No," I argued. "You drive. In two minutes, we'll find a spot to pull over and rest. In the morning, we'll have breakfast, then drive into the park. It's sixty-seven miles."

She frowned and started the car. "Where to?"

"Take a left. Go a block and turn right."

Soon after we turned south toward the park, I saw a gravel lane leading to a two track dirt road paralleling the railroad tracks.

"Turn left; down that gravel lane."

After driving down the dirt road for a couple hundred yards, Michelle found a wide spot and parked.

"Let's go to bed."

I led her around to the rear, boosting her up into the back of the pickup. I slid the side windows open, glanced at my watch, and turned out the dome light. It s 12:05. Three minutes later, both of us were sound asleep.

At about two fifteen, we awoke to bright light flooding our rolling bedroom. An instant later, our world was filled with the piercing sound of a locomotive whistle. My panicky thought was, *Oh my god, we've parked on the railroad tracks.* I surrounded Michelle with my body, to ease the blow of the train. For long minutes the S10 rocked like a canoe in a busy harbor. Then the train was passed. *We were alive.*

"My God, Paul!" Michelle whispered in my ear as the sound of the train whistle faded into the distance, "That may have been the scariest thing that's ever happened to me!"

"Shall we move?" I asked.

"I'm really too tired, Paul. Next train, we'll know that we won't die. I need sleep."

She grabbed the back of my neck and kissed me. "Good night, Paul."

"Sleep well, Michelle."

About four, another train roared past. That one was almost an adventure. No fear. I still rolled over and held her close. It felt fine.

We awoke to bright sunlight filling our sleeping space. We crawled to the ground at about eight. Michelle turned the little pickup around on the narrow dirt road and drove back toward the highway. We were surprised to see a police car with flashing blue lights meeting us head-on. A short, wiry cop in a huge western hat exited the cruiser. His big revolver was pointed at Michelle.

"Show me your hands," he commanded. "Keep 'em high where I can see them." Then, "Both of you. Hands on the dash."

He walked around to my side of the truck and trained his big gun on me. "Let me see your license, mister. Slow and easy."

"Sorry, sir," I lied. "Somebody stole my wallet last week and I haven't been home to replace it. Canceled all my credit cards, but can't arrange for a new license until we're back to Arkansas. Sorry."

He moved around the front to Michelle. Now the pistol was pointed at her.

"Ma'am. Your license, please."

"May I reach into my purse?"

"Do you have a weapon in there?"

"No. We don't do guns."

"Alright. Reach into your purse. Go real slow."

"Yes, sir."

She found her wallet and handed the license to the officer.

He took the license. "Iowa, huh?"

"Yes, sir."

"What are you doing here?"

"We're on our way to Big Bend National Park for a vacation."

"I mean what the hell are you doing on this road?"

"We drove into town late last night. We were exhausted so we stopped to rest. Thought we'd have breakfast and then head into the park."

"Why are *you* driving? Why not him?" He pointed the gun at me.

Michelle stared daggers at the little cop with the big gun. "When he lost his wallet we figured it would be better if I was driving. Besides, a woman can drive as well as a man."

"Some of them." He looked at me. "And what's your name?"

"Don. Don Swartz."

"And you're from Iowa?"

"Originally. We just moved to Arkansas."

He walked behind the truck and looked at the license plate.

"Alright. Makes sense to me. Seems like you ought to get yourself Arkansas driver's licenses. You probably have some kind of a time limit. Better get 'er done."

He focused his beady little eyes at me and tried to be polite. "I hope you recover your stuff, Mr. Swartz. You're a lucky man. Your wife is a damned sexy woman. Enjoy the park."

He backed his patrol car onto the highway and turned towards town as I shook my head.

Michelle glared after the police car. I could see fire in her eyes. It was all she could do to remain calm and avoid exploding. I could tell Michelle's mind was working on the stop from Barney Fife.

She shook her head, "It's a good thing that cop is dumb as a post."

"Why?"

"He could have dug up some big problems in our story. I have an Iowa driver's license. He should have run a check on my license and then looked for Don Swartz in Iowa. If he'd checked, we'd be on our way to his jail. If this guy had a brain, he'd be smelling fish."

"We need to leave this town. And we need to work on a better story," I suggested. "If he starts asking questions, we'll be pretty well trapped in Big Bend."

"Shit! I want to leave this town, Paul. Now."

"Give me a second." I looked a the map.

"Drive up to the corner and take a left. We'll go to Alpine first then go south to Big Bend."

Instead of driving south toward Big Bend, we headed west toward Alpine. On the edge of town, flashing blue lights filled Michelle's mirrors. The whoop of a siren penetrated our ears. Michelle pulled off the highway.

"Did the bastard hear me?"

The little cop walked up to the driver's door. This time his big pistol was in his holster. Michelle lowered her window.

"I thought you was goin' to Big Bend. You make a wrong turn?"

"No," I answered. "We changed our mind. Decided to go to Guadaloupe National Park instead."

"Strange. How'd you happen to change your mind?"

"We didn't like the way the day was beginning. Thought we'd drive for a while."

"Strange."

"Officer, neither of us liked the way you talked to my wife. She's upset and wanting to get away from you and this town. Now we'd like to be on our way, if it's alright with you."

"Sorry about that Mr. Swartz. I apologize to you Mrs. Swartz. Of course. You just head on your way."

We drove west at two miles per hour under the speed limit. Forty minutes later, we arrived at Alpine, Texas where we found a bakery cafe. We enjoyed their pecan sticky rolls and coffee. Then we searched out a pay phone and waited until ten o'clock to call Mom. Once we made our phone call we'd take the back road into Big Bend National Park. If the cop put two and two together, then perhaps four might be the wrong answer.

At 10:02 I used my phone card to dial George's number. He answered on the first ring.

"Hello."

"Hi, George."

"Good to hear your voice, buddy. There is someone here who would love to talk with you. I didn't tell her why I invited her over. She's been down in the dumps lately. I had to push pretty hard to convince her to leave her house. Maybe you can cheer her up."

I heard him say, "Someone on the phone wants to talk to you, Mrs. Hartman."

"Hello?" Mom said questioningly.

"Hi, Mom."

The line was silent.

"Paul?"

"This is Paul, Mom."

"Paul? My son? Is this really you?"

"This is me, Mom. I'm so happy to hear your voice. It's been a long time, Mom."

"It is you! Are you alright? Are you in jail? Are you coming to see me? Where are you?"

"I'm alright, Mom. I can't tell you where I am. It's better if you don't know. I'm sure you heard about our problem in the halfway house. Our drunken guard was trying to rape a woman inmate. I pulled him off. We had a fight. I hit him a solid blow and he fell and hit his head on the edge of the door. The guy fell awfully hard. It must have injured his brain. We had no choice but to run, Mom. It would have meant life in prison for all of us if we had stayed."

"I'm glad you ran, Paul."

"Anyway, I'm so sorry it happened. He was a bad man, but he didn't deserve to die and I feel terrible that I'm responsible for his death. Anyway, I wanted to let you know I'm ok. I'm in another part of the country and things are going pretty well. I was hoping you would do something for me."

Mom said, "Paul, I didn't like you being in prison and I don't like you being on the run for a murder, but you know I'll do anything for you. I know you are a good boy, Paul. What is it you want me to do?"

"I'm trying to start a new life, Mom. From what I've read, I don't think the authorities can access my social security records. I need some identification papers to apply for a new driver's license. I think you have a copy of my birth certificate and my passport. Could you put them in a big envelope and take it to George. I'll give him an address and he can send the envelope to a town we'll go through soon. I'd rather it came from George than from you. If you don't know the address then you won't be forced to tell someone like the FBI.

"Mom. I'm going to build a new life. I'm going to build an honest life. I served my time in the fraud case. I shouldn't have stolen that money. It was wrong and I'm sorry. But this murder of a guard thing was not my fault, Mom. I had to protect that young woman from the guard. She didn't deserve to be raped, and his death was an unfortunate accident. I'm going to start a new life, Mom. I need some identification papers to do it."

"They will be in the mail this afternoon, Paul. I believe you and I trust you. I know you'll do what's right. I love you so much. You will never know how much this mother loves her son. You will never know how good it is to hear your voice."

"Thanks, Mom. It lifts my spirits to hear your voice too. I'll call again, but not regularly. There's a good chance that the police will be watching your home and even listening to your phone calls. You must not say anything to anyone about talking to me or sending me anything. If they knew anything about this, you and I and George would all be in big trouble. Don't talk about this even to your best friend. If you and George talk, talk in person and not at your house. I don't trust the FBI or any government official. I love you, Mom. I have to go."

"Just remember, no matter what happens, Paul, I'll always love you."

She gave the phone back to George.

I told him, "George, Mom is going to give you some of my official papers. I need you to send them to Michelle Swartz at General Delivery, Fort Stockton, Texas 79735. Obviously, no one else in the world should know you did this and especially where you sent them. I'll drive to Fort Stockton next week sometime and pick them up. Thanks, George."

"Just a second, Paul. I'll send your stuff, but if you use any of that shit, the Fed's will have you back in prison in a week. Think twice before you use any of it."

I mulled that over for a minute.

"You're probably right, George. I'll be really careful and really desperate before I use any of my old ID papers. Thanks. It was great talking to you, my friend."

"You too." And he was gone.

I hung up the phone and turned to Michelle with tears streaming down my face. She put her arms around me and held me close. Then, we were walking back to the S-10. Michelle turned south down a narrow country road toward the back entrance to Big Bend National Park, while I stared out into the rugged wasteland.

XXXVI

Chisos Basin

Seventy-five miles south of Alpine, Texas, we stopped at the Maverick Junction Entrance Station and paid $20 for a week's park pass. The ranger gave us a brochure and told us to keep our receipt to show we had paid. Thirty miles later we parked at Panther Junction Visitor Center. We bought a book about cactus and walked a short nature trail near the visitor center. Most of the cactus in the book were growing right there, along the trail.

"Look, Paul. Look at the blooms. What are they?"

I saw a little sign that identified the lovely cactus as a prickly pear, "Gorgeous, aren't they?"

Michelle was thrilled. "The outside ring of petals is such a beautiful rich yellow."

"Look at the middle," I observed. "It gradually changes to a watery orange and the center is a bright red circle filled with brilliant yellow stamens."

"I've never seen such a fabulous flower," exuded Michelle.

I shared information from our book. "This says the prickly pear has needles about an inch long. These fronds look like them, but the needles are very short."

Michelle said, "Look at the sign. They're beaver tail cactus. Pretty cool."

Michelle murmured, "Strange. These lovely flowers seem to have a calming affect on me. I can almost forget about that cop."

"I just hope he doesn't start adding up his facts," I declared. "I'd hate to see your Iowa driver's license with the name Swartz on it lead that creep to escaped Iowa prisoners. It's a good thing we told him we were headed west. We're kind of trapped down here if they come looking for us."

Big Bend was in the northern third of the Chihuahuan Desert. The southern two-thirds were in Mexico. The ranger explained that the reason it was so dry was that there are mountains on three sides blocking the rains. The rain that does fall comes mostly in the summer, much of it from the Gulf of Mexico during the hurricane season.

We wanted to come back and see this park after a rain. The ranger told us that rain makes the desert alive with blooming cactus.

We asked about camping. The ranger said her favorite spot to camp was Chisos Basin unless we had a huge RV. From the visitor center, the road took us west and then south into the Chisos Mountains. On the way up through Green Gulch, we passed through grasslands with tall century plants and sotol. As we wound our way up into the mountains, evergreen sumac appeared. At 4,500 feet, we were seeing both evergreen and deciduous trees. High above us were masses of trees: junipers, small oaks, and pinyon pines. Michelle and I loved the pinyon pines. They grew in low rounded mounds. Their needles were short and in bundles of two. We learned that mature pinyon pines can be from 75 to 200 years old. Being around a tree that was very, very old gave me a feeling of awe.

The road turned down into Chisos Basin, giving us a marvelous view of the basin. The campground was in a giant bowl surrounded by mountains. Our car radio quit working. There was no way a signal could reach down into the little basin. As we wound into the bowl-shaped valley surrounded by rugged mountains the view was amazing.

Our tent went up with almost no conversation. Then, I leaned back against the picnic table and Michelle reclined against me. We absorbed the feel of these mountains and the beauty of this spot. Neither of us had ever seen mountains before. These weren't the Rockies, but they made an impression deep inside us. Our whole beings were celebrating our freedom and memorializing this place. We honored whoever had set aside this unique spot for us to experience.

As the sun sank low in the western sky, I broke up hamburger in a big skillet, added chopped onion. When the hamburger was brown, I dumped it in our aluminum kettle, adding carrots, celery, a can of green beans, a can of mushrooms, a can of tomato soup, and water.

Darkness descended as we finished our stew. Dessert was a slice of fresh wheat bread with butter and strawberry jam.

"I don't think I have ever felt this contented and peaceful, Paul," Michelle said. "We are so lucky to be here. Our whole life is awaiting us. I just know it's going to be good."

"Life can be nothing but good, with you and me together, Michelle."

For an hour we watched, with wonder, as the stars appeared in the moonless sky. We slept well that night in the peaceful basin surrounded with mountains, guarding us from the world.

XXXVII

Emory Peak

Stars were still shining when Michelle and I filled a plastic gallon milk jug and a couple of plastic bottles with water. We stowed the water in a day pack. Michelle made ham and cheese sandwiches with lettuce and a bit of mustard. I packed apples and bags of gorp that Michelle had concocted of peanuts, raisins, and M&M's.

Before morning light, we were dressed and breakfasting. We left camp in the dark, trudging down the road, searching for the trail to Emory Peak, a 7600 foot Texas mountain. Michelle soon focused a small flashlight on the trail sign.

Once we found the path, I said, "Turn off the light, Michelle."

"What do you mean, *Turn off the light?*" she asked. "We don't want to fall and break a leg, Paul."

"When I was a boy, my daddy taught me that when you walk outside at night you're better off if you walk without a light," I explained. "Your eyes adjust to the dark and you will really see much better than you can with a flashlight. Will you try it?"

"It doesn't make too much sense to me, Paul, but I'll try anything you say. You are usually right."

"Thanks for the confidence, sweetheart."

Soon our eyes adjusted to the dark. As our pupils opened, the starlight enabled us to travel nearly as fast as we would have in daylight. In the east, we noticed the sky turning a lighter shade of blue.

It was about four miles to Emory Peak. Michelle had read about the trail on the library computer in Del Rio and she had picked up a trail map at the park visitor center. We had talked to a ranger, who had hiked the trail many times. She had cautioned us to take plenty of water and to make an early start. Our goal was to be close to the peak by sunrise. We weren't disappointed. Michelle led the way, setting a good pace. We were near the summit when the sun burst into the clear Texas sky like a hot, red ball of fire. A low mist hung white over the valleys.

I took Michelle's hand and whispered, "Look at the fog rising up to the sky under the power of that warm sun."

"I never saw anything like this in Des Moines," she declared.

I reached in my pack for the book I had bought in the visitor center about the Chihuahuan Desert.

"Listen to this, Michelle. By a naturalist named Edward Abbey. He says, 'Half the pleasure of a visit to Big Bend National Park, as in certain other affairs, lies in the advance upon the object of our desire. ... Like a castled fortification of Wagnerian gods, the Chisos Mountains stand alone in the morning haze, isolated and formidable, unconnected with other mountains, remote from any major range ... an emerald isle in a red sea.' Does this look like, an emerald isle in a red sea, Michelle?"

"It really does, Paul. That guy, Abbey, describes this scene as if he's standing here beside us."

"The panoramic view is stunning," I remarked. "The ranger told me we'd have an expansive desert vista on all sides and she was right. Look to the south; on the horizon. She said those Mexican mountains are even higher than this one."

"Those peaks look really rugged," Michelle observed. "Maybe we should keep hiking. We could cross the Rio Grande and spend our lives safe in Mexico."

"We can't."

"Why not?"

"Mandi is in Del Rio. You don't want to leave her behind. Besides, we don't have enough water. We'd run out in a day."

"Can't leave without our dog."

"Mexico offers more problems than it solves," I declared. "It's nearly impossible to get back into the United States without a passport these days."

"Yours is coming in the mail. I could apply for one."

"Not a terrible idea. Might work if we decide to leave town someday."

The temperature was rising fast. An hour before, not far above freezing; now it was too warm for coats. We slipped out of our jackets, stowing them in our packs.

"Are you hungry, Paul? I think I need something to eat," Michelle said.

"What's your pleasure, pretty lady?"

"An apple might hit the spot. And you don't need to call me *lady*. I am a woman, not a girl or a lady, please."

"That you are!"

I quartered an apple and we each enjoyed a couple of sweet slices. Michelle held my sticky hand and licked apple juice off my fingers. Looking west, the high desert was bathed in golden light from the bright morning sun. The amazing view held us, as we experienced the brilliant colors coating mountain peaks, forest, and finally the lower desert country. In the southwest, in a valley between two ridges of the Chisos Mountains, I noticed a lonely ranch house.

Pointing at the far away buildings, I said, "That might be the Homer Wilson Ranch. Can you imagine what it must have been like settling in this country and trying to make a living here a hundred and fifty years ago?"

"I don't think I'd have been a ranch wife for anything," Michelle agreed. "Life must have been brutal. I read that most of the graves in the cemeteries around here are filled with people under 40 years old. And how many of the babies died young? How many of the kids were raised by just one parent? Remember the panel in the visitor center about all the families where the mother died and the father farmed out the children to childless families. Do you suppose those kids ever saw their real father and their brothers and sisters again?"

"What happened to your father?" I asked Michelle. "I sense that you and your mother are really close, but you never mention your dad."

She hesitated, then explained, "Mom and Dad split up when I was a little girl. My sister, Michelle, was born and Dad lost his job. Mom received more help from welfare if he was gone. I don't think they really loved each other anyway. They argued all the time. Finally, he just moved out. For a while he would come and see us occasionally. Then, when I was four, he left town for good. I never saw him again. I hardly remember him. I don't know where he is or even if he is still alive."

"It must have been tough."

"Eventually, we all moved in with Grandma. She loved us a lot, but it was never quite like having our own home. I always envied those kids who lived with their mother and father, especially mothers and fathers who loved each other."

She looked up at me. "How about you, Paul? What was your childhood like?"

I didn't hesitate. "I had a great childhood. Mom and Dad loved me and they loved each other. I never doubted I was an important part of their lives.

"Dad was a scoutmaster and I grew up as a Boy Scout. I learned to tie knots and build campfires and sleep in tents. My parents trusted me. I never had much supervision. As a ten year old, I rode my bicycle all around Carbondale."

"Grandpa Grant must have had some money. He had a cabin and a speedboat on a lake near there. Mom and I spent a lot of time at Grandpa's cabin. Sometimes, Dad came out after work. I learned to swim and fish and row the boat. They had an old, flat-bottomed, row boat. I rowed it all over the lake. Became a pretty good fisherman. I could almost always catch a mess of bream and I caught plenty of big bass."

Michelle asked, "What are bream? I don't think we have them up north."

"Actually, you do. Bream is a southern word for sunfish. Bream are eatin' fish. Do you like to fish, Michelle?"

"I never fished very much. They had some kind of a kid's fishing derby once. I borrowed a fish pole and used a bobber and a worm and caught one of those horny fish, the ones with thorns."

"Bullheads?"

"That's it. I caught a bullhead. He swallowed the hook and nobody could get it out. We finally just cut the line and let it go. That was enough fishing for me."

"I caught a few bullheads," I said. "If nothing else was biting I could always hook on a big juicy night-crawler and catch bullheads on the bottom. When we fished for them we used a long-shanked hook so they couldn't swallow it. Then, we just grabbed the hook with a pair of pliers and worked it out."

"It sounded like your mom is alone," Michelle suggested. "What happened to your dad?"

"When I was about twenty, Dad developed cancer in his lungs. They cut him open and took out a bunch of the cancer, but it still spread around his body. He died a few months later. I miss him a lot. It seems there is always something I need to talk to him about and I just can't do it because he's gone.

"Occasionally, I do something special and I think, Dad would be proud of me. He'd like to hear all about you and I sitting on this mountain. But, I can't tell him. It's like a big empty spot in my life. Then there are times when I do something lousy and I'm glad he's gone. I hope he doesn't know that I was sent to prison. I'm not real proud of that."

"I wonder if our moms feel that way about us now," Michelle pondered. "We are gone. They'd probably like to talk to us about something, but we are gone, like empty holes in their lives."

"You're probably right," I agreed. "We should find a way to communicate with our mothers. It felt so good for me to talk to Mom last week. Maybe I can write to her and send the letter to George. He could deliver it surreptitiously."

"Do it, Paul. Do it."

"How about you? Do you have a friend you could trust?"

"Friends? Yes. To trust with my freedom? I doubt it. My aunt Carol, Mom's sister comes to mind. I think I could trust her. She wasn't proud of me being sent to prison and I know she didn't like my dancing career, but she loves my mom a lot. Carol might deliver a letter and keep the place we sent it from a secret. I'm not sure I'd trust her to know our address. We could call her and talk to her. I think she'd be honest with me."

"Why don't we just send a letter to George with letters inside to our mothers?" I suggested. "That sounds safe. The law is probably watching our moms pretty closely."

"Sounds simple to me," agreed Michelle.

"We probably shouldn't send postcards from Big Bend."

"Funny man!"

After spending an hour sitting on the rock, sipping water, reminiscing about our childhoods, and watching the sun paint the mountains in red light and dark shadow, we hiked on to the summit. We surveyed the panorama from the peak. Then we followed the South Rim Trail to the east and then back north to Chisos Basin. By the time we returned to our campsite our knees were wobbly, our water was gone, and we were ready for a nap.

We were also hungry as a couple of hunting dogs. I boiled some water for macaroni and cheese and stirred up a package of instant Jell-O pudding. Michelle sliced apples and oranges. Soon we sat down to a mid-afternoon feast.

We crawled into our tent for a nap. Opening the vents sent a nice breeze moving through the tent. It was late afternoon when we emerged for a quick stroll around the campground to loosen up our stiff muscles.

The road to the Basin Campground has tight curves that prevent big motor homes and travel trailers from driving into it. That made this a special place for tent campers and people with small trailers, mini-motor homes, and pickup campers. I knew we were poor and we were camped among the poor and middle class folks of our society, but this was just where we wanted to be. The families in this campground were pleasant people, delightful people, people who cared about others since they knew what a struggle it is to make it in life. I thought of President

Teddy Roosevelt, who set aside Yellowstone as our first national park. I thought about how farsighted he was to realize that wild places are national treasures that must be protected from commercial mining and forest industries, so that normal people could have somewhere to go to rejuvenate themselves.

We were feeling safe, but our lives were about to take a turn.

XXXVIII

Snitch

Our fear of discovery seemed far away as Michelle and I planned relaxed days in this remote, West Texas national park. We celebrated Monday with a drive to Santa Elena Canyon where the Rio Grande River enters the park. We planned a hike up a trail into that awesome crevasse.

Santa Elena Canyon was impressive. The Rio Grande had cut its way through two thousand feet of rock and flowed peacefully along the bottom of the precipitous gorge. Where the trail ended, we sat on a rock near a sand beach, spending a peaceful hour allowing the magnificence of the yellow sandstone walls to penetrate our souls.

By noon, our morning pancakes had worn off. We dug out food from the cooler in our truck. We ate cheese and crackers, shared an orange, and drank cool lemonade.

Gazing across the Rio Grande, we were still tempted to slip across the river into Mexico. The prospects of avoiding the law in the United States were staring in our faces. If we crossed the river, we'd have the same problem as a terrorist going north. Traveling down into Mexico away from the border would be difficult. We'd need transportation and our Spanish was terrible. Michelle would lack a passport and I would have no personal identification at all. Nothing special was required to cross the border into Mexico. We knew, thanks to our country's new security plans after 9/11, coming back into the United States would require passports. Michelle and I decided that it would be easier and safer to stay in the USA until I had some kind of official papers.

On our way north, back toward our campground, we turned off at Tuff Canyon. We enjoyed the rugged view from an overlook and then hiked up the canyon for a mile.

Back on the road, skipping the turnoff to Chisos Basin, we drove for another two hours to Rio Grande Village Campground in the southeast corner of the park. Our bodies were hot and sweaty. It had been too long since we had stood under a shower. Shower-meters demanded quarters so we traded a couple of dollars in the general store for change. Soon, the grime was washed away. We walked into the warmth of the late-afternoon, wearing clean clothes on fresh bodies, feeling like civilized people again.

During the late afternoon, we found a rugged trail taking us along the Rio Grande to Boquillas Canyon where the river left the park. This was another place where water had cut through a thousand feet of rock. We wondered how such a little river had managed to erode such a huge channel in that mass of rock.

Finally, reluctantly, we turned the S-10 toward our campground. An hour later the sun was setting at the end of another day of precarious freedom.

"Michelle, I feel like we are workers who are relaxing, away from a stressful job."

"I know that feeling," she agreed. "It seems that for a few days we are relatively safe from discovery in a wild, lonely place."

The low sun turned the canyon behind us from its mid-day yellow to shades of red. The sky produced a unique show of baby blues and grays with sections of pink and peach.

As we neared the visitor center, a brownish-grayish animal flashing across the road in front of us, gave us another treat. Slowing the pickup, I turned, spotlighting the coyote in our headlights. The scrawny hunter stopped, turning to stare toward the light reflecting whitish-green in his wild eyes. He looked at us and seemed to say, "Welcome to my country, folks." Then the wild creature loped easily on its way, searching for other creatures of the night.

"Oh, Paul. That was a coyote wasn't it? I've never seen a coyote."

"Too small for a wolf. Too wild for a dog. Wrong color for a fox. I do believe we just saw a coyote."

"It was so free, Paul. There's something symbolic about that."

At the gas station at Panther Junction, I filled our gas tank while Michelle checked our cell phone.

"We have a signal on our phone, Paul."

We didn't get a lot of calls, so the phone was turned off most of the time. Besides, Big Bend National Park is so remote that there is no cell phone signal in most of the park.

Michelle checked the screen.

"It says we missed a call. I think it was from Tillie. Three seventeen. She called this afternoon."

"Did she leave a message."

Michelle finally figured out how to check for messages.

Hi, Paul and Michelle. This is Tillie. I probably should mind my own business, but you know me. This afternoon two guys in suits showed up at your door. They didn't look like them Mormon missionaries. They almost looked like cops -- like them FBI types on TV. Anyway, they, or some guys who look a lot like them have been parked up the street most of the afternoon. I thought you might like to know. Sorry, if I'm butting into something I shouldn't, but this situation is strange. Take care. Call me if I can help.

The look on Michelle's face changed. It was full of fear.

"What's going on?"

Michelle said, "Listen to this message."

She handed me the phone. I listened.

When I looked up, she said, "What's going on? How could they have found us? What'll we do?"

I said, "I don't have a clue, Michelle. I can't see any way the FBI could have found out we were in Del Rio."

Suddenly, the phone rang.

I answered. "Hello."

"Paul? This is Charles Black."

"Hi, Charles. What's happening?"

"Well, I don't know if I should get involved in this situation or not, but I like you a lot and Harriet thinks you should know what happened."

"Ok."

"Well, you remember last week you built some new shelves in Ken Miller's trailer?"

"Yes."

"Well, Ken is from Des Moines. He gets the Register, so he had seen pictures of those escaped prisoners who killed the guard in that prison escape last month. He found his old newspaper and looked again. He thought you looked a lot like one of those escaped prisoners. Yesterday, he called the Des Moines Police Department and told them. Last night he told Harriet and me about it. He was proud as a peacock. We told him he was nuts. We let him know you weren't the kind of guy who would kill anyone. Even if you were one of those escaped prisoners, it looked to us as if the guard was drunk and probably fell in a stupor and hit his head. We said if you was a killer, you wouldn't be out looking for birds. You'd be robbing banks or something. Harriet told him he ought to be ashamed of himself.

"Anyway, I wouldn't be surprised if the cops showed up at your door. I hope this doesn't cause you a bunch of trouble,

Paul. Harriet and I know you are a good man. We're glad to have you for a friend."

"Thanks, Charles," I replied. "I appreciate your confidence. I'm really surprised to be accused of being a murderer. That's the first time that's ever happened. I'll know what it's about if the police knock on my door. I have to run now. Thanks again. I'll be in touch."

I shared with Michelle what she hadn't heard from the other side of the conversation with Charles.

"It seems we have FBI agents watching our apartment, Michelle."

"Or a couple of Des Moines cops."

She looked at me. Fear filled her brown eyes. The look on her face was the expression I had seen in the eyes of a doe after it had been hit by a car in an Iowa park a decade before. Then the eyes of the woman changed. An unwavering look of determination replaced the fear.

XXXIX

The FBI On Our Street

"It seems to me that the guys parked in front of our apartment really might be FBI agents or Des Moines cops," I speculated. "I'd guess that at this point they're probably not 100% sure who I am. I'm hoping they don't even know that Mary Swartz and I are together. If not, they'll probably figure it out soon. Will they connect me with *Michelle* Swartz? I think these guys are very close to catching us, my dear Mary. We should pack up and hit the road for other places. What do you think?"

"We have nothing in that apartment I can't live without, Paul," offered Michelle. "Except that I love that dog dearly. She'll retrieve anything we throw. She'd give her life for us, Paul. Is there any way we could retrieve her before we clear out of Del Rio? Remember when you told me how traveling with a dog makes us look less suspicious?"

"Going back to Del Rio after a dog might not be very smart."

Michelle argued, "I have three or four hundred dollars due from pay and tips at the truck stop and we have about fifteen hundred in the bank. At this minute, we probably agree that that bank account was a terrible idea. We could use a couple thousand dollars. What do you think, Paul? Should we risk going back to Del Rio or should we be smart and drive to Mexico or California or Montana right now, while we still have a chance?"

"It's a four hour drive back to Del Rio," I suggested. "If we head north or west from here we'll gain a full day's head start."

For five minutes nobody talked. The only sounds were the life on the desert coming alive with the night. Then, "We might pull it off, Michelle. We know the Des Moines cops got a call from Ken Miller. We know he told them that he thought he saw a guy who resembled the picture of one of the escaped prisoners. I don't think they can be sure yet that it's me. If they had my body it would be easy for them. Run my prints and they have me. As long as we can avoid the FBI agents we're still on our tour of the USA."

My mind took me another way. "How does this sound? We leave our camp set up here. You stay with our camping gear. I'll drive to Del Rio. I'll withdraw our money from the bank, pick up your check from the truck stop, sneak into our apartment for Mandi, meet you back here tomorrow afternoon."

"Or," Michelle suggested, "**I** drive back, retrieve all the stuff, while you wait here? Who are they looking for? You and a long-haired blond."

"I can't let you take that chance, Michelle. If they get me, you can make it on your own, with your sister, Michelle's, ID.

Your license and Social Security card are keeping us viable. It makes no sense to send you back. Without you, I won't last a month."

Silence.

"Ok," declared Michelle. "We'll both go. Let's get packed," She pointed toward the road to our campground.

Silence.

"Alright," I agreed. " Let's retrieve our money and our dog. We'll drive back to Del Rio, get your check at the truck stop, close most of your bank account, call Tillie, and have her meet us somewhere with Mandi? Then we'll head west and north and lose ourselves in the American West. Let's go back to camp and pack up. I'm not going to sleep tonight. We'd just as well be on the road."

"I'm ready, Paul."

We drove back to the campground, packed our tent and sleeping bags, and drove into the night toward Del Rio. It was about two in the morning when we pulled into a campsite at Amistad National Recreation Area, crawled into the back of the pickup, and slept in our clothes until dawn.

I drove into town and circled the truck stop. I parked a half block away and we surveyed the cars. They were all pickups, semis, or cars with Texas license plates. We walked around the block and saw nothing that seemed out of place. Cautiously, we entered the cafe and headed for a corner booth. Michelle's boss was at the register. We stopped to talk.

Michelle greeted her with a tight smile, "Good morning, Marsha. How ya'll doing today?"

"Doing fine so far, Michelle. How about you? Did you have a nice holiday? What'd you think of Big Bend?"

Michelle's smile got a bit bigger. "We just loved it. The park's so big and so wild. We saw a coyote, a million kinds of cactus, lots of new birds, and those canyons are something else."

"I knew you'd like it. We go up there every chance we get. Missed you at work."

"I didn't miss being here. I'd really like to be independently wealthy, so I could just travel all of the time. In fact that's one reason I'm back today. Paul and I are getting antsy. We decided we're going to explore some more of Texas. Paul wants to go down towards the Gulf, see if we can find some special birds in those National Wildlife Refuges down that way. You ever been to Santa Anna National Wildlife Refuge or Corpus Christi?"

Marsha said, "It's real nice around Corpus, but I don't like all the people. Y'all will like camping at Padre Island, at least if it's sunny. The wind off the Gulf can be real cold."

Michelle continued to share our fake plans. "We want to visit San Antonio and the River Walk too. We've heard that's real nice. And then the Texas Hill Country west of Austin is supposed to be pretty. Have you ever seen those fields of blue-bonnets blooming in the spring?"

"I have. They are one of the most magnificent sights a body can imagine. Your timing should be great. That part of Texas is plum beautiful in the spring, Michelle."

Marsha stepped out from behind the counter. Michelle's boss encircled her waitress in a huge hug. "I'm real sorry to see you go, Michelle. You know we love you a lot."

"And I love you too, Marsha. I'll keep in touch when we get someplace permanent."

"Y'all want breakfast?"

"We came to say goodbye, eat a great breakfast, and get my pay. Would that be a problem this morning?"

"No problem at all, Michelle. Y'all sit down and have breakfast and I'll write you a check. We'll miss you. Come back and see us -- anytime. We'll always have a job for you, sweetheart."

Michelle said, "Oh, Marsha, would it be possible to get cash for that check. With us leaving town and all, the banks are sometimes hesitant about cashing checks and closing accounts."

Marsha said, "I gotta write you a check, honey, but I think we got enough in the till to cash it for you. We don't usually cash second hand checks, but I reckon this one ought to be good. Ha. Ha."

We ate ham and eggs and cheesy grits. Marsha gave Michelle a check for $463, which she cashed. Then we stopped at the bank and withdrew all but about $87 of the money in the account. That amounted to close to $1800. Living cheaply and working hard for more than a month had allowed us to save money in the time we had spent in Del Rio.

Now we needed to find a way to slip past the FBI guys and grab the dog. We were hoping to be clever enough to also collect the tools I had left in Tillie's garage.

Our first thought had been to have Tillie take Mandi for a walk. If the FBI man didn't follow her we could meet them somewhere and pick up the dog and say goodbye.

"Maybe she can leave her in the garage," said Michelle.

I dialed Tillie's number.

"Hello. This is Tillie."

"Hi, Tillie. This is Paul. Are they still there?"

"They are patient men, Paul. They just sit in their car and sip their coffee."

"Tillie, I'd like to come after Mandi and maybe pick up some of my tools. We don't want the hassle of dealing with the watchers. Could you put Mandi in the garage? I don't want you to be making trouble for yourself. I appreciate your confidence in us. You're a great friend, dTillie. Michelle and I are leaving town. We may go down to Corpus Christi and see some of the Texas coast. Someday, we'll be in touch again. Our rent is paid up for another two weeks. Sorry about leaving the mess in the apartment. Michelle and I love you a lot, Tillie. Just leave the dog in the garage and go back in the house or leave. We do not want you to be in trouble for caring about us."

"I'd love to give you hugs, Paul, but I'll do like you say. I think I can sneak Mandi out the back door and put her in the garage. Use the side door of the garage. The guys won't see you from where they're parked. Y'all take care, hear? I'm going to miss you two a ton and your dog even more."

"We'll be back some day, Tillie. Count on it."

XL

Slipping Away from Del Rio

Michelle dropped me off a couple of blocks from the house.

"If I'm not back in fifteen minutes, get the hell out of town. Don't stop until you are far away. Start a new life for yourself, Michelle. I mean it. There is no sense in both of us going down here. You don't want to spend the rest of your life in prison. Promise me you'll leave in fifteen minutes if I'm not back."

Michelle hesitated. Then said, "I promise. Fifteen minutes."

She had her hand behind her back. My guess was that her fingers were crossed.

I walked up the alley to the garage. Mandi was overjoyed to see me. I muscled her close to me to keep her from barking. She was wiggling in every joint a dog can move. When she settled down, I picked up my tools. Tillie had left $400 for the return of our deposit in my tool box. We'd get even with her later. In five minutes I was back at the pickup. Ten minutes later we were on our way out of town.

Michelle drove west to Comstock, picking up State Highway 163 north to Interstate Highway 10. In four hours, Michelle was collecting my mail in the Fort Stockton Post Office. Now I had my old birth certificate and passport. I had little hope that they would be safe to use to get me a real driver's license and a real job. If I used them, I'd have to pray that the police couldn't trace my social security records. My choices were to use my old papers, try for some brand-new forged documents, or to go on risking losing freedom every day at a minor traffic stop. We were sad to leave Tillie, Marsha, Charles, and Harriet. In our short stay in Del Rio, we had met more than our share of really wonderful people.

Michelle grabbed my arm, put her head on my shoulder, and murmured softly, "I always feel sad when I leave a place where I had a good time."

I reflected, "And I feel sad when I leave friends behind who we will probably never see again. Aren't you glad we were able to rescue Mandi from the FBI? I hear they don't treat dogs that well."

"I have a feeling we're on our way to something better, Paul. This is a big country. We'll find a place where we can actually start a new life. I just feel the truth of it."

Farm and Ranch Road 1053 headed northeast out of Fort Stockton. I liked the back roads. We didn't have to hurry, but we wanted miles between us and the FBI agents in Del Rio. I worried about when they would become impatient with us not returning. I worried about our finger prints all over the place. The Feds would soon know that Mary Swartz and Paul Hartman had been in Del Rio, Texas.

"I think we screwed up," I observed. " When the FBI guys become tired of waiting for us to return, they'll request a search warrant. When they go through our apartment they'll find our fingerprints. That will put them very close behind us. We should have wiped down the apartment."

"Think about it, Paul. We couldn't have done that. We needed to get out of Del Rio fast. Staying around one minute longer would have been pretty stupid. In fact it was probably pretty stupid to go back and get this fool dog."

Mandi was sitting on the floor between my feet. Her head was in my lap. Her big brown eyes slipped over to stare at Michelle who frowned and then broke into laughter.

"Sorry, Mandi," she apologized reaching out to rub the big black head. "I didn't mean it. You know I love you the most."

Mandi's tail beat a tune on the floor.

Then Michelle glanced at me. "We were really lucky, Paul. I'm just now beginning to relax. We'll figure out something when we arrive at where we're going."

"Where **are** we going, Michelle? Any ideas?"

"Do you mean tonight or next week?" she asked.

"Both, I guess. I suppose we should have a plan. I hadn't thought much beyond picking up my papers at Fort Stockton. It's been a long day and last night was kind of short. Is there a place to camp or a motel or do you want to set up our tent in a hollow somewhere off this ranch road?"

"Find something. I'm ready to stop."

I opened up the Texas map and the Texas Travel Book. We weren't far from a state park with a camp ground.

"This could be what we want, Michelle. I'm reading about the little town of Monahans up here on I-20. Just west of it is a state park called Monahans Sandhills State Park. The guide says they have camping and 4000 acres of *wind sculptured sand dunes.* They also have *one of the largest oak forests in the nation, stretching out over 40,000 acres of arid land. The forest is not apparent because mature trees (Harvard oaks) are seldom over three feet high, yet they send down roots as far as 90 feet to maintain miniature surface growth.* If we spent a couple of days relaxing there then the cops wouldn't catch us driving down any Texas highways. Our trail might become pretty cold."

Michelle offered, "Especially if I register as Michelle Swartz."

"Michelle, you are a darned smart woman. I don't know how I kept out of trouble without you."

"You didn't."

Our ranch road had an interchange with Interstate 20. We turned back to the southwest for ten miles and found Monahans. The dunes were impressive; the wind had sculpted gentle drifts of light, tan-colored sand high in the desert.

We had an early dinner of chicken noodle soup and peanut butter and jelly sandwiches. Michelle and I felt safe as we settled into our tent before sundown.

I was nearing a fitful state of sleep when I heard a soft, "Paul?"

I whispered back, "Yes."

"I think we did something dumb."

"Again?"

"Yes," she said. "When the Des Moines guy, Ken Miller, thought you might be one of the escaped prisoner, the name *Paul* gave them a link to Paul Hartman. If he was paying attention, the name Paul gave him a clue. I think you need to change your name."

"Does this mean I need to go to court?"

"Which court has jurisdiction?" she laughed. "Do you agree?"

"It's so obvious. I have to have a different first name."

"Think about it. Let's decide on a new name for you by the time we wake up?"

"I've got it."

"Already? That was fast. What name do you want? I'll see if I approve."

"Dean. Dean Swartz."

"Dean? Dean. Dean Swartz? I think I like it. Where did you get Dean?"

"My pledge father in my college fraternity was Dean Schwarz. Since I'm hanging around with Mary/Michelle Swartz, it won't take much to steal Dean's name. Dean Swartz will be harder for the cops or for anybody from Iowa to nail down."

Michelle rolled over on top of me. "Can I be the first to make love with Dean Swartz?"

I pulled her close to me. Michelle had excellent ideas.

While we were driving away from Del Rio and the mystery cops, our friend and landlady had decided that she had watched enough cop and lawyer shows on TV to know a little something about law enforcement. Tillie took a pail of water and a bottle of spray cleaner and gave our old apartment a thorough cleaning. She washed down the walls, the cupboards, the sink and counter tops, the bathroom, and the few pieces of furniture we had left behind. She cleaned the toilet and the shower. Then she walked from room to room checking to see if there was anyplace that could hold a fingerprint or a sign of our presence.

She looked up. The lights were all off. She got a chair, stood on it, and wiped the light fixtures and the bulbs with her wet rag. Now our apartment was clean and ready to rent again. There was not a fingerprint left belonging to either Michelle or me. Tillie walked to the garage and used what was left of her pail of water to wash off the saw horses and swept down the pile of two-by-fours I had left lying on the floor.

When the FBI agents became tired of waiting for us to come back from our long weekend, they would have no trace of Paul Hartman or Michelle Swartz in or around Tillie's apartment. The FBI may be good at finding fingerprints, but Tillie Teasdale was very good at cleaning.

In her house Tillie sat on her recliner and picked up her phone. She dialed our cell phone number. Our phone was off and it immediately jumped to voice mail. She heard, "Leave a message."

Tillie said, *Paul and Michelle, this is Tillie. I want you to know that it was so nice to be acquainted with y'all. You are high quality folks. I wanted to inform you that I have your apartment all ready for me to rent. I gave it a thorough spring cleaning, not that y'all are dirty people or anything. I wiped down every square centimeter of surface in the whole apartment. Why, there's probably not even a single finger mark left in the whole place. I like to be real clean, don't you know? Keep in touch someday. Love you both.*

XLI

South to Louisiana

Jonathan Wilson nosed his deep blue, Toyota Corolla sedan into a parking space in front of the Houma Courier. His 808 mile trip from St. Louis had been an easy two day drive. With the cruise control set at three miles per hour over the speed limit, nearly all of the traffic had passed him on his trip south on I-55. Jonathan remembered passing eight cars in two days of steady driving.

Under his seat was a legal sized envelope containing his birth certificate and the signed title for his Toyota. On the back seat was a new thick-walled cooler. Advertisements claimed it would keep ice for a week. Inside he carried a hunk of Provolone cheese, a tube of summer sausage, a small bag of apples, a couple of bottles of Pepsi, several cartons of yogurt, and a bag of ice from the Super 8 Motel in Waterloo. *I'm probably in trouble with the law again,* he thought. *The sign on the ice machine said not to fill coolers.*

Beside the cooler on his back seat was a cardboard box with a loaf of wheat bread, a jar of peanut butter, two warm Pepsis, and a small jar of strawberry jam. Stopping in a restaurant for a meal was not in his budget. Jonathan did stop at a McDonald's where he drank a cup of coffee and a refill.

It was still light when he had reclined his seat and slept in a rest area for a few hours. Later, in the outskirts of Memphis, he parked in a Walmart parking lot and rested among recreational vehicles until his growling stomach woke him up before dawn. He splurged at another McDonald's for coffee and a breakfast sandwich. The sun was strong as he entered Louisiana, pulling into the visitor center for a free map and some vacation literature about New Orleans. Jonathan had no goal. He had no idea where he was going. In a park in New Orleans, he fixed a summer sausage sandwich thick with free mustard he had picked up at McDonald's.

I told Rod, I was heading for the mountains of New Mexico. I should go east, he thought. As he was eating, he studied his Louisiana map. He thought New Orleans was as far south as he could go in the state, but the map showed a couple of roads winding west and south out of The Big Easy. One highway headed to the town of Houma. Its population was a little larger than Marshalltown, a central Iowa city of 25,000 people. *That seems to be a nice sized town. I wonder how they p*ronounce the name. *Houma. It must be a Cajun thing,* he thought. *Maybe I'll go there and learn to pronounce the name of the town. House he knew. Houma must be "How ma."*

In Houma, Jonathan gassed up the Corolla and checked the mileage. The twelve year old Corolla had used a total of 25 gallons of gas which meant he had averaged over 32 miles per gallon. When he paid for the gas, he asked the clerk the name of the town.

"Home-a," the gal said. "Dis is Houma, Looseana."

Jonathan bought a copy of the Houma Courier and began to study the want ads. At the rest area he had compiled a list of the things he needed to do wherever he decided to stop. He thought, *I have to find a cheap place to live. Then I need to apply for a Social Security card, register this Corolla, and acquire a driver's license. High on my list has to be finding a job. That will become a necessity very soon. Might be my toughest problem. People these days wanted resumes. They wanted to know where you went to school and where you've worked. This Jonathan Wilson guy, whom I've become has no usable record of schooling or working. I have no idea how I'll solve either problem. I know myself. I'm a worrier. I'll worry until I figured out a way to find that job.*

When Joe had decided to take up Angie's offer to share her apartment, he had called Danny and they bought the Toyota two door sedan. The twelve year old Corolla ran great. Broken plastic parts on the body and in the interior didn't bother Jonathan a lot. When he got established and accumulated a little extra cash he knew they were replaceable with parts from wrecked cars. It was a four cylinder with an automatic three speed transmission. The mileage was very good, so it was cheap to drive. Danny had changed the oil just before he sold it.

They had agreed that half of the Escort was Jonathan's so Joe had paid Danny $1200 for the rebuilt Toyota. Jonathan had almost $1700 left to help him get started in a new life.

"We'll keep in touch," Jonathan had promised. "I'm going west. I've never seen the mountains, so I may end up some place like New Mexico." He thought, *There aren't a lot of people I trust. My brother and I have always been close. Stan came to visit me regularly in prison. He never believed that phony drug charge. Stan Johnson was always in my corner. Someday, when things settle down I'll find a way to contact him.*

Jonathan and Joe had talked about Stan.

Joe commented, "Ain't he the guitarist? Plays classical kind of stuff?"

"That's him. When I find a place to live and save some money, I'll find a way to contact Stan and tell him where I am. This whole deal means a lot to me, Rod. You are a good friend and a great guy. I appreciate all you've done for me. Keep your nose clean. Make a good life for yourself."

The two escaped prisoners shared a parting hug. Jonathan brushed a tear from his eye as he drove west from Waterloo, Illinois into Missouri, and then turned *south* toward the Gulf of Mexico on I-55. He loved Rod, but once his friend began to drink, the cops might be looking for Bob Johnson in New Mexico. Bob Johnson thought, *Jonathan Wilson will be in a little Louisiana town a thousand miles from the mountains.*

XLII

A New Job In Houma

Jonathan was still worried about money. *I spent about $75 on gas and $25 on the cooler. So I have $1600 remaining from the $1700 I had when Rod and I split. I'm not counting the $500 from the money we stole from The Ranger. That's safe, tucked into the toe of a shoe in my bag. I need to rent an apartment, probably buy a phone before looking for a job. Maybe the job should be first. Then I can find a place to live close to where I work.*

Parking the Toyota on a side street near Houma's First United Methodist Church, curling up in the back seat of his narrow little Corolla, Jonathan spent his second night stuffed in the car like a sardine tight in a can. He felt the need to stretch out on a bed. He needed a shower to scrub his body and rid himself of his odor. Jonathan was very tired. Concentrating on his list of things to do, put him to sleep in three minutes. An hour before dawn, his eyes opened. The days were growing longer. Still, his body was ready to move out of the cramped back seat of the little car well before daylight showed its welcome face in the east. He drove to a modern gasoline station taking a clean shirt and clean underwear into the restroom with him. Ten minutes later he walked out feeling somewhat civilized after plenty of hard scrubbing.

He searched out the Bayou Cafe. It opened at 6:00 am. Inside, the Houma Courier was lying on a table for customers to read. Old guys and a retired-looking couple filled about a third of the seats. Jonathan sat in a booth and ordered coffee, pancakes, an over-medium egg, and sausage links.

Tracking down the want ad section of the newspaper from one of the empty tables, he began his search for a place to live. Sleeping on a real bed was moving higher on his list. The ads had plenty of apartments for rent at $700 - $1200 per month and two for $400. His $2100 wouldn't last long if he spent a thousand a month on rent. Actually, his money wouldn't last long at $400 per month. Jonathan needed a job. A bed and a job.

The job ads in the paper always carried the kicker, *Send a copy of your résumé to … .*

Sure, I'll just tell them I've been in prison for the last ten years, he thought. *Then they'll want to see my release papers. That should work real well.* Jonathan sipped his coffee. His eyes caught a sign in the outside window of the restaurant. He read the mirror image through the glass. ***Needed: Bus Boy and Waitress.***

A big, burly guy was walking around carrying a pot of regular and a pot of decaf coffee. He was giving instructions to the waitresses and filling coffee cups. He stopped at Jonathan's table and glanced at the empty beige cup with the chocolate brown trim. Jonathan figured he was the manager.

"Coffee?" the guy asked.

"That would be great," Jonathan held out his cup for the waiter to fill with regular coffee. "Are you the manager?"

"Actually, I own this place. Name's Owen. Owen Blanchard. Hope your service and food's ok. We's a bit short of help today."

"The pancakes were great. And I'm in no hurry. I just drove into town. I'm looking for a job and a place to live today."

"Y'all can go to work right now if you want to work. We need someone to bus tables."

"I can do that. I'll go wash my hands and you can share the details."

The job was twenty hours a week at $6.50 an hour. His pay also included 10% of the tips. Owen figured tips would be about $3 to $5 per day. Jonathan might have a few dollars left after he paid $400 rent on an apartment.

In a way, he liked the mind-numbing job of clearing the tables of dishes, stacking them in tubs, then loading the dishwasher. Jonathan wasn't as fast as the young waitresses who hurried around the tables at the Bayou Café, smiling and greeting customers. Keeping steadily at his work, he soon caught up with the morning crowd.

By 10:30, that crowd had slowed to a trickle. He had time to sit down with Nora, the mature waitress in the group, to drink another cup of coffee. Jonathan guessed Nora was about 40 years old. She wasn't beautiful, but she certainly wasn't homely. Jonathan and Nora worked well together. Soon they were beginning to enjoy each other's company. She had a 20 year old daughter who was a sophomore at the University of New Orleans. Nora showed him her picture. The young woman was a stunningly beautiful blond with a broad smile showing perfect teeth.

"Sarah Sue is majoring in International Studies. I'm very proud of her. She studies hard and makes very good grades. Being a waitress is not her goal in life.

"She is gorgeous. It must be hard for you to keep the boys away," commented Jonathan.

"Sarah Sue takes care of that. She likes boys well enough, but her goal is to earn a degree, work a year or two in another country in an embassy, maybe even in the Peace Corps, then go back to school for her master's, maybe even her doctor's. She won't let herself become really involved with a boy. She says boys are the difference between B's and A's. 'Boys mean B's,' she says."

"That must mean there are plenty of disappointed boys at the University of New Orleans," Jonathan laughed.

"You'd think so."

"Isn't college pretty expensive these days?" Jonathan asked. "How can you send your daughter to a big time university on a waitress' salary?"

"This job helps me buy her food and housing. She has a couple of pretty good scholarships that pay her tuition. For a while she had a part time job, but that didn't last long. Sarah Sue decided the job was like boys. It kept her from getting A's.

We finally agreed that I'd just work extra for a few years and her job could be studying. Her dad died when she was a high school senior. It's been tough since then, but we are making it work."

"Sounds like you have a daughter who makes you very proud, Nora."

"She does. I am very pleased with Sarah Sue. How about you? You just blew in on a north breeze. Owen said your name is Jon?"

"Actually, I'm Jonathan Wilson. I was doing some carpentry work up north near St. Louis. The boss and I had a bit of a disagreement. I decided I was tired of snow and big towns. Somehow my old rusty Toyota stopped in front of your restaurant. I'm needing a job and a place to live."

"Just a wandering man. If you are a decent carpenter, then this could be your lucky day, Jonathan Wilson. My real job is as an accountant for ARC Construction Company. There is a lot of repair work going on in Houma from the last hurricane. Randy Lee Rogers, he's the R in ARC, is looking for a guy who knows how to use tools to solve problems in repairing wind damage."

"That sounds challenging. Might be fun."

"If you're interested," offered Nora, "follow me and you can have a talk with Randy Lee. I'm going to work right now."

"I'm sure needing a job. This bus boy thing would barely pay the rent on a cheap apartment. I'll follow you, Nora."

XLIII

A Date With Nora

By noon, Jonathan had signed on as a carpenter. He had worried about not being able to find a job. Suddenly, he had two. He and Randy Lee had agreed on strange working hours, from 11:00 a.m. to noon and from 12:30 to 7:30, five days a week. The job included health insurance and a 401K plan that would begin after six months. ARC would match his contributions up to ten percent of his salary. The twelve dollars per hour seemed a little low, but Randy Lee assured him that raises would come quickly as he showed he could do the job and if they learned Jonathan and Randy were compatible.

Jonathan spent the afternoon buying a set of basic tools and finding a place to live. After he rented the apartment, he had eight hundred fifty-seven dollars in his wallet. All he needed was enough money to eat for a week or two until he began collecting pay checks.

The carpentry job included a pickup.

"You can use it to stop at the grocery store and drive to and from work," directed Randy, "but, generally, it should sit during the weekend unless I call you out on an emergency job."

Jonathan picked up forms to register his car and apply for a Louisiana driver's license. He would need to study the license booklet to learn Louisiana traffic laws and refresh his mind, especially since he hadn't driven much the last ten years. The hours were Monday through Friday from 8:00 to 4:00. That meant he would have to take off work to take his driving test. Randy Lee might not like it if he were picked up in the company truck without a valid driver's license.

Establishing a life was not going to be an easy proposition. As he studied the requirements to acquire a driver's license and a Social Security card, he realized how important his new birth certificate was. For a driver's license, he needed his birth certificate plus two secondary documents. Those could be a Social Security card, a health insurance card, or a payroll stub. Basically, he had to have a Social Security card.

Documents that would satisfy Social Security included a birth certificate and a health insurance card. In his job with Randy Lee, he would be receiving health insurance, so he would have the insurance card that he needed. That would be the key to toward establishing himself as a person. His smile broadened as he realized that the big problem in his life as an escaped prisoner was solvable.

Jonathan pondered about how his life was falling together. *Society doesn't make it easy for escaped prisoners to establish a new life,* he thought. *I wonder how quickly Randy Lee would have hired me if I had been legally released from the Iowa State Penal System. I might have looked for a long time before I'd have found an employer who was willing to hire an ex-con.*

On Saturday night Jonathan and Nora went out to eat at a Cajun BBQ restaurant. The place was full of families. It was loud and rowdy and the waiting list was forty-five minutes long. They stood outside in the warm spring air and talked for half an hour. Nora reached for his hand and his heart fluttered like a teenager's on a first date. They came across a bench and sat close together and shared stories of their lives. He hesitated for a while and then his reminiscences became real stories of Des Moines with fictional St. Louis locations.

He learned that Nora Breaux had grown up in New Orleans and gone to a community college majoring in bookkeeping and accounting. During her sophomore year, she had married a basketball player and had a baby girl while she was still in college. Her husband, Mel, was an alcoholic. When the baby fussed while he was drinking, Mel's meanness began to show. Nora called the police. They settled the violence and warned Mel to cool it.

Nora told Jonathan, "After the squad car drove away Mel beat me until I was unconscious as punishment for calling the cops.

"The next day I packed my car. My baby and I escaped by driving to Florida to live with a cousin. When Sarah Sue was in kindergarten, a friend sent me a clipping from The

Times-Picayune. Mel had been driving drunk one night when he drove his pickup truck into a bayou and drowned. I moved back to Houma and took a bookkeeping job with ARC. That's my life story."

That night in Houma, Jonathan and Nora ate fabulous BBQ ribs. They were spicy with Cajun seasoning, cooked tender and moist.

"These Cajuns know how to barbecue meat," praised Jonathan. "This is the best I've ever eaten."

"It's a traditional skill," agreed Nora. "Aren't we glad."

He drove Nora home. At her door, she held both his hands, reached up and kissed him goodnight and made him feel like he was eighteen.

"Y'all are trembling. Are you OK?" she asked.

"It's your fault. You just set my feelings on edge."

"I had a good time, Jonathan. Thank you for a pleasant evening."

"I enjoy being with you, Nora. Thanks for sharing your story."

As he drove back to his dingy little apartment Jonathan thought, *I like this woman a lot. I wonder what she might think if she knew that I was an escaped prisoner. What would she think if she knew that I was wanted for the murder of a prison guard? Should I end this relationship before it begins. She doesn't need to have another terrible man in her life who will accept her love and then beat her.*

On the other hand, he thought, *I know I won't abuse her. I don't intend to have anybody catch me. I'm on my way to having an ID. I'm working two jobs. I have a place to live. And I'm a long way from Iowa. It would take a real bad break for me to be caught. I think I'll ask Nora Miller to go out with me again. I'll see what develops.*

XLIV

Plans for Colorado

I sat at a picnic table in Monahans Sandhills State Park reading a book. It was May and it felt hotter than July in Iowa. Texas has a reputation for dry heat. I think they're right. In mid-summer Iowa people sweat a lot. In West Texas, the perspiration evaporates quickly. During these warm days, Mandi spent plenty of time panting. We saw a lot of her big, red drippy tongue. Even though we were in the Northern Chihuahuan Desert and the highs were in the 90's every day, neither Michelle nor I complained about the heat.

Michelle crawled out of the tent after an afternoon siesta.

"Whacha reading?" she asked.

"Easy Prey. A book I bought at a garage sale. It's by John Sandford. I read some of his novels when I was in prison. Most of his books are about some serial killer in Minneapolis and a cop, Lucas Davenport, who is Deputy Chief. They call him in on all the really tough cases. Davenport is good. In every book I've read he always gets his man, sometimes his woman."

"Hope he's not assigned our case," Michelle offered. "I'd hate to see him get his man or woman if it's you or me. Let's hope Davenport stays in Minneapolis and that Sandford doesn't write a new novel about Iowa called <u>Prison Prey</u>."

"It's just fiction, Michelle."

"Since you are a murder suspect," she asked, "who do you root for when you read his novels? The cop or the bad guy?"

I didn't hesitate. "The cop, of course. I never think of myself as a bad guy. ... Well, maybe when I think of the money I stole from the school district. The Ranger thing was an accident. He was not a good man, but I'm not happy that he's dead.

"The guys Lucas Davenport chases are really mean and nasty dudes. They deserve to be caught and sent to prison, or to be blown away."

We spent three nights in the little state park in the desert, walking trails with Mandi, lying in the warm sand reading, and sitting around a picnic table making travel plans.

One evening, Michelle asked, "Have you ever floated down a wild river in a rubber raft?"

"Actually, I've canoed down some pretty tame rivers. Do you have something in mind?"

"I read something in the library about the Arkansas River in Colorado," Michelle explained. "I thought the river was probably in Arkansas, but it comes out of the Rocky Mountains in Colorado, cuts through the mountains near Pueblo, into Kansas, runs through a corner off Oklahoma, and then flows through Arkansas to the Mississippi River."

"Doesn't the Salt Fork that we camped on in Oklahoma, run into it?"

"I think so. Wonder if it makes it salty?"

"What's special about the Arkansas River?" I asked.

"In Colorado, the Arkansas drops fast. There are wild rapids. People float the river in kayaks and rubber rafts. We could hire a guide to take us down the river on a raft. It's supposed to be an adventure as well as a really scenic trip. When the snow melts in the Rockies the river runs pretty wild. I'll bet in May, we would be floating down a torrent of spring melt water coming right out of the mountains."

"Sounds like if we tipped over, it would be like swimming in a bath tub full of ice cubes and water," I suggested.

Michelle went on. "We seem to be traveling north or west. If we aren't in too much of a hurry to find a new place to settle, then floating a river sounds like fun to me."

"We'll never have a better chance. Besides, if the cops catch us, they'll take all our money. What we spend, they can't take."

"Funny. Shall we do it?" asked Michelle. "This park is pleasant, but I've had enough of it. I'd like to go see the Rocky Mountains."

"I wonder where the FBI agents went," I pondered. "If they didn't find our finger prints in the apartment, then maybe we're ok."

"If they had our license plate number," Michelle reasoned, "they'd probably have us by now. Makes me nervous, but what can we do?"

"Just hope and pray that they haven't figured out our little S10 pickup. Not much we can do."

Michelle and I both felt rested and ready to travel. Early the next morning, we finished packing our pickup during a spectacular West Texas sunrise. Then, we were on our way out of the park.

We splurged for breakfast at a restaurant called the Huddle House. As we settled into a booth, we glanced around the room. The place was full of cowboys and oil field workers. We were smelling a mix of pancakes, cows, and oil.

Michelle ate pancakes; I had two eggs with thick gravy covering biscuits and sausage patties; all for less than five dollars.

"These pancakes aren't bad," Michelle whispered to me, "Although thick and chewy isn't nearly as good as your thin ones, Dean."

"Me and Aunt Jemima do make great pancakes. I'll give the black woman most of the credit."

"Your pancakes are still the best I ever ate," Michelle declared. "And I do appreciate you cooking meals. So many men are real sexists about cooking. I like it that you do your share."

I love this woman!

XLV

New Mexico - Path to Colorado

State Highway 18 took us northwest from Monahans into New Mexico. Michelle was still doing most of the driving. We were choosing roads that appeared as narrow lines on the map. Our plan was to drive north along the eastern counties of New Mexico to Colorado, a good route for us to see part of New Mexico and make easy progress toward Colorado. Our main goal was to put plenty of miles between us and the FBI agents in Del Rio.

The map suggested we would gain about 1200 feet in altitude during the day. To the west, we saw a glimmer on the horizon. We wondered if we were seeing the Rocky Mountains.

That night we camped near Logan, New Mexico at Ute Lake State Park. By mid-afternoon, we located a lonely campsite. After a warm spring day, the breeze off the lake cooled, as if we had plugged in an air conditioner. We hooked Mandi to her leash walking and jogging several miles on a hiking trail.

The next morning the sun rose as we drove into Logan to find Angie's Place for breakfast. The locals looked us over carefully, as we sat in the cafe that morning. I figured their eyes were drawn by the striking beauty of the woman sitting beside me. People in Logan made us feel welcome. We fielded questions on where we were from and where we were going. Our Arkansas license plate gave us a cover story for our past. A vacation in Northwestern New Mexico gave us a future.

Looking to the west, we saw morning light painting the Rocky Mountains with color. Cool air told us of the nearness of the peaks. Colorado was not far ahead. I kept glancing at the fuel gauge. Keeping our gas tank filled had become a habit. It was a long way between towns; not all of them had gasoline stations. When our tank got close to half full, we began looking for a place to fill up. Fences and scattered cows were often the only signs of civilization.

In Trinidad, the Rocky Mountains appeared close, large, and picturesque. Snow was capping the peaks, filling the valleys, testifying to the height of these spectacular mountains. We put Mandi on her leash and walked around this Colorado town.

Trinidad had a grocery store with a good meat market. We stocked up on groceries, including a couple of t-bone steaks. Enough of this camping food. Salads, baked potatoes, and steaks roasted over a bed of coals sounded like a tasty change for dinner.

We stopped at a trading post where a Navaho wool blanket with a repeating z-pattern drew Michelle in the door as if it were a magnet and she were a steel ball. I glanced at our pickup as a black Corvette drove by at a slow speed. Its door was decorated with a colorful sign that said, Trinidad Police. I watched the Chevy sports car drive past and then turned to follow Michelle into the trading post.

Michelle leaned toward my ear, whispering, "It seems strange calling you Dean. You don't seem like a Dean."

"Seems strange to me too. My pledge father namesake was a bantam rooster kind of guy."

"Not much like you."

I pulled her close to me and whispered. "I know it's impolite to whisper, but back to the blanket, haven't I been keeping you warm enough?"

"We haven't been camped beside snowdrifts so far, Dean. Besides, it's gorgeous. Don't you love it?"

"I really do. How much?"

"$70. Half price."

"Half of seventy or seventy is half price?"

"It was seventy dollars originally. Now it's thirty-five."

"Ok. Let's buy it."

"Dean?"

"Yes."

"I found something else."

"What?"

"This pillow. Isn't it beautiful? Don't you love the patterns and the colors? It would be adorable in our apartment and you can prop your head up when you read in bed."

"How much?"

"$30. It's on sale for half off too."

"Half of thirty?"

"Yup."

"We should have it."

Michelle threw her arms around me and gave me a kiss on the cheek.

"You're wonderful."

"It's probably your money."

"Thanks, Dean. I love you."

"Just my big bucks. Can we hit the road before we find something else we have to have?"

At the car, I asked, "We made it to Colorado. Where to now?"

"Any ideas?"

I studied the map.

"How'd you like to see a sand dune?"

"Sure. We've only found about three of them so far."

"OK. Buckle your seat belt and let's drive north. Then west. We're looking for Great Sand Dunes National Park."

XLVI

Great Sand Dunes National Park

The thermometer on the bank sign read 65 degrees; a typical crisp, sunny day common for Colorado.

"It looks to me as if we want I-25 North for about thirty-five miles to Walsenburg, then west about an hour to Highway 150. The Great Sand Dunes National Park is about twenty miles north. Sound right?"

Michelle drove to the shoulder. "Let me look. I picked up a flier in town. I think there's a scenic route, Paul ... err ... Dean. We can pick up Highway 12 just out of Trinidad; take the mountain roads past Spanish Peak and a couple of other really cool scenes. We'll go up the east side of the Sangre de Christo Mountains. We should see peaks more than 12,000 feet high; some geology similar to what we saw in Big Bend. There are giant igneous rock towers that have been formed by lava forced up through vents in a volcano. They call them plugs. Remember the rock fences where lava was forced into cracks to form dikes. It says these dwarf the ones we saw in Texas."

"How do you know all this shit, Michelle."

"I've been reading," she explained. "We have all these pamphlets and I spent some time in the library while you were wasting your time reading, <u>Birds of Prey</u>. That's how I know all this *shit*, Dean."

"That's <u>Night Prey</u>. And you never used to be interested in this kind of information about the natural world, did you?"

"No. I guess I was missing out on a lot of this kind of stuff. I like it. I feel good about learning so much. Maybe I'll be a naturalist when I grow up."

"You'd make me proud, Michelle."

"Let's go find another sand dune."

"Let's do it," I agreed.

"Find me the corner."

I did and soon Michelle was giving us our first taste of the Rocky Mountains.

"And you said these were the Sangre de Cristo Mountains?"

"Right."

"And what does that mean?"

"I'm not sure. Cristo would be Christ."

"Makes sense."

"Sangre?"

"Let me look."

We had a lot of travel literature.

"Here it is. Sangre de Cristo means Blood of Christ."

"The Blood of Christ Mountains."

"We are seeing a kaleidoscope of color with a topping of snow on the high places. I'm glad you suggested the shortcut, Michelle. This is stunning."

"I love the contrast between ranch land and forest and rugged mountain peaks. Look!" she exclaimed. "Look at the huge dike. It's like somebody built a giant rock wall that goes on and on in a straight line."

"It's way bigger than the ones we saw in Big Bend," I reflected. "Impressive."

"That must be Spanish Peak where it starts. It's huge. And alluring," said my alluring companion. "I read that the Tarahumare Indians believed that these summits were sacred and that all life originated here."

"I can believe they might be right."

Then I found something else.

"It says here that in 1594 Juan Humana and a band of conquistadores disappeared near the Purgatoire River. They were never seen alive after that."

"We'd better keep our eyes open."

"Think they're still alive?" I asked.

"Ha!"

"Look at that view, Michelle. It looks like a layer cake. A row of willow trees, a section of dark mountains with a white frosting of snow-capped Sangre de Cristo Mountains. A layer cake."

"It is. Aren't you glad we came this way?"

"And 72 degrees with clear, deep, baby blue sky," I commented. "It doesn't get any better than this."

"It beats being in prison."

"It's better for us and for society for you and me to be in the Sangre de Cristo Mountains, Michelle."

Our route took us through the little mountain town of La Veta. We picked up a bit of history at the Fort Francisco Museum; old rail cars on a short piece of track and a bunch of antique buildings. The place was closed, but peaking in the windows gave us a replica of life on the frontier a century or two ago. North of the fort, we made a hard left onto Highway 160, drove a dozen miles before picking up Highway 150. A sign pointed us toward Great Sand Dunes National Park.

Michelle asked, "Dean, are you sure we want to see another sand dune?"

"I'm thinking the west has a lot of sand and wind, piling the sand up all over the place. Do you want to skip this park and find a different place to camp tonight?"

"I'm tired."

"There's a campground at the park," I offered. "By the time we arrive, it will be mid-afternoon. I'm thinking we'd just as well stop. All of the dunes we've seen have been a little different from the rest. If we don't like the place, we can keep on going. If it's not a special spot, we drive on through and find somewhere to camp up north of here."

We had driven up the east side of the Sangre de Cristo Mountain Range, cut through a pass and now we were driving north on the west side of the Range. Suddenly, an amazing vista opened in front of us. Someone had painted a giant mural that filled our windshield. The afternoon light gave a sense of depth to the most remarkable set of sand dunes Michelle and I had set our eyes upon in our two months of exploring

Oklahoma, Texas, and Colorado as we ran from the law. I glanced at Michelle and she stared at me.

"This is the most awesome sight I have ever seen," she declared.

"I've never experienced anything like it," I added.

Day after day, and year after year, the steady west winds had lifted sand up the slopes of the Sangre de Christo Mountains. There, they slowed and dropped their load of sand. Now the dunes were like a huge mountain, cresting 600 feet above the valley. They were bigger than any mountain we had seen in Oklahoma or Texas. Behind the dunes, to the east were magnificent mountains, impressive in their own right and made more so by the spectacular dunes leading our eyes into those mountains.

"We should camp and spend some time here, Dean."

"We should hike to the top of these dunes," I challenged. "Can we do it?"

"Maybe we should explore a bit, then hike to the top tomorrow."

"Good plan. Find us a camp spot."

In an hour our tent was pitched and we had grilled and devoured our steaks.

We tied on tennis shoes, waded the creek, and headed for the dunes with our big black lab. I was wearing shorts and a t-shirt. Michelle wore short shorts and a pleasing to the eyes, halter top. God, she was sexy.

The skimpy outfit was a mistake. The higher we climbed in the dunes, the more the wind blew. The wind-blown sand stung my legs and my arms. It peppered my face with sand pellets. The blowing sand was worse for Michelle with her skimpy halter.

I thought both of us were in pretty good condition, but we were dragging before we had climbed a couple of hundred yards up the mountain of sand. Several times, we stopped to sit and empty a load of sand from our shoes. Sometimes, when we tired, we let Mandi pull us up the steep side of the dune. She loved the climb.

We found places where we could be sheltered from the wind. Touching a wall of sand, we watched the grains collapse into a miniature avalanche. As the wind abated, we climbed a little higher, huddling together, surveying the sunset from a ridge high on the dune.

The sun dropped below distant mountains, with Mandi snuggling between us. I caressed the soft skin of Michelle's shoulders. Her skimpy halter top distracted me from my love of nature, as we enjoyed our favorite time of day.

We already knew layers of clothing were a good idea for hiking in mountain country. That afternoon the lesson was re-emphasized for both of us. As the bright ball of sun slipped below the horizon, Michelle said, "I'm cold, Dean." I offered her my t-shirt, but she refused. "I'll be ok. I just think we should head back. I should have brought a sweater or a jacket."

We walked and slid down the dune for a few minutes. Then we stopped. Michelle was shivering. I slipped my t-shirt over my head and slid it over Michelle.

"No," she protested. "I don't want your shirt, Dean. I'm the one who did something stupid. Why should you freeze just because I didn't dress warm enough for a mountain evening?"

"It's not a problem, Michelle. I am plenty warm. You take my shirt. I'll be alright. Let's slide down this sand pile to camp and put you in a warm sleeping bag."

A half an hour later, we were back to the tent. I helped Michelle into a sweat suit and her sleeping bag. I found my sweats and a fleece jacket. Then, I lit the camp stove, boiled water, and made two cups of hot chocolate. By the time Michelle had finished the hot chocolate, her shaking had stopped. I packed our camp stove and dishes in the pickup and crawled up close to Michelle. My body was still warmer than hers. It didn't take long before she was warm and all three of us were asleep in the tent.

Next morning, it was cold. I heard somebody walking around outside our tent. *Are we in trouble again*? I thought. *How in hell did they find us here? Did somebody learn the license number on the pickup? I don't think they could, but who knows? Whoever it is, is moving around in a strange way.*

Carefully and quietly, I unzipped the window above my head, looking out toward the dune. Our intruder had four legs, big ears, and tan-colored fur. A deer was grazing in the meadow near our tent. I unzipped the window in the other end of the tent. A fawn and two more adult deer were undisturbed by our little green tent.

I kissed Michelle awake and held my finger to my lips. "Ssssh." I whispered. "Be quiet and look out the window."

Michelle sat up and looked out.

"Wow! Aren't they wonderful?" Michelle whispered. "I've never been this close to a deer before, Dean." "Are they mule deer?"

"I'm not sure. What do you think?"

"Look at the big ears. And that buck. His antlers look different than white-tails. I'll bet they are mule deer."

We watched the deer graze and play for twenty minutes until somebody in a camper disturbed them by walking down the road toward the restroom.

When the deer moved away, we dressed, ate Cheerios with bananas and milk, packed a lunch and walked toward the dunes. The sun took a long time to rise above the Sangre de Christo Mountains. We thanked God for the lack of wind. I dressed in a pair of shorts, t-shirt, and polartec jacket. Michelle had added several layers to her tank top. She carried an empty backpack for some of our clothes on the trip back to camp.

We saw interesting tracks in the sand. Some creature, probably an insect, left a trail that looked as if a miniature tractor tire had rolled along the sand. We found a strange little mouse track that had two, long back foot tracks slightly in front of two, tiny front foot tracks. Later, at the visitor center, we matched the tracks to those of a jumping mouse.

By ten o'clock we reached the top of the dunes. I had stripped shirtless and Michelle down to shorts and her tank top. We stowed our extra clothes in her pack. We spread our lunch on top of my t-shirt. Reclining on the sand, resting, munching gorp, drinking juice, enjoying warm sun and the wonderful panorama of sand all around left us with a wonderful feeling of contentment. We saw level plains and distant mountains to the west, but the magnificent Sangre de Cristo Mountains dominated the eastern sky.

We saw tiny people moving about in the campground and at the bottom of the dunes, but at the moment, we felt all alone on top of the world.

On the way down, we searched for steep slopes. Holding hands and spreading our arms, we slid down together in miniature avalanches followed closely by a big black dog. In an hour we were back at camp, ready for a good meal. I built a fire. Opening a can of baked beans, setting it in the fire to cook, I roasted a couple of hot dogs. This time, I didn't mix them with the beans.

The Great Sand Dunes National Park moved high on our list of the most beautiful places we had seen on our journey. We had never experienced a setting so resembling a painting when you saw it in real life.

I told Michelle, "We nearly overlooked this place. Are you glad we came?"

"I wouldn't have missed this for anything, Dean. It's a re-markable spot, isn't it?"

"I agree. I thought it sounded interesting, but the raw beauty of those dunes is beyond belief -- beyond expression."

We were thrilled with Great Sand Dunes National Park. Now we were on our way to the Arkansas River and another adventure. And so far, we were avoiding the law.

XLVII

Arkansas River By Raft

Michelle said, "Paul."

"Dean."

"Dean. I am troubled that we have no plan as to our destination or where we might settle down."

"So am I," I agreed. "I really enjoyed our time in Del Rio. I need a new place to live. I want the routine of going to work and living a normal life. Being able to open the door of our refrigerator and see food for the next meal makes me feel connected to something solid. The wild places of the West stimulated our senses. I think we both loved the dunes. The sound of the wind, the touch of the sand between our toes, the blast of the sand against our skin, the smell of the pine forests. I think those things fill our memories. My mind is playing the tune of the natural world."

"Our finances are solid," added Michelle. "We have gas money, we aren't hungry, and we pay for campgrounds every night. And the FBI guys watching our Del Rio apartment seem a world away. I agree. We need to sit down with some maps and figure out where we want to be."

The Eastern Colorado roadside was dotted with advertisements for rafting expeditions on the Arkansas River.

Michelle said, "Paul. I mean, Dean."

"Yes?"

"If they catch us, we'll probably never ride a raft down a wild Colorado River."

"You're saying we should do it now?"

"That sign says Dvorak's. That's the outfit the young couple we met at the sand dunes said was really good."

"I'm willing."

We booked a half-day trip for the next morning and then found a National Forest Service campground west of Nathrop along a sparkling mountain stream. The mountain air was cool; we wrapped ourselves in blankets inside our sleeping bags and threw the new wool blanket over the top. In the morning, frost covered the tent. We were cold. After we dressed, we looked for a restaurant for breakfast.

Matt, our guide, was long and lean, bronze and tough as leather. He agreed to take Mandi along with Mike, his big male black lab. The five of us had a wonderful time. The two dogs loved it when we dipped into huge waves that drenched all of us. The first wave dumped water down Michelle's neck and Matt had a chuckle as he gave her revenge by filling my neck with icy water on the next rapids.

Matt issued us paddles and gave us paddling lessons. He ran the oars. I think our efforts were mainly to make us feel that we were part of the crew. We both felt pride at conquering the river and finishing right-side-up at our take-out point.

A photographer had been sitting in the rocks above the first rapids. By the time we returned to the office, he had already printed a color photo of us. We saw looks of terror on our faces as we crashed into that first standing wave. The guy had a digital camera, had beaten us back to the office, downloading his pictures onto their computer. Two minutes later, he had pictures of us being drenched as we paddled through a huge wave. Our mouths were open in silent screams, both of us with closed eyes. Mandi was taking the wave as if she was a permanent bow ornament on the raft.

Photos were nonexistent in our recent life history, so we splurged and bought a photo. This was our first picture in what we planned to be many years together. If we ever found a place to call home, we could frame it or mount the picture with magnets on our refrigerator.

XLVIII

Free Camping

Matt understood that we were on a tight budget, that we were splurging to fit a raft trip into our finances. We talked about this being a camping vacation. He told us about a free campground up towards Denver.

"The place is called Rampart Range Road Campground," he informed us. "It's five miles from the nearest paved road. Take plenty of supplies. It it rains, you're stuck there until it dries out unless your S10 has four-wheel drive."

"No luck there," I replied.

"One other thing. People sleep in tents, but the bears there have a reputation of being pretty aggressive. If you sleep in your tent, make sure you don't leave any food in your tent or even outside your car."

"Don't worry," Michelle bragged. "P... Dean has pledged to protect me against bears. I'm safe."

"More power to you then, Dean. Do you have a gun?"

"I'm afraid we don't do guns," I responded.

"Probably a good thing. Unless you have a very big gun and you are a terrific shot, you'd just wound him and make him mad. A mad bear is trouble. The place is pretty and its free if you're heading in that direction."

"Thanks, Matt. We'll talk about it," I said.

Matt's directions were good. We did a lot of twisting and turning, but we finally found a free camping space at Rampart Range Road.

"This is a really strange name for a camping place, Dean. It's a pretty place though. I love the beauty and it's nice not having to spend money to sleep."

"Shall we set up our tent?" I asked.

"It's late. Let's check out the bears and maybe sleep in the tent tomorrow night."

We locked all our food in the front of the pickup. The three of us retired early and went right to sleep.

About 2:00 a.m. the truck began to rock. Mandi began to bark. She never barked. The hair on the nape of her neck stood straight up. I think mine did too. A huge black face appeared in the side window. I shined our big flashlight at the face. I yelled. Michelle screamed. Mandi barked. The face disappeared and the pickup stopped rocking.

"Oh, Paul. It was a bear, wasn't it?"

"I think he's gone. I think I saved you, Michelle."

"Mandi saved me. She's the one who barked."

"Do you want me to get out and chase him away?"

"No! Don't you leave this truck! We're going to stay right here, Paul."

"Dean."

"Dean. Your name is Dean. I know that."

"Until you get excited."

"I won't be able to sleep the rest of the night," she promised.

"Good. You and Mandi stay up and guard us from the bear. I'm going back to sleep. Goodnight, Michelle."

"Paul ... Dean, You can't go to sleep. You have to stay up and protect me."

"I chased the bear away. What more do you want?"

"Oh, Dean."

"Let me know if he comes back. I'll wake up and chase him away. Goodnight."

Michelle might have drifted off to sleep about three thirty. We woke up about seven and climbed down with Mandi. There were tracks. Big ones. From a big black bear. I found muddy, paw prints on our roof and on our side window where the bear had tried to figure out a way in.

"I'm glad we locked our food in the cab," commented Michelle.

"One smart thing," I responded.

Later, as we sat around the table drinking coffee, letting our breakfast settle, we discussed our future.

"I'm not going to spend another night in this campground with that black bear, Dean. That subject is closed. Neither

Mandi nor I will stay here so the vote is two to one in case you vote to stay. Now we should really talk about where we want to live."

"Do we really need to talk about it? It sounds as if we'll take a family vote and I'll lose two to one so why don't you just tell me what you and our dog have decided?"

"Oh, Dean. You're being silly now."

"No, you're being silly, Michelle. We've always discussed what to do and made our choices together. I don't understand why, all of a sudden you're making the decisions on your own. I'm going to take a walk. I'll be back in ten minutes."

I left her sitting at the table. Mandi bounded after me. I turned down a narrow trail and walked briskly, stepping between big rocks, accelerating off others. When I turned around and started back, twenty steps took me face to face with Michelle. She was crying.

"I'm sorry," she apologized. "You're right, Dean. I really just don't want to stay here tonight. I'm afraid, but you're right. We should talk about it. Is it all right with you if we go someplace else?"

I wrapped my arms around her. "I don't like to be told what to do. I thought being ordered around ended when I left prison. I'd rather talk about things, Michelle. I'd rather talk."

"Me too."

We walked down the trail with my hand in Michelle's. Back at the picnic table she asked, "How do you feel about leaving here, Dean?"

"I'm not afraid of staying, but if you and Mandi want to go, I'm willing."

"Are you just saying that?"

"No. Last night would scare anybody; looking into that huge face; giant teeth in our window. I'm ready for a place without bears."

"Thank you, Dean."

"It's ok. We really should talk about where we go from here. Colorado Springs lies just down the road. Denver to the north. There are a bunch of middle-sized Front Range towns on the other side of Denver. I kind of like Fort Collins. It's a teacher's college town."

"I liked Del Rio," offered Michelle. "It might have been too small. These Colorado towns are all much bigger than Del Rio."

"If we settle in one of these towns we should figure out how to establish ourselves in Colorado. Someday, we'd need a new license on the pickup. You should get a new driver's license."

"What about you?"

"I don't know. I'm kind of losing hope. I have my old birth certificate, my passport, and my expired driver's license that Mom sent me, but I'm really scared that as soon as I use them, the FBI will be on our doorstep. Maybe we should go into Colorado Springs and do some research."

Michelle said, "You like Fort Collins. It's eight thirty. What would you think about driving up to Fort Collins and doing our research up there? If we like it, maybe we could just stay there. What do you think?"

"I'll vote for that," I agreed with a smile. "If Mandi votes for Fort Collins, it's unanimous."

"She told me she's voting with you, Dean. Let's pack."

XLIX

Rejecting Colorado

"Dean. About driving today? I've never driven in big city traffic," confessed Michelle. "Would you mind driving around Denver?"

"I guess I can do that. I'll try hard to avoid a ticket."

"You'd better."

In two hours, we were in Fort Collins. We registered at a campground on the west edge of town as Mr. and Mrs. Dean Swartz. We needed jobs, a place to stay, and an address.

"I'm ready to work again," Michelle explained. "Playing tourist with you has been a learning experience as well as great fun, but I love working and I really enjoy seeing you after we've been apart for a few hours. That's when I fall in love with you all over again.

I was almost wordless. "Wow! Go to work. Find a job. I want to greet you after a day away."

The need for information led us again to the library. There, we found a copy of the Fort Collins Coloradoan. We perused the want ads and found furnished apartments from $400 to $2000 a month. All but one had the restriction, "No Pets." We wrote down the phone number of the $425 per month unfurnished apartment.

It was a one bedroom house that allowed pets and had a fenced-in yard and a garage. I wondered, *how are we going to furnish a house with appliances, beds, chests, table, and chairs?*

"Back to garage sales." said Michelle, answering the question on my mind.

She studied the want ads for jobs while I sat down at a library computer, looking on-line to find the requirements for a Colorado driver's license. First, I thought I would have to take a commercial driver's education course. Private companies had taken over the training and testing of drivers. Pay your money, pass the written and driving tests, then present your certificate to the state people for your license. Simple. Move the government out and private industry in.

Then I noticed the requirement that sent us to Wyoming. *All Colorado drivers must be photographed and fingerprinted.* When I showed Colorado's driver's license requirements to Michelle, we burst into a mix of tears and giggles.

My next search was for Wyoming's driver's license requirements. Wyoming required Michelle to present her Iowa license, give them twenty dollars and show them proof that she lived in Wyoming. Then, they would issue a Wyoming license. I would need some sort of identification (I had a passport and a birth certificate) and pass both a written test and a driving test. I'd also need proof of Wyoming residence. Then, I could qualify for a license. Wyoming had no fingerprint requirement. The big question still troubling me: Would they do a background check on me when I applied for a license that would reveal my history and show them my prison record? I needed to talk to somebody who knew about those things but wouldn't be curious about my questions. It sounded as if I was going to continue in limbo. At least Michelle could have a new license of her very own. We could license her and our car in the same state.

We drove back to the campground. Early the next morning, we were on our way up I-25 toward Cheyenne, Wyoming. An hour later we left the interstate in Cheyenne. We drove around town and found the library. This time, we searched The Cheyenne Tribune Eagle. It gave us a list of unfurnished apartments.

The headline on the newspaper was ironic. "TRIAL OPENS FOR BUSINESS MANAGER OF GOSHEN COUNTY UNIFIED SCHOOL DISTRICT #1. ACCUSED OF EMBEZZLING $400,000 FROM FINANCE COMPANY." Business managers were not to be trusted. First, Des Moines, then Del Rio, and now Cheyenne had problems with school business managers.

We rented a one bedroom apartment on the second floor of an old house, At one time, it might have been a real show place. At the top of the stairs, was a balcony and living room. We thought the place had character. We paid $350 a month plus a $250 deposit. The rent included all utilities except a phone.

The ad for the apartment said pets were "negotiable." The landlady told us that meant we had to pay an extra $100 deposit. If the dog caused any kind of a mess, we could lose up to $350. We didn't think Mandi would leave a mess. She had never had an accident in the Del Rio apartment. This place had a refrigerator and a stove that were both old, but they worked. The neighborhood was not the greatest, but the landlady didn't ask for references. We registered as Dean and Michelle Swartz.

We bought a pre-paid cell phone. Memory would be easy to add and nobody could connect us with the calls we made. Our initial plan was to spend a couple of months in Cheyenne and then move on.

We opened a checking account for Michelle in the First National Bank and Trust Company of Wyoming with a thousand dollars in cash. We had $4000 stuck in a sock in a backpack under our bed and another $3800 in another sock in another backpack behind the seat in the S-10. We had been living frugally and saving a good part of what we earned.

I stopped at the driver's license office, picking up an application for a driver's license and a booklet to study for the test. Michelle bought a Wyoming automobile license for the S-10. We decided Wyoming plates would be less conspicuous than the ones from Arkansas. The clerk explained that Michelle would need to turn in her Iowa license and purchase a new Wyoming driver's license within 60 days after she established residence.

"Thanks for letting me know about that," Michelle smiled at the helpful young lady. I didn't dream I'd need a new driver's license."

We debated whether it was safer for her to have a new license or to ignore it and keep our trail as small as possible.

"The Iowa license only has a few months to go, Dean. I think it's time to change. A new one is good for four years."

We both enjoyed cruising garage sales again, looking for neat things for our apartment. In a week we were settled in. Michelle had a job at the Flying J Plaza. The pay wasn't great, but the clientele were good tippers. Both the management and the customers loved Michelle. She was happy and she always had stories to tell when she came home.

Michelle talked with a couple of cops who stopped regularly for breakfast. One night she came home with some news.

"I was talking with my cop friends. Jerry and Vern are really nice guys. I asked them if they'd ever captured any notorious criminals?

"They told me about chasing bank robbers out in the country on a dirt road. The robbers went off the road and into the ditch. Vern said they just held up their hands and surrendered.

"He said it was a piece of cake. They had a hundred grand of the bank's money in the car. Then, I asked them if they ever caught any big time murderers. Jerry told about a guy from Florida, who had killed his wife, showing up in Cheyenne once. The guy applied for a driver's license. When they processed a computer check on him, they learned he was wanted in Florida.

The license clerk notified Jerry. He arrested the suspect. The guy sat in jail until Florida State Police came and picked him up.

"Aren't you glad you didn't try to pick up a license, Dean? You'd be on your way back to Iowa. I'd be terribly lonesome."

That shook me up. I had worked on several odd jobs the last week and had been just too busy to go after my driver's license. My goose would have been cooked.

We talked it over and decided there would be no risk for Michelle to buy a Wyoming license. Once she established residence, she could take an afternoon off and trade her old Iowa license and twenty dollars for a new Wyoming license.

L

Odd Jobs In Cheyenne

I was still cautious about attempting to find a regular job. I bought some card stock, and using the library computer, printed a hundred business cards. I posted cards at trailer courts and apartment buildings around town with a note that I would do odd jobs. Soon, I was again doing a pretty good business. We were earning enough to pay our rent, eat, buy gasoline, and pay for car repairs. Thank God we were both healthy. We couldn't afford medical insurance. A big health problem for either of us would have wiped out our cash in a hurry.

Neither of us cared much for Cheyenne. It was a military town, dating back to just after the Civil War. The Union Pacific Railroad and the military were the reasons for Cheyenne's existence. The railroad was the second biggest employer.

Most people in our neighborhood came home from work to sit in their air conditioned houses watching TV in the evenings. We didn't have TV so we were forced to do fun things to entertain ourselves.

I bought a cribbage board without pegs at a garage sale. I carved a pair of unique pegs from a scrap of blond-colored maple and two more from a scrap of dark walnut. We splurged on a deck of cards. Then I taught Michelle how to play cribbage. She quickly became a pretty good player. Every night, we played a game or two or three. We played for a penny a point with double score for a skunk. We paid our losses out of our pocket change and saved our winnings in jam jars. I thought I was pretty good at the game, but after two months in Cheyenne, Michelle's jar was definitely heavier than mine. Not only was this woman beautiful, she was skillful.

Anytime Michelle had a day or two off from work, we drove west of town to camp in the Medicine Bow National Forest. We loved the campgrounds in park-like stands of aspen and conifers. Lovely trails let us explore the rock formations in this high plains desert area. Mandi loved the freedom of running around without a leash.

One night I had a call from Ruth Rankin. She had a kitchen sink that wouldn't drain. I gave up our cribbage game and drove to her house. She and her husband, Karl, had bought a small, two bedroom bungalow. Neither of them were home much. Ruth was a sergeant in the Air Force and Karl had followed her to Wyoming, landing a job with an oil company. They had a two year old who was the epitome of the terrible twos. Kevin loved my tool box. He picked up a Crescent wrench and carried it all over the house. I hoped I'd find it when I finished.

Ruth had seen my card on the bulletin board at the laundromat. When their sink wouldn't drain, she called me.

"Neither of us knows anything about plumbing or taking care of a house," she said.

I showed her how to disassemble the trap. "This trap is designed to catch bad stuff that accidentally goes down your drain. Sometimes, like this one today, it fills with sludge. I'll just take this outside and use your garden hose to clean it up a bit. Let me take your dish soap along. It should cut the grease."

When I brought it back inside, I asked, "Do you dump grease down the drain, Ruth? The trap had a lot of grease coagulated in it."

"As a matter of fact, we dump all of our grease down the drain, Dean. Are you telling me I hadn't ought to do that?"

"Really bad. You are lucky the grease coagulated in the trap and not somewhere further down the line where it would be harder to get at. We usually pour our grease in a tin can and send it out with the trash."

The trap was shiny clean and when I re-assembled it, the sink drained like a dream. Ruth paid me twenty-five dollars.

Karl came home as I was leaving. Ruth asked me to join them for a cup of coffee and a cookie. The Wyoming sun was dropping low in the sky. We sat on their patio enjoying the end of the day. Ruth came from Franklin, North Carolina, a little mountain town in the Appalachians. I had spent a summer near Franklin when I was in college. We talked about Smoky Mountain National Park and of hiking the Appalachian Trail. Karl, Ruth, and I enjoyed our visit. We made a tentative plan for the four of us to go out for dinner a week later, when Michelle was off work.

However, our dinner date never happened. Michelle and I had a sudden change in plans.

LI

New Home for Joe

"You don't have much stuff, Joe," observed Angie. "I cleaned out a chest of drawers and half the closet for you; you're going to leave most of it empty."

"When we moved out of the Twin Cities we decided to travel light. Even Goodwill wouldn't take most of what we had left. I left a few things with my mom, but what you see is pretty much what I have."

"Well, what do you think of my house?"

"I love the brick," complimented Joe. "It looks so solid, like its been here for a century and it ain't going nowhere. You have your house filled with so much art work. I didn't realize you are rich, Angie."

"Rich, I'm not. I've bought most of the art at garage and estate sales for just a few dollars. It makes me pretty excited when I buy something like this little Hallmark cartoon sculpture of a pup, then clean it up and sell it to a collector for $200."

"Wow! You have a whole knick-knack shelf full. Are these all Hallmark statues? I like them. So colorful. Just cute."

"I like them too. I read some advice someplace -- maybe on TV -- If you're going to invest in art, buy pieces you really like. That way you can enjoy them while you own them."

"What about these little metal animals? Are they made of pewter?"

"Do you like them? They're pewter. And they are made by Hallmark also."

"I think they're pretty cool, Angie. You have great taste in art work."

Joe's eyes traveled the walls, seeing paintings filling much of the space. He loved some and others seemed to be gaudy collections of color. One prominent painting caught his eye.

"This painting is pretty abstract. What is it?" he asked. "It looks to me like the Pacific Ocean with a bright yellow sunset. A layer of yellow; tiny line of blue clouds; a layer of brighter yellow and a layer of steel-gray like the ocean with a touch of yellow reflected in it. I really kind of like it. The layers of color are kind of growing on me."

"Actually, it *is* the ocean, probably the Atlantic off the coast of France. It was painted by an artist named Judith Rothchild. I bought it at an estate sale for less than a thousand dollars. Then I started reading up on the artist. She was an American who studied here and then moved to France. Now she's barely dead and her works sell for $1500 to $100,000 to millions."

"How much is your sunset worth?"

"I'm really not sure. I'd guess it's worth at least $50,000, maybe a quarter of a million."

"Wow. That means you're rich."

"Hardly. It may be worth that if I take it to New York and sell it at an auction. Hanging on my cracked plaster wall, it's something I love. Someday, I might be motivated to try to sell it."

Joe scanned the room, amazed at all the art work. His eyes traced the quarter inch wide cracks like spider webs in the walls.

"You have big cracks in your walls, Angie. What's the deal? Looks like you had an earthquake."

"Those cracks are the main reason I was able to afford to buy this house, Joe. In 1968 a 5.5 magnitude earthquake shook St. Louis. It was centered south of here at the little town of New Madrid. The quake hit St. Louis hard.

"There's a story about a woman in St. Louis, talking on the phone to her daughter in Indianapolis. The woman told her daughter about the shaking. A minute or two later the daughter, several hundred miles to the east, felt the quake.

"The cracks in the walls came from that quake. That's why I could afford to buy this place."

"I can't believe nobody ever tried to fix those cracks, Angie. I think maybe I could fix them. Do you want me to give it a shot?"

"I don't know. They're kind of like a mole or a birthmark on the cheek of a beautiful woman. The mark makes her a unique individual. It makes her distinct and different from all the other beautiful women in the world. I hardly see the cracks anymore. In a way they make this house special. Let me think about whether I want to fix them or not. What would you do? How would you fill them? Could you make my walls blemish-free?"

"It might not be perfect, but a critic would have to look really close to see where the cracks had been. I'd take an old fashion beer can opener and make a trench behind the crack. Then I'd buy some of that fiberglass or plastic webbing that they use to cover the cracks on sheet rock. As I fill the crack the trench makes the sheet rock cement go behind the good plaster and keeps it from pulling out. The plastic web holds the two pieces together. Another smooth coat over the top and it will be just like new."

"You talk a good game, Joe. Can I hire you for the job?"

"I guess you can't. I'm out of work. I'm living with you for free. I have a driver's license now. My car is registered and insured. I have job applications out. Thanks to Angie Abbey I'm living in a solid house. Life is looking good."

"Moving between states is a big pain, isn't it? Having to get a new driver's license wasn't fun. I can empathize with you, Joe. Until you had an address nothing seemed to work for you."

"It didn't help that I let my license expire. I had to take the written test twice before I passed. I should have studied harder the first time. Failing a driver's test sure makes a guy feel stupid."

"I was a little surprised that you had to take the driving part, Joe. I thought since you had a Minnesota license all you would have to do was pass the written test -- even if your old license was expired.

Angie was asking too many questions. She was making Joe nervous.

"I don't know why, but I wasn't about to argue with the lady. 'Yes, ma'am. No, ma'am. Whatever you say ma'am.'"

LII

Revenge on Mary

"Dean, I love Wyoming."

I relaxed on the sofa, reading a book. Michelle put her arms around me, demanding my attention. I laid the book on the floor, pulling her into my arms. Who was I to refuse the chance to be close to this woman?

Her voice came softly from the middle of my chest. "Did I tell you what a wonderful time I had camping at Vedauwoo Recreation Area last week? Did I tell you how much I loved being able to look out at the Snowy Mountains? Especially, when the binoculars brought the mountains in close. They were spectacular; so much snow. Did I tell you that?"

"I think you might have mentioned something about loving the Snowy Mountains."

"Can we go camping in the Snowy Mountains? Can we go see them up close, Dean?"

"I think so. I think the Snowy Mountain Range is about an hour and a half west of here. Seems like there is a campground pretty close to Medicine Bow Peak. We could go there."

"I'd love hiking mountain trails, learning about the wildlife that lives there. If we hiked in the Snowy's we might see pikas. Do you know pikas, Dean? Have you ever seen a pika?"

"I think I know what they are. They are little rats. I don't think I've seen one."

"They aren't rats, Mr. Swartz. I've been reading about them. Pikas have big ears like little teddy bears and a screeching call. They're like a big mouse. I think they are a really special animal. I read today that they are farmers. They spend the short mountain summer gathering stacks of grass and storing them in rock passages for winter. When the heavy snows come, they have tunnels all through the snow joining their tiny hay stacks. They live in really cold places. They don't really hibernate just spend all winter living on what they stored in the summer. Isn't that cool?"

"That is cool, Michelle. I didn't know that."

"So can we go camping in the Snowy Mountains?"

"Do you want to leave right now?"

"Soon. How about I ask for two days off work and then we go?"

"We just returned. Didn't you like Vedauwoo Recreation Area?"

"It was a fine place. It was kind of cold at night. We should have brought an extra blanket; maybe that wool Navaho blanket you bought for me."

"I thought it was a marvelous place," I commented. "An amazing pile of big rocks and a wonderful pine and aspen forest.'

"I read that the Arapaho Indians called the place *The Land of the Earthborn Spirit*," explained Michelle. "They were right.

I could feel the presence of an amazing spirit living in those big rocks, as alive as you and me."

"What did you think of the climbers?"

"I'd be scared to do that, but it was so much fun watching through the binoculars. I loved looking at their faces as they were stretching to reach for handholds. They were concentrating so hard. Did you see the muscles on some of those guys? Their shoulders and arms looked woven out of straps of strong muscle fiber.

"I'd be scared to death if either of us tried that kind of climbing, but I loved hiking through the forest. All that prairie, dense pine forest, aspen groves surrounding massive rocks sticking up in the middle. The place had so much activity. Mandi liked the trails too."

"She just likes to go anywhere with us," I suggested. "I liked looking at the rocks. My favorites were those big ones that resembled giant toad stools. The pile of rock looked like it was splitting into ten-ton blocks that all fit together like a puzzle."

"I wanted you to know I loved it, Dean. Thank you for taking me there. That doesn't even count the Pasque flowers you found blooming. They were awesome. I thought it was too early to have flowers blooming and those were simply lovely."

"I used to photograph Pasque flowers in Iowa. I marked April 5 on my calendar because I could almost always depend on them to be blooming that week. There was a little patch of them in a goat prairie up in Hardin County. I'd drive up there almost every year in early April. I'd lie on my belly, trying to produce a picture better than what I already had. After a rough winter, I had a passion for seeing lovely spring flowers. And I took some fantastic photos."

"Anyway, thanks, Dean. It was a good time."

"I get a kick out of exploring new country with the woman I love and the dog I love."

Thirty minutes later we were in bed and sound asleep. Then alarm bells were ringing and I was running from the prison fence toward a brushy creek. My feet were flying and my arms pumping. Suddenly, I felt Michelle's hands on my shoulders. "Careful, Dean, you'll hit me. It's the telephone. Somebody wants to talk to the *handyman guy*."

I stuck the phone under the pillow and shook my head. "Sorry, I was dreaming. I was escaping from prison and running for all I was worth. Hope I didn't hurt you."

"I'm ok. Just answer the phone. Probably someone with a job. Our morning nap just became a bit shorter. A nice nap though, I feel better."

"I will too. When I wake up."

I took the phone. "Hello. This is Dean."

The lady had seen my card at the senior citizen center. She had a very dark room and wondered if I could put in a sky light. I didn't think that would be too much of a problem. I told her I could come over right away and look at the room and give her an estimate.

Michelle wanted to walk to the store and pick up a few groceries.

"I'll give you a ride on my way."

"No. It's a nice summer morning. I need the exercise. I'll see you back here in an hour or two."

"You probably won't want Mandi at the grocery store. I'll bring her with me. She can stay in the pickup while I work."

Michelle gathered her groceries and turned her cart up the ice cream aisle. Suddenly, she was staring into the eyes of a face from her past. A guy she had gone out with, sold sex to, and then blackmailed, stood between her and the ice cream. Memory of her work as a stripper in Des Moines was alive and staring back at her.

I should run, she thought. *But my feet are frozen to the floor.* Then he was beside her. His face close to hers.

"Mary?"

She was silent.

"I thought it was you, beautiful. You look just as gorgeous now as you did four years ago, baby. Only now you owe me big time. I lost my wife and kids because of you. I think you're going to pay me back for ruining my life."

"You ruined your own life, mister. You didn't have to take me out. You were a married man. You could have had all you wanted for free."

"My wife was nothing like you, Mary. She hated sex and she was built like a post. I've been thinking about that night with you for three years. I ain't never had nothing that good before or since. Now I walk into a grocery store in Wyoming and here you are, standing right in front of me."

His arm shot out. He grabbed her, moving her along the aisle.

Michelle spoke softly, "Let go of me! Let me go or I'll scream and you'll have more problems."

"No you won't, Mary. I read all about you killing a guard and escaping from a halfway house. You scream for a cop and you'll spend your life in an Iowa prison. I think you are going to entertain me for a while."

They left her grocery cart in the aisle. He slipped his left arm under her right and grabbed her wrist tight. His right hand put her forearm in a vise-grip.

"That hurts! Let me go!"

"Just smile. Smile and keep walking. Keep quiet. You might live to see another day, Mary."

The couple strolled arm and arm to the door. Outside in the warm Wyoming air, he walked her to a red Toyota sports car.

He grabbed both of her wrists, put his knee between her legs, forced it up against the car door.

"Kiss me, bitch."

She turned her head away.

"Fuck you."

"You'll have the chance."

"I'm God-awful pissed off at what you did to me, Mary. Your little blackmail scheme cost me my family and left me with the worst years of my life. For four years, I've hated you.

I can't believe I found you in a grocery store in Cheyenne, Wyoming. I should just put a bullet in you and leave you out by some lonesome ranch road. Nobody would ever find you and nobody would care."

Michelle thought, *Is this the last day of my life? Am I going to die? He is right. I can't scream. To scream and bring the cops means life in prison. Even if I escape, all he has to do is call the cops and they'll be on our tail quick as a flash. This guy is strong. I'm in big trouble. I need Dean.*

He opened the passenger door and shoved her into the front seat.

"I'm Greg, in case you forgot," he told her as he dropped into the driver's seat.

She remembered. *Greg Rogers.* Four years ago, she had taken him for almost two thousand dollars and then his wife had found out anyway. Now she wished she could undo it. She had to figure a way out of this. Escape did not look promising.

Greg reached under the seat grabbing a .38 revolver. He shoved the pistol into Michelle's breast. "This is going to be fun, sweetheart. You and I are going to have a real good time."

He was silent for about three minutes as he pulled out of the parking lot and drove through the streets of Cheyenne. It was quiet in the red car.

Then Greg said, "Maybe I won't kill you. Maybe I'll give you a chance to earn the rest of your life, Mary. I think I'm going to let you practice your profession on me. You entertain me right for a day or two and you might live through this experience, sweetheart."

Five minutes later, he pulled up and parked in front of a small condo.

"Now, Mary, you and I are gonna walk up to the door like we are a couple. I'll unlock the door and you will snuggle up to me and be real sweet. Remember, any trouble and you can talk to the cops. Understand, sweetheart?"

"I understand, bastard."

When they were in the apartment, Greg turned around to face his prisoner.

"Look at my eyes, Mary. Can you tell how angry I am?"

Mary looked at him and was silent.

Out of nowhere, Greg's right hand shot out. The slap was the hardest blow she had ever felt. She fell to the floor. A welt in the shape of his hand rose from her cheek.

"Now can you tell how angry I am?"

Greg grabbed a wrist, jerked her to her feet, and led her into the bedroom.

He opened a drawer, produced a set of handcuffs, and locked one end on her wrist. He pulled her roughly to the bed, locking the other end onto the wooden bed frame.

Michelle sat on the bed. Her arm hurt; the cuffs held her in an uncomfortable position.

The pistol was in Greg's right hand, his left was on his hip. He looked average in height, with strong shoulders and arms, a fat neck and a big belly that told of a hefty appetite for beer, burgers, pasta, and pizza.

"Can I ask you a question?"

"Yah. Sure."

"How did you know I was in Cheyenne?"

"I'd like to say I followed you here, but it was pure luck. My brother lives here. He's a good friend and a contributor to the sheriff. When my wife left me, he found me a job as a dispatcher in the sheriff's office. Ain't I lucky?"

"Does the sheriff know you are such an asshole?"

"You want me to hit you again, don't you?"

Greg reached back his hand as if to hit her. Michelle raised her free hand to stop the blow. His hand ripped down the front of her blouse. Buttons popped like popcorn in a hot skillet.

"You have the nicest tits I ever did see on a real live women, Mary, my love. I've been dreaming of them knockers ever since I first saw you."

Greg grabbed her bra and ripped it off leaving her heavy breasts hanging bare.

"God, you are gorgeous. You just hang on a minute. I need to slip my pants off. You just be patient, sweetheart. I'll be ready shortly."

Greg unbuckled his belt and unbuttoned and unzipped his pants.

"Do you know the penalty for rape in Wyoming, Greg? Think about what your doing."

"I **am** thinking about what I'm doing. Look at me. Isn't it obvious that I'm thinking about what I'm doing. Or what you're doing to me."

"Greg, you don't want to do this. Jail time isn't fun. Trust me on that."

"This is the West, Mary. The penalty for rape here is just a slap on the wrist. Besides, you aren't going to turn me in, are you? You know it means the rest of your life in prison for you if you do. I think you and I will have a good time and then if you're good enough, you'll go on your way and I'll be fine. Don't you worry your sweet little tush about me."

LIII

Russian Roulette

Greg Rogers slipped off his pants and underwear and placed the revolver on the bedside table. He turned toward Michelle to show her his endowment. She moved her knees to her chest and kicked out, connecting with both of her high-heeled cowboy boots. Her left boot caught Greg in the groin and her right heel hit home in his testicles as the toe smashed into his erect penis. Greg went down like a truck had hit him, screaming in pain.

Michelle rolled, reaching over to the bedside table with her left hand, picking up the pistol. She cocked the hammer and pointed the weapon at Greg's body. Her attacker was lying on floor, holding his crotch.

"Now, you son of a bitch. Roll over on your stomach. Either stop crying or keep it under control. As you pointed out, I am wanted for murder. One more won't cause me any additional problems. If you will be so kind as to use your foot to give those pants of yours a little shove toward the bed, I'll use the handcuff key and leave you here. If not, I'll gut shoot you and you'll spend weeks wishing you had behaved yourself and done what I told you."

Greg took a deep breath, stretched out, gently shoving his trousers toward the bed with his foot.

"That's fine. Now, I want you flat on your stomach with your fingers clasped behind your head."

Michelle slipped the gun into her right hand, reaching down with her left to find the key. She unlocked the cuffs from her wrist and the bed.

She opened the closet, taking a long-sleeved shirt to cover her nakedness.

"I really should kill you," Michelle suggested. "You are about the most worthless bastard God has ever created. You must be so disappointing to him. As it is, you might come out of this situation alive. I want you to crawl toward your dining room. Keep your penis on the floor. If I think it's off the floor, I'll put a bullet in your knee. Understand?"

Greg nodded and said a soft, "Yes."

He crawled very slowly into the dining room."

"Now, sit down and wrap your legs around the table legs."

Greg complied and Michelle locked the cuffs on his ankles. There was no way he could unwrap his legs from around the table.

Greg cried out in pain. "Mary, have some mercy. Please. This hurts like hell."

Mary suggested, "The other two choices you have are a bullet in the knee or a bullet in the belly, shithead. What will it be?"

Greg said nothing.

Michelle walked back to the bedroom, opened the cylinder of the revolver. The gun contained only three bullets. She dumped them into a pocket of her jeans.

She took the wallet from Greg's pants and removed five hundred-twenty dollars, a couple of credit cards, a debit card, and his driver's license. She stuffed the wallet back into his pants pocket and put the contents into her jeans along with Greg's car keys. A slip of paper with a bunch of account numbers followed.

In the closet she found a little safe with the key sticking out of the top. Inside, was almost two thousand dollars in cash, which she jammed into her jean pockets.

Dean and I are going to have to leave town again, she thought. *Just as things were going well for us. Moving is expensive so I guess Greg is going to help with moving expenses.*

She walked to the bathroom and took a wash cloth out of a drawer. She ran water on it and lathered it with soap. Every place she had touched, she wiped clean. She had the revolver in her hand as she walked into the dining room. Greg was still lying on the floor crying. She wiped the handcuffs free of her fingerprints.

Greg cried, "It hurts so bad, Mary. Can you at least call a doctor?"

"How about a funeral director, shithead?"

She spun the cylinder. "I want to kill you so you never bother me again, Greg, but I'm going to give you one chance. Your pistol had three bullets in it."

She spun the cylinder again.

"I'm going to give you a chance to live. Three out of six. 50/50."
She spun it one more time.

"If it lands on an empty chamber, you live. If not you die.
Fair enough?"

Michelle aimed the pistol at his head, just above his ear.
She held the gun with both hands.

Greg cried again, "No, Mary. I'm sorry. I'll do anything
you say. I'll give you anything you want. Please don't shoot me.
I don't want to die. There is money in the safe. Take it all. I
know you like nice things. Take my credit cards. You can buy
anything you want. Take my car. It's yours. I'll sign it over to
you. Just don't shoot me."

"Thanks, Greg. You really are a shithead."

She cocked the gun and held it pointed towards his head.
He covered his eyes with his hands and peeked to watch her
squeeze the trigger. He heard the click as the hammer hit the
empty cylinder. Greg burst into tears.

"Goodbye, Greg. If you ever see me in a grocery store
again, go the other way. If I see you first, I'll kill you."

Michelle walked out the front door of the condo, slipped
behind the wheel of Greg's red Toyota and drove home.

She found me waiting and worried.

"Where have you been?" I asked. "I've been so worried
about you. I drove to the grocery store and asked everybody I
could find about you. One of the carry-out boys said he saw a
beautiful woman leave with a tall chubby guy in a red Toyota. I
almost called the police. I didn't know whether to drive around

town looking for a red Toyota or to stay and wait for your call or to call the cops. What happened?"

"Can we talk later?" Michelle suggested. "We need to leave town. The short story is that I ran into a guy in the grocery store who recognized me from before prison. He kidnapped me and tried to rape me. He's tied up in his condo for a while. We need to dump his car and leave town. Can we wipe our prints from this apartment and talk later?"

I said, "Sure. Let's do it."

In an hour we had everything important loaded in the S-10, every surface of the apartment was wiped clean of prints, and we were on our way out of Cheyenne, headed east. We stopped for gas, using Greg Rogers' credit card to pay. We filled our cooler with food and put two hundred dollars on his card for other things we thought we might need, including a selection of flies and fishing lures. I used Greg's driver's license for ID. Then, Michelle stopped at the bank and wrote a check for the balance in her checking account.

The grocery store had an ATM. Michelle used the numbers he had kindly printed on the card in his wallet to take $500 from his bank account.

After wiping Greg's car clean of prints, I drove it to a reservoir east of Cheyenne, locked it, and gave it one more wipe-down. Michelle threw the keys into the water. Then we turned west on I-80 toward Laramie. As I drove, Michelle's story unfolded. I began to realize that mild-mannered Michelle was a mighty mean woman when she was riled up.

"I don't know what came over me, Dean. I was so fuckin' mad at that man. What gave him the idea he could kidnap me, handcuff me, and have his way with me? I should have shot him in the kneecap."

"No, you did just right. You must have scared the crap right out of him."

Michelle chuckled. "As a matter of fact, I think I did. When the gun clicked on the empty cylinder, he crapped all over the carpet and wet himself. The guy will think twice before he tries something like that again."

"No, he'll just try to be more careful next time," I reasoned. "Look out if you ever see him again. He'll devote his time to searching for you. Greg Rogers will try to kill you if he ever finds you again. The man will be trouble."

"You're probably right. He offered me all of the money in his safe not to shoot him. I had already taken about $2500, so I considered it a gift. I figure we have about $11,000 now. And most of it is legal money."

"If you count the last chunk as a gift."

"I do."

"Did you just promise to marry me, Michelle?"

"Any time you produce a legal ID, lover."

"We have to work on that," I answered. "Maybe it will end up to be a *legal-looking* ID. In the meantime I might have enough illegal ID in this wallet to pass for Greg Rogers, if the cops happen to stop us while I am driving. Or is that a real stupid thing to even think about?"

"It better be a real emergency," Michelle argued. "I have a feeling the cops might connect us to Greg Rogers and find out who we really are pretty quickly. We had better keep working at producing a legal driver's license for you. There must be a way."

Michelle reached in her purse and showed me a dark-colored revolver and a box of .38 caliber shells.

"What should we do with this?"

"You should have thrown the damn thing in that reservoir along with Greg's car keys. We don't want anything to do with a gun, Michelle. All it can do is cause us trouble."

"As if we aren't in trouble all ready."

"We should dump it in a deep lake."

"Maybe it will come in handy."

"If the cops find us with a gun," I argued, "we'll have serious problems."

"If the cops find us without a gun, we have serious problems, Dean. I liked the respect I had from Mr. Rogers when I had his gun pointed at him. I don't think I'd ever really use it, but it seemed to demand respect."

"We don't really plan to come in contact with the riffraff of the world," I argued. "We want to find a way to live normal lives and make our past history go away. Agreed?"

"You're right. When we find a nice deep lake, we'll see how fast this piece of steel will sink. In the meantime I'll store it under the seat. Ok?"

"A good plan."

"Speaking of plans, where are we going?"

"This pickup is pointed west. Look at the map and find us a destination."

"Or we can drive west and see where the road takes us. The farther west we go the less chance of running into Iowans."

LIV

Rainbow Trout

Michelle said, "I think I'm calm enough to drive if you want me to, Dean."

"Sure. Let's switch."

I pulled off at an exit. She took my place behind the wheel, driving west on Interstate 80. Mandi sat on the floor taking up most of my foot space. Our goal for the day was to increase the distance between us, Greg Rogers, and law enforcement. I made a list of what we needed.   We stopped and bought a few more groceries in Laramie. We had enough food so that we could spend a couple of weeks in the mountains. We wanted to stay away from people for a while. Our plan was to find a National Forest Service campground and stay put for several days. Later, we could disappear into the wilderness for a week. Avoiding our pursuers was our goal.

"Greg is going to be mighty pissed off when he finds a way to escape from those handcuffs," Michelle advised. "You can bet he'll either be on my tail or else he'll have had some tall tale to tell the law about Mary Swartz and how he became handcuffed around the legs of his table. My guess is that he'll have the cops looking for me as a murderer of a prison guard and for escaping."

We exited the interstate west of Laramie and picked up Highway 130. It was July and one hundred one degrees in the high desert. The Snowy Mountains sounded good. The daytime temperatures there would still be warm and the nights would be very cool.

We passed through the little mountain town of Centennial at about four o'clock in the afternoon. Minutes later, a sign directed us to a National Forest Service campground just west of town. Michelle braked and I said, "Keep going. Let's put another hour behind us before we stop."

A half hour later, we had climbed a thousand feet and driven only about ten miles as we followed a slow-moving semi up a narrow, curving, steep mountain road.

"I've had enough, Dean. I'm really tired." Michelle said. "There's a sign for another campground. Can we take a look?"

"Why not?" I said.

We turned left on a gravel road and wound our way down through lovely mountain country with open pasture mixed with heavily wooded fir and spruce forest. After about fifteen miles, we were wondering if we had made a wrong turn. Then we saw the sign for Nash Fork Campground. We stopped at the entrance, picking up an envelope to pay the $10 camping fee. The sign suggested the little creek offered trout fishing.

"Looks like the perfect spot to me," I said. "I wouldn't mind trying my hand at some trout fishing."

Michelle agreed. "I just want to leave this car, set up camp, and do some walking."

In an hour, we had pitched our tent, spread our foam pads and sleeping bags, and made a plan for dinner. I took a walk in the forest gathering a supply of firewood. Then I used newspaper and some dry twigs to start a fire. While Michelle read about some Colorado wilderness areas, Mandi terrorized the chipmunks, and I mixed up some instant pudding for desert.

"I have a hunger for fresh trout, Michelle. How does that sound to you?"

"I never ate trout, Dean. Can you catch one?"

"Can an eagle fly?"

"You taking Mandi?"

"Better keep her here."

"She won't be happy."

"Then you'll have to entertain her. I'll tie her to the picnic table. The chipmunks can work their revenge."

I strung the fly rod I had bought for $30 at a garage sale in Cheyenne the week before, tied on an eight-foot leader and a #8 hook. Then, I went for a walk in the grass, catching a half dozen grasshoppers that I stuffed into an old sock. Nash Fork Creek had a few deep pools and a number of shallow rapids. I could almost jump across it in places. I approached the stream cautiously to avoid spooking the trout.

Reaching in the sock, I pulled out a juicy grasshopper, hooking it behind the collar. It spit brown tobacco juice on my hand. I flipped the wiggly insect into the shallow riffle at the head of a deep pool. It drifted over the dark water making concentric rings as the insect struggled. The water dimpled and a foot-long rainbow trout swallowed the succulent insect.

My little graphite rod bent almost double as the trout sped round and round in the pool. In a quick run it swam through the riffle, leaping into the pool above. I tried to follow, holding the rod high enough to avoid a big midstream boulder. The trout made a run around the rock, turning back through the riffle into the lower pool. It was the fastest fish I had ever hooked.

Finally, the fish settled into the lower pool and fought like a bulldog until it finally tired, turned on its side, coming to me in the shallow water. The sides of this gorgeous fish had a large pink slash down the middle and the square tail was full of spots. The colors amazed me. How could a fish be so beautiful? Part of me wanted to release it to swim and fight again and another part of me could smell this fish cooking over our fire, tasting its firm flesh. The frying pan won. I gathered some dry moss, slipping the trout and the moss into the canvas, garage sale creel I had bought where I had purchased the fly rod.

In a half hour, I had four beautiful rainbow trout in my bag. I followed the trail back to camp. Michelle was still reading at the picnic table.

"What do you think of my catch, Miss Michelle?"

"They are so pretty, Mr. Dean. How can you kill them?"

"It is a thing people do, Michelle. We catch game and eat it so that we can live."

I used the fillet knife to gut the trout and cut off their heads. I did feel bad about butchering such beautiful creatures. Part of me hated to kill them and another part of me was pleased to be able to put food on our table.

Michelle said, "Dean?"

"Yes?"

"You went fishing again without a license."

"I did, didn't I?"

"Was that smart?"

"It was not at all smart."

"Maybe you shouldn't do that again."

"Maybe you're right. Maybe I should pack away my fishing tackle and we should eat these fish in a hurry."

The fly rod and tackle were soon packed in the bottom of the S-10. I coated the fish with butter and wrapped them in aluminum foil. Michelle had some potatoes baking. Before long we had trout and potatoes on the table. Neither of us hesitated in devouring the tasty meal. I said a little prayer to thank the trout for giving up their lives for us.

"Thank you, all you rainbow trout for giving up your lives so that Michelle and I might be nourished. You battled valiantly. May your souls rest in peace in whatever the hereafter brings to you. Amen."

Native Americans prayed to the spirit of animals they killed. It seemed like a good idea that day on Nash Fork Creek in the Snowy Mountains.

We cleaned up our dinner dishes and I buried the remains of the fish a hundred yards back in the forest. Then I began to work on verifying a strange suspicion.

"Come on, Michelle. I want to take a walk. Join me?"

"Of course, Dean. I have your undivided attention, when we walk together. Besides, I like to hold your hand."

We put Mandi on her leash and the three of us turned east, walking down the gravel road. When we drove to the campground, we came from the west on this road. This evening we walked east, crossing the bridge over Nash Fork Creek. After a half mile, we came to a stop sign and a paved highway. The road sign read, *Highway 130*. About four hours earlier, when we had decided to drive another hour, we had been at this same spot. Michelle had driven up the pavement following the slow-moving semi, turned south on the gravel, and circled back to the campground we had passed on the way up the mountain. In an hour of driving we had made one big loop.

"This is the highway we were on a few hours ago, Dean."

"Yup. I looked at the map a while ago. I suspected it might be the same campground we passed. Kind of funny, huh?"

"We did something wasteful."

"I guess we did, but it gave us a humorous ending to our day."

Back at our camp, I added some wood to our fire, nursing it back to life. Michelle dug out some marshmallows, Hershey bars, and graham crackers, adding another taste treat to the cool evening. She roasted the marshmallows to a gentle tan color and we ate s'mores.

As we crawled into the tent, we were laughing again at our foolish mistake.

"It's kind of like life," Michelle said philosophically. "It is not the ultimate destination that is most important, it's the trip you take in living it."

"I like your attitude, woman. No wonder I love taking this trip through life with you. I can't believe I am such a lucky man."

"You are not lucky. You are just a marvelous man, Dean. I'm the one who is lucky. I'm lucky to be spending my days with you."

"Do you think we'll find a way to live a normal life together someday?" I asked. "How much time will it take before nobody recognizes us and we stop having people come up to us in the grocery store or on a service call and say, 'I know you. You murdered a prison guard. Why aren't you still in jail?'"

"There has to be a place for us. Maybe we just need to keep heading west."

I rubbed my chin. "What if I grow a beard? Would that help me be less recognizable? Would you still love me?"

"I don't think I could love you any more or less if you grew a beard. Your face would be all scratchy and mine would be all bloody. Besides, you wouldn't be nearly as handsome as you look now."

Then she added, "Just joking, Dean. I think you might be real handsome in a beard. I also think it might make you harder to recognize. But, you would have to be really gentle when you make love with me. You can do that, can't you?"

"Just watch me beautiful lady!"

LV

Medicine Bow Mountain

The next morning we found a trail that led up the creek. We took an early morning walk before breakfast. The grasshoppers and dragonflies were wet and cold. Their blood hadn't warmed up yet. Some of them were covered with drops of dew condensed on their wings and antennae in the cold, moist mountain air. Purple larkspur and sunflower-like, arrowleaf balsomroot flowers in the meadow were frosty.

Mist was rising from Nash Fork Creek. Our eyes followed the winding line of the creek by the snake-like fog that hung above it, catching the sun. To the west we caught glimpses of the Snowy Mountains touched by the morning light,. We saw Medicine Bow Peak painted burnt orange by that early morning sun while it was still dark in our valley. It was as if God had poured huge pails of orange paint on the gray mountain, allowing us to watch as it slid slowly down the mountain-side. Gradually, the colors changed until the deep, dark rich gray was the dominant color on the flashes of rock we saw through the trees. A truly awesome sight. We felt the serendipity of the moment surrounding us. Good fortune was ours.

An hour and three miles later, we were back at our picnic table eating French toast and drinking coffee. Mandi was lying near Michelle with orders to leave the critters alone, as a couple of chipmunks were begging at our feet. I had to be careful or one of them would crawl up my pant leg. They seemed to be experienced beggars, expecting handouts, even though park rangers discourage feeding people food to wild animals. We understood the principle. Wildlife needs natural food to over-winter in this country. We tried hard to resist their advances.

Michelle said, "Dean, that dark gray rock above us intrigues me. Is there a trail that we can take to the top? I have never hiked to the top of a mountain. I think it might be fun."

"There was the one in Big Bend. Emory Peak?"

"That was different. We just hiked to the top of Emory Peak. It looks like we'd have to *climb* to Medicine Bow Peak."

"I think it's pretty much a trail," I conjectured. "Shall we try it?"

"Sure."

"If we pull back on this highway and keep going west, the road takes us up to Medicine Bow Pass," I offered. "We should be able to find a trail to Medicine Bow Peak from the pass. Shall we give it a try?"

"Sure. Should we leave our tent here and come back tonight or should we take it with us?"

"Ordinarily, I'd say, 'Leave it here,' but we never seem to be able to tell when we will need to travel fast. Let's pack up."

By late morning we were parked at the trail-head to Medicine Bow Pass. The road crossed the Medicine Bow Mountains at 10,800 feet above sea level. The sign at the trail head told us that Medicine Bow Peak was 12,013 feet in elevation. It also told us that Mandi was welcome, but she must be on leash and under control.

"Mandi'd be under control even if she wasn't on a leash," I said.

"Bring a couple of plastic bags, Dean. I wouldn't want you to be arrested for letting your dog poop on a mountain trail."

"What's the penalty for that?"

"In your case, life in prison."

"We have a huge amount of pressure on us to be good citizens."

""You better believe it, Mister."

We packed a lunch with bottles of water in our day packs and located the trail. It led through an open grassland with scrub pines and then to a mass of scree. The hunks of gray granite made interesting climbing as we jumped from boulder to boulder, making our way up the thousand foot slope. Soon, we were traversing carefully across a snow field, on a well-defined trail along the steep sloping ice. We didn't seem to be in danger of sliding, but still it made us a little nervous. We were glad to reach the solid rock as we approached the ridge. The view was magnificent. I don't think I have ever seen so much of the earth. A sign at the top named some of the peaks we were seeing.

"Look at that mountain far to the south on the horizon," Michelle observed. "I think that's Long's Peak. How far do you think that is from us?"

"I'd guess about seventy or eighty miles. Have you ever seen anything that far away, Michelle?"

"Of course I have, Dean. Look up at the sun. How far is the sun from us?"

"You know what I mean, smarty. I have never looked across the surface of the earth and seen anything so far from me that is on the earth. Many of those peaks that we see are other twelve thousand foot mountains, but Long's Peak is over fourteen thousand feet. There are probably hikers standing on top of Long's Peak, looking at us."

Michelle waved.

"Don't wave," I joked. "We don't want them to know we're here."

We dug in our packs for a granola bar. I sliced an apple and shared it. Food tasted especially good on Medicine Bow Peak.

The trip down was faster. We slid on our butts through much of the snow field. In the talus slopes, we jumped from rock to rock.

"You be careful, Dean. We have no insurance and if you break a leg, how would I haul you down this mountain?

"Besides, what would I tell people at the hospital when they wanted to know who we were?"

I stopped and waited for Michelle.

"You're right, Michelle. It would be stupid to have an accident."

Lack of a driver's license and a Social Security card were always threatening me. This was still the persistent problem I had to solve, before having no identification put me back in jail.

As Michelle caught up with me, we heard a high pitched screeching sound.

"Pika," we both exclaimed.

I looked above us. There were the big round ears of the little rodent sticking out over a rock above us. He puffed his cheeks and let out another of his strange short squeaks.

"I just love those little animals," Michelle smiled. "I keep thinking of them spending the winter here, crawling through all their tunnels in these rocks and stopping at their little hay piles for lunch. All the while the wind is whistling by above the snow. The temperature on the mountain is forty below zero and the little rodents are cozy in their snow tunnel."

We watched him watching us for a couple of minutes. Finally, he tired of us, scrambling into a crevice in the rock scree.

"Look here, Dean," Michelle exclaimed. "Here's a little pile of grass. Do you think this might be one of his haystacks?"

"Looks like it might be."

" These little farmers are incredible!"

"They are amazing," I agreed. "Every creature in this world has figured out its place in the environment. When I was in prison, I read about warblers. When they migrate, they take over different parts of a tree. Each of them specializes in a particular kind of insect or seed or flower. Birders with binoculars look up really high for some species and down in the lower branches for others."

"Maybe we should go back to college and become naturalists," Michelle suggested. "We could learn all about the little critters in the world, learn how to protect them, then share stories about them with other people."

"Or, we can just keep reading, learning all we can on our own," I reflected. "We can certainly do that until we settle down someplace safe."

We climbed carefully down the rest of the talus slope. I still thought that jumping from rock to rock might be the easiest way to travel.

As we neared the bottom, my brain was contemplating where we might be wandering from here.

LVI

Rawah Wilderness Area

We spread our maps on a picnic table and began to make new plans, searching for a place where we could avoid civilization for a while.

"Look at this, Dean. Just south and east of us in Colorado is the Routt National Forest. Right next to it is the Roosevelt National Forest. There is a place called the Rawah Wilderness area right about here." Michelle pointed at a spot just north of Rocky Mountain National Park.

"We could leave our S-10 parked and spend a week hiking in the wilderness area. We won't see anybody all week. We have plenty of dry food that we can cook in a bit of water. Pack light, have a blast, see all kinds of great scenery, stay out of sight of other people. What do you think? Can we go?"

"I think we'd probably run into a hiking club from Cedar Rapids," I laughed. "Let's pack our backpacks, Michelle. I'm ready to hit the trail."

"You can be so funny, in a weird kind of way, Dean Swartz."

We drove back to the east. Just past Centennial was a state highway heading south, eventually into Colorado. We had lunch in the little cowboy town of Walden. An outfitter there sold us a topographic map of the Rawah Wilderness area.

Our intention was to camp at Chamber's Lake, then make an early start into the Wilderness Area the next day, but we drove into a drizzly rain as we rose higher into the mountains. The higher we drove, the harder it rained. Every time we left the car, the chill entered our bodies. We had some pretty good rain gear made of Gore-Tex, but this was one of those days when the cold just permeated through me. We could not stay warm. Neither of us wanted to camp in the rain and be forced to start our hike with a wet tent in our pack.

Michelle asked, "Can we afford to splurge for a motel or a cabin tonight?"

"I was thinking the same thing," I agreed.

Then, we had trouble finding an affordable lodge with a vacancy. We passed a couple of places that looked really expensive and one that had a "No Vacancy" sign out. Finally, we turned into a cabin court that rented log cabins with kitchenettes. We figured we could pay as much as $50 for the night.

I slipped on my rain gear and hurried into the office. The lady who owned the place was Sally. She was really nice. Michelle wanted to see a cabin.

Sally said, "They are open. Go take a look. Number three is empty."

Michelle opened the kitchen cupboards and looked in the oven. She sat on the bed. It was a little soft, but it would do for one night. "This is so quaint, Dean," she declared. "I love it.

Maybe we could just rent it for the summer and live here. How much does it rent for?"

"Would you believe, $35?"

"It costs $20 in many camp grounds, Dean. Pay the money. I'm going to take a hot shower."

After showering, we jogged through the rain to a restaurant across the road and had a decent steak dinner for about ten bucks a piece. We looked around the parking lot and noticed that most of the cars had Colorado plates. We were in lovely mountain country that the natives knew about, but it was a secret to most tourists. We were glad to have found it.

During the night the rain fell steadily. We were cozy and warm in the log cabin and the sound of the rain on the roof made sleeping easy.

We awoke with sunlight streaming in the windows. I looked at my watch. 9:30.

"Wake up sleepyhead," I whispered in Michelle's ear as I kissed her cheek. We were both in an amorous mood and not in too much of a hurry to hit a muddy trail.

An hour later we were having pancakes and omelets with fresh fruit in the restaurant. The waitress gave us a rag to wipe off a table and two chairs. We ate outside on their patio, with our dog. Mandi looked so hungrily at everyone's food, that people gave her plenty of scraps. I don't think it was possible to fill her up. It was after noon before we found the trailhead and hefted our packs.

Serious backpackers have packs that are fitted to their bodies. Padded belt straps customize them to ride on just the right spot on their hips. Our packs were bought at garage sales.

Mine was a pretty fair pack, except it was rather old and beat up. The belt had some padding and the pack had several pockets to separate the stuff I carried.

Michelle's pack was a piece of junk. I think it was a K-Mart Special. We made sure that we loaded her light. She carried a one burner camp stove we had bought in a sports store and a couple of bottles of propane fuel. I had two more fuel bottles in my pack. We each carried a gallon milk jug full of water. Someday, if we decided we really liked wilderness camping, we wanted to buy a water purification system. Our backpacking tent came from The Ranger. It was tied on low, above my sleeping bag. Michelle's sleeping bag rode low on her pack.

She packed a big plastic bag of gorp -- raisins, peanuts, and M & M's -- in an outside pocket of her bag. Our food was divided pretty evenly. Serious backpackers had all sorts of dry and even freeze-dried foods. Ours, pretty much came from the grocery store.

I carried a cheap aluminum skillet, a couple of nested aluminum sauce pans, two spoons, two knives, two salad forks, a tablespoon, two metal plates, and two glass cups. I hated drinking coffee out of tin or plastic cups. A tiny plastic shampoo bottle full of dish soap, a dish cloth, and a dish towel rode in an outside pocket of my pack. Each of us had a tooth brush. Genuine backpackers cut off the handles to make them lighter. I filled a pocket of my pack with a cheap pair of good quality, light-weight Chinese-made binoculars that I had found on sale in a Cheyenne camera store for $30.

We figured that Michelle's pack weighed about 40 pounds and mine about 60. Our food supply was supposed to last us five days; we planned to be back in four.

The trail head had an altitude of around ten thousand feet. Blue Lake was a short hike up the trail. The rules of the wilderness area stipulated that no camping was allowed close to a lake, a stream, or a trail. We figured an hour's hike would put us at a camping spot somewhere near Blue Lake. We would have the rest of the afternoon to explore.

Cheyenne's elevation was over 6000 feet. Michelle and I thought we were acclimatized to the high altitude, but before we had walked very far, our bodies began screaming for oxygen. After two hours of hiking, we saw no sign of a lake. The trail just went up and up and up some more.

"Dean, I thought ... I was in pretty good shape," Michelle gasped. "I can't seem ... to breathe in enough air."

"I'm having an awful time, Michelle." I was almost breathing too hard to talk. I leaned my backpack against a pine tree, breathed deeply, and tried again. "We have hiked in the mountains almost every weekend all summer long. There must be a huge difference between the amount of oxygen in the air at 6000 feet and 11000 feet."

"Remember the sign we saw back toward the trailhead?"

"I do. The sign said, 'Blue Lake, 3.5 miles.' Someone carved a 1 in front of the 3. So now, it read, 'Blue Lake 13.5 miles.'"

"The carved-out version seems more like it," I said. "Is 13.5 miles the real distance?"

"It probably makes some difference that we are carrying fifty pound packs on our backs," Michelle reasoned. "Our hikes in Wyoming were day hikes. All we carried was water and a lunch."

We had been taking many short breaks. Wherever we found a convenient tree, we leaned back, stopping a minute to breathe. Then we walked a hundred yards and leaned against another tree, trying to inhale enough oxygen to continue. Every half hour we took off the packs, found a rock to sit on as we drank water and ate gorp to hydrate and replenish our energy.

Suddenly, the character of the trail changed. We entered a dense old-growth forest, following a wet trail along a creek. The air smelled invigorating and cleaner. Maybe it was just the dampness of the air coming off the stream. Wildflowers bloomed, fresh and lovely in the lush habitat.

"This must be the creek that leads from Blue Lake," I surmised. "The walking is easier. The ground is nearly level."

"This is almost fun," Michelle agreed. "I love the wildflowers. Look at these little flowers, Dean. The petals look like little pink elephants. Guess what their name is."

"No clue. I'll bet you can tell me."

"E*lephant heads*," Michelle explained. "I read about them a couple of weeks ago. July is supposed to be the best month for Colorado wildflowers. In a way, I'm glad Greg Rogers chased us out of Cheyenne. I really wanted to hike in the mountains. Now we have a chance to look at wildflowers. I wish I was a photographer with a good camera and a close-up lens. I'd love to make pictures of some of these mountain wildflowers. They are absolutely gorgeous."

"They wouldn't work in our house, Michelle. They really are beautiful, but their beauty would pale compared to you."

"You are so full of bullshit. I still love you, though. Let's put these packs on our backs again and see if we can find Blue Lake."

The trail took us on another steep climb with a couple of switchbacks. Then it leveled out, opening up to overlook a deep blue lake in a pocket surrounded by green meadows, random gray boulders, and high mountains.

Michelle put her arm around me. "Blue Lake is so pretty, Dean. Can we camp here for four days?"

"We can do anything we want to do, Michelle. It looks to me like the only flat place to camp is down there below the lake."

We bushwhacked down the steep bank. In an hour our tent graced a level spot in a meadow below the lake. Michelle put together aluminum foil dinners of hamburger patties, slices of potatoes, carrots, onions, and a fair amount of catsup. I hiked back down the creek to collect dry wood. We had our camp stove, but the dinners needed a campfire and a bed of coals.

By the time Michelle pulled our meals out of the fire, I was dozing off. We finished dinner and while Michelle cleaned up I filled her backpack with our food and threw a rope over a tall tree limb. I pulled the pack ten feet in the air to keep it out of reach of bears. We also made certain that we had no food in our tent. We didn't want a hungry bear breaking into our tent trying find a cheap meal.

I lay down to read. Before I had finished a page, I was asleep. Michelle struggled to remove my clothes, helping me into a pair of sweats and my sleeping bag.

"You have to be tired, too, Michelle."

"Just slide your butt into bed, Dean. Sleep, so you can protect me from the bears. We'll talk tomorrow."

Before dawn, I slipped out of the tent to mix up eggs and milk for French toast. I fried some link sausages finishing by sautéing them in a bit of orange juice and honey.

"There is the most wonderful smell drifting into my bedroom," said a voice from the tent.

I slipped the sausages onto a tin plate, covering them with a paper towel; setting a pot of coffee on the burner.

Stabbing one of the sausages on a fork, I handed it through the tent flap to my companion.

"I am amazed, every time I see you in the morning, Michelle. How can you be so beautiful, the moment you wake up?"

She ate her sausage and kissed me. "You say all the right things, and you cook food that is out of this world, Dean. How did you make plain old sausages taste like honey from the Gods?"

"It's an old family recipe that I promised never to reveal to anyone, except my wife. Marry me and I'll give you the secret, woman."

LVII

The Murder of Our Dog

After finishing our French toast and another cup of coffee, we loaded our belt packs with fruit and granola bars, setting out for the mountains. As we circled the lake, our trail was blocked by a drift of snow from Hanging Lake above us to Blue Lake below. Looking through my binoculars, I saw a wild mountain stream emptying into Blue Lake from the bottom of the long narrow glacier. In the middle, about halfway down I spotted an opening. Michelle, Mandi, and I hiked to that upper opening. Peeking inside was spooky, but when we looked down we saw the stream dumping into Blue Lake below us. Michelle and I summoned our courage, zipped our jackets, ducked into the opening, and walked down the icy stream through the magnificent snow tunnel.

The cylinder surrounded us with solid, dripping ice. The ceiling was low. I walked hunched over to avoid scraping the top of my head on wet ice. The place was scary and exhilarating. On the warm July day, standing in the snow tunnel was like being in a defrosting freezer. Drops of water showered our faces. We were glad for our Gore-Tex windbreakers.

When we reached the bottom, Michelle was shivering. All three of us were soaked and laughing when we reached the bottom, emerging from the tunnel at the lake shore with wet feet, feeling pleased with our bravery, proud that we'd made it through the spooky ice tunnel. All of us celebrated warm sunshine and mellow mountain air. We found a grassy spot nearby and sat on a couple of big hunks of granite to share a granola bar three ways.

Our peace was fractured by the blast of a rifle echoing across the lake. The splat of a bullet hitting the ice tunnel behind Michelle's head caught our attention. A yell from above helped us locate the shooter, a guy in jeans and a plaid hunting jacket, holding a rifle.

"Mary, you've pissed me off the last times we was together," screamed Greg Rogers. "I'm through fooling around with you, sweetheart. You and your new boy friend are going to die."

"How in hell did you find us up here, Greg Rogers?" Michelle yelled back.

For a moment I was confused. *Who was this guy threatening our lives?* Then, it clicked. *This is the dude who tried to rape Michelle in Cheyenne.*

I reached for her hand. *I hope Michelle doesn't feel the shake,* I thought. *I'm scared. We could die out here on this mountain.*

Michelle and I backed down the slope, a step or two toward the snow tunnel.

"It wasn't easy, sweetheart. I found out you were with a guy who drove a blue S-10. Just made some big circles around Cheyenne. I almost lost hope that you'd be so stupid as to stay around. Then, yesterday I found your pickup.

"Last night, I slept in my car. You were nice enough to leave it in a spot where the cops found it and came looking for me at my Condo. I didn't tell them about you -- just blamed my embarrassing condition on burglars."

I whispered to Michelle, "Keep moving toward the tunnel. We're going to make a run for it. Be ready."

Greg continued his bragging. "You are so God damn dumb. Why would you stick around this country? Why didn't you kill me when you had a chance?"

Michelle answered, "I didn't think you would be dumb enough to cause us more trouble after you looked so stupid the last time we met, Greg."

"Who's dumb, Mary? You're the ones who are about to be filled full of lead and spend eternity at the bottom of this lovely little lake."

I yelled up at Greg, "Are you going to shoot those back-packers on the trail behind you too?"

The hefty man glanced behind him and we ran for the ice tunnel. As Greg looked back at us and saw us running down the steep slope, he raised his rifle to his shoulder. We were moving and he wasn't a great marksman. His first shot missed. Then we were in the tunnel. We heard another dull thud and a whine from Mandi. We saw the big black retriever drop in the mouth of the snow tunnel. I reached down and pulled her limp body inside, into the cold stream of water. The exit wound in her chest was massive. Life had left our lively, loyal friend.

Michelle screamed, "Mandi!"

I was mad. I had never been so angry. "That bastard will pay," I told her. "Come on! Right now we have to move, or we're dead too."

I peeked out to see what Greg was going to do. He was running down the steep incline toward the entrance at the bottom.

"Let's go for the top."

I grabbed Michelle's hand. We ran up the slippery, wet, rocky stream bed. Half way up, we fell and continued our scramble on hands and knees. By the time we were 3/4 of the way up, Greg was at the bottom. He fired again. Water and chips of ice showered us. Another shot splashed in the creek behind us. Then, we were at the upper entrance of the tunnel and out.

"Now what?" I asked. "Do we spend all day running, until he hits a lucky shot?"

Michelle unzipped her belt pack and pulled out Greg's .38 revolver.

"Here. I brought this along in case we had a bear in camp."

"This won't do much against a bear and I told you to throw it in a lake."

"It might stop Greg if he's close."

We stepped to the downhill side of the opening and waited for Greg. Soon, he came out of the entrance. His first glance was up the hill.

I yelled, "Freeze or you're dead."

Greg stopped and slowly looked back over his shoulder. He saw the pistol aimed at his chest. I could almost hear his brain calculating his chances of shooting me before he died.

"Just drop the rifle, Greg. You might live to see another day."

He hesitated, then threw the rifle in the snow.

"Now, take off your belt, and throw it in the grass."

He did.

"Lie down and put your hands behind you."

I handed Michelle the pistol and used Greg's belt to tie his hands securely behind him. Then, I grabbed the index finger of his right hand and bent it back to his wrist.

Greg's screams echoed through the empty wilderness as the pain of his suddenly broken finger filled his body.

When his screams died I told him, "That's for shooting our dog. Was she a problem for you?"

"My finger hurts like hell. I ain't never had pain like that before. Why did you break my finger, you son-of-a-bitch?"

I kicked him in the ribs. "Answer my question or I'll break another one. Why did you shoot our dog?"

"I figured it would make you feel bad."

I pushed his face into the wet snow, took the pistol from Michelle, and cracked his left hand, hard, with the revolver. More broken bones.

Three minutes later, when he stopped screaming and whimpering, he asked, "Why did you do that?"

"I figured it would make you feel bad. Isn't that why **you** do things?"

"Give me the gun," demanded Michelle. "I'm going to kill the bastard."

Greg turned his face toward us and watched me hand the revolver to Michelle. Icy snow was dripping off his three day beard.

"Please!"

Michelle pointed the gun at Greg's back and cocked the hammer.

"Nooo!" he screamed as he closed his eyes.

I gently pushed the gun to the side as she squeezed the trigger. The gun barked and a bullet made a dull thud into the snow above Greg's head.

The chubby, would-be assassin began to sob again.

"Please! Anything!"

"Mary and I are real tired of you messing with our lives," I told him. "We loved the dog; you shot her out of pure meanness. The logical revenge for that shot is your death, Greg. Can you think of anything else? What would you do if you were in our shoes?"

Silence.

"Greg?"

"I'd probably kill you."

"We can do that. It would be easy for us to kill you right now. Without lying to us, can you think of something we can do to convince you to go home and leave us alone?"

Silence.

"Greg? Any ideas?"

"Let me live. I promise to God I'll leave you alone. I promise. I want to live."

"And what's your story to the cops?"

"I'll tell them I fell and broke my hands."

"Won't work. They're going to find you with your hands tied behind you with your belt and your feet handcuffed together again. What are you going to tell the cops?"

Silence again.

"Greg?"

"I'm thinking. ... I'll tell them I was robbed."

"And the perpetrators?"

"Two big black guys."

"Bad story. It's racist. You need to move beyond racism, Greg. How about a five foot tall, slender blond, who you never saw before. You tried to rape her and she grabbed your gun, tied you up, and broke your bones. How's that for a story? Better yet, make her a brunette. And she was driving a red mustang convertible with Nebraska license plates. Can you tell that story to the cops, Greg?"

"I can. I will."

Michelle said, "I want to kill him. He murdered Mandi and he tried to rape me."

I said, "Ok, Greg. Mary wants to kill you. I want to punish you and receive a sincere promise to leave us alone. One more bit of punishment."

"Please, don't break any more bones, mister. My hands hurt so bad."

"The promise."

"I promise to leave you alone. If I see either of you accidentally, I'll go the other way; pretend I don't know you."

"And your story."

"I'll tell the cops I tried to rape this brunette and she took my gun and broke my fingers."

Michelle looked at me. "What about his rifle?" she asked. "I think it is a bad thing for us to have around."

"It might be useful for some target practice," I suggested. "I think either one of us can shoot better than *Asshole*, here. Let's go over on the other side of the lake and do some shooting. I think I can hit him from a couple of hundred yards away with this fine weapon."

"Maybe we should check his pockets first," Michelle suggested. "Let's see what he's carrying with him this time. He gave me a bunch of his money last week. Do you suppose he found a new supply?"

Michelle emptied his pockets and found a set of car keys, a box of rifle shells, a wallet with a new driver's license, a credit card, and about twelve hundred in cash.

"You can have it," Greg offered. "Just don't start shooting at me. I don't want to die. You just leave. I'll wait till you're gone and you won't ever have to worry none about me again."

I let the silence ride for two minutes.

"Ok, Greg. Your last punishment. For the dog."

I reached into his back pocket and pulled out the handcuffs I had felt there. I cuffed his feet together.

Pointing up to the west," I asked, "See that mountain above you?"

Greg looked up.

"Yah."

"There is a lovely view from the top. After you climb up to the peak and look it over, you can walk back down. Then you're free to go back to Iowa or Cheyenne or wherever you want to go. Just don't go north. We're thinking about going toward Canada and we don't want to have to kill you."

"Alright."

"One other thing, asshole."

"Yes?"

"If we find out that you tell the cops a thing about us, then one or both of us are going to find you and you will die a very slow, painful death, Greg. Understand?"

No response.

I kicked him in the stomach.

"Understand, asshole."

"I understand."

"Get the hell out of here, Greg Rogers."

"I can't do that, mister. I can barely walk with these handcuffs on my legs. Please."

"Go, Greg. Don't turn around. Don't look back until you're at the top. Another word and Mary will put six shells in your pistol and play another game of Russian Roulette with you."

Greg looked up at the mountain and frowned. I saw a flash of happiness that he wasn't going to die today, followed by a look of raw hate. This was the third time Greg Rogers had been embarrassed by Michelle or me. He would never ever forget. He turned and started to shuffle slowly up the mountain.

"Greg."

He turned.

"If I ever see you, it will be the worst day of your life, mister."

When he was a couple of hundred yards away I said, "Shall we go?"

"Can I cry for Mandi first?"

Michelle sat on the wet grass beside our big black Labrador retriever and ran her fingers through her hair. Then she smoothed it down and caressed the long black ears. She stood, hugging me close, sobbing on my shoulder.

"Why did he have to shoot Mandi?"

"He's evil, Michelle. He's the kind of a man to avoid. Let's take care of our dog. We'll find a spot away from the lake and the trail; bury her and cover her with a big pile of rocks."

Michelle reached into her pocket; handed me a gas receipt she had taken from Greg's wallet. On the back was scrawled, *Mary* and underneath was our license number from the pickup. Our eyes met.

"I wonder how good his memory is," I whispered to Michelle as I wadded the paper in a ball and stuffed it into my pocket.

"We may have to do something about our blue S-10. Maybe we need a new image, Michelle."

Mandi was lying in the icy water of the creek. I picked up her wet body and threw her over my shoulders in a fireman's carry. I carried her up the slope to a big pile of rocks. We moved enough to make an empty spot and laid our big Lab inside. Then we gathered more rocks and covered her up several feet deep.

We walked back to camp hand in hand. There, we stuffed our camping gear into our packs and hiked back to Blue Lake.

I looked at Greg again through our binoculars. He was a tiny figure, high above us, moving higher.

I emptied the .308 Winchester and tossed the shells in Blue Lake. We watched as they danced their way out of sight in the clear water.

"I really like this rifle, Michelle. I've always wanted a nice gun like this."

I grabbed the barrel and swung hard. The rifle made a graceful pattern as it circled through the thin air, landing with a gentle splash far out in the blue water.

I told Michelle, "I really wouldn't feel good using a gun that belonged to Greg Rogers."

"Maybe someday when we settle down and have a place of our own, I can buy you a rifle; you can do some hunting."

The last time we saw Greg Rogers, he was high above us on the mountain, as we were walking down the trail toward our blue pickup.

Two hours later we were at the parking lot. We quickly packed our gear in the S-10.

"I'll drive his car, Michelle. Follow me. We'll leave it just off the road someplace."

I took a pair of gloves out of my pack. *No use leaving finger prints in his car,* I thought. Sliding into his driver's seat, I glanced at the passenger's seat. There was a 4x6 photo. It was a selfie Michelle had taken of herself and me and Mandi and our blue Chevy S-10 pickup. On the back our license number was scrawled in an uneven script. I put the photo in my coat pocket, closed my eyes, and sat for two minutes.

Backing onto the road, I turned east, toward Fort Collins. After five miles I turned south on a forest service black-top, driving five miles into the mountains. I parked Greg's red Toyota at a trailhead, in the back of a National Forest Service campground. I opened the hood and switched a couple of spark plug wires. Then I thought of Mandi. My Swiss Army Knife was suddenly in my hand and my body was prone on the front seat. The knife sliced through all the wires I could reach under the dash. I slipped back into the S-10, closing the door gently.

I sat down beside Michelle. She drove back to the highway. I flipped his keys into the rocky ditch. Michelle pointed the pickup back up the Poudre River Canyon toward the west and the pass.

Just before we stopped at the little town of Gould, I asked Michelle to stop at the Moose Visitor Center.

"Dean, we don't have time to stop and be tourists. We need to travel."

"Just stop. Please. We need to talk for a minute."

"What?"

"I found this on the seat of Greg Roger's car."

I handed her the picture.

"My God! I forgot about this. He must have taken it out of my bag or my pocket. I never even looked for it."

"All he had to do was check out motels or restaurants. He could show them our picture and the picture of our pickup."

"'I'm looking for my sister. We were supposed to meet out here and missed connection.' That'd work. I'm so sorry, Dean."

"One little mistake. We covered our tracks really well except for this damn picture."

"I'm sorry."

"I know you are. I'm not blaming you. Now we know how he found us. Will he remember our license number?"

"Maybe we should sell our Chevy."

"Maybe we better go to Utah first. Our trail will be tougher for him without the photo. We might still be in good shape, if his memory isn't fantastic."

It was midnight when we drove down a remote backcountry road in the Grand Mesa National Forest, northwest of Black Canyon of the Gunnison National Park. Pulling into Jumbo Campground, we found an empty campsite and set up the tent by car lights. I spread our foam pads and sleeping bags. Michelle fixed a couple of cheese sandwiches; we split an orange and a soda. Ten minutes later we were asleep.

LVIII

Louisiana Living - Jonathan and Nora

Jonathan Wilson couldn't believe his good fortune. He had driven homeless, friendless, and jobless into the South Louisiana town of Houma. Two weeks later, he had an apartment, two jobs, a bank account, and the best two friends he had had since before prison. Randy and Owen, his two bosses were both younger than he was. Both men trusted him and treated him more like a friend than an employee. Except for Frank, the foreman, the carpenters at ARC were all at least ten years younger. They were easy going and seemed to never take things too seriously, but the jobs always got finished. Randy started the third week by giving Jonathan a fifty cent raise.

"Y'all deserve it, man. You work well with all the guys and you figure out ways to solve any carpentry problem we face. I'm just happy as a tick on a dog's ear to have you working for me, Jonathan. Besides Nora seems easier to get along with since you been here. I don't think she knew you too well when she sent you to me, but she picked you as a winner right away -- for both of us."

Jonathan's relationship with Nora had been good for both of them. They spent most of their free time, as well as working time, together. She was serving as his tour guide and was introducing Jonathan to springtime in the Swamp Country of Louisiana.

Saturday afternoon after his third week, he and Nora were sitting beside the canal on a park bench.

"Do you like to fish, Jonathan?" she asked.

"I love to fish. As a youngster, my family fished and in high school, my brother, Stan and I had traveled with our parents on regular fishing trips to the lake country of northern Minnesota.

"As a child and a young adult, Stan and I spent much of our spare time fishing. I remember getting together with a couple of buddies on warm summer day. The four of us pooled our money to fill the gas tank of my old Chevy. We bought three dozen day-old bismarcks and donuts. We drove to a lake that had a reputation for great crappie fishing. At a little stream along the way, we stopped and seined a pail of minnows. Seining minnows was an important part of our fun.

"We must have caught a hundred crappies that day. They weren't very big, but they bit fast. After awhile, I tied a streamer fly on my leader and caught dozens of crappies without minnows. The fish were pretty small. We released all of them. Ate all the pastries though. We were so sick that we had to stop about every five miles on the way home."

Nora said, "Randy has a canoe and he'll let us use your company pickup to haul it. There's a lake a few miles west of town, in the Mandalay National Wildlife Refuge. We could take Randy's canoe and go fishing for a day. There are really big pan fish in Lake Hatch and the large-mouthed bass will make Missouri's biggest bass look like babies."

"Sounds good to me. When do you want to go?"

"Do you have a fish pole, Jonathan?"

"No. That's something I haven't bought yet. I guess I'll have to go shopping. I'll buy a rod and some basic tackle."

Sunday morning, the sun was painting the clouds red, orange, and gray as Jonathan and Nora turned off Highway 27, parking in the lot beside Lake Hatch. They carried the fifteen-foot red plastic Coleman canoe to the water, returning for Jonathan's new ultra-light spinning rod. He had filled the reel with four pound test line, tying on a yellow and black Beetle-Spin with his first fisherman's knot in twelve years. His hands remembered the motions as he cinched the knot tight on the little rubber grub and spinner.

"Y'all are in trouble, Jonathan."

"Why? What's wrong?"

"You ain't gonna be able to handle a big Louisiana sunfish with that little rod and that tiny little lure. And if you hook one of the big bass in this lake, they'll tear that little rod of yours apart and break that line faster'n a gator can eat a swimming beagle pup. You should've bought a rod with some backbone an' at least a twelve pound test line. I love you sweet-heart, but you ain't too bright when it comes to fishing in Louisiana, honey."

"You're probably right, Nora, but I bought it. I guess I'll give it a whirl."

Jonathan sat in the stern, steering the canoe a half a mile to the south. The canal opened into a beautiful lake. Nora tied on a small hook. With her teeth, she squeezed a split shot onto her line a foot above the hook. She snapped a long, thin bobber about four feet from the hook. Baiting the outfit with a big juicy nightcrawler, she made a perfect cast, the bobber settling just outside a patch of lily pads.

For two hours it made no difference what they used. Nora's bobber didn't move and Jonathan didn't have a strike as he cast the weed edges with his lure, letting it settle, making steady retrieves.

Suddenly, Jonathan felt resistance. He gave a jerk, feeling the hook bite into something solid.

"Snag," he announced.

He jerked the rod a few times, feeling the snag begin to move. The fish yanked its head from side to side, fighting the pressure of the little rod, then making a run toward the middle of the lake. The drag on the little reel screamed as it gave line to the big fish. Luckily, the fish had moved the fight to the deep water, instead of the brush-filled water near shore.

Twenty minutes later, Jonathan grabbed the lower lip of the huge bass, lifting it into the canoe. He held it up with both hands as Nora took pictures with her cell phone.

"You and your dinky little rod caught our dinner for tonight, Mister Jonathan. You are really pretty amazing at this game. I didn't think you had a prayer of landing that bass."

"I was very lucky, Nora. If that largemouth had headed for the brush, there was no way I could have stopped him. When he decided to head for deep water, I knew I had a fighting chance. You're right, though, I need a rod with a bit more heft and a line that is three times as strong if I'm going to fish for bass that size. How much do you think he weighs?"

"I've seen plenty of ten pound bass caught out of here. This one is much bigger than a ten pounder. Maybe, ... , thirteen pounds. Maybe even fifteen. Put some water in that plastic pail. We'll keep the fish in it. It should stay alive for an hour or so. You hooked it in the lip so it's not hurt bad, just worn to a frazzle."

An hour later they paddled back to the landing, where they loaded the gear on the truck.

Nora wasn't just a fisherwoman; she could cook too. She added Cajun seasoning to a breading. Then she fried the bass fillets to a golden brown. Jonathan judged the fish to be the best he had ever eaten.

"Purely delicious," he exclaimed. "You're a multi-talented woman, Nora."

Jonathan's mind bounced up and down like a yo-yo. At the top, his life was spinning with pictures of the perfect day of fishing, paddling, and companionship. He was playing mental images of easy times with Nora. Being with her was a delightful highlight every day. The bottom of the yo-yo of his life spun with reflections of the lies he was living. He thought of the trust Nora and his two bosses placed in him. What would happen if any one of them learned his real history? Like his wallet and his pocket knife, a constant fear hid within him that a law enforcement officer might identify him as an escaped prisoner and murderer. He tried to keep the spinning disk near the top, keeping his attitude upbeat. With Nora, that wasn't hard.

LIX

Utah and a New Identity

I was warm. No, I was hot. Michelle had rolled over half on top of me. One of my feet was outside my bag. The foot outside my sleeping bag was my built in temperature control system.

The sun was already above the mountains. It filled the tent with light and heat. I rolled Michelle gently off me and lightly kissed her on the forehead. She smiled. Her eyes did not open.

Slipping out of my bag and into my shorts, I unzipped the door of the tent. It seemed like a day for a simple breakfast. I found a couple of envelopes of instant oatmeal and lit the gas stove. I set a pot of coffee on one burner and a covered pan of water for the oatmeal and dishwashing on the other.

The aroma of the coffee must have drifted into the tent. I heard a stirring; before long a disheveled looking woman crawled out of the tent.

"God, you look beautiful in the morning." I leaned down, kissed her and pulling her to her feet as I stood straight again.

"Want some coffee?"

"Absolutely! What wonderful culinary delight are you mixing up for me this morning."

"It's called 'fruit of the oat.' You have a choice between 'Maple and Brown Sugar' or 'Apples and Cinnamon.'"

Michelle said, "Either one would be great, Dean."

I pulled a packet from the box, poured it in a cup, adding boiling water. Then I fixed one for myself and poured two cups of coffee. It wasn't much, but it started our day.

We washed the cups and spoons, packed up, and hit the road. Michelle drove.

We were on an old, beaten up blacktop road with sharp corners and steep drops that made me nervous. We hit a construction area and the road suddenly turned into gravel. Michelle rounded a curve too fast and the S-10 skidded. Suddenly, we were out of control and sliding sideways. I reached for the steering wheel to help her control the skid. I resisted the impulse, instead I shouted, "Turn into the skid, Michelle. And for God's sake, slow down."

Michelle was a good driver. She had already pulled us out of the skid by the time the words were out of my mouth. She had turned into the skid and accelerated. We were back under control. Then she did slow down.

"Sorry, Dean. I was going too fast. Guess we aren't in a hurry, are we?"

"I'd agree to that. You're a great driver, Michelle. I'm just not a good passenger on this kind of a road. I'm awfully nervous sitting in the passenger seat when we have a hundred foot drop on my side. It doesn't matter who is driving. I really don't like high places in a car."

The mountain face on our left, looked solid. I couldn't see the top. On the right, the precipitous drop looked daunting. I was glad that Michelle had slowed down.

It helped when I decided to focus on the scenery instead of the road. Snow-capped, mountain-filled vistas opened to us as we rounded corners. The views were breath-taking. Below us a mountain stream roared down the canyon. I was watching fast water boiling over hunks of red rock when a flash of baby blue caught my eye.

"Michelle! Pull over when you find a wide spot. I saw something strange. I want another look."

"What?"

"Don't know," I said. "Something in those trees back there at the bottom of the canyon was a bright blue -- not a natural color."

Michelle found a wide spot on a straight section of road. We parked and walked back up the road to the curve.

"There," I said, pointing to the bottom of the canyon. "I think it's a car. See those skid marks on the gravel? It came around that curve too fast and lost it. Let's go down and take a look. I don't think it happened too long ago."

Our trip down the steep slope was not easy, but twenty minutes later we were approaching the smashed car. The Ford was a mess. We could hardly tell it was a car. It's trunk was buried in the stream. It was still a bright blue. The hood was out of the water. The front half of the car was charred badly. All the blue paint was burned off the front half. The hood was a dull white, as if it had been dusted lightly with white spray paint. The back half of the Ford was sitting in the creek. It was still baby-blue. The driver was pretty much unidentifiable.

"What's the smell?" asked Michelle. "It smells like grilled meat."

As we approached the car, the driver came into our view. Since the car was lower in the back, the man's body was leaning back against the seat. The driver was still buckled into his seat belt. He was badly burned; hardly recognizable as a man.

"My guess is he never felt the fire," I said. "I think he was very dead by the time the car stopped rolling down the mountain."

Michelle put her head on my shoulder, closing her eyes. She said, "This is awful, Dean. There's nothing we can do here. Let's climb back to the road and find a pay phone. We should call the cops."

I held up my hand. "Just a minute, Michelle. Take a look at this guy. It could be me. How tall is he? Just a little heavier, maybe."

"Dean!"

"Seriously, look at him. Let me see if I can find some ID."

I reached through the shattered window. Reaching around the burned body to his right rear pocket, finding his wallet. It was singed, but still together. The wallet tore as I opened it, but his body and the seat had protected the contents. The dead guy was Alan Sibley. His address was an apartment in Salt

Lake City. From his Utah driver's license, I learned that Alan was forty-one years old, divorced, six foot two inches tall, had brown hair and weighed 230 pounds.

I read the information to Michelle.

"If I were a bit heavier, this could be me," I repeated to Michelle.

In the wallet I found a Social Security card, a Visa card, and twenty-two dollars in cash.

In the glove compartment was a scorched registration card for a blue, 1989 Ford.

"Dean, are you thinking what I think you're thinking?"

I nodded. "I think you can call me Alan Sibley, sweetheart. Can you learn to love a new man?"

She smiled. "I can love you with any name you take, Mr. Alan Sibley."

I took out my wallet and emptied the things I wanted to keep. I left my expired Iowa driver's license, and twelve dollars in cash. Then, I threw my wallet in a puddle on the floor of the back seat. I pulled the key ring from the ignition, pocketing all the keys, but the one that went to the car.

Pointing at Alan Sibley's hands, I commented, "Nobody's going to take any finger prints off this guy. I think the Iowa cops are about to close the case against Paul Hartman, escaped prisoner and cop killer."

"Let's leave this place, Dean, ... , er, Alan," said Michelle. "A car driving down this lonely road right now would spoil everything. Besides, I don't like being around death."

"One minute, Michelle." I fingered the key and ran my hands over the steering wheel. A good cop might find Paul

Hartman's finger prints and his wallet in the blue Ford and, just maybe, have more evidence that the dead guy was me.

We climbed back up the bank and drove to a little country store. They had a pay phone outside. I called 911. It connected me to the Mesa County Sheriff's Office in Grand Junction. I explained that I'd had my 89 Ford stolen while I was camping and hiking. I gave them a description and the plate number.

"I have a ride back to Salt Lake City," I told the officer. "The car was only worth about $500. I hitched a ride and I'm going to take it. You can call me in a day or two at home if you find the car."

I gave him the phone number from Alan Sibley's wallet and thanked the dispatcher. After I hung up I wiped the phone clean of my finger prints.

We drove to Salt Lake City to find the dead man's apartment. For the rest of the day, we sat in our parked pickup, watching the apartment. We saw no action. Late that night, I dug out the extra keys from Alan Sibley's ring, finding one that opened his door. A bed might feel really good tonight.

The place was a pit. He did have some clean sheets. We made a run to a grocery story and picked up some cardboard boxes. Then we began to pack up Sibley's stuff. This guy didn't seem to have much. We found a fairly new computer and a big TV set.

"Do we want a TV and a computer, Michelle?" I asked.

"We could take them to Goodwill, pawn them, or fill our pickup with them, Alan. How soon are we planning to set up a place of our own?"

"We need to make some new plans. We don't want to spend too long around here. Maybe we should take anything worthwhile with us and figure out a place we want to locate for a while," I suggested.

The phone rang. After three rings, I said, "Answer it, Michelle."

"Hello."

"Mr. Alan Sibley please."

She handed me the phone.

"This is Alan."

"Mr. Sibley, this is Deputy Ryan. I'm with the Mesa County Sheriff's Department.

"Your Ford was found at the bottom of a ravine this afternoon. The car thief wrecked it and lost his life. The man was an escaped prisoner and a murderer from Iowa. You might be lucky he just stole your car. He was a real bad fellow."

"Wow. That's scary. I appreciate your call, Deputy Ryan. I liked that old Ford, but I guess I'll have to go car shopping. Thanks for your trouble."

"You're very welcome, sir. Sorry I didn't have better news. Let us know if you need anything else from us."

Michelle and I shared a high five and a big hug. I was on my way to becoming Alan Sibley.

In an hour we celebrated again.

I heard Michelle scream from the back bedroom. "Dean. Come here!"

It was the kind of scream that says, "Eek, a mouse!" or "Oh, Dean. I've cut my finger! Really bad."

I sprinted to the bedroom. Michelle was sitting on the floor behind the bed.

"Are you ok, Michelle? What happened?"

"Look what I found, Dean. There was a tin box under the bed. And look what I found inside."

She held up a sheet of paper. "Here is your birth certificate, Alan Sibley."

She handed it to me and reached into the tin box. "Look at this, Dean. A passport. Let your hair grow a bit longer and frown a bit and you will be a more handsome version of Alan Sibley."

In the morning we filled big plastic bags with anything Sibley had that was usable that we didn't want. We filled some more bags with trash and located a dumpster. In his desk we came across a phone number for his landlord. I called and told him I planned on moving to southern Utah. If we had a refund check coming he could send it to Alan Sibley, care of General Delivery, Bluff, Utah."

"No, I don't have a job," I answered. "but I have a cousin down there who says she knows a rancher who needs a guy. I'm tired of living in a big city. Thanks."

By mid-morning our pickup was loaded with Sibley's TV and computer and even some of his clothes. His trousers had to be cinched up a bit with a belt, but otherwise Alan's clothes were a good fit.

We bought a newspaper, checking the used car ads for a different truck. A *FOR SALE* sign for the S-10 looked good in the side window. A week in a cheap motel might let us handle all of the details to set up a new existence as Mr. and Mrs. Alan Sibley. We were closer to a real life together now than ever before. Some medium-sized town in Utah would become our new home. Both of us were ready to stop running.

LX

A Teaching Certificate

I was anxious to hit the road, but Michelle was still messing around in Alan Sibley's apartment. I climbed back up the stairs and opened the door.

"Are you ready to go, Michelle? I've seen enough of Salt Lake City."

"Come here, Dean. I'm finding some interesting stuff about our Mr. Alan Sibley."

She was in the extra bedroom that Alan had been using for an office and a lounge. It had an Apple Computer, a file cabinet, a recliner, and a messy desk piled high with paper. Michelle was sitting cross-legged on the floor with the file cabinet open in front of her.

"This is very interesting, Dean. This guy has a degree from Colorado State University in Greeley. Guess what his degree is in? You'll never guess."

"What?"

"Business education. Alan Sibley majored in business education. The guy was going to become a teacher. Actually, he taught in Salt Lake City for four years. Then he became so involved in rafting and skiing that he gave up his teaching career to bum around the rivers and the slopes. He guided river trips in the summer and taught skiing in the winter. He blew out a knee two years ago and he has taken some courses to renew his teaching certificate. Here it is."

She handed Dean a formal looking sheet of paper from the file.

"Alan Sibley has been substitute teaching a couple of days a week. The rest of his time he spent hiking, skiing, biking, rafting, camping, and kayaking.

"Take a good look, Mr. Alan Sibley. You are fully certified to teach in the state of Utah. Practice that signature, Alan Sibley. And, if you really want to teach again, I found a week-old letter from the Alamogordo, New Mexico school system. They want you to set up a time to come to Alamogordo to have an interview for a teaching job.

"I turned on Alan's computer to look up reciprocity between states. I'll read it to you. Listen to this, *If you have a teaching license from another state or another country, you can teach now and apply for a comparable New Mexico teaching license under interstate reciprocity.*"

"You, Mr. Alan Sibley, have a teacher's certificate from Utah and I think this means that you can teach in New Mexico. What do you think?"

My mouth was gaping. I had never even dreamed of being a teacher again. I had known my teaching career was over the day I was convicted and sent to prison. Michelle had found the documents that declared that I, Alan Sibley, was licensed to teach. She had thought through the possibilities. My thinking process had not yet caught up. My mind was full of questions. *Could I step back into the classroom again? Was I ready to handle a bunch of kids? What would it do to my students if they found out I was a convicted felon, an escaped prisoner, and wanted for murder in Iowa?*

Michelle was expecting words from me.

"Living a lie is becoming more and more complicated," I observed. "I loved teaching. I was so upset with myself when I screwed it all up. I let my students down. To me, being a good example of how to live your life was a primary part of being a teacher; showing the kids by *your* example how to live *their* lives; then giving them the tools they need to be successes in their work. I don't know that I had ever put it into words, but that was how I felt inside.

"Now here I am lying and cheating my way into the possibility of being a teacher again. I don't know if I can do it, Michelle. I don't know if I am man enough. I don't know if I can risk disappointing another group of students by risking their exposure to a teacher who doesn't exemplify the values he teaches them. I don't know if I can do it, Michelle."

Michelle looked at the tears on my cheeks. She put her arms around me and said, "You are a good man, Dean. I love you."

We stayed wrapped around each other for five minutes.

Then I said, "Let me think about this situation for a few days, Michelle. We need to give plenty of thought to where we go from here. Staying in this apartment doesn't seem safe to me. Alan must have had friends. Passing myself off to strangers as Alan Sibley might have a good chance of working. There is no way that his friends or relatives are going to believe that I am Alan Sibley. We need to leave this town. Maybe we could send emails to people on his address book to let them know he's out of their lives.

"This idea of assuming someone else's identity is an opportunity, but it's also very risky business. This could be the fork in the road moving us into a terrific life or it could be a path that hurts a great many other people. If we aren't very careful and very lucky, we could easily end up back in jail."

"I think you, or we, have two choices," reasoned Michelle. "We can steal Alan's ID and go to some little town in Oregon or California where Iowan's never go and set up a new life. Or you can try to use his teaching credentials and do what you love to do."

For about three minutes it was quiet. I was memorizing a knot in the floor board. Then I said, "I'm thinking about being a teacher again. I'm thinking I could do it."

"I'll email the assistant superintendent and tell her you want to be removed from the substitute list."

"Good plan. Then we'll contact Alamogordo."

Michelle threw her arms around me. "This is great for you. Go for it, Alan Sibley. I think you can do it. I found a couple of other loose ends about Alan Sibley that we better clean up if this guy is going to leave Salt Lake City."

"What's that?"

"There were a set of keys on his desk and another in his jewelry box. The set on his desk includes an apartment key and an attached ring of keys that I think might be for a camper of some kind. The key ring includes a Ford key and a key that is marked with a storage company tag. The matching car key in his jewelry box has a dealer's tag that says, 2004 Ford/F150/White."

"Let's go for a little walk, Michelle. I'm thinking I saw a Ford pickup with a camper on the back. It was parked in front of this apartment."

Outside the apartment was a white, ten year old F150 Ford pickup. It had a super cab with a small pickup camper on the back and a little blue Liquid Logic Kayak on top. The key fit the lock. This outfit was another surprise.

One of the keys on the ring fit the camper. It was the kind that expanded upward to make it almost tall enough to stand in. I found the button and raised it from traveling height to camping height. Inside was a one room house with everything a person would need for living on the road. It had a two burner stove, a microwave, a refrigerator, a little television set, a tiny closet, table and two bench seats that made into a bed, with another bed over the cab.

The place was a mess. Clothes were scattered everywhere, blankets and pillows were thrown in a pile on the cab-over bed, dirty pans and dishes filled the little sink and the counter. This

Alan Sibley wasn't the neatest guy. Maybe that comes from living as a bachelor for a while.

Michelle said, "This is so neat. Oh, I don't mean it is neat and clean. It has everything we need to travel around the west. Since we are taking over Alan Sibley's life, does it mean all of this is ours?"

I glanced down. "I don't know about all of this, Michelle. Things are happening really fast. We obviously have some decisions to make about what happens next. Our first priority has to be to stay out of jail. If we tangle with the law in any way, we don't have a chance in hell. Let's sit down and think about all of this."

We threw the dirty clothes and blankets on the upper bed and sat at the bench seats by the table.

"Other than when I was embezzling money from our school district, I've spent my life operating on the principle that if something was ethical then that was the way I was making my decisions. Is it ethical to take all of this shit that belonged to Alan Sibley?"

I looked at Michelle and she stared back.

"I didn't feel any moral compunction in taking things we needed from The Ranger. The guy was a prick. And he was dead. And there was nobody close to him who would inherit his stuff. I didn't feel any remorse at all with taking what we needed from our prison guard.

"Alan Sibley is another question? We don't know the guy. We don't know his family. Does he have parents who are going to drop in and see him? Was he married? Does he have kids someplace? We don't know if he had a girl friend."

"I see what you mean," Michelle agreed. "Taking this guy's stuff might be wrong. On the other hand if you are going to become Alan Sibley, leaving a bunch of his things here in Salt Lake City will surely make somebody start to investigate what happened to him. That would lead them directly to us. Maybe we should just get the hell out of here and forget we ever met Alan Sibley."

"We didn't exactly meet Alan Sibley. And the police already have my wallet and ID. If Sibley turns up missing they *will* connect it with me and their search will narrow down again to a fairly unpopulated state where it might be pretty easy to track down a couple of strangers."

"Are you saying I am stuck with being in love with Alan Sibley? My love life is becoming pretty complicated."

"I have the same problem, Mary Swartz. First, I loved you. Then it was your sister. Now I am on the way to being in love with Mrs. Michelle Sibley. This is so confusing."

LXI

An Old Girlfriend

Michelle and I were sitting in Alan Sibley's pickup camper pondering our situation.

"I think we're stuck with our plan," Michelle declared. "You need to become Alan Sibley. I need to be your girl friend, Michelle Swartz. We should keep the stuff that we need and haul most of his stuff to the Goodwill Store or the pawn shop. Our plan was to leave town as soon as possible. I think we still need to do that, but we have to cover our tracks and make it look like Alan is blowing this place and making a new start."

"Makes good sense to me," I agreed. "I'm still a bit concerned about his next of kin. I don't like the idea of stealing from a real person."

"Dean, how much money do we have?"

"I'm not sure. Something like $10,000, I'd guess."

"How much is all this stuff of Alan's worth?"

I did some mental arithmetic.

"Maybe $10,000."

"Let's go back upstairs," suggested Michelle, "find out who this guy is; find out who his friends are, who his relations are, what he does, everything about him. I'll log onto his computer and write a story of his life; find out who his next of kin is. Someday, we send that person $10,000. It can be anonymous. Alan Sibley will disappear from the life of somebody who loves him, but someday that somebody will open a package with some money in it."

"I like the idea," I nodded.

"I can see it," she fantasized. "His grandmother opens a let-ter. *Hi. I knew your grandson and I owed him a bunch of money. I just learned that he died three years ago and here is what I owed him plus interest. He was a great guy. I loved him a bunch. Yours truly, John Doe*"

"It might make us feel better."

"Let's find out who Alan Sibley was."

"Agreed," I said. "Do it quickly. I have a funny feeling about this place. It would be so easy for someone who knows him to drop in to see him. I doubt if I look enough like Alan Sibley to pass for him among his friends."

I took two steps toward the apartment house when Michelle stopped me.

"Wait a second, Dean. There is another key on this ring. Maybe we should investigate it. It says, McJams Storage. The address looks like southeast Salt Lake City. Let's go upstairs and do a MapQuest on his computer. See if we can find it."

An hour later, we were parked in front of a drive-in storage unit.

The little key opened an overhead garage door. The small storage unit held a variety of first class sports equipment. There was a mountain bike that must have cost a thousand dollars and a beautiful narrow wheeled road bike, downhill and cross-country skis, and a rubber raft with some big oars that seemed like a great way to travel wild mountain rivers. In a corner was a bike rack that would fit on the hitch of the Ford. Plastic storage tubs contained a wet suit, top quality winter clothing, an expensive pair of binoculars, some really quality walkie-talkies, and an expensive set of rain gear. Alan Sibley scrimped a bit on his car and his pickup, but his fun gear was the best available.

I looked at Michelle. We were both astonished.

"What do we do with all of this?" I asked.

"We can't just leave it. If Alan Sibley was leaving town, he simply wouldn't leave this kind of equipment behind."

"You're right. I really don't want to be saddled with his toys, but we have to take them with us. I guess we'll figure out what to do with it all as we go."

"I feel like it is Christmas morning in a rich person's house," Michelle smiled. "I have to act as if I like all my Christmas presents, when really, I like and want only a few of them. I didn't ever imagine me becoming a skier or running a raft down a dangerous river. I love that pickup camper though, Dean. I'm a bit tired of pulling myself out of that sleeping bag and crawling out of the tent every morning."

"Are you a biker?"

"Not much. You?"

"I used to bike to school quite a bit in the spring and fall," Dean reflected. "The kids thought it was kind of funny having my bicycle in the back of the classroom. Sometimes, I'd bike to the grocery story, save gas, and exercise a little. We have two great bikes here. We might have some fun with them if you want to give them a try.

"The big problem is that our mobility has tended to keep us out of trouble. Every time we keep more things we become bogged down with extra weight and volume and trouble."

It became quiet in the little storage shed as we pondered our problem.

Michelle finally broke the silence. "Lets fill our S-10 with some of this and go back and do our study of Alan Sibley."

I turned on his computer. Alan must have been a trusting type of guy because nothing was protected with passwords. His email told a story. He had messages back and forth from about a dozen people. Most of them seemed to be from people who lived outside of Utah. That was good because they were less likely to show up at our door.

Michelle was looking at me. "Dean, you haven't shaved for two days."

"I'm sorry. I'll find Alan's electric razor and try it out."

"I don't mean that. You might look real good in a beard. Also there are two other good things about you and a beard. You might look just a little different than Alan Sibley so if you see someone he knew, the beard might explain the difference.

"Also the FBI might not recognize you quite as easy. I think you should grow a beard."

"I started two days ago, smart woman."

Alan didn't have a phone with a land line. We had taken his cell phone from his pocket and we checked it for messages and automatic numbers. He had friends from Wyoming and Idaho, not many from Utah. He was really a loner.

Alan appeared to have a woman friend. Marsha Slater was married with two elementary school kids. Hopefully, she had protection on her computer because some of the earlier messages had some pretty graphic stuff about their physical relationship. She had finally broken it off in late spring. Marsha had told Alan that she just felt too guilty. She loved him, but she still loved her husband and, especially, her two girls. The guy was a Mormon and she didn't like his domination of her. Marsha was torn between ending her marriage and supporting her family. Finally, it became too much for her. She had told Alan in an email that it was over. She said she was changing her email address and Alan should stay completely out of her life.

Alan had dabbled with pornography on his computer. He liked big-breasted women. They turned up all over his computer. He had a nice file of pictures of Marsha; she qualified nicely in that big-breasted category.

Michelle was searching his file cabinet while I did the computer study. She pulled repair and upkeep records on the vehicles, sales receipts, warrantees, college transcripts, pay records, phone bills, and Master Card receipts. He had a file of letters from his mother, father, and sister. A newspaper clipping showed that Alan's parents had died in a car crash about ten years before. His sister Barbara, lived in New York City. They saw each other once every two years and wrote or emailed about twice a year. Someday, Michelle and I would answer an email from Barbara and tell her I was looking for a new job out of state.

Michelle also found a thick file titled, *Pictures of Marsha*. She had posed in about every position imaginable in the mind of a horny man. The 8x10 pictures were very good, leaning toward quality art. Alan was an accomplished photographer; Marsha was a beautiful model. Michelle found a couple of Nikon cameras, a great assortment of expensive lenses, and a padded Manfrotto tripod with a ball head.

"Sometimes I think we are learning too much about this man, Dean. We are invading his privacy. He's dead and we are digging through a slightly perverted life."

"If I hadn't traded wallets with the dead man in the wrecked car, I wonder who would be going through Alan Sibley's effects. Would another stranger be gathering his things together, discovering all the secrets of his life? Would his sister, Barbara, from New York City be the one? Maybe we are doing this guy a favor. Nobody who knew the guy will ever know what went on in his life. I don't think any of what he did was illegal. It's just that his private life was perhaps a bit different than his public life. Is that a problem?"

Both of us jumped a foot when the door bell rang. We were quiet as mice.

"Alan, are you there?" said the sweet sounding female voice. "Open the door please."

Michelle didn't pause. She slipped off her blouse and her jeans and opened the door a foot.

"Can I help you, ma'am?" said the gorgeous former prostitute and prisoner, standing in her bra and panties.

The woman's eyes painted Michelle from neck to knees. She swallowed and said, "My name is Marsha. I need to talk to Alan Sibley please."

"Alan and I are pretty much busy right now, ma'am. Would another time be better or would you like for me to give him a message from you?"

The woman took in Michelle's fantastic figure and backed up a step. Then she said softly, "I was going to tell him I missed him and thought we might talk about restarting our relationship, but it looks as if he has moved on to greener pastures. Tell him it was great."

She turned to walk away and Michelle said, "Marsha. Alan and I talked about you and if he was here, he'd say you was a very special part of his life. He'd say he loved you more than a mountain trail. And he'd say he figured that you'd have a special place in his heart until the day he died, but he needed to go on and he thought you needed to continue your life without him.

"I think he is leaving Utah so that you and he can both be free. He's taking me with him, but he's always going to love you. I hope I can make him love me as much, Marsha.

"Good luck to you now. You take care of them girls."

Marsha turned and walked down the stairs. Michelle gently closed and locked the door.

I looked out a corner of the window at a white Cadillac Escalade. A sexy woman in a short skirt and a plunging blouse unlocked the door with her remote and slipped into the driver's seat. I watched Marsha rest her head on the steering wheel and cry. Two minutes later, she started the engine and drove slowly down the street of the quiet neighborhood.

LXII

Selling the S10

I put my arms around my half-naked Michelle. "You are such a tactful woman. You left that woman knowing she was loved. She knew she had been a very special part of Alan Sibley's life, that he was moving on without her and that she might live without him. Wow. You, Michelle, are brilliant."

I decided to continue the little play that Michelle had started. I took her to bed and pretended I was broken-hearted at losing Marsha, but that I was ready to try starting a relationship with Michelle. She did her best to convince me that no one was better. She succeeded.

Afterwards, I had another surprise. As I was lying on my stomach with my hand dangling over the side of the bed, my hand touched something hard. I slipped to the floor and reached under the bed. There was a .22 Remington rifle with a scope and a strap and a six shot clip. Behind it was a .308 Winchester lever action rifle and a Winchester 16 gauge pump shotgun.

"Remember, I said I wanted to take up hunting someday, Michelle. Look at this. We have an armory under the bed."

"I thought you were the guy who threw the rifle in the lake because you didn't want any guns."

"Should we go find a lake?"

"I don't care if you keep them, Dean. I still have the pistol you wanted me to throw away."

"I thought you got rid of that."

"I figured I might need it since I was sleeping with a man who was wanted for murder. Seriously, you said we ought to travel light. You might think about that with all those guns, Dean."

"You're right. We shouldn't take them with us. Maybe we can find a gun show or a sport shop to sell them."

Ten minutes later, I was dressing. I reached into Alan Sibley's sock drawer and had another surprise. My hand touched another hard object. It was a big box of .22 caliber long rifle shells. Looking a little further, I found a Beretta .22 caliber pistol tucked into the back corner, a neat little gun. I could have a good time plunking targets with this pistol.

"Michelle, this Alan Sibley was a real outdoorsman. He has every toy a guy could want. Look at this little semi-automatic pistol. If I weren't a hardened criminal, I could have fun with this."

"Get rid of it, Dean. Get rid of all of them."

I emailed the Superintendent of Alamogordo High School. I told him I was interested in the job and would like an interview. He must have been sitting at his computer. In fifteen minutes, he wrote back saying he was very serious about hiring me as a

business and math teacher. He had been having trouble filling the position and if the interview went well, I'd have a good
chance at the job. I told him I would try to gather up some
loose ends here and would be down there in a week. It was
Wednesday and I set up an interview for the next Tuesday. I
had six days to drive to New Mexico and psych myself up for a
teaching job.

We made two trips with the S-10 to the Goodwill store.
Then we made a trip to a gun shop with all of Alan's guns. We
sold them for $1000. Their value was probably twice that, but
the dealer needed to make some money and we wanted to get
rid of the guns. Michelle told him her brother-in-law died and
she didn't want the guns. Michelle made the salesman a deal to
include a $35 Concealed Carry Class with the sale. She was de-
termined to keep the little pistol that she had stolen from Greg.

"Sell it," I told her.

"It saved our lives," she argued.

"He probably turned in the serial number as a stolen
weapon."

"That means if we sell it to the sports shop or if I use it in class,
they catch me either way. Right? I think I'll use Alan's Beretta before
we finalize the deal. The ammunition is cheaper anyway."

"And we'll throw the little pistol of Greg's in Salt Lake?"

"Sure."

I saw her crossing her fingers.

On the way back from the second trip to Goodwill, a guy in a
beat up old Toyota saw our for sale sign. He waved us over to
a parking lot.

"How much do you want for the pickup?" he asked as he circled the vehicle and kicked the tires.

Michelle said, "We want $2000, but I don't think you'd pay that much. I think it's worth around $1700, It runs great, doesn't use any oil, and averages 25-30 miles per gallon on the highway. It's a solid little truck and I hate to sell it, but we have a full sized pickup and we just can't afford two."

The guy said, "My name is Henry Fallon. I'd give you $1900 cash if you'll deliver it to my house in Moab."

"That's kind of a strange request, Henry. What's the deal?"

"Two things. My bank's in Moab and I live there. I can't drive two cars to Moab."

"Makes sense. You have some earnest money to put down then."

Henry pealed off three, hundred dollar bills. "I have $300. If I don't follow through you can keep it."

"How do you know you can trust us."

"I have a nose for honest people, lady. I can tell you two is honest as a sunrise on a clear day."

Michelle said, "I'll miss this little truck," She reflected, "but you just made a deal, Henry. We'll drive it to Moab on Friday or Saturday for sure. Do you have an address and a phone number?"

Henry gave her his card and they shook hands on the deal.

"We'll need cash," she said. "We're closing our bank accounts."

"No problem."

Later, Michelle and I talked.

"I do hate to sell that little truck, Dean. My old client, Greg, knew what it looked like and he might even remember the license number some day. It will be good to remove those plates from circulation."

"We can do just fine with the pickup and camper for a while," I observed. "We'll probably notice the high gas prices. Hopefully, we won't be traveling as much any more. If that teaching job works out we could have found a long-time home. Then you can marry me and we'll live happily ever after."

LXIII

A Des Moines Connection - Dulac, Louisiana

It was Tuesday morning when Randy called Jonathan into his office.

Have I screwed up? Does he know something about my past? He took a deep breath. *I guess I'll find out.*

"Sit down, Jonathan."

He sat in a beat-up arm chair.

"Jonathan, we won't be working next week. About 15 miles south of Houma is the little town of Dulac. Actually, it's an Indian village where the Houma Indians have lived for centuries."

Randy told Jonathan, "The Houma Indians are the tribe that the government left out when it was giving Indians the aid that federal laws allowed. The people couldn't read or write. Their children weren't allowed in the segregated White schools and the Blacks didn't think the Indians were dark enough to go to their schools. They were pretty much left out of the whole public education system until 1963."

"Was that the year when the Civil Rights Bill was passed."

"That's it," agreed Randy. "Luckily, the Methodists recognized a need. They created a Mission Center in Dulac. Work groups from all over the country travel to Dulac to help the disadvantaged people there. The first class began in 1932; seventy-five students, ages six through twenty. None of them had ever been to school before, so everyone was in the first grade. Classes were held in an old-fashioned, high-ceilinged overseer's home. Miss Wilhelmina Hooper taught and lived there. Sometimes, classes were held out on the porch or in the yard under an oak tree. Besides teaching school, Methodist workers taught religious classes twice a week. The school was for all Indians, regardless of their religious beliefs. Miss Hooper was assisted in the early days by a Miss Hoffpauir.

"Hurricanes have hit Dulac hard so there is always plenty to do repairing damage from winds and floods. Men and women from our United Methodist Church in Houma go down on a regular basis to work on projects. I go along and kind of organize work crews. My construction company will go on vacation next week. Most of the guys drive down to Dulac, stay in the bunkhouse, and give their time. You're welcome to come if you like or you can take the week off. No pressure."

Jonathan didn't hesitate. "I'm real happy to have a job and a good guy to work for, Randy. I'd be pleased to help out for a week."

"You have to remember one thing, Jonathan. You can't put your values on these people. I know you're from up north. I appreciate your work ethic on the job. But, don't judge these people by how much they are doing or aren't doing to help themselves. They often don't know what to do. I've worked on a house for two days while the residents either stay out of my way or just ignore me. Other times the people who own the house will jump in and work shoulder to shoulder with me or even try to tell me what to do. Just remember you're working for God in Dulac. My thinking is that Jesus said we were supposed to help those who were less fortunate. That's all we're doing. We're making their lives a little bit better than they might have been without us."

"I'm not proud," confessed Jonathan. "I'm really lucky to be where I am. I think it will feel really good to give back a little, Randy."

A week later, Jonathan and Nora were working together on a beat-up shack of a house a block from the canal in Dulac. The place had been hit hard by the winds from a couple of hurricanes and then heavy rains and floods had left mold growing in the walls. A work crew of volunteers from Wisconsin had torn out most of the sheet rock and sprayed bleach in the wall and under the floors to kill the white, wooly, mold that was growing in every dark damp space. The family had used government flood relief money to buy sheet rock and two-by-fours. None of the corners of the building were square, so fixing anything required ingenuity and extra cutting.

Jonathan and Nora were working together with a crew from someplace up north. He could tell that by the accent. Jonathan thought they might be from southern Iowa or northern Missouri.

Brian Morris was nearly six feet tall; weighed about two hundred forty pounds. His long black hair had a natural curl and was neatly trimmed. He had his own chargeable Black and Decker drill. It was shiny and Brian was careful to avoid scratches or heavy dirt. He wore a brand new nail apron with a handful of screws in one pouch and a brand new twenty-five foot tape measure in the other.

His wife, Connie, must have had a nice figure as a teen-ager. At forty-five, she was fifty pounds overweight; her once sexy figure was gone. *Her face was rounded and pleasant. She carried a friendly, smile that made people happy to be around her.*

The third member of the crew from up north was a pretty teen-ager who might have been a high school senior or college coed. Keisha Piper was pretty right now. She wore a t-shirt that was too tight, but Jonathan didn't care. He wondered if she would develop into a portly matron as her friend Connie had. Somehow, he didn't think so. The youngster was a lovely woman and she took care of herself. She had come to breakfast this morning dressed in a sweat suit and dripping with perspiration after a five mile jog. Running in the warm morning air thrilled her, after leaving Iowa in a snow storm. Her breakfast of yogurt and fruit was not the kind of food that makes a person gain weight.

Brian held a piece of sheet rock while Jonathan screwed it in place. Brian said, "I can't believe these people are just sitting there watching TV while we are fixing up their house. They are really a lazy bunch, aren't they?"

Nora responded, "One of the rules here is that we aren't supposed to judge the people we are helping. Get acquainted if you can and listen to their stories if they want to talk. None of us knows what these people have gone through. Who knows how we might act if we were in their shoes?"

Jonathan asked Keisha to help him mark a pencil line down the center of each stud. Then he showed her how to use his electric drill to set the screws about eight inches apart. She had trouble at first, but soon the youngster handled the power tool like a pro. Jonathan and Nora could tell she felt really good to be doing the job. She finished screwing the sheet in place and then helped Jonathan measure for the next one. Brian had some experience with sheet rock, but he wasn't really good at the process. Jonathan double checked his measurements while Nora held the tape for the Northerner.

"Where is it that y'all live, Brian? Was it Iowa?" Nora asked.

"Yeah. We live in a little town in the southern part of the state. Osceola has about 4000 people. We aren't far from Missouri. We're right on Interstate 35. Our biggest claim to fame is a gambling casino with flashing lights that you can see from the interstate. The original state law was that a casino had to be built on a steamboat. The law said that during the warm weather months the boat had to make a run every week. I'd be out Crappie fishing on West Lake and suddenly the steamboat would crank up its engines, untie its lines, and make a run to the southwest corner of the little lake. It would screw up the fishing for an hour before the big boat returned to its berth.

"I work for a rural electric cooperative in Osceola. It was a nice town to raise our kids."

"Jonathan here is from Missouri," reflected Nora. "You ever been to St. Louis, Brian?"

"Sure, I've been to St. Louis. My sister lives there. What part of the town did you live in, Jon?"

"Which part does your sister live? I've lived several places in St. Louis, mostly in the suburbs."

"Sally lives in the northeast part. I can find the place if I have to but don't ask me to describe how. I just follow MapQuest and it takes me right to her front door."

"It is a big town," declared Jonathan. "Actually, I haven't spent much time in that part of St. Louis. I'm kind of like you. I can usually find someplace if I'm forced to, but I'm not really too familiar with that part of town. This MapQuest thing kind of passed me by. I probably should buy a computer and take a class in how to use it. So far I haven't really seen the need; seems like my friends who have them spend less time fishing and more time sitting in front of a screen."

"There's some truth in what you say, Jon. On the other hand, they give you so much power. Osceola is a little town about a hundred miles south of Des Moines. At home, the paper boy drops the Des Moines Register on my front porch every morning at 6:00. Some of my friends are too cheap to subscribe to the paper, so every morning they sit and drink their coffee and read the newspaper on their computer.

"In fact that's the way I'm following the Iowa news while I'm here. I have some stories I'm trying to keep up with. One is about a big jail break that happened last spring in Des Moines. Four people killed a guard and escaped from a halfway house. They never really found a trail for any of the four escapees. That was kind of strange. Then there were other strange things about the escape. They learned that the guard who was killed had been drinking and there was a sack of beer cans beside his body. It was a weird case; I wondered what really happened.

"This morning, I read the Register's news stories on line. The cops captured one of the escapees in St. Louis. The guy started to talk and gave up one of his buddies. They had been living together near St. Louis and when they split about five months ago, the guy's buddy had headed for New Mexico. Now the FBI and New Mexico police are looking for the second guy."

Nora glanced at Jonathan. Then looked away.

He caught the glance. This woman he loved was doing some mental arithmetic.

By lunchtime the wall was nearly finished. They ate sandwiches, veggies, and cookies.

Brian pulled Pepsis from the cooler and passed them around.

"That tastes so good," he said as he downed half the Pepsi and reached for another cookie.

Connie said, "I need to walk back to the bunk house and use the rest room."

Brian said, "I'll come along."

Keisha was sitting in the living room talking to the folks in the family. The mother and their twelve year old boy were watching TV with grandma and grandpa. Grandpa had a chronic disease that confined him to bed. Keisha was taking the *get acquainted* suggestion seriously. She was asking questions about life in the bayou country of Louisiana.

"Maybe I'll take a little walk," said Nora. "Do you want to join me, Jonathan?"

LXIV

Discovered In Dulac - Jonathan

Nora and Jonathan walked down the quiet village street for two blocks before either of them spoke.

Finally, Nora said, "Should I be afraid of you, Jonathan?"

"Afraid? Have I done something that has made you afraid?"

"Not since you've been in Louisiana. Have you done anything before you came here that should make me afraid?"

"You are holding my hand. You don't act afraid."

"You never told me about your past, Jonathan. All I know is that you came from St. Louis and you came about the same time that the escaped murderer left St. Louis. Two plus two usually equals four. Do you want to tell me about your past? I have a history of picking men who are terrible people. It wouldn't surprise me if I managed to find another one."

Jonathan was pretty much wordless. They walked in silence for two more blocks. In the west, was a grassy marsh; the warm winter sun bathed the grass. They watched ducks swimming in open water and a long-legged white egret fishing near the shore.

Nora was still holding his hand; that gave him courage. He kept opening his mouth, but no words came out. He thought, *What can I say? This woman has absorbed a lot of hurt in her life. I care about her. I don't want to add to her pain.*

He tried again. "Nora, I don't know what to say. I'm living a lie. I'm not going to lie to you any more. Ten years ago I was living in Des Moines. I was happily married. I had a job and two wonderful kids. The All-American family. Then our son involved himself in the drug scene. I think he tried all kinds of stuff and he hung out with a nasty bunch of guys. One day the police picked me up for speeding. The cops wanted to search my car. I had no problem with that, so I said, 'Sure. Go ahead.'

"They found a big bag of marijuana under the spare tire. I assume it belonged to my son. Before my trial, I was out on bond and he was staying with some of his buddies. He'd never talk to me about it. All I could do was tell the police that the stuff wasn't mine; that I didn't know anything about it. The police and the jury didn't believe me. They sentenced me to twenty years in prison. While I was in prison my wife had a better offer. She divorced me and married a guy with a job and an available body. I haven't seen my son or heard anything about him for eight years. My daughter is in college now. I'd love to be able to send her some money to help her along her way, but I can't figure out how that could happen.

"I served eight years and tried to be a model prisoner. They put me in a new halfway house that was supposed to teach us how to live on the outside. One of the four prisoners there was a woman. She was gorgeous. One night an asshole of a guard tried to rape her. One of the prisoners pulled him off. They had a fist fight. The guard fell; hit his head on the door. It wasn't much of a fight. The guard was drunk. We didn't know what to do. We probably should have called 911. Maybe the paramedics could have pulled him back to life. We kind of panicked and took off in the guard's truck.

"My buddy and I drove to St. Louis, bought some false ID, and here I am.

"I guess the next step is for me to start running again. You don't need to worry about me hurting you. I'm not that kind of a guy. The last time I hit someone, I was a freshman in college. Some guy threatened to shave my balls and I hit him in the mouth. He went down flat on his back and when he came up he was ready to fight. I was lucky. Three guys held him back and convinced him that it had gone far enough. Lucky for me. The guy was a boxer. He'd boxed in the Golden Gloves Tournament in Des Moines and won his middle weight class. Later, we became pretty good friends.

"Anyway, you don't need to worry about me hurting you."

For another two blocks, it was very quiet. Nora and Jonathan had wandered near the canal. A great blue heron was sitting on a post and a fishing boat was slicing the smooth water as it headed north.

Jonathan finally said, "I'll get out of your life. I'll pack my stuff and leave. Or if you feel you need to turn me in I guess you can do it. I'm a little tired of running. My big problem is that I fell in love with you."

"You fell in love with me under false pretenses, Mr. Jonathan Wilson, or whatever your name is. I didn't fall in love with an escaped prisoner and a murderer. I fell in love with Jonathan Wilson who was the kindest guy I ever met.

"I suppose you wonder why I'm still holding your hand. I'm mad because you lied to me, but I understand why you couldn't tell me the truth. I knew y'all weren't a bad man. Even after I figured you were one of the escaped prisoners, I knew you were a good person. I am mad, but I still love you. If I have anything to say about it, I'm not going to let you get away. From me that is."

Nora wrapped her arms around Jonathan Wilson and they held each other for a long time as they stood in the street beside the blue water of the canal. The piercing whistle of an ocean-going fishing boat finally broke the trance and a couple of sailors yelled and waved at them from the boat.

Jonathan raised his hand and returned the wave. He and Nora turned and began a slow walk back toward the house they were repairing.

Brian was nowhere around when they returned. He should have been back.

"Do you think he figured out who I am?" asked Jonathan.

"No way. I knew your schedule. I knew when you left St. Louis. I knew something wasn't quite right with your history. Brian doesn't know anything about you. Besides, he's dumb as a post. He couldn't figure out that a wading bird ate fish."

Nora and Jonathan greeted Keisha and the three of them went back to work on the sheet rock. An hour later Brian and Connie wandered into the house.

"Sorry, we're so late. It was so calm back at the bunk house, we laid down on my bed for a minute. The next thing we knew it was two o'clock. We had a wonderful nap. Then we kind of lost our directions on the way back here. I didn't know who to ask or what to ask about. Finally, we spotted your old rusty Toyota and knew this was the place.

"You guys are almost done with the sheet rock in this room. Good job. You didn't even need us."

"We're glad you're back, Brian," said Nora. "Y'all can do some of the heavy lifting that a Southern Belle shouldn't be doin'."

Brian and Connie didn't seem to have a clue that Jonathan was the murderer running loose in New Mexico. That guy's name was Bob Johnson. This Jonathan guy was a carpenter from Houma where the group was going for barbecue on Wednesday night. He was a really nice guy. The thought of Jonathan being a murderer and an escaped prisoner never crossed the minds of the people from Osceola.

Jonathan and Nora made it a point to avoid teaming up with the Iowans for the rest of the week.

LXV

A New Trailer and An Old Friend

Possessing a large amount of stuff troubled both Michelle and me. That is strange to say because this woman had lived much of her life in pursuit of owning things. She especially liked fine jewelry, but now that she had almost none, she really didn't seem to care. After years in prison, both of us were ready to settle down and live normal, peaceful, productive lives.

If we could pull off this teaching job charade and make a real life out of one of the biggest lies ever invented, it would be a miracle as amazing as if Hellen Keller had been restored to sight. If we could turn two careers of crime into lives that made contributions to society, it would be a resurrection, not unlike Jesus Christ's; perhaps more like the woman at the well. "Go and sin no more," Jesus told her. I always figured that Jesus' prostitute friend had done that. Michelle and I were trying to do the same thing. Maybe we needed some religion. Later. First, we had to tell some more lies. Then, we might seek forgiveness.

We debated about what to take to New Mexico. Starting over at garage sales was one option. Keeping the best of Alan Sibley's furniture and other possessions was another. Trying to transport everything we might need was a third option. If we did that we would have to rent a trailer or a truck. Renting something in Salt Lake City and leaving it in Alamogordo seemed like a bad idea to both of us. A record of our travels was not a good thing to leave behind.

Every time we had stopped for a month or for a few weeks, we had hoped that might be the place where we would settle. At each of our temporary homes, we had found people we liked and respected. We had invested ourselves in people and places. In the end, we had always pulled our anchor before it had really stuck in the rocks. Each time, we had left in a hurry in order to preserve our lives and maintain our freedom.

Invariably, we had had my lack of identity hanging over us. A driver's license, a social security card, a passport, even a library card seemed to be pieces of paper that I would never have. Now, I had a driver's license. I had a Social Security card and the magic Social Security number that I needed in order to apply for a real job. I had a library card for the Salt Lake City Library. And I even had a passport that Michelle had found under Alan Sibley's bed. I was ready to face life with a name and an identity that could carry me on to the life that Michelle and I were seeking.

"Just think about how lucky we are, Michelle. We are on the way to freedom. We can do almost anything we want to do. We have to be a little more careful than the average American, but we can be productive people. We can have a house. We can have kids. We can dream of a future. We can have careers and be part of society. We can do charity work and help those who haven't done as well as we have. I am excited as a little boy at Christmas."

Michelle smiled at me, "More. You are more excited than that little boy, Alan. I am too. If I were a chicken, I'd lay an egg."

"You're making fun of me, but I've been thinking about guys I knew in prison who served their time and earned parole and were dropped back into society. Those guys had terrible problems. One black guy, Charles Jackson, was released from the Iowa State Penitentiary in Fort Madison. He moved back to Illinois. Nobody would hire him. After six months, he still didn't have a job. He didn't own a car. He couldn't even rent a house, because he had once committed a crime. It didn't matter that he had served his time and paid his debt to society. Nobody would trust him. Finally, he was facing the possibility of setting up on a corner, begging for food money. He couldn't take it. He stole a car and robbed a bank. He wasn't very good at it. The cops gave chase. There was a high speed pursuit. Some kid stepped off the curb in front of Charles. His car skidded and he was killed as it crashed into a tree instead of the kid. Charles Jackson was a hero. He was stuck at the bottom of our society and couldn't find his way out. When he had to make a choice between hitting a kid or a tree, Charles Jackson chose to be a hero.

"You and I are lucky. Nobody knows we are criminals. Everybody assumes we are just working people who need jobs and a place to live. If we had served our time and been released on parole, we might have been just like Charles Jackson. With no jobs, all we could do is find some kind of a criminal activity to keep us alive. This whole prison process doesn't really rehabilitate people, does it?"

Michelle is a good listener. I was lucky to have her too. "You're right, Paul. This adventure of ours looks like it might be ending soon. We might have a better chance than your friend, Charles Jackson."

She looked around the apartment at the couch and chair, the queen-sized bed and chests, and the kitchen table and chairs.

"What about this stuff? I almost think we might be better off if we abandoned our travel light principle and take a bunch of this to New Mexico. I'm wondering if we shouldn't go at this move as if it is going to be our last one.

We both agreed that renting a truck or a trailer and leaving it in Alamogordo would be a stupid thing to do. Someone on our trail could easily follow us with our rental records.

We called a U-Haul business and priced the rental of a small truck or a big trailer. We could rent a small moving truck for about $1000 for four days. An enclosed trailer with unlimited miles would cost less than $50. Neither one of us had much enthusiasm about spending a long day driving to Alamogordo, a second day finding a place to live, unloading, driving back to Salt Lake City, and then making the trip to New Mexico again in our pickup. That scenario would cost us four days of time and about 2300 miles of exhausting driving. It would also cost us about $350 more for gasoline than if we made just one trip. There had to be another way.

We found a local farm equipment store that sold utility trailers. They were on sale for about $800. That seemed like quite a bit of money, and when we arrived in New Mexico, what would we need with a trailer? We had a good Ford pickup. We left in a quandary.

Halfway home we had another answer.

"Stop, Paul," Michelle ordered. "Look at that little two-wheeled trailer back there with a 4-sale sign on it."

"Trailer: $225."

It was homemade out of an old axle and a Ford pickup box. It looked to be in great shape. The trailer was painted with a fresh coat of bright red paint and had a wooden frame that extended eighteen inches above the old pickup box. It reminded me of my dad's old trailer that had made dozens of fishing trips to Canada.

It had a fairly long tongue and a steel bed that didn't show any rust. An old guy with an oxygen tank was riding a lawn mower around the yard. When he saw us looking at the trailer he drove the mower beside the driveway and shut it off. He must have been 80 years old. He was wearing bib overalls, a plaid shirt, and a cowboy hat and boots.

"You needin a trailer, folks?" he asked.

"We were planning a move and buying a little trailer might be the most sensible way to go. Besides, everyone needs a trailer sometimes. We have a pickup, but it has a camper on it most of the time. It isn't the easiest job to keep putting that thing on and off. The trailer might be just the ticket."

"This little trailer follows better than a hunting dog at heel. She has fresh grease and decent 15" tires. They ain't new, but they are way better than them little tires that turn a million times each mile."

The old man looked me in the eyes and said, "I'm Clem Romney. How about you?"

"My name is Alan Sibley. I'm pleased to meet you. This is my girl friend, Michelle."

He paused and looked me over again. "By golly. It sure is a small world. I thought I knew you. Your pappy, Donald, was a great friend of mine before he died, son. We worked a lot of jobs together building pole buildings up in Wyoming. He was hurt on the job and moved to Salt Lake City. I tried to find him when I moved here ten years ago, but he'd passed on by then. I talked to your sister. It sure made me sad that he was gone. And I ain't seen you since you was about ten years old. You probably don't remember me.

"You favor old Donald a might, Alan. Sure can tell you have Sibley blood running in your veins, although you sure have plenty of your ma in you. I'm right pleased to meet you.

"If you have a hankering for that little trailer, I'll give you a special deal on her. For you, the price is $200, son. I just pull the axle and box off an old wrecked truck from the junk yard. A few bolts and a couple of welds and I have me a pretty good trailer. It has a one and seven-eighths inch ball, just like your little Chevy. The lights oughta just plug right in. I sell about one a month. Helps me supplement my Social Security; gives me something to do.

"God, I'm pleased to meet you. What are you doing for a living these days? I heard you was rafting the rivers a few years ago."

"That's exactly right, Clem. I spent two decades rafting; taking tourists down the Colorado. In the winters, I taught skiing up on the Wasatch at Powder Mountain. Then I blew out my knee and had to give it up. I renewed my teaching certificate. I think I have a job up in Oregon. It's kind of late in life to get serious about a teaching career, but it seems to be the best option I have and I know I'll enjoy it. I always did like kids."

I reached into my wallet and dug under my driver's license for two folded up hundred dollar bills.

"Clem, you don't know how good it is to meet somebody who knew my dad. It's tough filling in the holes in his life that he never had a chance to tell me about. I might come back down here and look you up sometime. We'll have dinner and talk about Dad."

Clem grabbed my hand with both of his and held on tight. "You're a spittin' image of what he looked like about thirty years ago, son. My old mind is a flood of memories right now.

"Good luck to you and your pretty woman, Al. I sure can't believe how much you look like your pa."

Clem pocketed the two hundred dollars, slipped his oxygen back in his mouth, and started the mower.

I hooked the trailer on to the little Chevy, snapped the chain to the loop under the hitch, and plugged in the lights to the standard trailer outlet on the truck. We checked the lights, turn lights, and stop lights. They all worked perfectly.

As we drove away and waved to my father's old buddy, Michelle smiled broadly and said, "You sure look like your pa, Alan Sibley."

LXVI

Alan Sibley's Finances

By Thursday afternoon, we had the trailer and the camper load-ed with many of the treasures from Alan Sibley's apartment and storage shed. A couple of big tarps were over and under our new possessions, rope woven over the top. I stopped to tell the manager of the rental units that we were moving out.

"Looks like you're two months behind on your rent, Mr. Sibley."

He printed out a receipt. The total was $128.40. I paid him with cash.

As we left, the thought of the old bill filtered through my head.

"Michelle, I just thought of something that could be trou-ble. Did you check to see if Alan Sibley had any big bills that he was paying every month. I'd hate to have some credit company follow us to New Mexico wondering why we aren't making a payment. Maybe we should make certain that I have my bills all paid."

There were Visa bills in a kitchen drawer and a file folder held records of past payments. Alan was paying about $40 a month on a $2300 Visa bill. His interest was nearly $30 per month. I called the toll free number on the bill and found out the exact amount it would take to pay off the bill. Then we searched his check book for other payments that were being made. The truck and car seemed to be debt free. Michelle found the titles in files marked CAR and TRUCK. He did have a small payment to a credit union for his TV set.

The title to his car gave me a copy of Alan's signature. I spent twenty minutes practicing for forgeries. Then I wrote checks from his account to VISA and his credit union. I called and asked for a balance from his checking account. He had $823.19. We made a trip to his bank and deposited $2500 in cash to cover the two checks.

"It seems kind of strange to be making deposits to pay this guy's bills, Michelle."

"Think of it as your bills, Paul. You're taking all his stuff."

We need to find a ledger and start an accounting system.

"You're an accountant. You can do that, Alan."

Michelle checked the rest of Alan Sibley's files while I was running errands. When I returned, she had more information.

"Paul, here are insurance records for his vehicles. We should cancel the insurance on his car. Both vehicles have liability and comprehensive coverage. He has a $20,000 policy on his life that has a little cash value. The beneficiary is his sister Barbara in New York. Her address is here. Do you suppose that since we have taken his existence, we ought to keep up his responsibility to the sister he doesn't like?

"That's one we better ponder on for a while. Let's see where this leads first. If our plan doesn't work, then the proceeds might go to his sister when the truth comes out."

"Makes sense, Paul. Here is something else that is interesting. The guy has a stock account with a broker in San Francisco. It has about $45,000 in stocks and bonds. I can't tell where it came from, but it's a bunch of money. What do we do about it?"

"Wow!" I exclaimed. "Does this fit with the guy who pays a minimum payment and a huge amount of interest on his Visa bill."

"Makes no sense to me," observed Michelle.

"I really don't want to steal from this guy or from his estate," I reflected. "I don't feel bad about keeping his pickup and camper and as many of his things as we can use, but it looks as if his sister deserves to receive most of it. Maybe we should make a list of all of the valuable assets that we take from him. Someday, we can send his sister an envelope of cash."

"I like that thought," agreed Michelle. "This guy is dead and he's giving us a chance to have a fresh start in life. I think we should do it and then keep living frugally. When our finances are solid, we'll send his sister a bunch of money. Hopefully, she'll have to wait a few years. I don't mind living on a tight budget for a while, Paul -- as long as it's with you."

This was becoming more and more complicated. We wanted simple. I guess life is never simple.

We gathered Alan Sibley's important papers and records and put them in a file box. The S10 made many trips to the recycling center in the apartment complex with bags of Alan Simpson's things. Then, it made trips to Goodwill. When the junk and the usable pieces we didn't want were gone, we finished packing the camper and the trailer with items we thought we could use along with anything we might sell later.

By evening, we were east of Moab, camped at Big Bend, a Bureau of Land Management primitive campground along the Colorado River. There wasn't room in the camper to sleep, so we set up our tent and spread our sleeping bags. Then we drove both pickups into Moab and found Henry Fallon. He had the $2200 in cash ready. Henry was all smiles. He loved our little S10 and he was proud that we confirmed his judgment that we were good and honest people.

"I never miss. I can always tell honest people. It's just something that shows up when I look a person in the eye.

"Where are you folks headed now?"

"I have a good shot at a teaching job up in Oregon. Hopefully, we'll stay there for a long time."

"That's real good country. You'll love it. Ain't as pretty as Utah's red rocks, but in its own way it's mighty pretty country. What part of the state are you heading for?"

"It's a small town outside of Portland," I lied. "It has one of those Indian names. I always have to look it up. And it's not a done deal yet. So far, all I have scheduled is an interview, no firm deal."

"You better learn to call them Native Americans, Alan. These days, not being politically correct can cause you some trouble with folks. Sometimes, they don't like it if you call them Indians. Funny world we live in, ain't it?"

"I'll remember that, Henry. Hope you enjoy the S10. We loved it and we'll miss it. Take good care of our little truck."

We removed the plates and put them in the pickup. I was planning to cut them in little strips with tin snips and drop the pieces in several garbage pails.

The Chevy had been in Michelle's name, so she had signed the title over to Henry Fallon. We shook hands and drove back to the campground.

Before the sun set, we were on top of our sleeping bags. By midnight we were snuggled deep down inside. The temperature in the west cooled off at night. The cool air hanging around the mountain peaks sank into the valleys, surrounding us, making for pleasant sleeping conditions.

LXVII

The Arches

As we drove down Highway 128 toward Moab, the low, morning sun was behind us. We had a long drive to Alamogordo. Since we were doing it in one trip we weren't worried about driving it all in one day. As long as we were in Utah, both of us wanted to see more of this beautiful country. Our first leg was back toward Salt Lake City. We were only a few miles from The Arches National Park. One of the books I read when I was in prison was Edward Abbey's, <u>Desert Solitaire</u>. Abbey wrote the book about his experiences as a park ranger in The Arches. The book painted the Arches as one of the most unique places in the country. Michelle and I wanted to see this special park.

We paid the entrance fee, picking up a pamphlet that included a road map and descriptions of the highlights of the park. At the visitor center we learned that an earthquake split the prairie and moved the level of the visitor center below the level of the rest of the park.

From the visitor's center, we drove up a steep road to the upper section of the park. About a mile into the park, we came to giant rock fins that were called South Park Avenue.

"Can't you just imagine some giant, sitting down, reading the day's news on these huge red rock tablets," exclaimed Michelle. "These are amazing, Paul. All of those huge rocks are parallel to each other, as if God just set them there like pages in a book."

"They are magnificent, but maybe you should start calling me Alan. Paul died in a car crash in Colorado."

"You're right, Paul … er Alan. I'll practice."

At a roadside pull-off we looked back to the southeast. We saw a huge mountain on the horizon. The pamphlet said it was the 12,721 foot Mount Peale and that it was the tallest mountain in the La Sal Range.

"Look, Alan. It says here that early Spanish Explorers saw the white on the top of the mountain and mistakenly named it La Sal, thinking the top was covered with salt instead of snow. Sal is the Spanish word for salt. I guess I knew that."

Soon we came to Balanced Rock. which resembled a giant ball balanced on the nose of a seal. We were almost frightened to walk under the rock.

Michelle gave me a report from the pamphlet. "It says the ball is 58 feet tall and rests on a perch 73 feet in the air. The ball of rock weighs 3,600 tons. I don't want to walk underneath it. It seems ready to fall at any minute."

We took a spur road to the northeast.

"This is supposed to take us to some arches, Alan."

She gave me a big smile. "Did you hear me? Alan?"

"Gotcha. You call me Alan. I'll call you Michelle, not Mary. We can do this sweetheart." I smiled back.

We parked and walked a trail. Michelle was excited. She had Alan Sibley's Nikon digital camera and she was learning how to use it.

"I wanted to be a photographer, Alan. Now I have a great camera and I'm not sure how it works. I set it on A. Does that stand for automatic?"

"No, I think it stands for Aperture priority. That means you set it on a certain f-stop and it adjusts the speed to give you a good picture. You can try it that way, but on the old 35mm camera I had ten years ago, the pros always shot on M, for manual. They said if you are smarter than the camera, then you should choose both the f-stop and the speed."

"That makes no sense at all, Alan Sibley. We need to talk about this some more when we have time. I'd love to shoot like a pro. Maybe I'll read the instruction manual while we drive to New Mexico."

"I'm sure you'll figure it out, Michelle. You seem to always figure out anything you really want to know. If I land this teaching job and we settle in Alamogordo, maybe, you can take a photography course. In fact, I think you should find some kind of a community college program for naturalists and enroll. You already know quite a bit about the plants and animals and geology of the west from what you've read and seen the last three months."

"I love nature hikes, Alan. Do they pay people to take folks on nature hikes? I hear being a naturalist doesn't pay much, but if you have a great job as a teacher, I'm thinking we could live on your salary. I wouldn't have to make a huge amount of money. Would that be OK with you?"

"That should be no problem at all," I agreed. "We've been living frugally. We're maintaining a pretty cheap lifestyle. I don't have the job yet. It's too soon to start spending my salary. Worst case scenario, I can work at a real job now and we can move on."

Michelle let out a little scream. "Look, Paul. There's an arch. She took out her pamphlet. I think it's called The Spectacles. There is a North Window and a South Window."

We walked along the paved trail to where we had closer looks at the two arches. Then, we found Turret Arch and drove on to a second parking lot. A half mile trail took us to a view of Double Arch. Michelle kept snapping digital pictures of the arches. I could tell she was improving. Her sense of composition was instinctive. She seemed really tuned in to the gentle light of the early morning.

"You have a great eye, Michelle. I can't believe you are using Alan's tripod. Isn't that kind of heavy?"

"I was reading one of Alan Sibley's books on nature photography last night after you went to sleep. It said that most good nature photographers shoot 98% of their pictures off a tripod. It gives stability and the prints are much sharper than if you handhold. I also read that publishers don't want any pictures shot after nine o'clock in the morning or before four o'clock in the afternoon. The light is much better early in the day and late in the afternoon. What time is it now, Alan?"

"Nine thirty, Michelle. Time for all great photographers to quit shooting pictures."

"You're right," she agreed. "We have a long trip. Do you suppose we should hit the road?"

"I do. I also think this is a region we should return to. The Arches aren't that far from New Mexico. This park will be a good place to come on summer vacation."

"Or even spring break. That's one nice thing about teaching in high school," Michelle suggested. "Summer vacations will give us a good chance to explore the country."

We turned south, but we didn't travel far.

Michelle said, "Look, Alan. Here's a place called Natural Bridges National Monument. It's only a few miles out of our way. Can we go see it? Do we have time? I'll bet I could take some great pictures there."

We camped at the Natural Bridges that night.

After following the circle drive in Natural Bridges National Monument and hiking a couple of short trails, we drove to Blanding, Utah. At the library, Michelle looked for used books in the book sale while I used a library computer. Checking the headlines from the Des Moines Register, I found a headline, Escaped Prisoner and Killer of Guard Found Dead in Colorado Canyon. In a paragraph toward the bottom of page six, the article described an interview with Helen Hartman. It suggested that my mother was heartbroken at my death.

Michelle and I used our phone card to call my friend, George Dunkelberg in Carbondale. A half hour later Mom was with him when I called him back.

"Hello?"

"Hi, Mom."

"Paul?"

"You have other kids?"

"No, but I thought you were dead. This isn't a mean joke, is it? Is this really you, Paul. Really?"

"Don't believe everything you read, Mom. Sometimes newspapers publish false information. My wallet and my fingerprints were in that car. We found it at the bottom of a ravine and the dead guy looked too much like me. I gave him my old driver's license that you sent me. They must have thought that the dead guy was me. I'm alive and well, Mom."

"This is wonderful, Paul. You'll never know how good you've made me feel today."

"I'm glad, Mom. Sorry you had to go through this. Thinking I was dead. Sorry, Mom. Wish I could give you a hug right now. One thing."

"Yes?"

"Are you a good actress?"

"I was in plays in high school."

"Can you pretend to be heartbroken over my death; Like you were last week?"

"Right now I have a huge smile on my face."

"Pretend, Mom. Pretend. It can help keep me free."

"For your freedom, I can act sad, Paul. Never forget how much I love you." She glanced over at George.

"Your friend, George is overhearing our conversation as well. I'll tell him he has to act sad as well. He's been pretty mopey.

We had a memorial service last week. We cremated your body and spread your ashes on a bluff above the Mississippi River. It was a very nice ceremony. You'd be amazed at how many friends you have around here. The church was full and I have a stack of cards, such nice messages. I'll save them for you."

"Amazing, Mom. Keep acting sad."

"I already quit acting sad, Paul. I've been smiling and telling people you're in a better place. Now I know it."

"Thanks, Mom. I need to go. Love you."

"I love you so much. I hope things are going good for you."

"Looking up. I think life is going to be wonderful. Goodbye."

"Goodbye, Paul. Thank you so much for calling. I'll keep acting like you're dead. I can do that."

I hung up the phone and glanced at Michelle. She looked at me and began to giggle. "I heard that. So you've been cremated. Your ashes spread on a bluff above the Mississippi. Your mom is pretending to be sad. This is crazy, Paul. Crazy."

LXVIII

My Second Teaching Job

My stomach was doing gymnastics; I was in a cold sweat. It was the first day of school and I was scared. My royal blue button down dress shirt and diagonally striped necktie felt strange. The buttoned collar and the snug-fitting tie felt restrictive at my neck. Michelle thought my tan slacks and brown sport coat looked sharp. New black dress shoes glowed with fresh polish, but felt strange on feet that had been in hiking boots or tennis shoes for many months. Short walks had helped my feet adjust to the new shoes and the new shoes to form to my feet. Most folks don't know how much abuse a teacher's feet take in seven hours of teaching. I had bought good shoes; I hoped they were well broken in. A decade ago I had worn dress clothes every day; today, I felt a little self-conscious.

Some teachers wasted the first and last days of school. To me that would have been asking for trouble. I was ready to teach. As a new teacher, I was required to turn in lesson plans each week to be approved by the lead teacher in the business department. My plans were in, approved, and I was eager to begin my new teaching career.

As the bell rang, I took my position at the door for hall duty. Having teachers on duty at their doors helps to maintain order; it stops problems before they begin. This was a school rule; just common sense. Kids were less likely to cause trouble if there were teachers in the halls. Teachers at their doors were also helpful to students trying to find their way to class on the first day.

I nodded and said good morning to a stout, curly-headed youngster, who I guessed to be a sophomore. He didn't even look up as he walked past me down the hall. Another student had opened his locker, reaching to put notebooks on the top shelf when the curly-headed kid shoved the locker door and knocked notebooks across the hall.

"Why don't you pay attention when you open your locker? Keep out of my way."

I walked that direction down the hall. The stout boy who hadn't responded to me had his hands balled into fists. It looked as if I might need to break up a fight on my first day.

Stopping to pick up his notebooks and glancing at the sour look on the other boy's face, the offended boy looked the sour-puss in the eyes and said, "This is the first day of school and you look like your day isn't going too well already, Karl. Is something bad going on with you?"

Karl frowned again. "I guess my day started out wrong. I'm just pissed off. I'm sorry."

"I'm going your way. Is it alright if I walk to class with you? You can talk about it if you want to."

The two boys walked on down the hall talking. I went back to my post by my door. These kids might be alright.

Five minutes later another bell rang; I walked into my first class and looked at the well-scrubbed faces of twenty-two juniors who filled all but two of the twenty-four seats in my classroom. Since the noise level was high, I thought perhaps I should quiet them down before starting my class. I glanced from face to face. Some of my students bore a look of fear that might be similar to the feeling inside me. I wondered about the fear they might have had if they had known their new teacher was an escaped convict and a murderer. I frowned and immediately forced the slight smile back onto my face, purging the thoughts of my past. I guessed that some members of my first class were wary of this new entity in their school. I was a stranger; it might take a while for them to trust me.

I saw students who seemed to be filled with quiet confidence; I saw faces that I read as brash cockiness. I made eye contact, offering a smile to each of the youngsters. Usually, a smile reflected my own. I saw the backs of heads as a large number of my class members were involved in loud conversations. As I opened my mouth trying to control my first class, one of the boys I had judged to be cocky, lifted his voice above the noise, "Hey guys, give Mr. Sibley a chance to teach."

Many of the backs turned to face me. I said, "Thanks. I *am* ready to begin our adventure in the world of business."

That brought a collective groan.

"Good morning. My name is Mr. Sibley. All of you know that already if you looked at your schedule. This is Intro to Business. You're probably here to find ways to apply all you've learned the first two years of high school to make you a rich man or woman by the time you are 40."

"I'm planning to marry a rich man," said the blond in the front row who had a perfect complexion and even teeth that shined white, probably from several expensive years at an orthodontist.

"What's your name, young lady?" I asked.

"I'm Heidi Truax," she told us.

"What do you all think of Heidi's business plan, class?

Three or four people started to talk at once like in those talking heads news programs on cable television. I moved my hands like windshield wipers and said, "I'd like you to raise your hand and be called upon before you respond, please. That way we can have discussions that include the slow thinkers as well as the quick reaction people."

I called on the pretty red-head in the back row with a figure that could distract a careless teacher.

"Your name, ma'am?"

"I'm Alicia and I agree. I want to go to a good college and meet a rich man."

I called on a quiet looking guy from the second row who had his hand raised to the level of his face.

"I'm Todd." He turned to face Alicia. "Heidi and Alicia, I think your business plans suck. Over half the marriages end in divorces. I think you need to marry for love -- after you finish your college education. Then, when you and your Mr. Rich Guy Husband split up you can run the business that you receive as a divorce settlement."

The class had a good laugh at Todd's conclusion.

"Thanks for your comments folks," I responded. "I can tell I'm going to like teaching this class. You are filled with imaginative ideas. I'll try to find ways for you to share them. And I'll try to give you some new theories to think about.

"I need to know who you are. Please write your name on the seating chart. If you can sign it so your name is right side up for me to read and in the right spot, you'll earn a five point bonus grade immediately.

"Also, I'm passing around sheets of recycled paper that are clean on one side. I want you to take one and write your story. Tell about yourself -- what you like, what you hate, what you read, what you eat, what are your hobbies, who's in your family, your best friends, best courses, and future plans -- school and work. You have only one sheet. It's worth five points; I'd like it today before you leave class."

I gave them copies of my syllabus and explained what was expected of them and what I hoped they would learn. I issued a textbook to each student as I asked them to tell me the book number plus what they dreamed of doing in ten years. Then, I began a short lecture on the first chapter, ending with a reading assignment for the next class.

By the time the second semester had started, Michelle and I were convinced that Alamogordo, New Mexico might be the place for us to live our lives.

LXIX

Mothers

"I'm lonely, Alan."

"Really? Who do you need besides me?"

"You know I love you, Paul. You know I love every minute we're together. I understand why we can't be too close to other people. We'd have to start telling lies and pretty soon one of the lies would catch up to us. The more we're around other people the more chance we have that one of our lies won't fit with someone's knowledge of the way it really is. I understand all that.

"Still, I'm missing a closeness to other people. I'm talking about friends; people we associate with at work or in class. I have two classes this spring at the community college. The business class is awful. I feel terribly alone even before I walk through the door. And when I leave, I feel even worse. Most of the students are way younger than me; many of them already have friends in the class. There is an eighteen year old fresh-man boy who makes little passes at me and is obviously in love with my breasts. I think a couple of the girls are jealous because of the attention this kid pays me.

"The teacher is married, but he keeps hinting that I'd do better if I stayed after class for some extra help. I'd earn an A for sure if I'd see him after class and do one of my old dances for him."

"You said you liked your environmental biology class," I said. "Is it still going well?"

"It's a highlight of my week, Alan. One day we gathered needles from high in a tall pine tree and from low on the inside of the same tree. The teacher has a machine that calculates the surface area of a group of ten needles. When we compared and ran some kind of statistical analysis on the computer, we found that the top needles were significantly smaller than the lower needles.

"We had to formulate a conclusion. I postulated that the bottom needles received less light so they had to be larger to create enough photosynthesis to feed that portion of the tree. I don't know if I was correct or not, but it made sense to me. I really like a couple of the girls in that class and the teacher is wonderful. She's kind of a biology nerd, but she knows everything about biology and she does a terrific job of putting us in situations where we can't help but learn.

"Oh, Paul. I mean, Oh, Alan," Michelle chuckled. "I miss my mommy. I miss my mommy and I miss my little sister, Michelle. I know Michelle is dead and I'll never see her again, but I want to see my mommy. I want to hug her and hold her."

She exploded in tears and wrapped her arms around me. She wrapped her arms around Alan Sibley, the fake man who I had become. Her tears flowed over the shoulder of Paul Hartman, the man who had been a trusted teacher, a convicted swindler, an accidental murderer, an escaped convict, the man this magical woman had grown to love.

I felt like sand on a beach being pounded by ocean waves. The problems continued to pound and I, like beach sand, must continue to absorb their force. Actually, I had been thinking about a possible solution for Michelle's problem. And Michelle's problem was my problem as well.

"I know how you feel," I agreed. "I miss my mommy too. Let's do something about the problem of missing our moms. Sometimes I wake up in the night with wild ideas. A couple of days ago I woke about 3:00 a.m. with a thought. Have you ever heard of the Road Scholar program?"

"No. I don't think so."

"Road Scholar is a new name for Elderhostel. They offer hundreds of programs for seniors who can go someplace and take classes to learn just about anything. Our mothers are both old enough to participate as Road Scholars. These week-long classes are held all over the world. In April, there is one on natural history and birding at Big Bend National Park. What if our mothers signed up for that Road Scholar program? One of the sessions ends on March 14. Our spring break starts on Friday, the 13th of March. You aren't superstitious are you? Our moms could both go to the Road Scholar Program. We could pick them up at the end and hang out together in Southwestern

Texas for a week. Actually, we can have about nine days together. Do you think we can set this up without bringing the FBI down on us here in New Mexico?"

"There must be a way. Did your dream tell you a safe process to set up this meeting of the moms?"

"It could be fairly simple. What if we picked up a bunch of $100 bills, address two small manila envelopes on the computer, one to each of our moms? We'll put $2000 in each envelope, and put them in a larger envelope addressed to my friend George Dunkelberg in Arkansas. He could send one to your mom and take the other next door to mine. We could tell them to register for the Road Scholar program at Big Bend and buy plane tickets to El Paso on Saturday the 7th. We could even check on the flights from Des Moines and Carbondale."

"Sounds terrific, Paul. Let's do it. It will be wonderful to see Mom and meet your mother and let them know that they are going to be grandmothers."

The apartment became suddenly quiet, like silent prayer time at church.

Finally, after two full minutes spent processing the new information, a tiny voice came from my mouth. "You ... you're thinking of becoming pregnant?"

"I *am* pregnant, Alan Sibley. Sometimes these things happen without thinking about them."

I wrapped my arms around Michelle. "Maybe you'll marry me now?" I asked.

"Maybe we should do it when our moms are here," she answered.

It had been over a year since Mary Swartz had seen her mother and more than two years since my mom had visited me in an Iowa prison. Thinking of being together after two years thrilled us both. The thought of becoming a father dazed me. I didn't know what to say. I knew what to do. As I held Michelle in my arms, she must have felt me tremble.

"Are you still alright, Alan? How do you feel about being a father?"

"I'm speechless, Michelle. I'm thrilled beyond anything I have ever felt in my life; I'm very scared. I like the idea of being a father. I love the dream of raising a little boy or girl with you. Risking my life the last year with you has been an adventure, the best year of my life.

"Risking your life has bothered me every day of the year," I continued. "Most of me has loved each minute with you. Another part of me has been afraid that we would screw up and you would go back to prison because some crazy guard had a power crush and tried to rape you. When he hit his head and died you should have stayed and explained what happened. You'd be free by now. You'd have a free life ahead of you, Mary Swartz. You'd have your own name. You could see your mother any time you wanted. You could have married and raised a family. Your child would have no danger of having its parents arrested and sent to prison while he or she spent years in a foster home.

"I'm thrilled to be a father, Michelle, and I'm scared to death to be risking the life of a child whose parents are escaped prisoners. How can I think of fathering a child when I know one slip-up means the child's father will spend his life in prison for murder? How can I do that, Michelle?"

Again it was quiet for a moment. Then Michelle said, "You don't have too much choice, Alan. I'm pregnant and you're the father. I'm going to have a baby. If you are thinking about an abortion, Alan Sibley, it's not going to happen. This baby is in my body. If it was in someone else's body she might choose to abort it. I'm going to risk the getting caught thing, Alan.

"I love you and I love our baby. He or she is a part of you and a part of me. Life is full of risks. We've had a year of facing more than most people face in a lifetime. For me, being with you and having a part of you growing inside me is worth all the risks we've taking this past year."

After a pause so I knew she was done, I said, "Tell me how you really feel, Michelle."

I had no words to add so I took her in my arms again and held her head to my chest.

"Will you marry me now?" I whispered in her ear.

She pushed me away and stared into my eyes. Her eyes were twinkling like magnified stars from the milky way on a clear night.

"I'll be your wife, for all your life.

I'll love you true, never make you blue.

I'll have your babies, all the way to Hades.

Together, we'll both stand tall.

Forever, I'll love you, Paul."

Michelle kissed Alan and said, "Won't our mothers be surprised when they arrive in El Paso and we invite them to our wedding and tell them they're about to be grandmothers?"

LXX

Letters Home

Helen Hartman's phone rang. It was after eight in the evening on a cold Monday night in January. Freezing rain had coated the sidewalks and streets in Carbondale. Paul's friend George Dunkelberg had spread sand on Helen's sidewalks and driveway so the glare ice was maneuverable, if a person was very careful.

"Hello," she answered.

"Hi, Helen. This is George. I'm fixing a pot of tea and I was hoping you might bring some cookies over so we could have a snack before bedtime."

"Why don't you come over here, George? The sidewalks are treacherous."

"I have something new, Helen. I just have to show it to someone and its too big to carry. I'll wear my ice creepers. I'll come over and escort you to my house."

Helen paused for twenty seconds, pondering her neighbor's offer. Finally, "Well, alright. Give me five minutes to slip into some jeans. I hope this is important. I'm in my pajamas already."

"You'll be glad you came, Helen. I promise you. You'll be glad you came."

The young man and the almost retired woman slid down her sidewalk and up his. They were both grateful when they walked into George's living room.

He poured tea and she spread a plate of brownies with nuts and thick chocolate frosting on the coffee table.

"The smell of those brownies is enough to make a person crave sex," smiled George, "if that relationship really exists."

"I certainly know nothing about that," responded Helen Hartman. "I used to have a Bichon who loved chocolate. Every time that dog ate it she became deathly sick. And she ate it every time she could find it. That little dog would figure out how to climb to the tops of kitchen counters, if a plate of chocolate chip cookies or a chocolate candy was there. Kichon was her name. She would be going wild right now."

The two neighbors settled back and enjoyed their brownies and tea.

Finally, Helen couldn't take it any more. "Alright, George. You have something new today. What is it? Show me."

He set his tea cup on the coffee table and held his finger to his lips. Then he whispered quietly in her ear. "We're going to do this quietly because sometimes walls have ears. Paul wouldn't want anybody else to know about what's going on. We can pretend later that I have a new refrigerator."

Then he said out loud. "I'll show you my surprise later, Helen. We'll just talk for a while first.

"There is an article in today's paper that you may want to read. Take a look at the editorial page."

George picked up a manila envelope from the coffee table, handing it to Helen. Again he put his finger to his lips to seal her comment.

The flap was lightly sealed and Helen opened the letter. It contained a sheet of white paper. Two stacks of currency fell out on the coffee table. She rifled through them counting twenty, hundred dollar bills held together with clips.

She looked at George and mouthed, "What's this?"

He shrugged. "That's lovely perfume you are wearing, Helen. Is it lavender?"

"Yes."

She opened the letter and began to read silently.

Dear Mom,

It's been over two years since we've seen each other. That has been way too long for me.

I've been doing really well. I have a great new job that is something I love. It pays good money. It is honest work and I'm not doing any bad stuff on the side except avoiding the law and trying not to be arrested for breaking out of jail.

Several bits of news. First, I've fallen in love with the woman who was with me when I escaped. Actually, I loved her before I escaped. That might have been why I couldn't let the guard rape her that night.

The $2000 in the envelope is honest money, Mom. My friend and I have earned it. She's working part time and is going to school. I want you to meet her. You'll love her as much as I do. Her name is Mary. She has a new name now and I won't say it until you meet her in person. I have a new name too. That might take you a while to become used to using.

Don't be too excited about the money in the envelope. We've already planned for how you'll spend it. First, we want you to buy a round trip airline ticket on American Airlines from St. Louis to El Paso, Texas. Maybe George can give you a ride to St. Louis. The flight you'll want will leave St. Louis on the morning of April 2 and return on April 13.

Also, you are going to sign up for a Road Scholar Program. (That's the new name for Elderhostel.) They are programs where people over fifty go to study good stuff. The title of this one is "Birding and Nature Studies." It takes place in Big Bend National Park. Its program number is #17973. It starts on April 4 and ends on April 9. We'd like you to request a roommate, Adel Swartz. That's Mary's mom. The phone number that you can use to register is toll free 977.426.8056.

If this works out, we will spend some time together. We have several other surprises for you.

Don't be too quick to recognize us at the airport, Mom. We will watch closely for the cops before we approach you. We have started a good honest life and we'd hate to spoil it. Keep an eye out for anyone who looks like he or she is following you. If you are suspicious then take a baseball cap out of your bag and wear it. We'll find a new way to make contact. In fact, we want you to write your cell phone number on a piece of paper. If there is a problem drop it near a trash can close to the luggage pick up. We'll find it and give it a call. That can be our plan B.

DO NOT share this letter or any of this information with anyone. It's OK to tell your closest friends about the Road Scholar Program, but wait until the middle of March to talk about it. George is my trusted friend and you can tell him that we are going to be together sometime. Don't let him read this letter. The less he knows the better it is for him. Tell him he is my dearest friend and that I will be forever indebted to him. In the spring you can tell him about the Road Scholar class.

We have a couple of great surprises for you, Mom. We'll see you in April.

Paul

Helen Hartman folded the letter and placed it and the $2000 carefully in the envelope, then slid the envelope into her purse. She took a sip of her cooling tea. From her purse, she removed a cotton handkerchief with a picture of a deer in a forest scene, wrapped her face in it, and began to cry. George slid beside her on the coach.

After about three minutes he asked, "What's wrong, Helen?"

Helen Hartman leaned over next to her neighbor and friend and whispered, "I'm so happy. Paul is alive. He's not in a grave in the desert. I'm going to see him. Oh, I'm not supposed to tell that to anyone. Promise you won't tell, George."

She looked up at George. "Maybe it's OK. I'm going to need a ride to the airport, George. Could you give me a ride to St. Louis?"

"Of course. You know I'd never tell anybody anything."

Des Moines

When she stopped at her recycling bin, Adel Swartz's hands were full of mail. She dealt the envelopes into the green tub like a black jack dealer at one of Iowa's casinos. Adel slipped a Wells Fargo envelope to the bottom of the stack, a move that would mean trouble in the casino.

That would be the house payment, she thought. *I hate it that my local lender sold my loan to Wells Fargo. They might have a great team of horses on their ads, but doing business with huge banks seems unethical after what terrible things they did to the economy of our country.*

Two more window envelopes dropped into the bin. At the bottom of the stack was a medium sized manila envelope. It was thick and had a real stamp and a written address, but its upper left corner was blank. Adel's first glance made her think it was from a business that was trying to make it look personal. Then she felt the heft of the envelope and stared at the neat penmanship on the address.

Mary! she thought. She ripped open the flap. A stack of money fell into the bin as her wrinkled hand closed around a second stack and a white sheet of paper.

Adel Swartz slowly unfolded the paper and read the handwritten letter.

Dear Mom,
  I miss you more than I can tell you. And I love you more than you will ever know. It's been way too long since I've given you a hug. I want to

sit beside you and tell you all about the good things that have happened to me the last year. I want to know all about what is making you happy and sad.

I've been doing pretty well. I told you I was in love with the guy who I escaped with. That love is stronger than ever. We're learning to love the good in each other as we embrace our humanness.

He loves me, Mom. He worships me. He treats me with respect, even though he knows all about my past. We're actually becoming pretty upstanding citizens in our community. Anyway, we are great for each other. We are kind of like a real small AA group. We keep each other out of trouble.

The $2000 in this envelope is honest money, Mom. My friend and I have earned it. I'm working part time and going to school. My friend is working at a really good job. I want you to meet him. You'll fall in love with him too. I've been calling him my friend. You probably know his name is Paul. He has a new name now and I don't want to say it in case somebody sees this letter who should not see it.

Don't be too excited about the money. We've already spent it for you. First, we want you to buy a round trip airline ticket on American Airlines to El Paso, Texas. You need to leave Des Moines on the morning of April 2 and return on April 13.

Then you are going to sign up for a Road Scholar Program. (That's the new name for Elderhostel). They sponsor programs where people, usually much older than you, go to study good stuff. The title is "Birding and Nature Studies" and it takes place in Big Bend National Park. Its program number is #17973. It starts on April 4 and ends on April 9. We'd like you to request a roommate, Helen Hartman. That's Paul's mom. The phone number that you can use to register is toll free 977.426.8056. (There may be an age limit so tell them you are 51 if they ask.)

If this works out, we will spend some time together. We have several surprises for you. Don't be too quick to recognize us in the airport, Mom. We will watch closely for the cops before we approach you. We have started a good honest life and we'd hate to spoil it. Keep an eye out for anyone who looks like he or she is following you. If you are suspicious, then take a baseball cap out of your bag and wear it. We'll find a new way to make contact. In fact Paul says you should write your cell phone number on a piece of paper and drop it near a trash can close to the luggage pick up. We'll find it and give it a call. That can be our plan B.

I love you tons, mom. DO NOT share this letter or any of this information with anyone, except it's OK to tell your closest friends about the Road Scholar Program, but wait until the middle of March to talk about it.

My love to you always,

Mary

Adel Swartz reached down and picked up the stack of bills. She felt a huge smile come across her face and tears stream down her cheeks. She hugged the letter and money to her chest and began to dance, twirling gracefully across the concrete floor of her garage.

Then she glanced at the post mark on the envelope.

Paducah, Kentucky. Only about three states away. Maybe I can see her again someday.

LXXI

Having a Stake in My Game

Hank Hanson taught biology at AHS. Our classrooms were adjacent. Hank was a big guy. He could have played guard on the Green Bay Packers football team except for his bad knee. He carried 240 pounds on his 5' 10" frame.

As a freshman at New Mexico State, Hank was fifty pounds heavier and on his way to becoming an All-American. That was the year he was the Big West Conference's Offensive Lineman of the year. NMSU ended its fine season by playing Idaho State in the Humanitarian Bowl in Boise. The Aggies were ahead 35-16 in the fourth quarter. A set of reserve linemen were standing on the sideline ready to enter the game, so the fans could give the varsity a round of applause. On Hank's last play of the season, a 310 pound defensive tackle landed on top of him. The offensive tackle's leg was under Hank's knee when the Idaho State tackle crashed down on Hank's ankle. The tear in the ligament required extensive reconstructive surgery. Hank worked hard at rehabilitation. After a redshirt year he spent the next three years playing as a reserve. He finished school with a master's degree in biology education. For the next twelve years, Hank built a reputation as a demanding, but caring and fair high school biology teacher.

Hank and I controlled the hall in front of our classrooms. Kids learned that they didn't want to tangle with the two of us. Our hallway was about as orderly as a place can be with 300 teen-agers streaming past in the three minutes between classes.

We also shared a common prep period. We usually spent part of it drinking coffee and talking about our history, our futures, our life outside the classroom. Sometimes our discussions even strayed into politics. Actually, we talked mostly about Hank's history and my lies about things I remembered about Alan Sibley, the ski bum and white water rafter. Thank goodness, Michelle and I had taken the raft trip in Colorado. It made my lies easier to fabricate. Many days, I hurried home from school, fired up Alan's computer, writing the stories about my life that I had told to Hank that day during our prep period. I had a growing file titled, "The Life of Alan Sibley" By Alan Sibley.

My bad knee stories kept me away from skiing. I had done a bit of cross-country skiing in Iowa, but lies about my downhill skiing were tough to invent since I'd never had the experience. Michelle and I spent many Saturday afternoons watching TV coverage of skiing competition, concentrating on learning everything we could about the sport.

One day Hank asked, "Did I hear you were a big time skier, Alan?"

I responded with a modest, "That part of my life ended when I messed up my knee. I don't even want to talk about it."

Luckily, Hank liked to talk about his super year of college football. I steered the conversation his way whenever he brought up the subject of skiing. Sometimes, I'd talk about a wasted life as a ski bum, but never about the actual skiing.

One warm Saturday in the fall, I dressed in a pair of shorts and a sweatshirt as Michelle and I decided to go for a walk. She glanced down and said, "Nice legs, Alan."

I stopped and looked at my smooth legs.

"Wait a minute, Michelle. I can't go out looking like this."

"Sure you can. It's a nice day and you have great legs."

"That's the problem. My legs should have big scars from surgery. I had a terrible skiing accident, remember? I should have a huge scar on my knee. If we meet somebody we know, two plus two will add up to five."

I pulled out a pair of jeans and gathered up the three pairs of shorts I owned.

"Let's take a trip to Goodwill; see if they can use three very good pairs of shorts. I'm not going to make this mistake again."

Hank and I had many experiences that drew us together and made us good friends. One day, we were almost finished with morning hall duty when we saw Bob Marske, a 6'2" 120 pound freshman walking up the hall toward us. He was swaying badly. Bob bumped the lockers with his right shoulder. Six steps later he glanced off the lockers on the other side of the hall with his left shoulder.

As he came between Hank and me, Hank gave a nod, I nodded back and took Bob's left elbow as Hank took the right. I asked, "Are you alright, Bob?"

Bob gave no response and the three of us moved down the hall, Hank on one elbow, me on the other with long, lanky, Bob Marske between us, barely skipping his toes on the tile floor.

We sat Bob gently in a chair in the principal's office. Hank talked to Steve Rodriquez, our principal, about connecting Bob with some medical help and contacting his parents.

I sat down beside the sick, slender sophomore and asked, "What did you take, Bob. We need to know, so we can help you."

Bob wasn't talking. Sometimes his lips moved, but he wasn't able to form words.

"Thanks guys," assured Steve. "We'll handle it from here."

Hank and I were glad to pass the problem on.

We learned later that Bob's mother, a single mom, came from work and took him home. The next day Bob was back in school, acting as if nothing had happened. Hank and I were glad. I hoped the kid had experienced a free lesson on the effect of drugs on his body. Everybody screwed up in life. Many people don't get caught or somehow, like Bob Marske, they don't suffer any bad consequences. They go on with life after a stunt that helps them to know better the next time.

Other people, like me, do something illegal and in my case immoral. Then their whole life changes. If I hadn't had that fluke prison escape, I'd be out walking the streets as a free man. And because of my prison record I'd be either unemployed or have some flunky job with no future.

As it was, the probability was high that I would soon be married to the most sensational woman I have ever known. I was doing a job I was trained to do, that I loved dearly. I was financially pretty well off and I was about to become a father.

I had two major concerns. The first was Michelle. If the two of us were together, one mistake on my part could write her a fast, one-way ticket back to the pen. I could live with more prison time, but I didn't want to live with the guilt if something I did sent her back.

Still, we had a mutual loving relationship. Those are not easy to find. We'd been together for a year. We'd had some disagreements, but both of us were willing to give some and take some. I didn't remember a single incident when a disagreement led to either of us shouting at the other person.

I loved this woman's spirit. I loved her body. I loved her soul. And I loved the fact that she reciprocated my love. If I believed she would be safer without me, I would have sent her away. I think I felt that we had survived a year of freedom together and had developed into a pretty good team. We had taken what life had given us, made choices that had kept us free, and moved toward having a real chance for spending the rest of our lives together.

If some unlucky event ended our time together and sent us back to an Iowa prison, we'd face it. Both of us knew that we had no guarantees of a future together. Unless Michelle decided to go off in her own direction, I couldn't end it. Marrying this woman, having our baby, and continuing to build a life for Alan and Michelle Sibley and their child was what I wanted.

The other huge problem that scared the hell out of me was my students at AHS. I was beginning to build some relationships with some quality young people. The ethics of business were emphasized in every class I taught.

If something happened that opened up my past to these kids, what would they think? *Mr. Sibley teaches ethics and really he's an embezzler. Ethics really isn't all that important is it?*

It wasn't just for me that the charade had to keep working. Michelle and our child-to-be had their lives on the line along with mine.

And now the web we were weaving had spread to ensnare a hundred kids who looked at me as an example of how an ethical person lives his or her life. Having them find out that they had a criminal for a teacher would be terrible for them to deal with.

My little web also included my principal and superintendent. These two men had investigated my phony background, deciding Alan Sibley was a pretty decent guy. They had allowed me to work every day with kids entrusted to their care. If my real life came out, the two men who hired me would have their butts in a fan.

I realized that other folks had a stake in my little game. They didn't know it, but many innocent people were better off if my real identity stayed a thing of the past.

LXXII

A Mutual Acquaintance

Michelle kissed me on the neck and spoke into my ear. The melody from the acoustical guitar filled the air near our table in the funky little bar along the Rio Grande. I moved my mouth close to her ear and whispered, "How long since you spent a Saturday night out on the town, sweetheart?"

"Long before I knew you, Mister Sibley," Michelle whispered back. "Seems like you and I have spent our life together scrimping and saving every penny we could lay our hands on. Partying has never been in the cards. Also, we always seem to have this fear of meeting someone who knows us or knows about us from our past lives."

Hank and Angie Hanson were having dinner with Michelle and me in the Eldorado Bar along the Rio Grande. It was our first night out with the first real friends we'd made since I'd started teaching in Alamogordo.

I liked this talking in the ear stuff. I nuzzled her neck again and whispered, "This isn't really the kind of place where

I'd expect to meet somebody from Iowa. I think we're pretty safe."

Michelle responded a little louder, "Whispering is not nice when we're out with friends, Alan. You're giving me chills. We are here to talk to Angie and Hank. Behave!"

The bar was funky. Slick tiles in a tan and brown pattern covered the floor. The walls were rough stucco. Wooden posts held up a bamboo ceiling which gave the nightspot a cheap, authentic Mexican look. Two of the stucco walls were painted a gaudy red-orange color. Bright abstract paintings in basic colors of yellow, green, blue, and red filled rectangular canvases on open wall spaces. Each of the wooden poles supported a candle-lantern made from a red-clay, field-tile reflector. Strings of red chili peppers hung from any available spot.

The four of us sat around a square table with a diamond-shaped table cloth. In the center was an ugly little candle that burned in a pleasant yellow flame.

Every part of the place felt like the southwest. Sixty percent of me was in a little Mexican cantina. The other forty percent in a western tavern. My companions added to both feelings. Hank, the biology teacher, had a well-trimmed mustache and goatee. He wore a big round-topped Stetson, like John Wayne's, a dark green canvas shirt, black jeans, well-worn and polished cowboy boots, and a broad belt with a huge silver buckle decorated with a bucking bronco. Hank had won the belt as All-Round Cowboy in the Ardmore, Oklahoma rodeo of 1990. My friend, Hank, was a man of the west.

His wife, Angie, was a gorgeous woman. Her quick smile caught the humor in any moment. Women liked her and her smile made every man she met fall a little bit in love with her. Angie wore her black hair long and straight. Thin bangs blocked a bit of her dark, intense eyes. She wore a deep blue blouse that looked Mexican. The shiny silk left one shoulder bare. This drew a glance from every cowboy who hadn't already found her eyes or her smile. Her skirt seemed to be made in layers of bright materials from a fiesta. Fancy engraved patterns in the leather high heels marked her cowboy boots as items of quality.

Michelle was lovely. Her azure blue dress had intricate hand crocheting in bright colors across her chest. On Michelle, this $15 Mexican style dress from a garage sale looked startling. The outfit drew every eye in the room to her figure and the bright colors brought another lovely piece of Mexico into this funky Alamogordo bar.

In my jeans and long-sleeved, black, garage sale shirt, I was the plain person in the group. It was a shiny silk material. I felt comfortable in it. Michelle thought I looked great.

The featured entertainer at the bar was an acoustical guitarist named Stan Johnson. He stunned us with his performance. The guy could make his guitar talk. His songs, at first, were unrecognizable. Then, after a few moments, I began to recognize a bit of melody that brought an old tune singing in my head. Listening to one of his songs was like meeting a stranger and minutes later hearing a nuance in voice or seeing a mannerism that opened my eyes to a friend from my past, causing the person's identity to flow back into my brain. Perish that thought. Meeting an old friend was a constant fear for Michelle and me. Meeting an old friend could spoil our lives and send us both back to prison. I sat back, holding Michelle's hand, letting Stan Johnson's guitar carry me safely back to places from long ago.

When the music was over I bought a CD of Stan's music and the four of us talked of our history and our dreams for the future. We gave our new friends a little of our history -- really, the lies we were learning. Michelle had her sister's name, her sister's driver's license, her sister's high school diploma, and her sister's good looks. She didn't have to lie very much. She avoided the Des Moines, Iowa part of her history. Her old home town was never mentioned in her conversations.

I had Alan Sibley's name, his driver's license, his social security number, his pick-up camper, his college degree, and his teaching certificate. Using Alan's credentials I had landed my teaching job. It was a job I was prepared for and a job I loved. I knew enough about Alan Sibley to talk a little about my background. My other big fear was that one of Alan Sibley's real friends would show up and wonder why I was calling myself by the name of his friend.

Most people enjoy talking about their histories. Michelle and I were learning to be good listeners. People loved telling us their stories. We were developing a talent for asking questions that encouraged people to talk about themselves.

"Tell us about your college days. Who were your friends? What were your favorite courses? What do you like to do in your spare time?"

The answers to our questions helped us to know Angie and Hank. They began to feel that Michelle and I cared about them. So many conversations involve everyone listening for a chance to jump in with, "I … ." Our friends enjoyed the chance to talk about themselves and we could see them developing into longtime friends.

Angie was a third grade teacher until she became pregnant with Josh and Gretchen their twin four-year-olds. She told us she really wanted to go back to work when they started full time kindergarden.

Her twins could read, do some basic math, and speak Spanish and English so well that they weren't always sure which language they were speaking. Michelle and I were taking Spanish as an evening course. The twins were far ahead of us.

Alan Sibley's college transcript included five semesters of Spanish. Paul Hartman had taken two years of Italian in college and a year of Spanish in high school. The two languages are so closely related that I found myself picking up Spanish pretty quickly. Michelle also had a year of high school Spanish.

"I really didn't apply myself in high school," she told our friends. "I didn't care much about having an education then. I just wanted to be beautiful and have the interest of plenty of boys."

Now, she was better than I was at speaking Spanish. Michelle was really smart when she was motivated; she was trying very hard to learn all she could about everything. I was proud of her.

The superintendent in Alamogordo had seen five semesters of Spanish on my transcript and was impressed. I think it's one of the reasons he hired me. I tried to cut his expectations by telling him that I had never really used the language, but I thought it would come back pretty fast. At home we tried speaking nothing but Spanish for three nights a week. My fluency in Spanish was another of those little lies that we were determined to keep from catching up with us.

We learned that one of Angie's hobbies was making pottery. She sold much of it through a shop in town and gave some of it to her friends. She promised us a set of coffee cups. We were excited, looking forward to having some of her beautiful work.

Hank and Angie were hikers and nature lovers. We enjoyed their stories of hiking in the mountains. We figured our story of the shooting of Mandi would top any of theirs, but we couldn't tell it.

"We love White Sands National Monument," said Angie. "We go there quite a bit. Maybe you two can come along some day, if you don't mind hiking with a couple of four year olds."

"We'd love to," volunteered Michelle. "Hiking with kids must be a blast."

Michelle and I exchanged a quick glance. We both thought, *there's another set of sand dunes we haven't seen. Maybe we need to go on a side trip.*

Angie and Michelle hit it off well. As Angie began to talk about White Sands, she quickly learned that Michelle was genuinely interested.

"You should be there on a calm morning after a windy night. Seeing fresh animal tracks in the smooth sand is so much fun. Trying to figure out who made them and what the little animals were up to is a blast for the twins; especially Josh. He loves it. Finding the tracks of a jumping mouse thrills him. It has two long prints from its hind feet that are usually in front of the smaller tracks of the front feet. The next set of tracks may be a meter away. Josh says, 'Look, Mommy. Jumping mouse made BIG jump!'

"Gretchen could care less about wild animals. If we go hiking, she spends her time reading. She looks funny walking down a trail with a book in her hands."

As we talked, Stan Johnson was making the rounds of the tables. He seemed to care that his audience had enjoyed his music.

I shared a story from my early teaching career that I adopted to a convention I went to in college. "I remember going to Chicago for a convention of business teachers. A group of us bought tickets to a play staring Hugh O'Brian. Before the play we saw the famous movie and TV star walking up the aisle. A few minutes later, he walked back down, my friend slipped to the aisle to ask Hugh O'Brian to autograph our programs.

"Mr. O'Brian said, 'I hope you all enjoy the play. We've worked hard on it and we want you to have a great time tonight.' It always impressed me that a famous star would have the goal of making sure folks in his audience enjoyed his work."

"Stan Johnson has a huge talent," suggested Angie, "but he acts as if giving us a good time is his major goal."

The musician stopped at our table and pulled up a chair between two beautiful women.

"Have you heard me play before?" he asked.

We weren't members of his fan club, but Angie had been to one of his concerts.

"We just bought your CD," Michelle bragged as she held up the disk. "If we have the chance we'd love to attend a concert."

"Are you a native of New Mexico." asked Angie.

"No, actually I grew up in a small town in Northern Iowa. Later, I played in bars and an occasional concert in Des Moines.

I felt the shudder move through to Michelle's hand. *Here we go again,* I thought. *I remember you. I saw your pictures in the paper. You're the escaped prisoners from Iowa.*

"I've been doing pretty well on the road," explained Stan. "I'm making expenses and putting a bit away in a savings account. My main purpose for traveling to the southwest is finding my brother. His name is Bob Johnson."

I was feeling Michelle's bare foot on my leg.

"There are about three million men in this country named Bob Johnson, so my chances aren't great, but it is something I have to do."

Hank said, "I suppose this means you want to know if any of us know a Bob Johnson. I think I know three."

"Then you probably don't know my brother. I'm guessing he changed his name. He was wanted for a crime and the charges have pretty much gone away. If I can find him, I think I can bring him back into the realm of free Americans. He will face a few minor charges in Des Moines. He's a convicted criminal, but I know he's really a good guy. And I know him pretty well.

"Let me show you his picture. This was taken almost ten years ago, so you may have to mentally subtract some hair; add a little gray; maybe some facial hair."

Stan passed around his picture, giving us each a business card with a cell phone number.

Michelle and I looked at the picture of our friend and partner in our escape from the halfway house. Each of us struggled to keep a straight face. We tried hard to produce looks that said, "Here's a man we have never seen before." My stomach was doing gymnastics as I said, "Sorry, I'll keep my eyes open, Stan."

Michelle added, "He looks like somebody I might have known years ago, but I can't place where. I know I haven't seen this guy for a long time. I guess everybody looks like somebody else. One of our friends always said Alan looked like Gene Hackman, the movie star. I've never thought so. I think Alan is much more handsome."

"I'd really appreciate it if you'd give me a call if you see him," requested Stan. "And thanks for saying the nice things about my music. I enjoy playing and I love making people relaxed and happy. Good luck to you all."

We looked at his business card. "Stan Johnson, Acoustical Guitar Music." It included an address in Des Moines, a cell phone number, and an email address.

Michelle and I exchanged glances. We were both wondering, *Shall we talk to this guy?*

I glanced at Angie and Hank. They were busy staring in each other's eyes. I peeked at Michelle. She checked our friends and then mouthed, *He knows.*

I gave a faint nod of my head.

Neither of us had to make that decision about whether to contact Stan. As we left the bar, Hank and Angie walked ahead. Stan Johnson came up behind us, walking between us, he spoke softly. "I know who you really are. Call me, Mary and Paul. We need to talk." He turned and walked back into the bar.

LXXIII

Facing the Music – Or Not

Our standard operating procedure when we were threatened was packing up, leaving town, and disappearing into the mountains. Michelle and I stayed awake much of the night discussing our options. The problem was that for the last seven months, we had developed as close to a normal life as we had ever visualized for ourselves. If Stan Johnson was going to turn us in to the law, he could have done it without telling us, *I know who you really are.* All he would have had to do was dial 911 and we would have been on a flight back to Iowa with FBI agents.

"I think he's for real," Michelle announced. "He's Bob Johnson's brother. Stan wants to find him and bring him back to Des Moines to face charges. I think he is offering us the same deal."

"Then the next question is, *Do we want the deal?* Do we want to give up our fake life and start all over as ex-cons trying to build a life somewhere where everyone knows we are ex-cons? What do you think, Michelle?"

It was quiet for a long time.

Then, "I like the life we are living," declared Michelle. "I want to marry you and have our baby. I want to earn a college degree and be a teacher's wife. I want to raise our kids and watch them play basketball or tennis or even soccer. I want to retire and go see our grandkids and travel the country. Can we travel the world or will our fingerprints and real identities somehow show up?"

"I don't know." I reflected. "I do know that I agree with you. I want this life we have started here to continue. Let's sleep on it and talk to Stan Johnson tomorrow; see what he says."

"As if I could sleep."

Sunday morning at five, we met the paper delivery guy at the door. By eight we had read the big Sunday edition of the Alamogordo Daily News and done all of the puzzles. Sunday mornings we had gotten into the habit of going to church; not that Sunday. I called Stan's cell phone before nine. Neither Michelle nor I could stand the wait. We arranged to meet at a bagel and coffee café at ten. We were there twenty minutes early. Actually, we drove by twice and saw nothing unusual. Then we parked three blocks away.

I parked and left Michelle in the driver's seat. "I'll call you by 10:15. If I call you Mary then get the hell out of town, regardless of what else I say. If I'm not in jail, we'll meet in Bixby, AZ in a week. If I call you Michelle and ask you to come, that means I think it is safe for you to join us."

I walked to the bagel shop, while Michelle drove three blocks on the other side of our meeting place and waited in the pickup.

Stan came at 9:55. We talked about the weather until twelve minutes after ten. Then I went to the restroom and called Michelle.

I said, "Hi Michelle. I can't see any sign of a trap. Come and join us. We'll listen to what Stan has to say."

Michelle was still cautious as she walked into the café. She looked over every face in the crowd for an FBI type; then she sat down in the booth beside me.

Stan had a lot to say. He had been on tour; looking for his brother Bob Johnson for almost six months.

"As I told you last night, I want to find my brother; offer him the chance to come back to Des Moines and become a free man. Someday, he will do something and the police will capture him. Bob is not a violent man, but I worry that he might get in a situation where some hotdog cop hurts him during an arrest. He could be desperate enough not to go back to prison, that he might do something aggressive. I don't want my brother injured or killed. He's a gentle man. Prison was tough for Bob. He won't want to go back.

"If I can talk to him, I think I can convince him that turning himself in is the best way to win back his freedom.

"I can't say what's the right thing for you two to do. Apparently, you have some kind of a life here in Alamogordo. It was pure luck that I saw you last night at the bar. I saw Mary as I was playing and thought *I think that woman is Mary Swartz?*

"I had your pictures in my pocket. I look at them every day. I'd be thinking, 'These people could be a link to Bob.' When I saw Mary, I almost lost my place in the song I was playing. It shook me so bad to see people who might help me find my brother.

"I hardly slept last night. I wanted to talk to you so badly. You are my first chance. Tell me. What do you know about Bob?"

I paused a moment to gather my thoughts. Then I answered, "Not much, I'm sorry to say. I knew your brother was a good man. I always thought he got a bum rap in his drug conviction. I saw a lot of drug dealer types in prison. Bob Johnson was not one of them. He never accused his kid, but I think he knew that the boy set him up and wasn't man enough to step up and take the fall. The kid must have been a weasel to let the guy who raised him go to prison for seven years for the bad stuff the kid was doing. He must have been a genuine jerk."

"Actually, my nephew is a scoundrel. Dave Johnson, got busted on another drug charge last fall. He didn't have his old man to get him out of trouble, so he was sent to prison. That's where he is right now. To his credit, he finally admitted that the drugs in Bob's trunk were his. Dave stepped up to the plate, just seven years too late. I talked to Bob's lawyer and he finally did the right thing. He moved that all charges against his client be dropped. If Bob shows up in court, this thing will be over forever. He will have a clean record and my brother can start a new life for himself. I think they'll even forget about the jailbreak charge. Judging from the resolution of Rod's situation, they figured out that the guard was drunk; the court believed the attempted rape scenario."

Michelle said, "Wow. That is so wonderful. I am so happy for Bob. Now we need to find him. The only thing I know is that I heard him and Rod talking about heading south where it is warmer."

I offered, "Rod said, maybe they could pretend to be brothers traveling together. What name was Rod going by?"

Stan opened a notebook from his pocket.

"Rod bought a new birth certificate from a guy in St. Louis. He never would admit who the guy was. Rod's new name was Joe Jorgensen.

"He wouldn't tell the cops what Bob's new name was. He said he couldn't remember. *I just kept calling him Bob,'* he told them. After Rod was released, I talked to him. He told me the name. Jonathan Wilson. He told me to look in New Mexico for Jonathan Wilson."

"I wonder how much Bob trusted Rod," conjectured Michelle. "Bob told me he wanted to go south where it was warm. If he told Rod he was heading west, that could be right or it could have been a false lead because he didn't trust our friend, Rod, to keep his mouth shut. Maybe you should do some shows in Arkansas or Louisiana or Alabama. Put up a lot of posters with your name and picture big. Maybe he'll find you. In the mean time, Paul and I will keep our eyes open around here."

"If the cops are looking for Bob in New Mexico," I reasoned, looking at Michelle, "maybe you and I ought to be really careful. They probably have our pictures too."

"I'm glad I found you two," Stan declared. "I don't seem to be any closer to my goal of finding my brother, but maybe you're right, Mary, uh Michelle. Maybe I should play some bars in the south. I've never been to New Orleans. How would a lyrical guitarist fit in with a bunch of jazz musicians?"

"Your music would fit in anywhere, Stan."

She slid the CD we had bought across the table. "Will you autograph this? Your music is delightful, Stan."

Stan shook hands with Alan and Michelle gave him a hug. He gave them another card with his cell phone number and email address on it. Give me a buzz if you find out anything. Good luck to you both. You're good people. I can tell."

LXXIV

Gospel and Boudin Sausage

Nora Miller drove toward the town of Ville Platte, Louisiana. Jonathan Wilson rode beside her in her Mazda CX-5 SUV. His eyes scanned the Louisiana countryside. Their route meandered between verdant pastures, speckled with Black Angus cattle. Long-legged white birds that seemed to have been lightly sprayed with tan-colored paint, lingered around the cows like third graders around their playground teacher.

"See those long-legged white birds," Jonathan observed. "Out in the pasture near the cows. Is there a relation between the birds and the herds of cattle? They look like they're hanging out together."

"Cattle Egrets." explained Nora. "They were given that name because the birds follow herds of cattle. There's a symbiotic relation between the Egrets and the cows. Did you notice that some of the Egrets actually ride on the backs of the cows? They pick fleas and ticks off the big mammals. The flocks follow herds of cattle and catch insects disturbed by and disturbing the grazing animals. Both the cows and the Egrets benefit from the deal."

"Another question," said Jonathan. "I take it you like gospel music?"

"Doesn't it sound great? Don't you love the nine speaker Bose system in this car?" asked Nora. "The sound is as pure as you can buy in a car. It's as if we were in church listening to live music."

"I love the solid sound. I wonder about the gospel music."

Glorious tones of Louisiana gospel music flowed from the speakers of the car radio of Nora's new Mazda.

"Folks use gospel music to show their love of Jesus," explained Nora. "They're calling upon Jesus to be with them. Most of these people are poor. They feel good knowing that Jesus will be giving them support; making things better for them."

Nora and Jonathan listened to a choir from Arkansas call on the Lord to send down his spirit. The perfect tone from the speakers on the radio system on Nora's new Mazda projected lively notes of southern gospel music. Hymns about the love of Jesus drifted from their open windows.

Nora continued, "Songs telling about the golden streets of Beulah Land gave country people assurance that the next life will be better."

"What do you think of the music?" asked Jonathan. "Do you like it?"

"Jesus gives hope to these people, Jonathan. I'm not thrilled with the music, but I like it all right. What do you think about gospel music?"

It took a minute or two before Jonathan found the words to respond to his own question thrown back at him.

Finally, he said, "Something about the music troubles me."

"Troubles you?"

"I think so," suggested Jonathan. "The music is telling folks that this life may be awful, but just wait until you die. Then you'll meet Jesus. He'll take you to a place of joy and happiness and good fortune. *'Blessed are the poor, for yours is the kingdom of God.'* God means for you to be poor in this life, but in the next you'll be surrounded with gold and beauty.

"And I'm hearing a lot of ME in it. Jesus loves ME. He's MY precious king. Thank you for all you've done for ME. You've rescued ME. You've set ME free. I'm listening to a lot of these songs on your radio and most of this music is professing a religion about ME."

"And you believe?"

"I believe God wants us to be happy, healthy, and prosperous in this life. He wants us to notice when others are down. He or she wants us to do what we can to make sure people have the basics of life. I believe that means, a good place to live, good food, medical care, a quality education, and things government can do to make this life tolerable for everybody."

"Jesus gives these people hope, Jonathan. Their religion encourages them to hope for a better life. They can picture bountiful living, if they let Jesus' love surround them."

"Here or in the next life?"

"Heaven is something to look forward to."

"After you die?"

"That's when heaven comes. Do you think heaven comes here on earth?"

"I think so. And maybe I'll go to a better place after I die. How can I tell?"

"The Bible tells you. Read the Bible."

"It seems to me," argued Jonathan, "that Jesus wanted people to be loving to the least of those who we come across in this world. I think my religious philosophy is that by loving and caring for poor folks, I love and care for Jesus. The radio religion disturbs me."

"Disturbs you?"

"Actually, the whole concept of eternal life bothers me a little. The songs we hear, talk about Beulah Land and streets flowing with gold. Riches in heaven. It's garbage. Religion was a way for rich planters to send their slaves to church where the slaves learned a gospel that says it's ok to be poor. God wants you to be poor. He wants you to receive your reward in heaven. It was a clever way to control the slaves. Now it's a clever way to control poor folks, so they don't revolt against rich people."

"It's hope, Jonathan. It's hope. Their God gives them hope for eternal life where they will have all they can eat and be forever with Jesus and God."

"I think it's control. I think we are going to disagree about this, Nora."

"I can see your point, Jonathan, but I still think it's good for people to have hope. It doesn't hurt for us to talk, but for now we mostly disagree, my love."

Nora glanced at the green road sign. "We're almost to the town of Ville Platte," she observed. "I want to make a stop near there."

"What's at Ville Platte?"

"I'm glad you asked," said Nora. "I have a surprise for you. Hungry?"

"Starved."

"Ever eaten Boudin?"

"What?"

"Boudin."

"Not when I knew it. What's Boudin?"

"Boudin sausage is a melange of cooked pork, rice, onions, and spice," Nora explained. "They pack it into a chewy casing that needs a sharp knife to sever. Once it's cut, the filling tumbles out. We'll go to T-Boy's. Their boudin is glistening-moist with the perfect combination of al dente rice. The pork is gently seasoned, but is still hugely piggy. You'll love it."

An hour later Nora and Jonathan slid from the bench seat of a picnic table. They had devoured a half pound of Boudin sausage, half a loaf of fresh white bread, and three beers.

"What'd you think, Jonathan?"

"You couldn't tell? Boudin sausage is delectable. Will it be coming out as the new special feature at McDonald's?"

"Did you have enough to eat?"

"No more food for a few days, I hope."

"Ok. No more food. Come on. I want to show you a beautiful woman."

"I already found one of those."

"This one might be worth your while, mister."

"So is the one whom I already found."

LXXV

Evangeline

"Have you read Evangeline, Jonathan?"

"If I did, I was eighteen and in Howard Girsch's English literature class in high school."

"If you were seventeen and were studying *American literature* you might have studied Longfellow. The man was an American poet, not an English poet."

"Sorry. I should have paid more attention."

"Longfellow had a friend, Nathaniel Hawthorne. You might have heard of him. Hawthorne told him a story about a young Acadian girl in Canada," explained Nora. "In about 1740, Emmeline Labiche was about to be married to her lover, Louis Arceneaux. Remember what it was like being seventeen?"

"Maybe not. I can remember sitting in English class beside Maggie Foster. I borrowed her shoe and calculated the area of the sole. Then I divided her weight by the area of her sole. I did the same thing for me and concluded that her weight per square inch of sole was more than mine. I proved to Maggie that women are heavier than men. Might have been when I missed Evangeline."

"That might have been when you missed Miss Maggie Foster too, Jonathan. Women don't like to be told that they are fat."

"Maggie knew she wasn't fat. She was trim and solid. She played basketball and the piano. She was an athlete and she was smart. I was a little bit in love with her, but she fell a lot in love with Bill Snider who was a senior. I never had a chance. She liked me, but I was always just one of her buddies.

"Anyway, tell me more about Evangeline or Emmeline Labiche. Did she marry her lover?"

Nora went on with her story. "The day before Emmeline and Louis were to be married, the British decided that the Arcadians had to leave Canada. The plan was to ship them to places in the colonies. Before they left, the two lovers agreed to meet in Louisiana. When Emmeline found her way there, the lovers had been separated, Emmeline couldn't find Louis. She searched for years with no success. Finally, one day she spotted her lover alongside Bayou Teche in St. Martinsville. Louis was standing beneath the spreading branches of a live oak tree.

"She ran to him and embraced him. Louis did not respond. Both of them were engulfed in tears as he told her, 'I cannot be your husband. I am betrothed to another.' They separated again. Her heart was not broken. It was crushed. The beautiful woman was demented forever. She wandered until she died, never recovering her mental balance."

"We should go to St. Martinsville," suggested Jonathan.

"Great idea," agreed Nora, with a twinkle in her eye. "We should see the Evangeline Oak that still stands along Bayou Teche. I want you to see the grave of Emmeline Labiche. The grave is actually the burial place of the beautiful Arcadian, but it bears the names of two other beautiful women. Some people say the grave is empty. I think the Arcadian is buried there.

"After Henry Wadsworth Longfellow heard Hawthorne's story, he penned an epic fictional poem about the tragedy. The name of his heroine was Evangeline. Her name is on the grave as a tribute to Longfellow's story. Years later the tale became a movie. The star was a hot-blooded Hispanic by the name of Dolores Del Rio. The cast of the movie contributed the statue in the image of the movie star. That means that a third beautiful woman guards the grave."

"I need to spend some time on the Web," said Jonathan, "and have a look at this hot Spanish movie star."

"She's a gorgeous woman, Jonathan. I hope you don't fall in love with her."

"That would be fickle. I'm in love with someone else."

"And who would that be?"

"Another Cajun beauty."

"Maybe you should marry her."

"Maybe I should. She knows all the worst about me."

"And do you think she'd marry you anyway?"

"I haven't asked her yet."

"Maybe you should ask her. I'd hate to waste my time on some guy who is going to marry another woman."

"Ok. I'll ask her."

Jonathan reached into his pocket. His hand come out with a sparkling diamond ring. He took Nora's hand in his own and slipped the ring on her finger.

"Will you marry me, Nora?"

The tears turned on like a faucet. They flowed down Nora's cheeks as she leaned her head to Jonathan's chest.

A moment later, she lifted her head, looked Jonathan in the eye, and touched his nose with her index finger. "You rascal. All this talk and you were planning to ask me to marry you all the time."

"So will you marry a guy who is an escaped prisoner and possibly a murderer?"

"Don't say that! You aren't a murderer! You didn't hit the guy. And the only reason you escaped from prison is so that you wouldn't get stuck with a life sentence. Yes, I'll marry you Jonathan. You promise never to mention being a murderer or an escaped prisoner again, and I'll marry you. Under those conditions, the answer is yes."

"Always conditions. Ok, I'll agree."

He kissed her.

Nora said, "I have a plan."

"Yes?"

"How about if we get married Friday in St. Martinville?"

"Ok."

"I have reservations for Friday and Saturday night at a bed and breakfast right beside Evangeline Oak Park."

"Have you got the church reserved?"

"I've talked to the priest and I think he might marry us Friday afternoon if that would work with you."

"I think I can get off from work. Let's do it. Honeymoon in St. Martinville?"

"That's my plan."

"How did you know I was going to ask you to marry me?"

"The ring surprised me, but I pretty well knew you were going to propose, Jonathan. You are an open book, darling."

"Does this mean I won't be able to have secrets?"

"No secrets," she demanded. "I like open books."

"Shall we drive to St. Martinville? I want to see Dolores Del Rio."

"Let's go. Just remember. You're committed to me now."

"We have a deal."

They drove through Lafayette. Nora turned off the interstate.

"Where are we going?" asked Jonathan.

"I think you should take me to bed."

"It's three o'clock in the afternoon."

"You just asked me to marry you. I think you should take me to bed."

"I'm willing. Where are we going?"

"There's an Econo Lodge here that is really cheap and has pretty decent ratings."

Nora drove them to the motel.

They checked in and took a shower together.

"You are making my body very clean, Jonathan."

"I like clean woman, Nora."

He kissed his fiancé.

"You're very good at kissing in the shower."

"You're not so bad yourself."

"Could you wash my back some more," asked Jonathan.

She wrapped her arms around him using much of the little bar of soap between his shoulders and thighs. He used another bar on her shoulders, back, buttocks, and thighs.

He kissed her again. The soap was nearly gone when Nora pushed him away.

"I think we should dry off and check out the bed."

An hour later, Jonathan looked up at Nora and said, "I lied to you, Nora."

"And I was beginning to trust you. Fess up."

"I told you I wouldn't want any food for several days. The exercise has made me hungry."

"Shall we dress and find some food."

Nora stopped in the lobby. "Look at this, Jonathan. Do you like guitar music? This sounds interesting. 'The acoustical guitar of Stan Johnson. The Station: Premiere Live Music Venue.' We could eat and listen to music."

She glanced at Jonathan. He was pale.

"What's wrong? Are you alright?"

Jonathan couldn't talk. He stared at the poster.

Nora put her hands on his cheeks. "Jonathan?"

Finally, still looking at the poster, he said, "This guy. . . . This guy's my brother."

"The one you went fishing with when you were making up lies?"

"That part was true. Stan Johnson's my brother. I love him. I thought I'd never see him again. He's right here in Lafayette."

"Is it going to cause us problems if we go listen to him? Will he turn you in?"

"No. I would trust my life to Stan Johnson. I've been trying to figure out a way to contact him. All I have to do is go out to eat. He'll be there."

"Jonathan. You're crying."

"I can't help it. I'm so happy, Nora. It's my brother. It's you. It's life.'"

"Let's go find The Station," suggested Nora. "Let's go find your brother."

LXXVI

Brothers Reunited

As they closed the doors of Nora's Mazda, Nora and Jonathan heard the notes of the lyric guitar wafting from The Station. The music carried familiar memories to Jonathan's ears, memories of years of youth, parents at work, two teens, home alone, tentative chords drifting through the little house in Ankeny, Iowa.

They waited for a table, "So we can see the musician, please," requested Nora.

Nora's hand reached out to steady Jonathan as introductory chords of a song drifted through the room. The guitar spoke the words, "Blue Moon, ..."

"Blue Moon." Nora repeated. "He has a lovely touch, Jonathan."

"I shouldn't have pestered him so much about all the noise. He played all the time. Now, he's terrific. Nobody does it better."

"I'm impressed. Your brother's really great."

They slid into the booth side-by-side, so they could see Stan. Jonathan's face was in the shadows. Stan's eyes were looking down on his strings, concentrating on his chords. The music rang through the bar. Jonathan detected sadness, something he had never heard in his brother's music.

Nora ordered two beers along with guacamole and chips. They ate and drank slowly, listening to tunes that moved Jonathan to wipe tears from his eyes with his fists.

"What's his favorite drink?"

"Probably a frozen strawberry margarita, with the rim dipped in powdered sugar."

Nora wrote a note on her napkin.

Mr. Johnson. My friend and I would like to buy you a frozen strawberry margarita with the rim dipped in powdered sugar during the break. We're in the booth in the middle of the right side. Please join us.

Nora

Twenty minutes later, Stan stared down at his brother.

"What the hell took you so long to find me, Robert?" asked Stan Johnson in a soft voice.

"I felt a hunger tonight," answered Jonathan in an equally soft voice. "Nora suggested a place with a lyric guitarist playing. I told her I'd heard enough lyric guitar music as a teenager to last a lifetime."

Jonathan pointed at the bench across from him. "Sit down, Bro."

Stan sat and said, "You came anyway."

"Nora was in the mood for food and music. Stan Johnson, this is my fiancé, Nora Miller. My name is Jonathan Wilson. We probably shouldn't talk about my old life right now."

"You'll never know how hard I've been looking for you Robert, ... Jonathan. I can't believe I found you."

"You didn't find me. I found you."

"No. I've been doing concerts all around the west and south, hoping you'd see one of my signs and come to a performance. I stumbled across a couple of your buddies out west. A guy and a girl with whom you left Des Moines. They seemed to be doing really well. You don't want to know any more about them. Right?"

"You're right," said Jonathan. "It's better for all of us that I know nothing about them. Makes me happy to know they're doing well. They're good people. Are they married?"

"They're living as if they are. They showed up accidentally, at one of my concerts. I recognized both of them."

"What about Rod?" asked Jonathan. "Have you heard anything about him. He worries me."

"You had a well-founded worry. Rod was drinking and his girl friend figured him out, turned him in to the cops. The prosecutor in Polk County charged him with some minor offense, gave him six months in jail. He should be a free man very soon."

"Unbelievable!"

"But true. Hey man, I have to go back and see if I can still play a guitar. Can we talk when I'm done?"

"Of course."

Nora wrote on a napkin. *"ECON LODGE; ROOM 413".*

They all slid out of the booth.

"So good to see you, Bro. You're looking great. And you have a lovely fiancé."

"You can follow us to our room when you're done."

"Can I kiss the bride?"

"Not yet. First, you have to be my best man. Friday at 3:00."

Nora hugged Stan and kissed him on the lips. She said, "I'm happy for both of you, Stan."

Stan turned and hugged his big brother. "I love you, Robert," he whispered in his ear.

Nora reached over to take Jonathan's left hand in both of hers. They smiled at each other as the notes of Stan's next tune filled the room with a joy that replaced the sadness of his performance before the break.

"What's that tune?" Nora asked. "I should know it."

"Smile.'"

"Smile. What's the use of crying? Good choice, Stan Johnson."

LXXVII

The Wedding

It was midnight when Nora Miller and the Johnson brothers gathered around a table in Room 413 at the Econo Lodge.

"Ok," said Stan. "Tell me your story. Halfway house to here."

"It's a long story, Stan. It started when our guard, Roger Stewart tried to rape Mary Swartz. Paul Hartman came out of our room and stopped the attack. They exchanged blows. Roger fell, hit his head on the door. We tried to revive him, but the guy was dead. We stole his SUV, drove to Roger's house. Then, we stole his Ford Ranger pickup and some other stuff we thought we might need. Rod and I headed south to St. Louis, sold the SUV, bought a couple of cheap cars and some phony ID's. Mary and Paul went their own way. Later, Rod and I split up. I drove to Louisiana, took a job busing dishes, met Nora. She found me a carpentry job that's really a good one.

"Yesterday, I asked her to marry me. I found out she had it all planned. Next Friday, June 25, 3:00 p.m. St. Martin de

Tours Church. St. Martinville. She even had the priest lined up. I think the woman lives inside my head. I love her, Stanley. When she looks at me, it's like she thinks I'm magic."

"That seems to go both ways," Stan suggested. "How did she find out you were really an escaped prisoner? How did she handle that?"

"Our construction company took a week off from work. Most of our people gave our time to a United Methodist Mission project in the little town of Dulac. There was a group from Iowa working down there. One of the workers had been following news of the prison escape on his computer. He began sprouting facts. Nora put them together with what she knew about me. It was enough to convince her that I was one of the escapees. At lunch she took my hand and we went for a walk. She made me tell her the whole story. Nora was almighty pissed, but for some reason she still loved me."

"And she asked you to marry her?"

"You have that wrong. I asked her to marry me. That was when I learned that all the plans were made before I asked her. The woman is a mind reader."

The conversation lulled. Finally, Stan put his hand on his brother's knee and looked him in the eyes. Stan said, "I think you need to turn yourself in, Bob. Serve a few months and set yourself right with the law. That way you won't have some blood-thirsty cop shooting you."

Jonathan looked at Nora. "What do you think?" he asked her.

Nora thought for only a moment. Then she shook her head. "We've started a pretty good life, Stan. Both of us like the way all the details are fitting together. Personally, I'm willing to give it a try. I think both of us have hope that we can keep going without anyone discovering Jonathan's past."

"She speaks for me as well, Bro. I'm inclined to risk it."

"I'm not going to argue with you. I just wanted you to know the option. Can we get one more person in the loop?"

"Jackie?"

It was ten minutes after one when Stan called Jonathan's daughter, Jackie Johnson, in Des Moines.

He heard a weak, "Hello..."

"Hi, Jackie. This is your Uncle Stanley. Sorry to wake you. I need you to prevail on a friend. One who wouldn't mind having you wake him or her in the middle of the night to make a private call on that person's phone. You and I need to talk and it would be better to do it on someone else's phone and with nobody listening. You can say your battery died on your phone."

"Now?"

"The sooner, the better."

"It just so happens I can do that pretty quickly. Call you back in two minutes."

Stan's phone rang forty seconds later.

"Hello."

"What's going on Uncle Stan? You're so mysterious. Did something happen to Dad?"

"Just a second, Jackie."

He handed the phone to Jonathan Wilson.

"Hi, Jackie."

"What's going on, Uncle Stan. Tell me."

"This isn't Uncle Stan, sweetie. He and I grew up together with the same DNA so our voices sound alike."

"Daddy? Daddy! That's you. Are you alright?"

"I'm doing well, Jackie. Stan and I found each other a few hours ago. We are both pretty excited. I have a request."

"Anything, Daddy."

"I was wondering if you might be free Friday afternoon to come to your father's wedding."

"Wedding? Wedding?"

"You keep repeating yourself. I met a wonderful woman. We fell in love with each other. This week I asked her to marry me. She had the whole thing planned out already. Her name is Nora and she has me all figured out."

"Daddy, I'm so happy for you. Oh.... Does she know about your past?"

"She knows all about me. And she still loves me."

"What about Stan? How did you find him? Or how did he find you?"

"That's an amazing story. Stan has been doing shows across the south, hoping to track me down. Nora saw a poster in a motel in Lafayette, advertising Stan's show. She asked if I'd like to go listen to a lyric guitarist play. I saw the sign and nearly fainted when I saw Stan's face."

"Where are you, Daddy?"

"Lafayette. Lafayette, Louisiana right now."

"Uncle Stan told me you should turn yourself in," Jackie suggested. "He says they won't really press many new charges against you. He says you'd be out in six months."

"We've talked about that a lot. I like the life I'm living here, Jackie. Nora and I want to keep the lifestyle we've been living. It won't stay the same if everyone learns I'm an ex-con. We would love it if you were a part of our lives, beginning with next Friday. Nora would like you to be a bridesmaid. Could you do that for us?"

"Oh, Daddy. You know it would thrill me to be together with you and your bride. Just one problem."

"What's that?" Jonathan asked.

"I don't know where you live. Are you planning to send me an invitation?"

"This is it. You fly to New Orleans. Come as soon as you can and we'll spend some time together."

"You're living in New Orleans?"

"Close. I don't think I'll tell you any more over the phone. Just call Stan on a friend's phone or buy a cheap cell phone and use it when you call me. We'll come pick you up. Read up on Evangeline. We'll do a bit of history study while you're here."

"What are you talking about, Daddy?"

"Just a hint. We'll talk later."

"You're crazy, Daddy. I can hardly wait to see you."

"You can't believe how much I've missed you, Jackie. This week may be the happiest of my life."

"You have a new name?"

"I do, but all you have to call me is Daddy. Does that work for you?"

"Daddy?"

"Yes?"

"My husband, Larry, is listening to my side of this conversation. He knows all about what happened to you. The drug charge, prison time, the escape, all of it. Is it alright if he comes to the wedding with me?"

I frowned and looked at Stan and Nora.

"He's a good man," whispered Stan. "I trust him."

Nora nodded.

"Can you swear him to secrecy?"

"He's safe, Daddy. He can call you Daddy too."

"You're funny. I want to meet him and my grandchild."

"Grandson. I had a little boy. He's a year old. His name is Robert."

"I can hardly wait. Call me with your flight information. We'll pick you up. I love you."

"I love you too, Daddy. More than you can ever know."

Jonathan awoke and looked at the clock. The time was seven twenty. He lay in bed with his arm around Nora Miller, holding her close to him. She seemed to be sleeping, but then he heard her whisper, "I need to call Sarah Sue, let her know for sure that I'm going to have another bride's maid."

"For sure?"

"I told her that Jackie might be here if we could find a way to invite her, without anyone finding out about you."

"She knows about me?"

"Sarah Sue and I have no secrets, Jonathan. She's my daughter. Don't worry. You're safe with her."

"This is scary. In twelve hours, the number of people who know my story and my whereabouts has gone from one to five. Are we going to tell the rest of the wedding guests?"

Nora thought for a few minutes.

"I could talk to the priest at confession. Then he could never tell."

"I'm a United Methodist."

"Doesn't matter. It's me who's confessing."

She thought for a moment. Then said, "No. 'I'm marrying an escaped prisoner' doesn't sound like something he needs to know."

"Good. Makes me feel better."

"One other problem," said Nora.

"Yes?"

"I'm not sure I'd like having a fake name," she declared. "Nora Wilson sounds alright until I start thinking about it being a name you bought from a bad guy in St. Louis."

"I've been thinking about the name Wilson. I don't like it either," I agreed. "What would happen if we both took the name Miller?"

Nora turned and grabbed his hands. "Wait! I've got another idea. My maiden name was Nora Duval. What if we both took my maiden name?"

"Jonathan Duval? Jonathan and Nora Duval? I like the sound. Let's look into it. Perhaps you'll have to get a court to change your name back to Duval first. Then we can work on changing Wilson to Duval for me."

Nora said, "I've heard Louisiana is one of about nine states where the man can take the woman's name at marriage. My daddy would be proud to have his name carried on to our children."

Jonathan kissed her. "It's a deal."

"Anyway, I need to call Sarah Sue."

"I'm going for a walk," said Jonathan. "You call."

Twenty minutes later Nora and Jonathan sat at breakfast.

"What did Sarah Sue say?"

"She was thrilled. I knew she would be. She and I have to go shopping for new dresses."

"Dresses?"

"A wedding dress for me and bridesmaids dresses for her and Jackie."

"Want me to come along?"

"The groom doesn't see the wedding gown until the wedding."

"I'm glad for that."

"Your turn will come. You'll need a new suit. I'll help you with that."

"This thing sounds sexist."

"That's the tradition, buster. Everything revolves around the bride. You do have a job. Call Randy Lee. See if he'll be a groomsman so we have a balanced photo of our wedding party.

We need to make a list of guests and call them. I'm thinking of about twenty people."

"Sounds as if you have everything under control."

"Should make it easy for you."

Two months later, Mr. Jonathan Duval and Ms. Nora Duval were living in Nora's apartment in Houma. Nora seemed to feel a bit nauseous much of the time.

LXXVIII

NM Teacher of the Year

When we invited our mothers to fly to El Paso for the Road Scholar program, we were ecstatic to surprise them with invitations to our wedding and overjoyed to announce that Helen and Adel would soon be grandmothers. During our week together, we sensed the changes in their feelings, from a mutual fear for the safety of their children to a sense of hope that their children and grandchildren might lead fairly normal lives. The growing expectation of regular contact with us was another bonus for the two women who had raised us, loved us, and backed us up in spite of our shortcomings.

For eighteen years, our lives soared, like a pair of golden eagles flying over New Mexico's Red Rock Country. Michelle Sibley earned her degree in wildlife management at New Mexico State University. For a decade, she worked for the state of New Mexico as a wildlife biologist. After starting her work life as a teenaged prostitute and spending time as a waitress, she loved and treasured the respect she was earning in her new career. Michelle not only gained respect and esteem among the professionals in her field; she delighted in taking young people on field trips, opening developing minds to the world of nature.

Our son, Andrew, is sixteen and our daughter, Abigail, celebrated her fifteenth birthday in February. There have never been two prouder parents than Michelle and me. We love our two children immensely. Abigail is an excellent mathematics student who does very well in all her classes. Her logical reasoning skills make Michelle think she might end up as a lawyer. Her beauty rivals that of her mother.

Andrew's love is history. Exploring the events of a particular time in the world stimulates our son. Figuring out why nations were formed or reasons wars broke out in the world gives him a sense of satisfaction. He loves to read, especially historical novels and the works of great historians. He does well in other classes, but his study of history consumes our older child. Neither of our children ever showed up in one of my business classes. But, they love going on field trips to the mountains led by their mother.

Besides being skilled basketball players, they have teamed up to win some USTA tennis championships. At a tennis tournament, Andrew divides his time between playing matches and sitting in the shade curled up with a thick historical novel.

My second chance at a career in education delighted me. I give my all to teaching my students efficient business practices, while at the same time moving them ahead as competent people. As a prisoner, I had never dared to hope for two more decades in the job I was born to spend my life doing.

Then, in my seventeenth year of teaching in Alamogordo, the superintendent made an announcement to the news media that threatened the life-style we had developed.

One morning in the late spring, Michelle picked up the Alamogordo Daily News. I was trimming my beard when she yelled, "Alan! Did you know about this?"

"What?"

She stomped into the bathroom. "Listen."

She read.

Alamogordo business teacher, Alan Sibley was selected today as New Mexico Teacher of the Year. New Mexico's Teacher of the Year acts as spokesman for the teaching profession for New Mexico. Sibley will travel to Washington, DC this spring for the official recognition ceremony with the President of the United States.

Alan Sibley enters each class with the comprehensible goals of teaching business skills as well as assisting each of his students in developing his or her own individuality, self-assurance, and integrity as a person in our complex society. In his application composition outlining his philosophy of teaching, Sibley related: "The significance of families and teachers working closely together can never be underrated. Both strive for the ultimate goal of making students successful learners."

The New Mexico Public Education Department and the New Mexico Teacher of the Year program are pleased to have such an excellent, compassionate professional as

*Mr. Alan Sibley as our representative in the National
Teacher of the Year competition.*

"I didn't even know you applied for this, Alan," reprimanded
Michelle. "This has to be one of the dumbest things you've
ever done."

"I thought you'd be honored."

"If you were not Paul Hartman, this would be super
cool. I'd be jumping up and down, kissing and hugging you.
This is going to lead to our demise. It's going to screw up
our family. We need to sit down with Andrew and Abigail
to explain that their parents are criminals. Your students
are going to be disenchanted with you and everything you
taught them. You just put your superintendent and principal in trouble for hiring you. The FBI is on their way to
locating two escaped prisoners and murderers. So stupid,
Alan Sibley. So stupid! You're a smart guy. What were you
thinking?"

Silence floated through the room like an iceberg in the
North Atlantic.

After many nights of quiet discussion in bed, Michelle and I
made the decision that our best course was to risk the life we
had developed. We were going to continue as we were and pray
that the award did not bring the collapse of our family.

Four days after the press announcement the phone rang.

"Sibley's. This is Alan."

"Congratulations, Brother," came the sexy voice of what sounded like a middle-aged woman. "Good to hear your voice. It's been a long time."

I hesitated. "I'm sorry. I don't recognize your voice and I don't know anyone from New York."

"This is Barbara, your sister."

"Barbara? I can't believe it. I thought I'd lost you."

"I lost you. I haven't heard from you in two decades."

"I moved out of Salt Lake City and lost your contact information, Barbara. Sorry."

"Barbara. You haven't called me Barbara for a long time. What happened to Barb?"

"You said, 'This is Barbara.' I thought maybe you go by Barbara now."

"Actually, I do. You can call me Barbara, Bro."

"How are you doing?"

"I'm doing very well. I married a chef about twenty years ago. He and I were divorced after twelve shitty years of married life. Hope your marriage was better than mine."

"I'm really sorry about that, Barbara."

"Me as well. The other problem was that I married within my group of friends. When we broke up I not only lost my husband, but I lost my friends. They went with him."

"That's tough. I'm married to a fantastic, intelligent, and beautiful woman," I explained. "She and I are a good match. She's made me a better person than I was when you last saw me. She and I respect each other. We have two fantastic kids, Andrew and Abigail. I would bore you, if I started telling about how great they are."

"Congratulations on your marriage and your family, Alan. I'm jealous. And congratulations on your Teacher of the Year award. I remember when you were a ski bum and a river runner with a teaching degree. I never thought you'd amount to shit. I'm amazed at this award. I'm happy and proud that you finally put your life together. If you get to New York come see me."

"How long has it been, Barbara? How many years since we've been together?"

"You must have been thirteen or so the last time I was home. Let's find a way to connect before another thirty years go by, Alan. Do you have my phone number on your phone now?"

"I do. And you have mine."

"I'll give you my email address. Send me an email. We'll communicate. Do you have a pencil?"

"Sure. Go ahead."

"barbara10011 at gmail.com. Shoot me an email. I'll tell you about myself."

"Thanks so much for calling, Barb. My life is better with you in it."

"Mine too. With you. Sounds like you've really settled down. Don't think you're the same man you were a few years ago."

"You're right about that. You probably won't recognize me. Keep in touch."

"I will. Goodbye, Alan."

"Goodbye, Barbara."

LXXIX

Detective Alexander and the Teacher of the Year

The desert was warming. The school year was coming to a close. I had missed a bunch of days after receiving the honor of being designated New Mexico Teacher of the year. I returned from Washington, DC with a picture of me shaking hands with the President of the United States. My schedule included about one day a week of traveling around the state appearing at school districts and being an advocate for good teaching. My pet line was, "Parents, teachers, and students must work together at achieving the goal of helping our kids learn everything they can learn and become the best people they can be." My talks also touched on the theme of making post-high school education available to every student who desired more education without accumulating debt that would never leave them.

My work was winding down with the school year. It appeared that I might bite the bullet and end the year without anyone figuring out that I was an escaped prisoner from Iowa.

Then the doorbell rang. Andrew and Abigail were at a track meet and Michelle and I were having a rare, quiet evening at home. I turned on the porch light, peeking out to see a man in a dark suit. He could have been a Mormon missionary, but I guessed not.

This is it, I thought. *We've had some good years, but now it's over.*

I opened the door. "Can I help you?" The screen door stood between me and the tall, closely shaved man with the short, neat, dark hair.

"Alan Sibley?"

"Yes."

"I'm Abe Alexander." He held out his wallet with an ID and a badge. "Iowa Bureau of Criminal Investigation." That's what it said on his badge also.

"Could you and I talk for a few minutes?"

"My kids are gone. My wife is here. I assume this is private."

"I'd prefer it that way."

"I'll send her to the neighbors. Can you wait a minute?"

"Sure."

I left Abe Alexander on my porch, closing the front door. I pulled Michelle to her feet.

"This guy is an Iowa cop. Get the hell out of here. I don't want him to see you. Go, Michelle. Now. Go out the back door, drive to Angie and Hank's. Stay there until I see where this is going."

Michelle didn't hesitate. Without a word, she grabbed her purse and left.

I opened the front door and invited Abe Alexander into my living room.

"Sit down, Mr. Alexander." I motioned the agent toward the couch.

I sat in a straight chair.

"How can I help you."

"I saw your picture in the New York Times. Congratulations. New Mexico Teacher of the Year. That's quite an honor."

"I was humbled."

"You must be a hell of a teacher, Mr. Sibley."

"I love teaching. You can't imagine how much fun it is to have a kid coming into my class who isn't fired up about education, seeing him or her leave with a solid background, thinking about going on to college or to some advanced school. It's so much fun seeing kids soar."

"Congratulations."

"Thank you."

"You probably know why I'm here."

"I have no idea."

The investigator reached in his suit pocket, pulling out a picture from the New York Times and another glossy photo about the same size. He handed them to me.

I studied the two pictures, noting the similarity, making no comment.

"What do you think, Mr. Sibley? These two guys look alike?"

"The guy has a resemblance to me."

"Younger. Less wrinkles," observed the agent.

For almost a minute, the room was quiet.

"I think it's you. I think it's you, Paul Hartman."

"What?"

"I think you're Paul Hartman, a guy who murdered a prison guard and escaped from a halfway house in Des Moines."

I said nothing.

"Do you have anything to say for yourself?"

"You appear to have your mind pretty well made up, Mr. Alexander. What can I say?"

"I'd like my pictures back please."

I handed him the photos.

"Now I have your fingerprints. I can compare them with Paul Hartman's. Then, I think we can go back to Des Moines and put you back in prison, Paul."

Again the room became very quiet.

"Do you have anything to say for yourself?"

"You already asked me that."

"And?"

"What will you gain by taking me back to Des Moines? The guard was drunk. He tried to rape Mary Swartz. I couldn't let the bastard do that. I pulled him off. We had a fight. Roger Stewart hit his head on a door and we couldn't bring him back. He was dead. The guard was a bad man. We were all very sorry that he died. None of us had much choice. We had to run. I understand you arrested Rod Dodge and the judge gave him six months in jail."

"You got that right."

"If you arrest me and take me back, you're going to screw up everything I've taught to a couple of thousand students over the past twenty years. Every kid who's been in my class learned how important ethics are in business and in life. I embezzled a bunch of money from the Des Moines School District. It was a terrible mistake. I was tremendously ashamed. That was one reason that every one of my students has left my classes with integrity built into his or her being. If you arrest me and take me back to Des Moines, then you'll tell two thousand youngsters that it's all a lie."

"You have a point there."

"Besides, there are a superintendent and a principal who hired me. If you arrest me and take me back to Iowa, two fine people will be destroyed and will lose their jobs."

"So what do you expect me to do, Mr. Alan Sibley?"

"Ideally, you do nothing. I think you know I'm not a threat to society. The best place for me is right here in Alamogordo, teaching business to high school students. I'm good at it. I've done nothing dishonest in the last eighteen years. I've done a terrific job of educating youngsters."

"Your old school district is down a hundred grand thanks to Paul Hartman, their ethical business teacher."

"I've been thinking about that money," I suggested. "I've been saving. I'm close to having enough to pay them back. If

I keep on teaching I might be able to come up with a loan and return the $100,000."

"Paul Hartman? Alan Sibley? A teacher certificate in the name Alan Sibley? How in hell did you do that, Paul Hartman? Did you commit another murder? Did you kill a business teacher named Alan Sibley? Tell me your story."

I paused. I was caught. Bad things would happen to a lot of innocent people if everything I did was made public. I put my hands in front of my face. Then I took a deep breath and opened my palms to Detective Abe Alexander.

"Ok. Here's the story. I spent a year driving around the country trying to stay away from the Des Moines Police and the FBI. I kept trying unsuccessfully to find a new identity. One night I set up my tent in a campground in Western Colorado. The next morning I drove down a gravel road, saw fresh tracks sliding into a ravine. At the bottom was a beat-up, half-burned, blue Ford with a dead man in it. In the guy's wallet was ID for Alan Sibley. Sibley was almost my age and size. His body had been severely burned. Nobody was ever going to get a fingerprint. I put my wallet in Alan Sibley's car, took his house keys, and called the sheriff to report a stolen car. A deputy called me later, in Salt Lake City, told me a murderer and escaped prisoner from Iowa had stolen my car, that the guy had died when it crashed into a ravine."

"Pretty lucky."

"Saved my butt. Alan Sibley had an application out for a teaching job in Alamogordo, New Mexico. I followed up; they hired me as a business teacher. I've been saving to pay his sister the value of the property that we took that belonged to Alan Sibley."

"You're married?"

"Yes."

"Your wife know about your past?"

"She does. And she still loves me. Strange, huh?"

"And you have two kids?"

"Teenagers."

"They know?"

"They'd be devastated. Think I'm perfect."

Quiet again. Five minutes listening to the ticking of the grandfather clock across the room.

I looked at Abe Alexander. The detective was contemplating the ceiling through closed eyes.

Finally, he sat up straight, put his elbows on his knees, looking across the room at me.

"Mr. Sibley. I think you're right. We have nothing to gain by putting you in prison for a year. I'm going to go back to Des Moines and talk to a judge whom I've worked with. I'm going to suggest that he issue a sealed order pardoning you for any crimes you might have committed during the jailbreak and releasing you from your remaining prison time. It seems as if you've been doing a hell of a job as a teacher, Mr. Sibley. The world will be better if you keep doing it."

The detective stood and held out his hand. The two men shook hands and Alexander walked to the door.

"Good luck to you. I'll talk to the judge; probably recommend a condition of payment of a hundred grand to your school district in Iowa. Don't go away."

As he opened the door, I touched his shoulder.

"When you talk to the judge, sir, will you ask him if he'll clear the charges against Mary Swartz?"

Author Biography

Jim Riggs received a BA from the University of Northern Iowa and a master of teaching degree from Northwestern Oklahoma State University. For thirty-five years he was a high school math teacher and tennis coach in Iowa. As a teacher, he strived to recognize goodness and strength in each individual.

An avid outdoorsman, he and his family loved exploring our national parks, several of whom are featured in this novel. Writing is a relatively new passion. Jim began writing his memoirs, family history, poetry, and fiction.

Jim and his wife recently moved to Hilton Head Island, South Carolina, where they live on a salt marsh overlooking Broad Creek. They enjoy watching the tides transform the area from a grassy mud flat into a reed-filled lake, observing the assortment of long-legged wading birds, and taking morning walks on the island's beaches.

98245679R00300

Made in the USA
Columbia, SC
22 June 2018